MULTIVERSE:
Exploring Poul Anderson's Worlds

BAEN BOOKS BY POUL ANDERSON

The Technic Civilization Saga
The Van Rijn Method
David Falkayn: Star Trader
Ride of the Terran Empire
Young Flandry
Captain Flandry: Defender of the Terran Empire
Sir Dominic Flandry: The Last Knight of Terra
Flandry's Legacy

To Outlive Eternity and Other Stories

Time Patrol

The High Crusade

MULTIVERSE:
Exploring Poul Anderson's Worlds

edited by
Greg Bear and
Gardner Dozois

Multiverse: Exploring Poul Anderson's Worlds

This is a work of fiction. All the characters and events portrayed in this book are fictional, and any resemblance to real people or incidents is purely coincidental.

ISBN: 978-1-4767-8059-7

First Baen printing, June 2015

Distributed by Simon & Schuster
1230 Avenue of the Americas
New York, NY 10020

Printed in the United States of America

10 9 8 7 6 5 4 3 2 1

TABLE OF CONTENTS

MULTIVERSE:

Exploring Poul Anderson's Worlds

INTRODUCTION: MY FRIEND POUL

by Greg Bear

POUL ANDERSON and I first met around 1968, became friends in the seventies, traded correspondence on an irregular basis—and then I intruded on Poul's life by marrying his daughter!

Strangely, he didn't object.

I never knew Poul Anderson to pull rank or lord it over anyone, not even his headstrong son-in-law. He was polite reason incarnate, difficult to rile, and a sweet, sweet man. Not that he didn't have grit. There was a hard and flinty conviction in Poul, sometimes expressed, but usually made obvious through accumulated experience. Family discussions over long evenings could get boisterous, sometimes about politics—on which we had more than a few disagreements—but more often about science.

My first debate with Poul about science happened way back in 1973 or '74. Somehow or other, in our correspondence, Poul had questioned the viability of icy rocks in the rings of Saturn. He thought that even way out there the ice would eventually sublimate in the vacuum. We politely went back and forth on this until I plunged deep into my copy of the *CRC Handbook of Chemistry and Physics* (one of the essential bibles of hard sf writers in that day) and dug up obscure tables on ice sublimation. At the temperature of Saturn's rings, sublimation is nearly zero. Ice behaves like rock out there. Poul graciously acknowledged this result, and I breathed an immense sigh of relief!

And somehow, I think I rose in his estimation. Later, when queried by his daughter (before we were married) about the physics of an artificial world in my first novel, *Hegira*, he said, "He does his homework."

After the appearance of my first cover story in *Analog*, "A Martian Ricorso," at a science fiction convention in 1976, Poul gave me a thumb's up across a crowded hotel lobby. I glanced around and behind me, wondering to whom he was *really* gesturing to.

Delightful affirmation! Science fiction writers have always been remarkably supportive and tolerant. Poul was exceptionally so, certainly for me.

On another occasion, in the late seventies, we spent a fine hour around a table in a convention hotel bar discussing black holes and singularities with other writers—over beer, of course. Beer makes an excellent lubricant for scientific discussions. It also helps eliminate tritium from one's body after an unfortunate laboratory accident—or so we learned from physicist John Cramer. I'm sure Poul would have approved of that prescription.

After I married Astrid, Poul and Karen provided technical assistance on several of my novels. For both *Eon* and *The Forge of God*, Poul helped me design the right orbits for astronomical objects. Karen supplied me with tips on history and various Greek usages and words.

Ten years later, Poul, Karen, and Poul's geologist brother John spent a memorable evening going back and forth with me about the ideas on genetics and evolution I was using in *Darwin's Radio*. Wonderful discussions! And pointed enough to make me sweat. Honing one's arguments in such company was essential to making that novel work.

Poul and I served in Jerry Pournelle's and Larry Niven's Citizen's Advisory Council on National Space Policy. That continued through the late nineties. Astrid and I attended Contact conferences with Poul and Karen, served on many convention panels together, frequently discussed writing and publishing—

And yet Poul and I never collaborated on a story. He certainly enjoyed collaborating with other writers, and likely would have gladly done so with me—but somehow, it never happened. During the time it could have happened, Poul was producing some of his finest and most ambitious novels, and so perhaps it would have been impolite to interrupt that streak. Still, it would have been fun.

If there had been a few more years . . .

Yet in many ways, Poul *did* collaborate with me—at a fundamental level. The influence of his novels and stories has been immense since I was a young teenager. *The Broken Sword* strongly influenced my vision of the Sidhe in *Songs of Earth and Power. Tau Zero* was, in my estimation, one of the finest science fiction novels of the last half of the twentieth century.

And his personal influence—gently guiding but never admonishing, informative about both business and science, about science fiction, history, and the history of science fiction—was incalculable.

Many writers find writing an arduous task. They'd rather do anything else—except work for a living. But Poul genuinely enjoyed writing, sitting alone in his small office, meeting his characters once again—old friends—and continuing their stories. He also greatly enjoyed being with friends and family. He was proud of his wife and daughter and his grandchildren.

I wish Poul had been with us longer, of course—his death moved me deeply. I miss him to this day. He would have been immensely pleased that his granddaughter Alex attended the Clarion West writer's workshop, a prestigious six-week boot camp for writers. He would have been equally pleased that his grandson Erik is now writing scripts for comics—and making more money on his first contracts than I did!

And Poul would have been very proud indeed that Astrid has sold a mystery story (to *San Diego Noir*, edited by Maryelizabeth Hart) and is currently working on a novel with her collaborator, Diane Clark.

For more than twenty years, I had pretty steady access to Poul Anderson. We still get together frequently with Karen, who lives down in the Los Angeles area now, and help manage the estate. Poul's legacy rolls along in so many ways. And so it is with great joy that I have read the stories in this collection.

This book is something of a miracle: tribute and collaboration, festival and continuity, an amazing gathering of many of the finest science fiction and fantasy writers of our time—brave writers all—

attempting the very difficult if not the impossible job of writing a tale set in one of Poul Anderson's many worlds—and succeeding!

Huzzahs and beer are definitely in order, with or without tritium!

OUTMODED THINGS

by Nancy Kress

***NANCY KRESS** began selling her elegant and incisive stories in the mid-seventies, and has since become a frequent contributor to* Asimov's Science Fiction, The Magazine of Fantasy and Science Fiction, Omni, SCI FICTION, *and elsewhere. Her books include the novel version of her Hugo- and Nebula-winning story,* Beggars in Spain, *and a sequel,* Beggars and Choosers, *as well as* The Prince of Morning Bells, The Golden Grove, The White Pipes, An Alien Light, Brain Rose, Oaths & Miracles, Stinger, Maximum Light, Crossfire, Nothing Human, The Flowers of Aulit Prison, Crucible, Dogs, *and the* Space Opera *trilogy* Probability Moon, Probability Sun, *and* Probability Space. *Her short work has been collected in* Trinity and Other Stories, The Aliens of Earth, Beaker's Dozen, *and* Nano Comes to Clifford Falls and Other Stories. *Her most recent book is the YA novel,* Flash Point. *In addition to the awards for* Beggars in Spain, *she has also won Nebula Awards for her stories "Out Of All Them Bright Stars," "The Flowers of Aulit Prison," and "Fountain of Age," and the John W. Campbell Memorial Award in 2003 for her novel* Probability Space, *and another Hugo in 2009 for "The Erdmann Nexus." She lives in Seattle, Washington with her husband, writer Jack Skillingstead.*

Here she takes us back to the frontier planet Roland, the setting for one of Poul Anderson's most famous stories, "The Queen of Air and Darkness," to examine the question of what happens to changelings stolen by the "fairies" when they return to human society. And are faced with a difficult choice of worlds.

> *"People had moved starward in the hopes of preserving such outmoded things as their mother tongues or constitutional government or rational-technological civilization."*
>
> —Poul Anderson, "The Queen of Air and Darkness"

It was difficult to hear over the barking. All the dogs—and there were so *many* dogs—seemed to have started howling all at once. The patient turned her head toward the window, which Luke had opaqued before the session began. He leaned toward the girl.

"Anne?"

"Something's happening."

"Those dogs bark all the time." He hadn't yet told anyone how much he disliked dogs; a therapist was not supposed to have such silly weaknesses. And here at Christmas Landing, the animals were necessary. Maybe. Luke preferred to put his faith in the mind-shields.

"That barking is different." She rose, a pale, doughy, difficult girl that he was coming to like very much, even though she took time away from what was supposed to be his main duty here. "I want to go see."

The session was almost over. Luke said, "I'll come with you," and stood. For a moment, dizziness took him and he put a hand on the edge of the ugly, utilitarian table to steady himself, but Anne didn't notice. That alone was a measure of her distraction; this was a girl who usually noticed everything, reacted intensely to everything, embroidered everything with the colors of her own over-romantic soul, all beneath a stolid exterior that misled nearly everyone about who she actually was.

Anyway, very few sixteen-year-olds would notice the symptoms of an old man's hidden disease.

Anne moved lightly to the door—for such a big girl, she could move with surprising grace—and pulled it open. Luke followed her through the corridor, as ugly and utilitarian as his borrowed desk in his borrowed office.

Most of Christmas Landing looked ugly to him. The entire planet had only hosted human settlements for a hundred years, and half of Roland's scant million people were crowded into Portolondon. This pioneer outpost at the edge of civilization had not had much time to beautify itself, being too occupied with, first, survival. Next, with its business as a market town for the farmers and fur trappers and miners who labored in the open country to the east and west. And then, in the last months, with Project Recovery. Accustomed to the greater age and comfort of Portolondon, it had taken something special for Dr. Luke Silverstein to uproot himself in his present condition and come here.

The something special ran past them.

"Oh!" Anne gasped. "Shadow-of-a-Dream!" And Anne went after her, all grace gone in comparison with the other girl, who once again had shed, or forgotten to put on, her clothes. Luke followed more slowly, apprehension shifting in his chest like some emotional tectonic plates. The dogs' barking grew hysterical.

In the Arctic circle's brief summer, hot and feverish, entire corridor walls were rolled open. Luke's borrowed office, at the edge of the town farthest from the bars and brothels and clamorous equipment that received grain and ore and furs, gave onto a wide strip of bare dirt that, supposedly, would one day be planted as a park. Beyond the strip of dirt, the shield shimmered faintly, jamming all electromagnetic signals not aimed at the high tower rising above Christmas Landing. Beyond that shimmer, wending its way among the shiverleaf bushes and vivid sprays of firethorn, a figure moved. The dogs, kept inside by the restraints on their collars, dashed forward to throw themselves against the unseen barrier.

Luke, like the two girls, watched the alien approach—but what did one of them see?

When Luke had first arrived at Christmas Landing, Police Chief Halford had driven him from the spaceport to the city. "The port is shielded," had been almost her first words to Luke, "and so is the entire perimeter of Christmas Landing. But this rover and the area in between is not. You probably won't see anything, but just in case you do, be aware that the illusion is not real. Most of the Rollies can't project farther than three or four feet, but a few can. The talented ones, if you call that talent." She had snorted derisively and made a gesture considered filthy in Portolondon. That, plus the dismissive "Rollies," made him dislike her. However, he kept an open mind. For one thing, the outlying settlements had been losing their children to the natives for nearly twenty years, and anger was to be expected. For another, he was paid to keep an open mind.

So he said mildly, "What might I see?"

She scowled. "I thought they briefed you."

"They did. I'd like to hear it from your perspective."

"My perspective is that the Rollies are kidnappers who used brainwashing to steal away our kids, less than half of which have been recovered. *Your* perspective is to straighten out the ones who have." She jerked the rover into motion.

Definitely dislikeable—and to call the aliens "brain-washers" was to call a tsunami a "beach wave." Luke had turned his attention to the countryside, in case he might "see something." He had not, except for the wild beauty of the largely unexplored and completely untamed northern wilderness. Such an alien wilderness, bright with strange summer colors, even though Luke Silverstein had been born in Portolondon, in the second generation of settlers on Roland. But Portolondon was far from any native sentience. Not even Christmas Landing had believed there was any native sentience on Roland, until recently. All the stories from outwayers had been dismissed as folk tales, superstitions, fanciful embroideries by humans living too much in isolation on their remote farms and ranches and trapping posts.

Nor had Luke "seen anything" in the month since. The elusive natives with their peculiar talent came nowhere near Christmas Landing. Meanwhile, the recovery teams had gone out twice and brought back six children, all under two years old. These six, like the others recovered so far, had gone back to the outwayer farms from which they'd been stolen. Luke had started therapy with the four older ones who had not gone home. And also with Anne, who was Police Chief's Halford's unlikely daughter.

Mistherd, Fire-Born, Cloud, Shadow-of-a-Dream. Or: Terry Barkley, Hal DiSilvio, Laura Simmons, Carolyn Grunewald. Terry had completely renounced his other name, a renunciation that was part of the extreme bitterness the police chief considered normal and Luke considered problematic. Hal, an exuberant eight-year-old orphan with astonishing adaptive capacity, was adjusting well to human life. Laura, eleven, said little and cried at night, although not for the parents whom she didn't remember and who were too afraid to reclaim her. But she, too, was coming along, having attached herself to a kindly refectory cook who was teaching her to bake. It was Carolyn—Shadow-of-a-Dream—who genuinely worried Luke.

She stood now, lovely in her nakedness that was both more innocent and more sensual than merely an unclothed human body. Every taut muscle strained toward the approaching figure. Every muscle—and what else? The shield deflected electromagnetic radiation, including brain waves, but Luke was not convinced that humans knew as much about their own brains as researchers claimed. Who, for instance, had known that what the aliens had done was even possible?

The figure stopped. Through the shimmer of the shield Luke saw an upright, vaguely reptilian creature: lean, scaly, long-tailed, big-beaked, with two small forearms and two heavy hind legs meant for speed. Behind the beak, its face was flat, with two eyes at the front and a third on the top of its head. *Once there were aerial predators on Roland*, he thought, inanely. In a curious way, the ugliness of the native matched the ugliness of Christmas Landing. It came closer and whistled something: high, fluted, oddly musical.

Carolyn gave a wordless cry and plunged forward, across the strip of bare dirt and through the shield. Without a moment's hesitation, Anne followed.

Alarms sounded. Police, already alerted by the barking dogs, raced belatedly down the corridor from the opposite direction. Only two men—Christmas Landing had diverted much of its constabulary to Project Recovery. By the time the cops reached the shield, which stopped radiation and dogs but not people, Luke had already reached it himself.

Carolyn, laughing and crying, threw her arms around the scaly alien and fluted back. Anne stood transfixed, her pale eyes wide as Roland's larger moon. Luke groaned inwardly. Anne should not have experienced this, it would make her therapy so much harder, and as for Shadow-of-a-Dream . . . Luke stepped through the barrier.

Dizziness took him, and he fell to his knees.

The angel was neither young nor old, male nor female. All white:

wings, skin, robe. Not soft but infinitely compassionate, it held a hand out to Luke and said, "There is nothing to fear."

"I know," he said, and a sob broke from him just as one of the cops seized him roughly and dragged him back behind the shield, and the Angel of Death vanished.

"I don't think you realize how brave it was of the alien to come here," Luke said carefully to Police Chief Halford.

"I don't think you realize what a spectacle you made of yourself out there," Halford said. Disgust rimmed her features like frost. It didn't help that she was right. But so was Luke.

"Consider, Chief Halford. A native, alien to us, comes to the conquerors of her people without the only protection she knows, all because she wants to assure herself that the human girl she raised is well and not being mistreated. That takes enormous courage in any species."

"If that's what you assume her motive was."

"Shadow-of-a-Dream said it was."

"*Carolyn* is deluded—that's the whole point of this therapy, isn't it? If this were up to me, Dr. Silverstein, you would be on the next transport back to Portolondon. But Terry wants you to continue 'helping' Carolyn."

Luke wasn't surprised to hear that sixteen-year-old Terry's wishes carried so much weight. In this pioneer society, sixteen was formally an adult. Carolyn's parents were dead; she and Terry were lovers; Chief Halford had no other real options for dealing with Carolyn. Luke also knew, without being told, that he was to continue seeing Anne as well because Anne herself wished it and she, too, was sixteen.

He said with deliberate mildness, "I'll see Carolyn now."

"Terry is with her."

"I don't do therapy that way, Chief Halford."

"Then you won't do it at all. He says she won't come without him."

There is more than one control freak here. But he said only, "Send them both in."

The two youngsters held hands. Carolyn wore clothes, jeans and a loose blue shirt, although her feet were bare, the soles hard as leather from fourteen years of running barefoot in the wilderness. They were both so beautiful, Luke thought, conscious of his own wrinkled skin and bald head. He had never gone in for cosmetic enhancements. Carolyn's long brown hair, streaked with sun-gold, fell around her shoulders. Terry's blue eyes burned with anger.

The first three seconds and he was already faced with a problem. *She* wanted to be addressed as "Shadow-of-a-Dream"; *he* would be furious if Luke used the name the aliens had given her—the name she had been called by for most of her life. He said, "Hello to both of you."

"Hello," Terry said. The girl said nothing.

"Terry, it's not usual to do therapy with a third person present."

"We aren't usual," the young man said.

"True enough." Terry was extremely intelligent. His fury at discovering the alien deception that had ruled his life raged in him, a fire undiminished in a month of burning. He had refused all scans of his own brain. ("No one will invade my mind ever again!") The English language that his captors had insisted all the stolen children learn or retain was soft-voweled, slightly slurred on the consonants, and this somehow made his bitterness and anger seem even more dangerous: a blaze deceptively softened by gauzy curtains that might themselves ignite.

Luke said to the girl, "What did you see when you went beyond the shield?"

She looked at him mutely.

Terry said, "I know what she saw: the Queen of Air and Darkness. That's what we were told to call her, you know. Starmother, Lady Sky, The Fairest—an ugly reptile, a liar—all lies!"

Luke said, "Is that what you saw, Carolyn? The Queen of Air and Darkness?"

"Of course it is!" Terry said. "Don't you understand? Her presence is how they kept us like you keep dogs—come when they whistle, do what they order, bring more children to fair Carheddin under the mountain, lies lies lies—"

"Terry," Luke said, "I'd like Carolyn to answer, please. What did you see?"

Anguish distorted the lovely face. Luke held her eyes steadily. She was torn between what she wanted to say, whatever it was, and her love for this boy, whose will was stronger than hers. A long moment passed; Luke did not relinquish her gaze. Finally she turned to Terry.

"Mistherd—"

"Don't call me that!"

She looked down at her bare feet and fell silent, but obstinacy lurked in the set of her mouth. Was she strong enough to do without him? Luke said, "Carolyn, if you would prefer to talk to me alone, I'm sure Terry will understand."

"I won't," he said, at the same moment that she clutched his hand tighter and whispered, "No."

Not strong enough. Luke tried a different approach. "We have some new information about how the aliens cast their illusions. Dr. Cardiff's analyses of Laura's and Hal's brain scans may help us deal with any future incidents, if they happen."

"They will," Terry said grimly. "They're still out there, just in a new location. They won't give Roland to us that easily."

Us. All his life Terry had been "Mistherd," devoted to the Queen's cause. You could not change sides that completely, that fast, without extreme psychological stress. Luke might well be treating the wrong patient.

He persisted with the cooling balm of objective fact: "We've known for centuries that the brain projects its own electromagnetic field. It's pretty weak, but it's there, and in a few people it has even been put to practical use. Dowsers, for instance, can sense magnetic changes associated with the presence of a water table. Apparently the aliens highly developed an ability to manipulate each other's much stronger fields, as a means of communication, when their science developed along biological rather than physical lines. From the first stolen children, they learned to manipulate our electromagnetic fields as well, saturating the human brain with neuropsychic forces that set up feedback loops which—"

"What?" Terry said.

Luke had forgotten whom he was speaking to. The boy was intelligent, but he was also illiterate. Luke sought words to explain. "There are stories that lie in all human brains. The same stories that have turned up in one form or another in every human society, on every planet, from the beginning of time. They're called 'archetypes.' They involve gods, rulers, great warriors, terrible monsters, enchanted palaces, songs and feasting—all the illusions you experienced out there."

"All the lies," Terry said bitterly.

"They were not lies," Carolyn said.

Both men stared at her. She kept her eyes cast down, her mouth set in a stubborn line.

"Of course they were!" Terry exploded.

She shook her head.

Luke said quickly, "What do you mean, Carolyn?"

Silence. Terry started to speak and Luke raised his hand. For once, the boy subsided, his eyes on Carolyn. Just as Luke decided she was not going to answer, she raised her head.

"They were illusions. But not lies. Because we really *did* experience the illusions. We saw them and heard them." All at once she began to sing:

"Cast a spell,
Weave it well
Of dust and dew
And night and—"

"Stop!" Terry shouted.

"Mistherd—"

"Don't call me that!"

She put her hands over her face and started to cry. "Flowermother came to see if I was all right! She came in her own body and she came even though she thought humans might kill her or capture her. She came because she cares about us. And even after I went through their shield she stayed as herself. Do you understand, Mistherd? She cast no illusion in my mind!"

The girl looked directly at Luke, all of Roland's pagan wilderness in her eyes, and said, "You asked me what I saw. I saw the alien who raised me and loves me and came to see if I am all right. That's why she came. And—" the girl drew a deep breath—"and my name is Shadow-of-a-Dream."

Later, after they had gone, the girl in tears, Luke sat alone in his office. He sat for a long time. Finally he activated the commlink and sent a message to Chief Halford.

"I think you should put a twenty-four-hour guard on Carolyn Grunewald. She may try to go back to them."

Dogs were never fooled by alien illusions; evidently their brains were too different. Chief Halford was accompanied by her mastiff when she came to Luke's office, although privately he doubted that she actually needed it. Some people's minds seemed impervious to illusions, even the illusion of goodwill created by common courtesy.

"You failed," the chief said. "Carolyn is refusing to see you again, and not even Terry can persuade her."

"That was a risk I had to take. The greater risk was having her run."

"Why would she do that? Why would anybody do that? I don't understand!"

The plea might have moved Luke if it had been less belligerent, or if he hadn't felt so weak. This was not one of his good days. It was so difficult pretending to not be sick, pretending to not be old. He was not moved by Chief Halford, with her small glaring eyes and self-righteous scowl, but he owed her an answer.

"The aliens' neuropsychic projections can create the illusion of seeing whatever archetype you most desire," he said gently. "Why *wouldn't* that tempt a person?"

"But it's not real!"

"No."

"Then the girl is insane. Or you misdiagnosed her."

"I didn't diagnose her at all. I merely alerted authorities that I thought she might run and was therefore a danger to herself. As I am legally required to do."

"Oh, I know, you follow all the rules, doctor."

He had her pegged now: a fear biter. She was like certain dogs—hopefully not the mastiff lying by her side—that attacked when afraid. Chief Halford's fear was not for herself but for Christmas Landing, for the humans so tentatively established on Roland, and for Anne.

The attack came next. "Why didn't you tell me that you are dying of an inoperable brain tumor?"

Anger rose in Luke. "Medical records are supposed to be confidential."

"Nothing in Christmas Landing is hidden from me!"

She actually believed it. Luke would trace the leak later, and someone would be in deep trouble for it. Now all he said was, "Total knowledge is an illusion."

It went right over her head; she was not built for irony. She rose, looking down at him—to gain an advantage?—and said, "I don't want you to see Anne anymore."

"That's really up to her. As you've pointed out to me, sixteen is legal adulthood on Roland."

"We'll see about that." She banged the door as she left, and the mastiff growled at him.

No, not one of the good days. And only half over.

The chapel in Christmas Landing was dusty. No one had cleaned the tile floor or the deliberately simple stone altar, with its two unlit candles. But a fresh bouquet of firethorn and driftweed lay on the dusty stone.

Colonists to Roland came for various reasons and, when only two or three ships from other planets might reach Roland each century, the colonists came permanently. There were the usual fortune hunters, adventurers, and scientists. Most emigrants, however, came to isolate a cherished way of life from corrupting influences. These had their own churches, temples, mosques, shrines. The small chapel, deliberately free of anyone's symbols, was designed for the rest, those who might want a place of comfort or meditation or merely silence. Apparently few did.

Luke stopped just inside the door. In the dim light, Shadow-of-a-Dream lay at the foot of the altar. For a heart-stopping moment, he thought that she was dead.

Then it seemed that his heart *was* stopping. Dizziness took him and he clutched at his chest. This was it, then, not his brain but his heart . . . The machine eventually wears out . . .

It was not the end. A brief vision, quickly gone, and he found himself slumped on a plain wooden bench, the girl kneeling beside him.

"Healer, are you all right?"

"Yes . . . I . . . "

"I will bring help!"

He groped for her hand. She was naked again, save for a garland of the same flowers as lay on the altar. "No . . . no, please . . . " He didn't want the infirmary, the inevitable fuss and restrictions and pity. Especially not the pity.

She said, with sudden and incongruous hardness, "You do not want anyone to know."

"No." His breath came easier now.

"You are afraid they will keep you somewhere against your will."

"Shadow-of-a-Dream—"

She gave a harsh laugh, whirled around, and was gone in a flurry of firethorn petals and sixteen-year-old scorn.

When he could breathe regularly again, he hobbled to the altar and picked up her bouquet. It smelled fresh and alive.

Anne sat across from him, slouched in an old padded chair. In one sense, Luke thought frivolously, the problem was aesthetic. Both Terry and Carolyn—Mistherd and Shadow-of-a-Dream—had looked wrong in this bare, ugly room that was temporarily his office. Their former lives were evident in every movement of their lithe bodies, in every glance from their forest-sharpened eyes. Even when she was dressed, Shadow-of-a-Dream wore the wilderness. Whereas poor Anne Halford looked like she belonged here.

And yet, she did not think she did. The same archetypical visions that Terry raged against, that Shadow-of-a-Dream longed for, existed deep in Anne's brain.

"I saw a fairy," Anne said, "but tall, maybe seven feet. Dressed in robes of starlight and petals of flowers. Light danced all around her, but shadows did, too. I saw the Queen of Air and Darkness."

"You saw an illusion," Luke said.

"I know that, doctor."

But she didn't want to know it. He said gently, "You would have liked it to be real."

"Yes, of course. Wouldn't we all?"

No. He waited. She had something to say and she was going to say it. His head hurt, and the dizziness came more frequently now. But he forced himself to concentrate; they had reached that critical point in therapy where the patient was ready to open up. There would be a rush, maybe an explosion, of words and feelings. But when words came, Luke was nonetheless surprised at how Anne began.

"My mother goes to church."

Anger in the young eyes, bitter from a lifetime of being considered a disappointment to her overbearing mother.

"I didn't know that," Luke said. Another surprise, but it shouldn't have been. People were always more complicated than they appeared, with hidden corners that led only to more shadowy passages. Even Police Chief Halford.

"She goes to church every Sunday and she believes in God. I asked her how she knew that wasn't just an illusion, and she said she didn't know directly, but she had faith, which was belief in what could not be known directly. I said that was a good definition of 'illusion.' She said no, she knew which was faith and which was direct experience, but if I wanted to believe in the Queen of Air and Darkness, I was muddying that distinction, by taking direct experience of deception for truth. I said there was more than one kind of truth and she wasn't capable of seeing that psychological truth, the truth of fiction and poetry, has its own validity. I said the really intelligent mind could hold both the truth and untruth of the alien illusions in mind at the same time. She said that was semantic hogwash. I said she was incapable of seeing it because she was incapable of doing it. I said she was an idiot. Then we had a big fight."

Luke was startled. He'd expected an outburst, but not this eloquence. Anne sat there—mulish, belligerent, more subtle than he'd expected. Obviously she had thought about all this, perhaps even rehearsed it. She was intelligent and very unhappy. Luke would have to tread softly.

"How did the fight end?"

"I moved out. I'm sixteen, you know. I took a room in the transition dorm."

This useful structure, unique to Christmas Landing, provided three months' free lodging to anyone who asked for it. The intention was to house newcomers to Christmas Landing while they organized their lives as outwayers, the farmers and ranchers and miners in the hinterlands who supported Roland. The transition dorm also housed those same outwayers who had failed in those endeavors and were returning, usually broke and sometimes broken, back to Portolondon. Several families reclaiming their stolen children had stayed in the transition dorm, as did the inevitable drifters, petty criminals, down-on-their-luck gamblers. Luke could imagine what Chief Halford thought of her daughter's living there.

"Anne," he said gently, "have you thought what you might do when the three months are over?"

"Yes. I went to Dr. Cardiff and offered myself as a liaison with the natives. I said I would go live with them and report back, and that way his scientific team would get another perspective on them than just talking to people like Mistherd."

He was staggered. "What . . . what did Dr. Cardiff say?"

"He said no."

Of course he had. Project Recovery was bringing children back, not sending them out. And no matter what this frontier town said, to Luke, sixteen was still a child.

Anne leaned forward in her chair. "You think it's a stupid idea, too."

"Not necessarily." She was looking for a fight, but she wasn't going to get it from him. "In time, it may be a viable one. But neither the natives nor we may be ready for it just now."

"'May,' 'may,'—aren't you ever definite, doctor?"

"Yes," he said, and she got the joke and smiled. The tension dissipated a little, but only a little.

"I'm going now," she said. "The session's over."

"Yes, it is, but Anne—don't go thinking that I'm in the same camp as your mother. I think your . . . your interest in the natives and their abilities shows a genuine intellectual curiosity. And I believe you are stable enough to tell the difference between illusion and reality."

He was rewarded with her rare smile. "Thanks." And then, fiercely, "All that people like my mother can think to do with illusion is wall themselves away from it. Instead of exploring what good it might bring to us."

It had not brought anything good to Mistherd, or to Shadow-of-a-Dream. Neither of them, however, had Anne's obstinate clarity. At the same time, Luke was afraid that, in the effort to keep her from stopping therapy, he had offered her too much encouragement. Perhaps he should not have taken this assignment; he was too sick, too old. His head hurt.

"I'll see you Tuesday," he said to Anne. All at once, and very unprofessionally, he was eager for her to leave.

"Yes," Anne said.

But Tuesday she was in the infirmary with flu, Luke was in bed at his hotel with chest pains, and Shadow-of-a-Dream had vanished.

◈ ◈ ◈

"She could not have left Christmas Landing," Chief Halford said. "I've reviewed the surveillance data on every penetration of the perimeter shield. All authorized."

"I thought," Luke said, "that you'd assigned her a twenty-four-hour guard."

"We did. A dog, of course; we can't afford personnel for wayward girls!"

"What happened to the dog?" Luke sat in his hotel room, as utilitarian as everything else in Christmas Landing, and tried to appear healthier than he was. He had doubled his medication, but if he went to the infirmary, he would never come out. That was not how he wanted to die.

Chief Halford—it suddenly occurred to him that he'd never heard her first name—said, "The dog was drugged."

Luke was impressed. "Where did Shadow-of-a-Dream get drugs?"

"Her name is Carolyn and I haven't yet found out where she got the drugs. You know Carolyn better than anyone—where do you think she might be in Christmas Landing? Dr. Cardiff and his team are very anxious to have her back."

I'll bet they are, Luke thought. And so was the chief, whose reputation would not be helped by this. Luke looked at her as steadily as he could manage.

"Chief Halford, the human brain is more plastic than we once thought, especially the brains of children. Children damaged in freak accidents have shown the ability to modify neural connections in ways completely impossible for adults. I'm sure Dr. Cardiff told you this after he examined the brain scans of Hal DiSilvio and Laura Simmons." Fire-Born and Cloud, that were.

"He did, but it isn't very relevant to what I'm dealing with here, is it? Do you have any idea where Carolyn might be?"

"No."

"Thank you." She left, scowling, a competent woman only trying to do her job, and faced with forces she could not comprehend.

But we all do that every day, Luke thought. Life itself is too complex for us to fully comprehend, let alone death.

In fact, humanity had gone backwards in its ability to deal with death. Once death was carried around as a constant companion, a silent shadow that might at any moment choose to speak. People died so much younger, and so much more frequently. In childbirth, as infants, of untamed diseases, of harsh environments. There was no choice but to live with the shadow, acknowledge it, and from that had grown death's opposite: stories of heroism and transcendence, of Valhalla and Paradise and the Elysian Fields, of beauty so strong it diminished one's inevitable fate. From the acknowledged shadow had come the once-and-yet-to-be Arthur asleep in Avalon, had come Apollo blinding in his beauty, had come the Queen of Air and Darkness. Illusions, and yet more than illusions.

It hurt to move. Luke did so slowly, gathering only what was necessary: a warm jacket, strong boots. In the hotel lobby, a mastiff eyed him. He ignored it and went out into the street. The night was clear and moonless, the stars dimmed by the lights of the city. He caught a robo-taxi and it took him to the transition dorm.

Only on the way did he realize it was Saturday night. Onto the streets near the hotel, outwayers spilled out of the bars, into the bars. They called to each other raucously, young people who lived with hardship but not usually, thanks to modern technology, with death. In the bright holos of Christmas Landing, under the dim stars, there were no shadows. Even the northern auroras seemed faint.

It was quieter close to the transition dorm, located near the city perimeter to make outgoing expeditions more efficient. Most of the transients were partying in the quarter he had just left. Luke made his slow way through the lobby, then up in the elevator to the room listed for A. Halford.

"Yes?" Anne's wary response through the closed door. Ready to be angry, but with another note underneath.

"It's Dr. Silverstein. Please let me in, Anne. I need to see you."

Silence. Then the door opened, almost defiantly. Luke understood. They were conducting a test.

Anne was dressed in clothes a little too warm for the evening. The guard dog assigned to her lay beside the bed, eyeing Luke. Luke gazed back, and he knew. Painfully he squatted beside the dog, looked directly into its eyes.

"Hello, Shadow-of-a-Dream."

They were first shocked, then afraid. "How did you know?" Anne demanded. Shadow-of-a-Dream had resumed her human form, which of course she had never lost. The girl was not a shape shifter. Only the human mind was.

Luke addressed not Anne but the beautiful, naked child. "It was in the chapel—do you remember?" *A brief vision, quickly gone, and he found himself slumped on a plain wooden bench, the girl kneeling beside him.* "I thought I was dying, and I saw the same vision I'd seen from your alien caretaker, the one who raised you, outside the perimeter of the mind shield. Only this time *you* sent it, didn't you, Shadow-of-a-Dream? Your own brain, worked on all those years and perhaps possessing more talent than most—you can cast the illusions, too. Not far and maybe not for long, but you can do it." *Brains more plastic than we once thought*, Cardiff's report had said, *especially the brains of children.*

Both girls, one so clearly the child of civilization and one so much the opposite, both stared mutely. Luke said, "What did you do with the dogs?"

Anne said sulkily, "Drugged. Hers and mine. We will not be guarded like criminals!"

Luke said, "You got the sleeping pills from the infirmary. While you supposedly had the flu." He didn't ask how she had faked the symptoms; it was easy enough with various ingested substances, and she was a researcher.

Anne said, "Don't try to stop us!" But she was no threat. It was Shadow-of-a-Dream who held the long, wickedly sharp knife—and where had she concealed it when she wore no clothes?

"Shadow-of-a-Dream," he said quietly, "you don't need that. I'm not trying to stop you. I want to go with you."

Three figures walked slowly down the corridor, open on one side to the warm summer night. The figures passed two or three people, all of whom saw a boy and girl holding hands, accompanied by their large mastiff.

The strip of bare land beyond the corridor was not surveilled; the mind-shield was deemed strong enough to keep out illusions. These illusions, however, were inside the shield. Had anyone been watching from the windows of Christmas Landing, three dogs wandered over the dirt, as dogs always did. The ground was littered with dog poop.

The mind-shield, a faint shimmer in the starlight, was under surveillance. But the dogs were not there long. They passed through the shield, and alarms began to ring. Within Christmas Landing, people responded.

"Run!" cried Shadow-of-a-Dream. Luke ran, but only a short distance was necessary.

"Go," he gasped, and collapsed to the ground, thinking *I didn't need boots and jacket after all.*

Shadow-of-a-Dream stopped. She looked at him, and in her eyes he saw comprehension.

Did the girl think then of Terry—Mistherd? Did she regret that he would not join her and Anne in the wild and enchanted Carheddin under the mountain? Terry's bitterness would never permit that. More, he would consider Shadow-of-a-Dream's return to the natives an act of weakness. But which was stronger: the mind able to reject illusion, or the one able to embrace it while still recognizing it for what it was?

Luke had a last glimpse of Shadow-of-a-Dream, lovely and wild and pagan and alien, before she vanished. The men who ran toward him through the shield saw only two shiverleaf bushes, among the many that grew just beyond the outpost. Luke saw only the stars above, not dimmed at all. He saw only the dark night, and the darker one approaching.

And then he saw the Angel of Death, as he had seen it once before on this spot, and then once again in the chapel. Shadow-of-a-Dream's last gift, coming toward him in a blaze of white light, holding out her long slim hands. Compassionate and welcoming, erasing all illusion of fear.

AFTERWORD:

I FIRST read Poul Anderson when I was fifteen. My mother had given me for Christmas the two-volume *Treasury of Science Fiction*, edited by Anthony Boucher, which I still have (it's a bit battered from umpty-umpty moves). The volume included Anderson's "Brain Wave," in which the Earth in its movement through space moves out of an "inhibitor field" that has been affecting electromagnetic activity in the human brain for millions of years. All at once everyone is much, much more intelligent. So are the animals. This story knocked me out with its inventiveness and scope. So I reread it while looking for a universe to borrow for this anthology story, and it still knocks me out.

However, for this anthology I chose instead "The Queen of Air and Darkness," the 1972 Hugo winner. This also is concerned with the human brain. It's a gorgeous story but, unlike "Brain Wave," it does not carry its characters' fates past the revelation of what the aliens have been doing. Even in 1972 I wanted to know more: What happened to Mistherd back in "civilization"? To Shadow-of-a-Dream? And what about the fact that the human civilization Anderson had created for Roland was far less attractive than the alien illusions? It was lovely to have a chance to write this story and thus to create some answers.

A final note on writing "Outmoded Things": Gardner Dozois is an experienced editor. I signed the contract for this story in August, 2010. This manuscript was not due until the following June. But Gardner knows writers, and so every single month he sent out a reminder: "Only nine more months until your story is due! Eight more months! Six more months and, oh, incidentally, Harry Turtledove and Stephen Baxter have already turned theirs in! They get a gold star!" It was lovely to have a chance to write this story—and the editorial nagging didn't hurt, either.

—Nancy Kress

THE MAN WHO CAME LATE
by Harry Turtledove

ALTHOUGH HE *writes other kinds of science fiction as well, and even the occasional fantasy, Harry Turtledove has become one of the most prominent writers of Alternate History stories in the business today, and is probably the most popular and influential writer to work that territory since L. Sprague De Camp; in fact, most of the current popularity of that particular sub-genre can be attributed to Turtledove's own hot-ticket bestseller status.*

Turtledove has published Alternate History novels such as The Guns of the South, *dealing with a timeline in which the American Civil War turns out* very *differently, thanks to time-traveling gun-runners; the best-selling* Worldwar *series, in which the course of World War II is altered by attacking aliens; the "Basil Argyros" series, detailing the adventures of a "magistrianoi" in an alternate Byzantine Empire (collected in the book* Agent of Byzantium)*; the "Sim" series, which take place in an alternate world in which European explorers find North America inhabited by hominids instead of Indians (collected in the book* A Different Flesh)*; a look at a world where the Revolutionary War* didn't *happen, written with actor Richard Dreyfuss,* The Two Georges, *and many other intriguing Alternate History scenarios. Turtledove is also the author of two multi-volume Alternate History* fantasy *series, "Videssos Cycle" and the "Krispes Sequence." His other books include* *the novels* Wereblood, Werenight, Earthgrip, Noninterference, A World of Difference, Gunpowder Empire, American Empire: The Victorous Opposition, Jaws of Darkness, Ruled Britannia, Settling Accounts: Drive to the East, In the Presence of Mine Enemies, The Bridge of the Separator, End of the Beginning, *and* Every Inch a King; *the collections* Kaleidoscope, Down in the Bottomlands (and Other Places), *and* Atlantis and Other Places, *and, as editor,* The Best Alternate History Stories of the 20th Century, The Best Military Science Fiction of the 20th Century, The Best Time Travel Stories of the 20th Century, *and, with Martin H. Greenberg, the* Alternate Generals *books. His most recent books include the novels* The Big Switch *and* Supervolcano! *He won a Hugo Award in 1994 for his story, "Down in the Bottomlands." A native Californian, Turtledove has a Ph.D. in Byzantine history from UCLA, and has published a scholarly translation of a 9th-century Byzantine chronicle. He lives in Canoga Park, California, with his wife and family.*

In the autumnal story that follows, a bittersweet return to the world of Anderson's landmark fantasy novel Three Hearts and Three Lions, *he shows us that sometimes you* can't *go home again, even if you want to more than anything else in the world.*

ALIANORA CARRIED A BUCKET to the well in the tiny green at the heart of the village. She needed the water. She'd used what there was in the house the night before to soak green and yellow peas. She aimed to cook up a big pot of pease porridge, and enliven the flavor with chopped onion, bits of salt pork and some fennel she'd got from a wandering trader.

Her long wool skirt almost stirred up dust as she walked along. Most village women embroidered flowers or bright birds on their linen tunics. She'd ornamented hers with dragons. Maybe—no, surely—they talked about her behind her back. Well, that was all right. They gossiped about one another the same way. And she joined in. In a place where great things never happened, what could you do but go on about small ones?

She knew about great things. She'd lived through a dragon's onslaught, something of which few mortals could boast. (Not that she *did* boast—what point to it?) She'd met elflords and sorceresses and high nobles of the human kind as well . . . and here she was, wed to the smith who'd forged the iron hoops that bound the bucket's oaken staves.

Sometimes she wondered whether the war against Chaos that had engulfed the whole world thirty years before was meant to bring nothing more splendid than countless villages, all of them places where great things never happened, scattered through plains and forests. But what better result could the war have birthed? If ordinary folk were able to live ordinary lives free from anything worse than ordinary fears, didn't things wag the way they should?

She smiled when she passed the smithy. Theodo waved back through the open door. He was never too busy to look out whenever someone went by. Part of that came from having two strapping sons learning the trade. Part sprang from life in a place like this. Anything that chanced was perforce noticeable and interesting, because not much did.

The smile stayed on Alianora's face as she walked on. Theodo was a good man, a kind man. He'd never struck her in anger, never once. He'd clouted Einhard and Nithard only when they'd really and truly earned it. His hands might be scarred and callused and hard, but they were gentle in the quiet dark. A good man. A kind man. Perhaps not the most exciting man God ever made, but . . .

"I've had enough excitements, enough and to spare," Alianora whispered fiercely. Her own work-roughened hands tightened on the bucket's handle. Having magic-dashing cold iron in the family, so to speak, wasn't such a bad thing even today.

No, not half. The blue gloaming that warded Faerie folk from the daylight they could not bear had retreated many leagues after Chaos' latest grand assault on the lands of Law went awry. Yet still you could see it on the horizon from here. It had even moved forward again, a little, once or twice, in the years since then. Law's nature, after all, was to forget and to forgive. Chaos did neither, it seemed, and found more agents within Law's borders to work its will than would ever be so in reverse.

Not that all wizardry was wicked. Oh, no! Alianora's smile subtly changed. Her daughter Alianna wore the white, feathered swan-may's tunic these days, and wore it wondrous well. Somewhere in the priests' holy Book it said there was a time for everything, and there as elsewhere the Book spoke true.

Alianora knew without—too much—resentment that her own time for the swan-may's tunic lay behind her. Three decades and four children (one tiny body had lain in hallowed ground since before its first saint's day, an unending sadness) had widened the hips to which that tunic once clung. She'd lost two teeth and gained wrinkles; encroaching gray streaked and dulled her red hair.

But when she dreamt of flying, she knew whereof she dreamt! Everyone flew in dreams. Almost everyone had to imagine what it was like. Alianora *knew* the wind beneath her wings, *knew* the joy of soaring on streams of warm air gusting up from the ground, *knew* the wonder of freedom and speed in three dimensions.

She glanced up into the watery sky to see if she might catch a glimpse of Alianna. No; wherever her daughter flew today, it was not near here. Just as well. Who didn't want to fly wide when young, to streak over the fields and the meadows and the dark woods beyond? A village was for settling down, for later. When you were Alianna's age, you thought later never came. You thought all kinds of things when you were Alianna's age.

Here was the green, and the stone-ringed well. Behind Alianora, Theodo's hammer rang against the anvil. The iron he beat into shape there wouldn't be cold, not yet. As always, she hoped he wouldn't come home nursing a burn. He was careful, but once in a while everyone slipped.

Four or five women stood near the well. Berthrada's twin blond boys toddled by her feet. One of them stooped and plucked up some grass or maybe a bug and stuck it in his mouth. She hadn't seemed to be watching, but she grabbed him, thrust a finger in there, and got rid of whatever it was. Mothers had, and needed, eyes in the back of the head. Berthrada swatted her son on the bottom, not too hard, and set him down again.

Alianora nodded to the women as she came up. They nodded back. It wasn't quite as if she'd been born and raised here, even if her husband had. She'd been places and done things they were just as well pleased not to know too much about. And the brief, form-fitting swan-may's tunic that had been hers and was now mostly Alianna's brought a whiff of scandal with it.

Still and all, she lived here quietly enough, as she had for many years now. She made eyes at no man but her own. Her sons would be catches; no doubt of that. So Ethelind, the miller's wife, said, "Have you heard the latest about Walacho and his poor sorry family?"

"What now?" Alianora asked sadly, working on the crank to bring up a bucket of well water. Any sensible man drank beer instead when he could; if you drank water all the time, you pretty much begged for a flux of the bowels. Walacho wasn't such a sensible man. He drank to get drunk, and when he got drunk he got mean. He did things he was sorry for later, which helped him as much as it did anyone else.

Before Ethelind could come out with—or embroider upon—the juicy details of his latest rampage, Berthrada pointed out to the edge of the woods and exclaimed, "Look! A stranger's coming!"

Ethelind shot her a dirty look. Walacho's ordinary folly would have to wait for another time. Strangers didn't come to the village every day, or every week, either. This one might give folk here things to talk about till the next one showed up.

He tramped along with determined strides, like a man who has been traveling for a long time and knows he may have to keep going longer yet. He was a big man, tall and broad through the shoulders. He wore a green plaid wool shirt with a stand-and-fall collar; sturdy, snug-fitting trousers dyed a blue not quite that of woad; and ankle-length brown leather boots. A scabbarded sword hung on his left hip, a sheathed knife on his right.

"Well, heaven knows I've seen worse," Berthrada murmured when he was still a little too far away to hear her.

"He's too old for you, dear," Ethelind said, also softly. She freighted the last word with poisonous sweetness.

No matter how catty that made her, it didn't make her wrong. The stranger's fair hair—so far, telling how much gray it held was hard—receded at the temples. Harsh grooves scored his forehead and the skin between his nostrils and the corners of his mouth. When you got a good look at it, his nose had a distinct dent.

When Alianora got a good look at that dent, it was as if someone had punched her, hard, on the point of the chin. She sagged. Her hands slipped off the crank. It spun backwards, and almost did clip her in the face. She wondered if she would even have noticed. She'd already been hit harder than that.

"Holger," she said, and groped for the stone wall around the well to help steady herself.

His eyes snapped sharply toward her. They were blue as she remembered, blue as a deep lake seen from the sky when she soared above it in swan's guise. But he had not known her till she spoke his name. Grief flamed within her for that.

"Alianora?" he said. "Is it really you at last?" Blood drained from his weathered face, leaving it lich-pale.

"Aye," she answered. She'd told him she loved him, there in the ruined church of St. Grimmin's. And he'd taken the sword Cortana, which he'd found hidden there, and he'd ridden forth on his great black horse, and he'd broken the forces of Chaos, for they could not stand against him and what he bore.

And that was thirty long years ago now, even if it sometimes seemed like yesterday. It might seem so, but seeming was not reality.

"My dear," he said. "My love." He took a step in her direction. The village women stared avidly, their eyes wide as saucers. Even Berthrada's twins peeped out from behind their mother's skirts.

Alianora straightened. It was like taking a wound. Once the first shock passed, you steadied—if it wasn't mortal, of course. "You never came back to me," she said, as if that were all the explanation she needed. Perhaps it was. No one died of a broken heart, regardless of how many people wished they could.

Holger's hands dropped. He had started to get his color back. Now he whitened again. "I couldn't, dammit," he mumbled, staring down at the grass and dirt between his feet. "The magics that brought me here swept me back to the world where I'd lived before. I was needed there, too, it turned out."

She believed him absolutely. That more than one world might require the services of such a hero . . . Well, who could doubt it? In the end, though, what difference did it make? Two worlds might need Holger, but so had she—then. "You never came back to me," she repeated, this time adding, "I thought sure I would never see you again."

He cocked his head to one side. A small, tight, crooked smile came and went. "You don't talk the way you used to," he said, sliding away from what she'd told him.

She knew what he meant. When he'd known her before, she'd had a thick back-country burr. It wasn't the way folk in the villages around here spoke. To fit in better, she'd softened the burr as much as she could.

"I've dwelt in these parts a long time now," she said, talking the way she talked.

"I know. I've been trying to get to these parts for a long time now." Holger stared off toward the horizon, and toward the blue Faeries gloaming darkening one stretch of it. "I've been to a lot of places—a lot of worlds. But Something or Somebody kept holding me away from this one. I can make a pretty good guess Who, too."

Alianora could make that same guess. If the Powers Holger had bested here had their way, they would never want to see him again. And, even if they'd lost their war to rule this world wholly, their strength was not to be despised.

"I wonder that you succeeded in their despite," she said, her voice softening a little.

"You'd better believe I did, kiddo. I don't give up, no matter what." He stuck out his chin. He was in good hard shape for a man his age—in extraordinary shape for a man his age—but the flesh under there still sagged. Well, so did the flesh under Alianora's chin. The earth dragged you down towards it, and then it dragged you down into it, and then . . . you found out for sure what came afterwards.

"Thirty years. I was thinking on that earlier today," Alianora said.

Holger nodded brusquely. "A devil of a long time," he agreed. "I made it, though." He looked at her as if she were the only thing in all the world—no, in all the worlds.

Once upon a time, that look would have melted her the way a mild spring morning melts the last winter frost. To a certain extent, it still did—but only to a certain extent. She was no longer who she had been in those dark and desperate days. Nor was he. She knew as much. She was far from sure he could say the same.

"So much time gone by," she murmured.

"Not too much. We still have a good bit left," he said.

She made herself meet that intent gaze. It wasn't far removed from crossing swords. "Thirty years," she repeated. "Thirty years of faring betwixt—amongst—the worlds for you."

"I was always trying to get here," Holger said. "Always." The word clanged in his mouth.

Alianora nodded. "I believe you." Even with the white tunic, she hadn't flown so far as she used to do. After the war, the sullen, sulking, beaten Middle World was no longer such a welcoming place. Since Alianna took wing in her stead, she didn't think she'd gone farther than a day's walk from the village. As gently as she could, she asked, "In all your wanderings, did you never, ah, meet anyone who made you want to leave off and bide where you found yourself?"

He looked down at the ground once more: dull embarrassment this time. "I won't lie to you. There's been a girl or three. You know how things are." He spread his hands. A swordsman's calluses marked his right palm.

She did know how things were. A knight errant spent his nights erring—that was what they said, anyhow. How the woman he loved—the woman who loved him—felt when he did, he could always worry about later . . . if he worried about it at all.

Holger raised his big head. Fierce intensity filled his stare. "But there was never anybody else, babe. Never really. Never so it counted here—" He touched himself on the heart. "Only below the belt, if you know what I mean." He chuckled.

Again, Alianora knew. Pity stabbed through her. "Why not, Holger?" she asked. "Why not, in heaven's name? So many long, dry years . . . "

She didn't think he heard, or noticed, that last. "I'll tell you why not. Because all I ever cared about in this miserable universe is you, that's why. Because I aimed to go on till I found you, no matter what I had to do, no matter how long it took. And here I am." His pride blazed like a forest fire.

Trying to deflect it seemed wisest. "All you ever cared for is me, say you? You know you speak not sooth. What of Morgan le Fay?"

He didn't flinch. She wished he would have. "Well, what about her?" he said roughly. "That was a long time ago, and in another country, and besides, I hadn't met you yet. I never would've busted my hump the way I did, fighting back to this world for the likes of *her*, and you can take that to the bank. But you, you're worth it."

He was convinced she was; she heard as much in his voice. He had to be, lest all he'd done and suffered this past half a lifetime turn to dust and blow away like fairy gold tried on an anvil of cold iron. "Surely life goes on wherever one wanders," Alianora said. "Surely, had you sought, you would have found many, or one at least, not so very different from me."

"No way. Not a chance." Holger had vast reserves of stubbornness. Without them, he never would have won Cortana, never would have had the chance to scatter the host of Chaos before him. Now . . . Now he said, "You're the one, the only one."

"Oh, Holger." Alianora tried to make him hear what he would not see: "I am no more the lass you wooed."

He wasn't listening. And he had his reasons: his eyes shifted away from her, and his yellow-callused hand dropped to the hilt of his sword. "Who're these clowns?" he ground out. "They better make tracks, kid. They mess with me, it's the last dumb stunt they ever pull."

Alianora turned to follow his gaze. One of the other women by the well must have hotfooted it back to the smithy. Alianora hadn't noted anyone leaving, but to say she was distracted only proved the weakness of words. Here came Theodo, a heavy hammer clutched in his fist. Behind him strode Einhard and Nithard, one with an axe, the other with a cleaver.

"Hold!" Alianora spoke quickly to her kinsmen. "This is the famous Sir Holger, come to call after all these years."

Einhard and Nithard broke into delighted grins. They knew she'd been friends with the paladin in the great days before they were born. Now at last they got to meet a hero in the flesh! Theodo's face was a study. He knew rather more than they did, and liked what he knew rather less. So long as Holger was gone and stayed gone, it didn't bother him—much. Now that he got to meet the hero in the flesh . . .

Seeing them lower their weapons, Holger also took his hand away from his sword, though not very far. He asked once more, "Who are these people?" This time, the question sounded cautious and formal rather than ferocious.

With relief, Alianora too chose formality: "Sir Holger, I have the honor to present to you my sons. The tall one is Einhard; the redhead, Nithard. With them stands my husband, Theodo."

Her sons rushed up to clasp the hero's hand. Theodo hung back a little, but only a little. He also set his hard palm against Holger's. He didn't pound the paladin on the back the way Einhard and Nithard did, or help try to lift him off his feet. The gray streaks in his beard excused his lack of youthful enthusiasm. Other things, perhaps, excused his lack of enthusiasm of any sort.

As for Holger . . . Alianora might have known—hellfire, *had* known—formality wouldn't be enough. While the puppies pounded on him and Theodo gave him more restrained greeting, he looked like a man who'd just taken a boot in the belly out of nowhere.

When the commotion around him eased a little, he stared over at Alianora with that astonished disbelief still all over his face. "Your . . . sons?" he said. He might never have heard the word before.

"Aye," Alianora answered stolidly.

"Your . . . husband?" By the way Holger said it, he had heard that word before, and didn't fancy it a barleycorn's worth. Theodo caught the same thing. He unobtrusively shifted the hammer from his left hand back to his right.

Alianora nodded. "Aye," she said again. It was the truth. Why should she not repeat it? Why should she want to weep when she did?

"But how did that happen?" Holger asked, still lost, speaking as if of flood or fire or other natural catastrophe.

"How do you think?" For the first time, irritation rose against sympathy in Alianora. "You were *gone*, Holger. Gone off the battlefield. Gone from human ken. Gone from the ken of other folk, too, as I have reason to know. Even smarting from their loss, the Middle Worlders laughed that I should have looked for aught else. So I came hither one day, and I met Theodo, and this is all these years and three grown children later." She raised her head and looked him full in the face. She'd essayed nothing harder since she last lay down in childbed, but she did it. "I would not change it now even if I could."

Einhard and Nithard blinked at her. They understood that they didn't understand everything that was going on. She sighed within herself. She would have a deal of explaining to do to them, and to Alianna. One of these days. Not today. Today had its own sorrows.

Theodo hung on to the hammer. How not? Alianora sometimes thought he set it down only to make love to her. Well, she never would have wanted a man who was not a willing worker. His grip eased a bit, though. He must have had his own fears about this moment, if it ever came. She'd slain some of them, at any rate.

"But . . . But . . . " Holger gaped like a boated carp. "I never gave up looking for you, looking for a way back here. Never once, never for a minute, never in thirty years. Now I make it, and what do I find?"

"That life went on whilst you were busy with other things?" Alianora suggested. His gape only got wider. She sighed again, out loud this time. "Holger, how could I know what you strove for, there in your other world? Even did I know, how could I guess you'd succeed?"

"You should've." Holger muttered to himself, scowling and shaking his head. He might bring out the words, but he had trouble believing them himself.

"Here. Wait." Alianora began bringing up the bucket of water again. "Your coming fair made me forget why I was at the well. I aim to stew up a great kettle of pease porridge, for supper this even and for as long after that as it may last. Will you come home and eat with us?"

He grinned crookedly—more the expression she remembered him wearing than the loss and rage that had been chasing each other across his features. "Bread and salt, Carahue would say."

"That's the Moor's custom, not mine, but I think it a good one," Alianora answered. After you ate with someone, trying to cut out his liver ought to be bad form.

"He's probably got himself a harem." Holger's grin widened. "Song girls and dancing girls and girls to peel grapes for him and drop them into his mouth. Oh, and about fifty-eleven kids, too. I bet he's fat, but happy."

"It would not surprise me. He always fancied the good things in life," Alianora said.

"Well, so did I." Holger looked straight at her.

More than anything else, that was what made her say, "Theodo, why don't you close the smithy, and you and the boys come home with us? 'Tis a holiday—an unlooked-for holiday, which makes it but the sweeter."

"Aye, I'll do it," Theodo said at once. He didn't want Alianora alone with Holger. She didn't want—she didn't think she wanted—that, either. Her feelings for him might be buried, but they lay restless in the grave. Best give them no chance to see light of day once more. And also best to give no one here the least excuse to think of scandal. Some of the women would regardless; they were made so. But no one else ought to be able to hearken to their vinegar tongues.

"Not a great big place, is this?" Holger remarked as they walked back to the house. He carried the water bucket. Theodo gave him a quizzical look when he lifted it, but at Alianora's quick gesture lowered his eyebrows and kept quiet. Holger had always been full of such small, strange courtesies.

"Grandest village for twenty miles around," Nithard said proudly. Holger nodded, polite as an elflord. If he also smiled for one brief moment, Alianora was pretty sure she was the only one who noticed.

She stirred the peas and strewed in salt. After adding the fennel—its spicy scent made her nostrils twitch—she cut the pork into little cubes. It went into the kettle, too.

"Will you chop some more firewood for me?" she asked Theodo.

"Aye." He went out to do it without a backward glance. Einhard and Nithard chaperoned Alianora better than well enough, even if they didn't realize that was what they were doing. They wanted every cut and thrust of Holger's adventures in this world, in the one where he'd spent some years, and in the others he'd passed through on his long, roundabout journey back here. To help loosen his tongue, they broached a barrel of beer Alianora hadn't planned on opening so soon.

Holger was a good talespinner, of the kind who could laugh at himself and his blunders: one more thing Alianora recalled from bygone days. She'd lived through some of his stories, and heard others before—how they came back! Others still were new to her. The feathered demons—or were they pagan gods?—who ate hearts and drank blood made her shiver in spite of herself.

Theodo had come back in with an armload of wood. Alianora scarcely noticed. Her husband got caught up in Holger's latest tale, too. When the knight paused to wet his whistle, Theodo asked, "This is truth, not just a yarn spun for the sake of yarning?"

"Truth." Holger signed himself to show he meant it. "Oh, sometimes neatened up a bit for the sake of the story, and maybe the way I remember it now isn't exactly the way it happened then, but . . . close enough for government work, they say in the other world where I lived a long time."

The phrase sounded odd to Alianora, but Theodo grasped it at once. "That is truth," he agreed gravely. "As near as a mortal man's likely to come to it, any road." He took up the beechwood dipper and poured himself a stoup of beer.

Holger refilled his own mug, not for the first time. He sipped appreciatively. "Mighty fine stuff," he said.

"I have a charm against souring I got years ago in the Middle World," Alianora said. "It works as well on this side of the border, so there must be no harm in it."

"Not unless you're the wrong kind of *microorganism*." That last must have been a word from some other world, for it meant nothing to Alianora—nor, plainly, to her kinsmen. Holger took another pull at the beer. "I saw a tavern near the well," he said. "If you can brew like this, I'm surprised you don't run it out of business."

"We would never do that!" Theodo sounded shocked. "Gerold needs must make his living, too."

"Besides, brewing a barrel of beer now and again is one thing. Brewing enough for a thirsty village, that's summat else altogether," Alianora added.

"Mm, I shouldn't wonder if you're right," Holger said after a little thought. "You always did have a good head on your shoulders, and not just for looks."

Alianora's cheeks heated. Theodo scowled. Then Einhard, not noticing anything amiss, said, "Sir Holger, will you speak more of these . . . Nasties, did you call 'em?"

"Nazis," Holger corrected. His face went hard. "Though Nasties is a good name for them, too. Some ways, I think they were worse than any of the evils that haunt this world, because the only devils that drove them boiled up from the bottom of their own shriveled souls."

He told some of what they had done. Only two things made Alianora believe him: that his voice held unmistakable conviction, and that no one could or would invent such horrors for the sake of making talk spin along. It was as if, for a time, a shadow hovered under the roof thatching.

Alianora got the fire on the hearth built up the way she wanted. She hung the cauldron of porridge above it. Then she said, "Shall we get out into the open air a while, to let it cook?" That made a fair enough reason, but she also wanted to escape the shadow that—she hoped—wasn't really there. She knew she would never eye a fylfot the same way after this.

"It is a trifle smoky in here," Holger said. Theodo laughed under his breath. Einhard and Nithard both smiled. With the forge always blazing in the smithy, they knew more of smoke than Holger would . . . or did they?

"What became of your pipe, wherein you burned the nickels' smoking-leaf?" Alianora asked him as they went out to the little plot of vegetables and herbs by the side of the house. A hen that was pecking at something clucked at the interruption and scuttled away.

"I gave it up. Didn't much want to, but I did." Sure enough, Holger's voice was plangent with regret. But he went on, "The miserable doctors have shown it steals years off the back end of your life. I still miss it sometimes, I will say."

"Doctors!" Theodo snorted scorn. "Me, I'd sooner go to a priest. He has a better chance of fixing what ails me."

"In this world, a priest would," Holger agreed. "Not in all of them, though. Some places, a sawbones knows as much about the way your body works as you do about shaping iron. He knows what's good for you, and he knows what isn't. And smoking isn't, and there's no way in the world—in any world—to pretend it is."

Theodo hoisted his tankard. "Next thing you know, you'll try and tell me beer is bad, too." He laughed. So did his sons and Alianora.

So did Holger, but he said, "There are people—bluenoses, we call 'em—across the worlds who'll tell you just that. I'm sure not one of 'em, though."

"I should hope not!" Theodo reached for the knight's mug. "Fill you up again?"

"Much obliged." Holger handed it to him.

Alianora went back inside, too, to stir the porridge. As Theodo dipped out more beer, he spoke in a low voice: "I do see why you cared for him. And if you think I'm sorry to have a long lead now he's back in the race, you're daft."

"Don't sound more foolish then you can help," she answered tartly. "There is no race, nor shall there be." There wouldn't have been a race had Holger ridden back from the battlefield, either. But that was a different story, one that hadn't happened. She'd done the best she could in the one that had.

All the same, she poured herself a fresh mug before following her husband outside once more. Sometimes the world needed a bit of blurring.

Holger had launched into another tale, about a folk he called Reds.

Einhard and Nithard listened, entranced. "Now, the measure of the Reds' damnation was that tens of thousands of their men took service with the Nazis against their own liege lord," the knight said. "The measure of the Nazis' damnation, though, was that almost every other realm in the world allied with the Reds' liege lord, wicked though he was, against them."

Einhard frowned. "Even the realms of Law? Did not this wicked Red serve Chaos as much as the Nazis' chief did?"

"He served Chaos, I think, yes, but less than the Nazis did." Holger gnawed on his underlip. "Things aren't always so black-and-white in that world as they are here. They—" He broke off.

A great white shape gyred down out of the sky toward the vegetable plot. Broad wings thuttered as the swan braked against air. Muscles in Alianora's shoulders tensed, remembering those automatic motions. Only a woman's muscles now, but still . . .

Suddenly the swan was swam no more, but Alianna, her bare toes digging into the soft, black dirt of the plot. She studied Holger with frank curiosity. "God give you good day, sir," she said; she'd always been a mannerly lass. "Who might you be?"

His eyes almost bugged out of his head. He started violently and shaped the sign of the cross on his chest. "*Jesu Kriste!*" he barked out.

For far from the first time that mad day, tears stung Alianora. Just so had Holger responded when she first transformed from swan shape to her own before him. Then he'd reckoned the very notion of magic all but incredible. He knew better now; else he'd never have found his way back to this world, this village. Too often, though, you forgot what a useless thing mere knowing could be.

Holger stared at Alianna. She'd just turned eighteen. Her hair was red, though darker than Nithard's. The spotless swan-may's tunic covered enough of her for decency's sake, but accented her sweet young curves.

"*Jesu Kriste,*" Holger said again, in a hoarse whisper this time, a whisper that struck Alianora as something close to true prayer. "Oh, *Jesu Kriste!*" Slowly, slowly, his gaze swung from Alianna to Alianora and back again.

Alianora knew what he was seeing, or thought he was seeing: her, as she'd been in the days when they were both young and everything stretched ahead of them. He stared down at the backs of his hands. The loose, age-freckled skin and the harsh tendons standing out like tree roots where the soil was washing away told him how lost those days were.

"Alack, the poor bugger!" Theodo murmured in Alianora's ear. He was thinking along with her again. After so long together, scant surprise there.

"Sir?" In the way Alianna repeated the word, she let her patience show. She had no notion what the sight of her was doing to this unexpected guest.

Alianora did what little she could: "Alianna, here before you stands the great Sir Holger, of whom you'll have heard me speak many a time. Holger, Alianna is the youngest chick in my brood."

Her daughter's face lit like sunrise. "Sir Holger? The famous Sir Holger? Come *here*?" She dropped him a curtsy more heartfelt than practiced.

Holger made heavier going of it. "Your chick? You said you had two—" He stopped short, looking absurdly astonished, and thumped himself in the forehead with the heel of his hand. "No. Wait. You did say you had three kids. You said, and either I didn't quite hear it or I didn't think what it might mean." He managed a ragged bow. "Alianna, you're . . . as pretty as your mother was." A tiny pause as he looked back to Alianora. "Is."

"Gramercy, sir knight," Alianna said. "She tells such tales of you, and of the days when you twain strove together against Chaos! I never thought to meet a grand paladin in the flesh!" She clapped her hands together.

"Here I am, such as I am." The old, familiar self-mockery sounded in Holger's snort. He held out his mug to Alianora. Almost plaintively, he said, "This got empty some kind of way. Could you fix that, please?"

"Certes." Alianora took it and went inside.

She gave the bubbling cauldron another stir. As she dipped up more beer from the barrel, she heard Alianna say, "Oh, Sir Holger, will you not grant us the boon of some tales of your brave adventures?"

"What do you suppose he's *been* doing?" Einhard sounded as snotty as only an older brother could. "If you'd stuck around instead of flying all over creation or swimming in a pond and sticking your tail up in the air whenever you spied summat tasty at the bottom—"

Theodo's rumbled "That will be enough—more than enough—of that" rose above Alianna's irate squeak.

"Yes, more than enough," Holger agreed as Alianora came out again. He nodded to her as he took back the stoup and drank from it. Then his gaze returned to Alianna. "I don't mind spinning out a few more stories if you folks can put up with listening to 'em." He might have been talking to all of them, but he had eyes for only one—with the occasional bemused glance at her mother.

Alianna couldn't have made a better audience had she rehearsed for the role. She laughed in all the right places. She clapped her hands some more when the story turned exciting. Whenever magic intruded, her eyes—they were green, not blue like Alianora's—widened.

Theodo blew on a fire with a goatskin bellows when he wanted to make it hotter. All unwittingly, Alianna had the same effect on Holger. He paid less and less heed to anybody else. Alianna basked in his attention, probably because, like Alianora at the same age, she wasn't used to getting much.

Alianora wasn't alone in noticing. After a while, Theodo said, "Sir knight, will you walk a little ways with me? Alianora, you may as well come, too." When their sons and daughter started to follow along, the smith held up a hand. "Nay, bide you here, an't please you. This is for the older heads. We'll be back betimes, I vow."

Einhard, Nithard, and Alianna all looked dissatisfied, each, perhaps, for different reasons. In the face of Theodo's stony stare, though, and Alianora's, they did not try to press their luck.

Holger didn't seem happy to cut short his latest yarn, either. But he did it with such good grace as he could muster. Theodo and Alianora led him along a narrow, muddy path through the fields—and away from the children. Holger did have the wit to wait till they got out of earshot before asking, "Well, what's this all about?"

"Sir knight . . . " Theodo stopped and scuffed one boot in the dirt. Then he squared his shoulders. Though shorter than Holger, he was nearly as broad through them. "Sir knight, I want you to understand I speak to you without meaning to offend. Can you do that, please?"

"Go on," Holger said grimly. "I'll try my best."

"For which I cry your grace." Theodo sketched a salute. "Now, I am but a simple fellow, and not a traveled man. I can only tell you how things seem to me, and how they'd look to other village folk."

"You can cut out the sandbagging." Holger's voice was desert-dry. When he saw Theodo and Alianora didn't follow the phrase, he explained it: "Say what you mean to say, and never mind all the 'simple fellow' garbage."

A ghost of a smile crossed Theodo's face and was gone before Alianora could be sure she saw it. "Right well said. I will, then: when a man your age, or mine, looks on a lass like Alianna the way you've looked on her this past hour and more, well, here in the village we make goaty jokes about it. Is it the same other places you've seen, or is it otherwise?"

Holger's cheeks flamed the color of heated iron. "I—I—I—" He tried three times, but nothing more came out. Then he tilted his head back and drained the stoup of beer, larynx bobbing as he swallowed. He took a deep breath, and another one. This time, he managed to speak: "I beg your pardon, Theodo. I did not know I was looking at her that way."

"Well, you were," Theodo said. Holger's eyes asked Alianora a silent question. Regretfully, she nodded. He had been.

He winced. He swore in the language Alianora used, and added things that sounded hot in what seemed like several others. "I must be a perfect jackass," he said at last. He met Theodo's eyes with a courage Alianora had to admire. "And to answer your question, they joke about pretty young girls and not-so-young men everywhere I've ever been. I expect God made those jokes about twenty minutes after He finished making the world—uh, worlds. Maybe even sooner."

"Mm, I'd not know about that," Theodo said uncomfortably. Like Alianora, like most of the villagers, he spoke little of God. Such things were more for priests than for the likes of them. She remembered Holger had always had an easier way with the Deity. She'd got used to it in the bygone days. No doubt she could again.

"Shall we go back now, before the children do come after us?" she said.

She looked to Theodo, but her husband only shrugged. It fell on Holger to answer the question. "Yes, let's," he said. "I'll behave myself, honest."

"We do understand the why of it, Sir Holger," Alianora said as they ambled toward the house once more. She almost said *dear Holger,* as she had so often while he was here before. But it would not do now. It most especially would not do right this minute. After a beat, she went on, "You've had yourself a whole great stack o' surprises since you came forth from yon woods."

"Surprises." Holger's chuckle was mirthless. "Oh, you might say so. Yes, you just might."

Alianora heard the pain that lay under the laugh. "I would not hurt you for the world, Sir Holger," she said, and came even closer than before to *dear Holger*. Theodo heard it whether she said it or not. He made a small noise down deep in his chest. She ignored it; she'd square things with him later. Meanwhile . . . "The world wags as it wags, not always as we wish it would. We move on. We change." She waved at the impatiently waiting Einhard, Nithard, and Alianna. Alianna waved back.

"Yeah. Right." Holger's forced smile likely masked tears. "Only I didn't, did I? I spent all those years wandering from one world to the next, or else in some of the places between them all. I was going to get back here, and nothing was gonna stop me no matter what. And I don't think I ever once stopped to wonder what in blazes you'd be doing. You were—"

"In amber in your mind?" Alianora suggested. She had a bauble from Theodo, a tear of the sun with a tiny ant trapped inside forever.

"Yes!" Agreement exploded out of Holger. "That's it. That's just it! And a whole fat lot of good seeing it now does me."

"Well, I am glad you came again," Alianora said: one more thing she would have to set right with Theodo. But it was so, even if not the way Holger would have wanted. Like anyone else, she had her own measure of vanity.

Nithard aimed a rather predatory grin at them. "Well, what were the lot of you going on about where we couldn't hearken?"

Deadpan, Holger answered, "What a rotten bunch of brats your mother's gone and raised—what else?"

Alianora's second son opened his mouth, then wisely closed it again without saying anything more. Some scrapes you not only couldn't win, you only made yourself look sillier when you tried. He at least had the sense to see as much.

Alianna, now . . . Alianna batted her eyes at Holger and

murmured, "Now, good sir knight, you don't mean that of me?" in tones that should have been sinful if anyone but their intended victim heard them—and were bound to be sinful if he alone did.

But Holger just threw back his head and laughed. All right, he'd been besotted for a little while, likely as much for what he remembered as for what he saw. As with any other man of his years, though, it was more his imagination that kindled than aught else.

"You ought to go wash your mouth out with beer, young lady," he said. "And if that doesn't work, somebody needs to turn you over his knee and paddle you."

Alianna gaped. Then she looked miffed, as any witch might when one of her spells fell to pieces instead of working the magic she had in mind. And then, after a few tense heartbeats, she laughed, too: she was good-natured-Alianora's good-natured daughter. If she didn't quite know yet how to keep a man three times her age inflamed, then she didn't, that was all. *Just as well, too*, Alianora thought.

"I hope you'll go on with your tales, Sir Holger," Theodo said. "They do make the time spin by." He said nothing, now, of not aiming them all at Alianna.

"I can do that," Holger said, but not before he held out the stoup once more to Alianora. "Will you give me a refill first?"

"Surely," she replied. "And after another tale or two, I think we shall pause to sup."

He sniffed and nodded. "Sounds like a plan. It's starting to smell mighty good."

He'd always been full of such small bits of praise, thrown out not for the sake of flattery or seduction but simply because that was his way. It was, Alianora thought with a twisted smile of her own, one of the things that marked him as a man from another world.

After she brought Holger the mug, she went back inside and fed the hearthfire a little more wood to keep the pease porridge above it bubbling. She tasted the porridge with a wooden spoon. In went a pinch of salt and a dash more fennel, but only a dash. It *was* getting there.

Outside, her husband and her children broke into guffaws at something Holger said. Theodo wouldn't have laughed unless the big man from another world wasn't leering at Alianna while he talked. Alianora sighed as she picked up a loaf of brown bread. It wasn't of the freshest—not expecting company, she'd baked day before yesterday—but it would serve.

She got out earthenware bowls, spoons shaped from horn, and one, for Holger today, of silver. That was another gift from Theodo, part of the family wealth and, even in these quiet times, a ward against werewolves. Not long ago, Holger had told of the one they'd tracked through Lourville, the town to the east. In those days, with the Middle World waxing strong, anyone even slightly susceptible to shapeshifting was likely to go were. Not so now. Still, silver kept virtues beyond value and beauty.

One more taste. Alianora nodded again. "Yes, we're ready," she said to herself, and walked to the door. "Can we stop the yarns long enough to eat?"

Trying to hold her sons back would have been harder. Stomachs with legs, that was what they were. Who was the king in fable who'd tried to hold back the tide? She couldn't remember if that was Canute or Louis XIV. Whoever he was, he wouldn't have had much luck with Einhard and Nithard, either.

Holger raised an eyebrow when she handed him the silver spoon with his bowl. His forehead corrugated. Yes, the years had scored him, as they'd marked Alianora—as they marked everyone. "You've done well for yourselves," he remarked: of course he'd understand what the precious metal meant.

"Oh, tolerable. Tolerable," Theodo said. He might be a smith, but he had a peasant's dread of admitting success, much less boasting about it. You threw your luck away when you did anything so foolish.

"Heh." Holger's single syllable said he understood that thinking down to the ground. He ladled porridge into the bowl and tore off a chunk of bread. Alianna had set out the honeypot beside the loaf. Holger grinned. "This is a feast!"

"Pretty good, all right," Einhard said. He was trying to eat and talk at the same time, and swallowed wrong.

His father thumped him on the back till he quit coughing. "Greedy like a hog, you are," Theodo said, but he couldn't make himself sound as angry as he might have wanted to.

Alianna said, "Sir Holger, you'll have seen riches beside which a silver spoon will seem as nothing."

"If you own your wealth, that's not so bad," Holger answered with a shrug. "If it owns you, that's not so good. I never had it in me to chase after gold or jewels or any of that nonsense. The treasure I was after—" He stopped short and upended his mug.

A considerable silence followed. Alianora unhappily considered it. At last, picking his words with obvious care, Theodo said, "For whatever it may be worth to you, you have my sympathy."

"Sympathy? It's worth its weight in gold," Holger said. Theodo started to beam, then frowned a sudden, stormy frown instead. How much would a word weigh? But Holger held up his hand. "Peace, please. Just a smart-mouthed crack. I know your words were kindly meant."

After another, briefer, pause, Theodo dipped his head. "Aye, let it go."

"Thanks." Holger ate a couple of more spoonsful of porridge. Then he said, perhaps as much to himself as to his companions, "It's funny, you know, when you spend so long looking for somebody who's all you ever wanted, and then you go and find her, and you see she's already got everything *she* ever wanted, and it isn't you."

A house, not one of the smallest and meanest in the village but not one of the finest, either? A garden plot? Chickens and ducks and pigs and a cow? Enough to eat, except at the end of the worst winters? *Is this all I ever wanted?* Alianora wondered.

But that wasn't what Holger was talking about, was it? A good, solid man with whom she'd made a life. Three children well on their way to turning into good, solid people themselves. A place where she belonged, where she fit in, if not perfectly, then better than well enough.

When you got right down to it, what more *could* you want?

"'Scuse me." Holger brushed past her to get to the beer barrel. He'd poured down a lot, and showed it very little. Well, there was a lot of him to soak up beer, and he'd always had that knack. Still, when he raised the stoup in salute, Alianora thought tears glittered for a moment in his eyes. "Here's to all of you," he said, and drank.

"To you, Sir Holger . . . dear Holger." Alianora returned the salute. "Without you, Chaos would have rolled over this land and swept all we have, all we've built, away for aye." She drank to him. Theodo and the children followed her lead.

"Yeah, well . . . " A sigh gusted from Holger. "I wonder if the

Powers here didn't finally let me come back to rub my nose in what a useless thing a hero is a generation after his war ends. The world goes on without him. What was the point to any of it?"

Alianora glanced at the kettle of pease porridge above the fire on the hearth. She took half a step toward Theodo, though she knew the motion would wound Holger. "This was the point," she answered.

"I guess it was." Holger sounded unconvinced, and who could blame him? Hero he might be—hero he was—but he had none of what Alianora enjoyed. He stared out through the doorway. Sunset reddened the light coming in. So too, perhaps, did escaping smoke from the cookfire. More got out through the hole in the roof above the hearth, but enough did linger to sting eyes and throats. Holger said, "I could show you a way to make all your smoke go outside: a *chimney*, it's called."

"Another day, sir knight," Theodo said, his eyebrows coming down and together at the strange word.

Holger looked towards Alianora. She said, "Is it that you came here for?"

"You know bloody well it isn't." He bared his teeth in another humorless smile. "But it seems to be about what I'm good for, doesn't it?"

Since Alianora had no answer to that, she spooned up some more porridge. The hard moment passed. Holger launched into another tale with the air of a man determined to push pain aside. Sunset gave way to twilight, which dwindled toward darkness. Shadows from the dying fire swooped around the walls.

Alianora lit a fine beeswax candle, and then, after a little thought, a second. Hang the cost tonight! The tilt of her chin defied Theodo to say anything. He was a bold man, but—wisely—not so bold as that. Even the candles' mellow glow could not come close to matching daylight, but it did help the red embers on the hearth.

Holger got to the end of his story. He blinked, maybe noticing the darkness for the first time. A cricket chirped outside. "Well," Holger said, as if it were a complete sentence. He blinked again. "We did walk past that tavern, right? You said a guy called . . . Gerold runs it." He grinned, pleased he'd come up with the name.

"Have we drunk the barrel dry?" Alianora squeaked in surprise. They'd applied themselves to it, aye, but that was a lot of beer.

"I don't think so," Holger said. "But the tavern'll have wine, won't it? Other stuff folks here don't fix for themselves, too. Gerold wouldn't make his living if it didn't."

"Well, aye. That's so." Theodo sounded grudging, and had his reasons: "Not the best crowd there—men who'd sooner guzzle than work, most of 'em. And always 'tis dearer to pay the taverner's scot than to brew for yourself. Wine may be sweet, but beer does well enough."

"Don't worry about that." Holger slapped one of the cleverly made pockets on his blue trousers. Whatever was inside clinked sweetly. "I'm buying."

"Mrmm." Theodo still hesitated.

"We thank you, Sir Holger." Alianora didn't. "If you're fain to fare to the tavern, thither we shall fare." They all walked out into the night together.

The tavern wasn't far. Nothing in the village was far from anything else. Stars, a nail-paring of moon, and firelight leaking out between shutter slats and through badly chinked walls and spilling from partly open doorways kept darkness from being absolute. All the same, Alianora planted her feet with care, trying not to step in a hole or a puddle or anything nasty.

A cat's eyes glowed green, then vanished. A dog growled a warning that faded into a whine when it decided it didn't want to take on so many humans after all.

"Right over here, y'see?" Theodo said in a low voice that wouldn't bother neighbors already abed. "Not so far from the well. It's—" He grunted in surprise. "The shape of it's wrong."

"Aye, it is," Alianora agreed wonderingly. The tavern shouldn't bulk so tall against the sky. It looked as if it owned two stories. She'd seen such things in her travels with Holger, but there wasn't a building like that in the village . . . or there hadn't been. The beam-ends of the roof were oddly and ornately carven.

"I know that shape," Holger breathed. "I wondered if the Old Phoenix would show up tonight. You don't always find it, but sometimes it finds you."

"How do you mean?" Alianora asked.

"It's one of those places between the worlds that I was talking about. It doesn't belong to any of them," Holger answered. "I can't explain it better than that. I don't think anybody else can, either."

The door opened. For a moment, Walacho's swag-bellied shape stood silhouetted against the light spilling out from within. It wasn't what the village drunkard had expected. But if it wasn't *the* tavern, it plainly was *a* tavern. That would do for Walacho. He waddled inside.

Before the door swung shut, Alianora glimpsed a bar, with a plump man—definitely not Gerold, who was on the lean side—standing behind it. In front were a few small tables. Walacho was heading towards one of them. At another sat . . . Alianora stiffened. Hair blacker than the night sky; a proud, harsh, beautiful face; long satin dress caressing every lush curve . . .

"That's Morgan le Fay!" she blurted, and knew not why she should sound so furious. Because the great sorceress had aged not a day these past thirty years? That should have been reason enough and more, but somehow her rage ran deeper yet.

The way Holger said "Yeah" made her understand why. He went on, "I'm not surprised to see her there. She's one the Old Phoenix would draw, sure as sure. And we've got a few things to talk about, the two of us. Uh-huh, just a few."

"Talk?" Alianora snarled the word, as if she'd been in the habit of transforming to cat herself rather than to swan.

"Well, that, too." Holger seemed sourly amused. "You don't want me, but you don't want me having fun with anybody else, either?"

"Not with her!" Alianora said. "When did she bring you aught but grief?"

"There were times, back in the day. There sure were." By the way he answered, he might not have thought of them for many a year, but that made the memories no less sweet.

"Perhaps—for her purposes. Never for yours." Alianora knew trouble when she saw it, no matter how seductive its package.

"That could be," Holger allowed, so he wasn't altogether blind. No, not altogether. He made as if to bow to her in the darkness. "If you want to play nursemaid, you can come in with me."

"When I came out, would I come hither and not into one of your other worlds?" she asked. Would Walacho's family have to make do without him, as if he'd gone into Elf Hill and emerged the next morning to find a hundred years gone in the wider world? They might prove better off, but that wasn't the point.

"You probably would. Most people do, most of the time," Holger said.

"That is not warrant enough," Theodo declared. He wasn't in the habit of speaking for Alianora; he'd learned she didn't fancy it when he tried. He did it now, though, and she liked it fine. Her children stirred. The Old Phoenix and the idea of adventure drew them. Well, naturally adventure drew them—they'd never known much. Alianora had, and knew she'd had a bellyful.

"I stay here," she said. If her voice roughened, then it did, that was all. She reached out and took the knight's hand. "Go where you would, dear Holger, and God keep you safe wherever it may be." Anger and jealousy flared once more. "Whatever else you do, mind yon witch!"

"Oh, I will. I'm not always as dumb as I look—just most of the time. And I've got more miles on me now. I'm not likely to be so stupid that way as I might've been a while back. I hope." Holger squeezed her hand hard. Then he leaned forward and brushed his lips across hers. "Good luck to you, kiddo, and to yours. You found what you were after. Me, I guess I've got to go look some more, don't I?"

He stumped toward the Old Phoenix, footfalls softening as he went away. When he opened the door, he stood limned for a moment by the light beyond him. He waved, once, then stepped inside. The door closed again before Alianora had to hear Morgan le Fay's voice.

She burst into tears anyhow. Theodo put his arm round her shoulder—less comfort than she would have liked, but as much as she could get. "If we're not going in," he said, "we'd better get back."

"Aye." She nodded. He would feel the motion even if he couldn't see it. "Let's do that."

Alianora woke early, before anyone else in the house, after a night of confused dreams. For a moment, she wondered if everything that had happened the day before was only a dream. But no. That was real. She knew the difference.

She tiptoed outside without disturbing her kin. It was still gloomy: twilight, with dawn coming but not yet come. She walked toward the well, far enough to discover that the tavern had its usual seeming once more. Someone sprawled asleep in front of the doorway; a tankard lay on its side near his head. Walacho: she knew his snores.

No sign of Holger. Well, she hadn't thought there would be. She turned around and went home.

Alianna was up when she came in. Even in the dim light, her daughter's eyes glowed. Alianora smiled to see her. She'd glowed like that herself, once upon a time. "Quite a day, yesterday," she said.

"It was! I'll remember it forever!" Alianna said.

"As will I." Alianora hesitated. Then, remembering, she asked, "Might I . . . wear the white tunic once more, for just this morning?"

Alianna set a palm soft with understanding on her arm. "Of course, Mother. Of course."

AFTERWORD:

FOR ME to talk about Poul Anderson is like a young guitarist talking about Hendrix or Keith Richards—he's one of the main guys from whom I learned my licks. What makes a story, how to tell a story, which words to choose to tell it as well as you can . . . What I know, I know in no small measure because so much of what Poul did rubbed off on me. I started reading him long before I started (and then soon stopped) shaving, and have been doing it ever since, always with enjoyment and always with profit. That we would become colleagues and, toward the end of his life, friends, shows me I've done a few things right in my life, anyhow. And that he and Karen would come to my house for dinner . . . Well, if you'd told that to my not-yet-shaving self, he would've said, "No way!" But yes. There may be something to this growing-up business after all.

—Harry Turtledove

A SLIP IN TIME

by S. M. Stirling

***CONSIDERED BY** many to be the natural heir to Harry Turtledove's title of King of the Alternate History novel, fast-rising science fiction star S. M. Stirling is the bestselling author of the* Island in the Sea of Time *series (*Island in the Sea of Time, Against the Tide of Years, On the Ocean of Eternity*), in which Nantucket comes unstuck in time and is cast back to the year 1250; and the Draka series (including* Marching Through Georgia, Under the Yoke, The Stone Dogs, *and* Drakon, *plus an anthology of Draka stories by other hands edited by Stirling,* Drakas!*), in which Tories fleeing the American Revolution set up a militant society in South Africa and eventually end up conquering most of the Earth. He's also produced the* Dies the Fire series (Dies the Fire, The Protector's War, A Meeting at Corvallis*), plus the five-volume* Fifth Millennium *series, and the seven-volume* General *series (with David Drake), as well as stand-alone novels such as* Conquistador, The Peshawar Lancers, *and* The Sky People. *Stirling has also written novels in collaboration with Raymond E. Feist, Jerry Pournelle, Holly Lisle, Shirley Meier, Karen Wehrstein, and* Star Trek *actor James Doohan, and contributed to the* Babylon 5, T2, Brainship, War World, *and* Man-Kzin War *series. His short fiction has been collected in* Ice, Iron and Gold. *Stirling's newest series include the* Change *works, consisting of* The Sunrise Lands, The Scourge of God, The Sword of the Lady, *and*

The High King of Montival, *and the* Lords of Creation *series, consisting of* The Sky People *and* In the Courts of the Crimson Kings. *His most recent books are the first two volumes in the new* Shadowspawn *series,* A Taint in the Blood *and* The Council of Shadows, *and a new volume in the* Change *series,* The Tears of the Sun. *Born in France and raised in Europe, Africa, and Canada, he now lives with his family in Santa Fe, New Mexico.*

Poul Anderson's stories of the Time Patrol were among the most popular and longest-running of his series, with almost a dozen Time Patrol stories and novels being published from 1955 to within a few years of his death. In most of them, Time Patrolman Manse Everard and his compatriots ride off to keep unscrupulous time-travelers from destroying the proper timeline by changing historic events in the past. In the suspenseful story by S. M. Stirling that follows, though, we encounter a situation so grim that Manse Everard himself *might end up needing a spot of rescuing.*

Prologue: Sarajevo, Bosnia
Austro-Hungarian Empire
June 28th, 1914 AD

THE SHORT, skinny young man was sweating as he touched the pistol. Part of it was fear, part a savage joy. Only moments now until he drew it and struck his blow for the South Slav cause.

Mehmedbašić had lost his courage at the last instant, Čabrinović's bomb had failed, then the cars had swept by so fast, so fast that there was nothing he could do. It had been as bad as the day the guerillas had rejected him as too small, too weak, to serve Serbia in the struggle against the Turks. But now the cars were here again, and stopped before him. The beefy Austrian in the light-blue uniform and plumed hat with his Czech whore by his side . . .

The hand about to draw the pistol fell to his side. A vast peace filled him, and he swayed, smiling, as if to the music of the angels his mother had believed in. Uniformed guards bustled about, the stalled engine coughed, backfired, and growled to life. The cars swept away as the crowd waved and cheered.

Gavrilo Princip slumped quietly to the ground.

There was a good deal of celebration that day, in honor of the Archduke's visit; it was nearly an hour before someone noticed that he had quietly stopped breathing. The Belgian automatic pistol had vanished from his pocket with his meager cash and the picture of his mother long before official notice was taken.

An appendix to the police report on the attempted assassination mentioned him as a possible member of the Black Hand, but the heir to the Royal and Imperial throne never bothered to read it.

I:

Venus
2332 AD

"MACH' MA *uns auf nach Wien!*" Wanda Everard said gaily. "Off to Vienna! Music, sinful pastries, architecture, nineteen twenty-six!"

She spoke in German and with a trace of the slurred lilting Viennese dialect you'd expect from a woman of that city's upper middle classes. One of the perks of membership in the Time Patrol was a system which could teach you a language in an hour or so.

"You look good as a flapper," Manse grinned.

She did, with a comely blond handsomeness that was wholly of her native late-twentieth-century California but would not be at all outré in Jazz Age Vienna. The skirt a thumb's- width above the knee and bobbed hair and cloche hat were one reason that they were taking their vacation in that decade, being a *lot* more comfortable than the corsets and long skirts that would be de rigueur in the halcyon days of the Belle Epoque. His own rather stiff collar and tie were probably more confining, but he'd fit in just as well, looking like exactly what he was: a Midwestern farmboy of German descent who'd grown into a big battered thirtyish man with a roadmap of experience on his face. Their covers would be as American tourists, whose dollars would be welcome in a capital still not recovered from the fall of the empire it had ruled.

"See you for dinner, Manse," Piet Van Sarawak said, grinning.

"Deirdre says the rijsttafel is coming along nicely. She's finally learned you can't scold a robot. Enjoy your week. Damn, but time travel helps with scheduling!"

Manse's friend was an Unattached Time Patrol agent as well, but he'd been born in this time and place, the terraformed Venus of the twenty-fourth century; he was slim and dark and dressed in a sarong.

Behind him, the open fretwork of the house walls showed a long stretch of lawn and garden, then slopes planted in vines down to the borders of a canal. The air was full of the scents of flowers and rock and an almost-eucalyptus tang that was not quite like anything on earth, and a rainbow of passing birds sang the intricate melodies men had designed them for. His wife Deirdre was pushing a three-year-old boy in a swing that hung from the branches of a great tree, her rust-red hair flying in the warm breeze as she laughed at the crowing child.

Good, Manse thought. *I was right to avoid Piet and her for a couple of years of their own duration-sense. She's had time to heal . . . not just from losing her world, but from learning that now it never existed at all.*

Their own ten-month Monica was in a playpen not far from the trunk, with the van Sarawak family manaq—a bioengineered hybrid of cat, dog, and chimp genes designed as a companion-nurse—curled up watchfully nearby. Manse felt a little bemused at the sight; as an Unattached agent of the Time Patrol he'd never really expected to be a father. He found he liked it.

"Yum!" Wanda said. "*I' bring dann de Sachatoatn von Demel mit.*"

Piet laughed and replied in English: "I didn't have that hypno, Wanda. What the hell did that mean?"

"I'll bring back some sachertorte from the Hofzuckerbäckerei Demel," Wanda said. "It's supposed to be legendary."

Manse smiled a little. Wanda was a Specialist, and in glacial ecologies at that; she'd had a lot less exposure to travel through human history than he had and it was fresher for her. Sometimes that made him feel like a bit of a cradle robber, but it also gave him some of the first excitement back. They mounted the timecycle, a smooth shape of not-quite-metal that resembled a wheel-less motorcycle as much as anything. He touched the control panel.

II:

Vienna
Austro-Hungarian Empire
June 1st, 1926 AD

"WHAT THE *hell*?" Manse said.

He felt Wanda's arms stiffen around his waist, and the little sonic stunner flew into his hand. The cycle was set for emergence in a warehouse owned by a Patrol front-organization, bought quietly in a half-abandoned suburb in the hungry year of nineteen-nineteen. There should have been someone to meet them.

Instead the timecycle *thumped* down on the stone pavement of a new-looking square, with buildings that were Art Deco-neoclassical-something-else-entirely all around it. People were streaming across the pedestrian parts, and the circular roadway was thick with automobiles and a few horse-drawn landaus. The air smelled of coal-smoke and exhausts and a little of dung. Not far away a flatbed truck carried a huge, clumsy-looking movie camera on a heavy tripod, grinding away with its lens pointed to the sky.

The screams and scrambling rush to get away from the machine that had appeared in their midst started immediately. The alarm spread a little more slowly than it might have, because everyone else was looking *up*. Involuntarily, Manse did the same. A dirigible was floating by about a thousand yards above his head, the rasp of the engines mounted in pods along its sides throbbing through the air. It was huge; his trained eye estimated the length as at least nine hundred feet and the maximum diameter at around two hundred, bigger than the *Hindenburg*. Fraktur-Gothic letters bore the name *Graf Zeppelin*, and the colors of Imperial Germany, black and white and red with the crowned eagle across it.

This is eight years after *the end of World War One!* his mind gibbered, even as his left hand dove for the emergency-departure switch.

And froze, for a single fatal second; a cold sweat broke out on his face and flanks. It was set to return them to the point of departure—and if what his subconscious had grasped was true, that would have put them both into a sulfuric-acid hell hot enough to boil lead, what Venus would have been if the world-shapers of the First Scientific Renaissance had never turned it into a second Earth.

A man in a uniform that included a tall shako-style leather hat ran towards him, blowing a whistle and fumbling at his waist for a pistol. Manse's snapped off a short silent pulse from the stunner. The cop went sprawling, bonelessly limp as the vibration-beam short-circuited his cortex; he'd wake up in fifteen minutes with a headache and some bruises. You could use it with a clear conscience. He shot again and again, at anyone who seemed to be coming *towards* them, while his left hand fumbled at the controls to change the setting to something on earth. Other uniforms were pressing through the crowd, gray cloth and rifles, the military. No need to be subtle, just get them up and out—

Crack.

The bullet ripped the stunner out of his right hand, taking skin with it. A few yards away a soldier in a pike-gray uniform blinked in surprise as he started to pull at the bolt of his Mannlicher rifle.

"Nein, ihr Cretins! Ich hab' g'sagt: lebendig festnehmen!" a voice screamed in nasal *schönbrunner Deutsch,* upper-class Austrian German. "No, you imbeciles, take him alive!"

Something hit him with stunning force and he toppled to land on the pavement; he'd been clouted in the back of the head with the butt-end of a rifle. Blinking, his vision contracting to a dimming tunnel, he saw Wanda stiff-arm a man away and slam her hand down on the control panel. The cycle vanished, instantly elsewhere in time and space. Behind it he could see the filming team, still cranking their camera, but now it was pointed straight at him.

The world went away.

III:

Elsewhere/When

WANDA EVERARD hovered ten thousand feet in the air and two centuries future-ward. Vienna sprawled beneath her, the neo-Baroque splendors of the Ringstrasse familiar, but enigmatic low-slung buildings stretching out beyond. A boomerang-shaped flying . . . something . . . curved silently towards her and she slapped the controls again.

Two centuries more, and a frantic sweep of her hand as a bubble of iridescent force started to close around the machine like time-lapse photography.

A jump, and she was over Vienna's ancestor, Roman Vindobona, in about the year the Emperor Marcus Aurelius died there. The Danube glittered a cold blue-gray beneath her, and she shivered; beyond it the wild Marcomanni laired in wolf-haunted forests. Legionnaires might see a glimmer, if they looked skyward at precisely the right angle.

Part of that quivering was shock. She turned up the protective field and the heater, and ate an energy-bar from the emergency supplies. That and systematic deep-breathing brought calmness back swiftly, buried rage and grief; besides Patrol training at the Academy she'd been in danger before, from animals and from men.

I've even been in something like this *situation before*, she thought mordantly. *Then it was San Francisco that wasn't the way it should have been.*

No more than a handful of Agents in the vast, labyrinthine organization that guarded a million years of history from homo erectus to the post-human Danellians had seen an alteration, an actual divergence in the time-stream. She was one; Manse Everard was another. Now she'd seen two, and equaled his record. Nobody had seen more than that. It was an honor she could have done without, and horror clawed at the edge of vision like things scuttling in the corners of her eyes.

"I will *not* think about Monica," she told herself.

Monica who now would never have existed, future-ward of *that* Vienna.

She could call the Patrol here; the standing-wave beacons were registering on the timecycle's control screens when she queried them.

Everything pastward of the moment of change would still exist. There were agents in every milieu, clandestine headquarters in cities, bases on the moon, spaceships inconspicuously orbiting, the Academy in the Oligocene, places like the resort in the Old Stone Age Pyrenees where she'd gone on her first long date with Manse. Tourists and traders and scientists . . . There was virtually no year since the emergence of the human race when the Patrol wasn't more-or-less active, and there were researchers farther back than that.

"Every step you take, I'll be watching you," she murmured, from the lyrics of a golden oldie she remembered from her childhood. "I never understood why anyone considered that a romantic song."

But I'm not a police type, she thought, as her hand halted on its way to call for help. *I'm a scientist, a Specialist and not even a Specialist in a period of history; I study ancient ecologies and the only humans I deal with are Pleistocene primitives. I'll be cut out of the loop, stashed somewhere safe—last time Manse had me involved only because* he *was in charge of the rescue project. They may decide that it's too risky to go after him, they may write him off. Monica needs her father too! Manse will be furious, but to be furious, he'll have to be rescued.*

Decision firmed, and she shoved emotion aside with an effort like hauling herself up a rock-face; the Patrol had its regulations, but you could get around them . . . if your insubordination *worked.* Then you were a hero. If it didn't . . . you were the goat.

"I'll be a *dead* goat if I can't pull it off," she told the bright spring morning of 180 AD. "Or never have existed. No need to worry about the exile planet!"

Which is full of Neldorian bandits and Exaltationists and similar low-lifes.

Patrol Court was the least of her problems. Other agents would be heading futurward "now", for a value of "now" that only the Temporal language could express, across the wave-front of actuating upheaval. They'd see the altered future; some of them would flit straight back downtime. They'd gather, assess the situation, and then they'd act. They might or might not spare crucial effort and personnel on rescuing those stranded here. Their first duty was to the timestream that led to the Danellians, after all. You didn't age in the Patrol and you never got sick, but you were most assuredly expendable.

She examined her mount. About four-tenths charge on the cells, which used a principle she didn't even begin to understand and which made nuclear fusion look like a water-clock. Hopping interplanetary distances as well as through time had drained them a bit, but they would be ample as long as she didn't go off-planet again. Her hand touched the controls, summoning menus, then tapped the actuator. This time she was over Vienna again, and in nineteen twenty-six once more, but at fifteen thousand feet and near sundown of the same day.

The city of the Habsburg emperors spread out below, the river gray, a haze of industrial smog merely giving it a blur. The machine detected a surprising amount of air traffic for this year, but most of it was well below her. Her optics cut through the gritty air, and the machine's memory showed . . .

About an eighty-six percent correspondence between what Vienna should *have been and what's below me now. Most of that difference is additional buildings on greenfield sites, and some redevelopment closer in.*

This city was bigger than it should have been. She'd uploaded information as part of her preparation for the week-long vacation they'd planned, before flitting back to Venus and Monica and returning on home to the Bay Area of the 1990s after dinner. Vienna had plunged from over two million people and rising in 1914 to about one and a half million after the end of the war, when it went from the capital of an Empire larger than France to an absurdly overdeveloped head on a minor Alpine republic's Heidiesque yodeling-and-goat-milk body. It had stayed around that number for the rest of the twentieth century and most of the twenty-first.

So that shrinkage didn't happen. This *city has something like two and a quarter, two and a half million people; and it's growing fast at the edges, flourishing, new factories and apartment buildings and suburbs. And there are five or six big dirigbles within detector range and that huge airport-hanger thingie there with a tramcar line running out to it. That's more airships than were ever in operation at the same time. Count Zeppelin would be over the moon. Something . . . I'd say something prevented the First World War. Either that or the Central Powers won it, and fast.*

She remembered a picture she'd seen once, of a mule belly-deep in the mud of the Western Front, its eyes full of the same weary terror and despair as the man who tried to haul it forward. A rotting body lay not far away in a shell-hole, and the cratered, corpse-saturated mud stretched away on every side, broken only by the occasional skeleton of a tree. And another picture, of a noisy crowd in Munich celebrating the outbreak of war, with a blurred but unmistakable Adolf Hitler waving his straw boater and cheering.

But that's the history that produced my parents and sister and me, and Manse, and our daughter. And the Danellians and the Patrol and everyone I've ever known and loved or liked or even detested.

She couldn't just scan and find where Manse was, though there were instruments that could. This was a scooter like countless thousands that plied the timelanes, not a special-operations reconnaissance vehicle. She had nothing but the modest sensors on it and another sonic stunner in the compartment that held the emergency medical kit and field rations.

But . . .

Yes. If they store his gear in the same location he's in . . . that's a big if but the impulse of whoever got their hands on him would be to keep everything safe and secret . . .

IV:

Vienna
Austro-Hungarian Empire
June 3rd, 1926 AD

"**COME** with us!"

A voice speaking German, but with a melodic Magyar accent.

The guards were sweating-nervous, and they clutched ugly bulky machine pistols with side-mounted drums. The muzzles in their perforated barrel-shrouds never wavered. Rumors about him must be circulating, but these were brave men and well-trained. More waited in the corridor outside, carefully not getting in each other's line of fire. Those weapons could chew him into hamburger in seconds and there were a couple of rifles with fixed bayonets just in case.

Manse Everard felt like groaning as he came to his feet. His neatly bandaged hand was still throbbing, but he could use it if he had to. They'd locked him in this cell that was like a room in a not-too-bad 20's hotel, and he'd seen nobody but a doctor who ignored everything but his injury, and silent orderlies who brought in good if rather heavy meals.

Now they went down corridors that were either unoccupied or cleared so that nobody would see him pass, and into an interrogation room that had the dingy beige ambience that bureaucracies seemed to prefer. Only one barred window showed, small and overlooking a paved courtyard; the lights were electric and harsh. One of them shone in his eyes as he approached the table where the officers sat, probably by no coincidence whatsoever.

"We will keep two of the guards," the man sitting in the center seat across the table said. "That is a dangerous man, if I've ever seen one. Agád, Lajos, *guard*."

He was about Manse's age, in an Austrian colonel's undress uniform; not quite the same as Manse knew from past missions in the early twentieth century, but still elaborate with braid and medals; all three of the officers had sword and pistol at their belts. Tall and slim, hazel eyes, a small brown mustache, sleek hair, an air of ironic detachment.

"They might hear things they shouldn't," the one to his left said, with a Mecklenberger rasp to his German.

Plain *feldgrau* Imperial German uniform with General Staff tabs, a captain by rank; massive pear-shaped head shaved bald above a bull neck, hands that could probably bend horseshoes, a monocle, an old saber-scar and one more recent that looked like the result of a shell-fragment. Those gorilla hands fondled a riding crop that had a steel core from the way it flexed.

The Austrian shrugged. "They speak only Magyar, apart from the words of command," he said. "As useful as mutes, in their way."

"We are wasting time," the third man said, his German fluent but with a harsh choppy accent that said it wasn't his native language. "This matter will be taken out of our hands soon. And probably lost for months if not years in quarrels over jurisdiction, and the incredulity of idiots who will try to fit this . . . extraordinary occurrence . . . into something they can understand. We have waited days as it is."

He was a square-faced blond with very cold light eyes, older than the other two and looking as much like a Balkan Slav as anything; the unadorned brown Ottoman uniform said *Turkish*, and a brimless

Astrakhan hat was on the table before him. The face had a teasing familiarity.

"Very acute, my dear Mustafa," the Austrian said. "*Das is ein Murks, aber gottseidank sind wir ja net in Berlin.*"

Which meant *It's a screwup, but we're not in Berlin, thank God.*

From the way the Mecklenberger snorted he was thinking the same thing, in a fashion much less complementary to his hosts. His lips formed something like *Schlamperei* silently.

The Austrian went on to Manse: "I can just see trying to explain this to the All-Highest . . . Do sit, Herr Everard. I understand you speak German?"

"Yes, I do," Manse said.

Absolutely no percentage in backing down before this bunch, he thought. *Central European heavies straight from Central Casting. But the genuine article off the Ruritanian Express, the thing all the books and movies were imitating or mocking.*

A slight eeriness gripped him as he looked at the hard, intelligent faces. If what he suspected . . . was virtually certain of . . . had happened, he was looking at men who had no right to be alive.

The German would probably have died sometime in 1916, hammered into the mud of the Somme or vanished without trace in Falkenhayn's corpse-factory around Verdun, where two whole nations had bled to death; the Austrian would have led his hussars into machine-gun fire trying to break the siege of Przemyśl or sweated and shivered to death with typhus in the mountains of Serbia; the Turk would have taken an Australian bayonet in the gut in the hills above Suba Bay or frozen rock-hard in the Caucasus snows or been bombed into bleeding fragments in the retreat from Meddigo.

I'm talking to ghosts that haven't died.

"Why have you detained me in this lawless manner?" he went on, doing his best to register starchy indignation.

The Austrian smiled. "Not only good German, but excellent Viennese!" he said, flicking a monogrammed lighter and extending a slim gold cigarette case to either side and then—surprisingly—to Everard. The Patrol agent took it; Turkish tobacco, and very high quality, soothing as he dragged the smoke in. Plus the Danellian-era longevity treatment made you immune to cancer, heart disease, and pretty well everything else.

Then the Austrian gave a little tuck of the head that was the seated equivalent of a bow and heel-click before he blew a cloud of fragrant smoke:

"Permit me; I am Colonel Freiherr—" Baron, roughly "—Rudolf von Starnberg of the Imperial and Royal Army. My colleagues are Hauptman Ritter Horst von Stumm of the German Reich, and *Binbaşı* Mustafa Kemal of the Ottoman Empire. All from the Intelligence sections of our respective services, of course, and here for the Three Emperors conference to keep watch for foreign agents, domestic anarchists, Serbs, and similar vermin."

"Why have I been detained?" Everard demanded again.

I should have taken the hypno for standard German, he thought; complete fluency in the idiosyncratic local version looked suspicious now. *But this was supposed to be a vacation, not a mission!*

"*Sie brauchen mi echt net für an Trottel halten, Herr Everard,*" Von Starnberg said, and held up a hand.

"Please don't insult my intelligence. Before we waste time with a tiresome protestation of how you are an innocent tourist from . . . Wisconsin, is it called? Please examine these."

He slid a folder across the table with one finger. Manse opened it and sighed. The stills were a little blurred, taken from the reel of a movie camera, doubtless the one on the flatbed. They were clear enough to show him and Wanda: him using the stunner, Wanda leaning forward and her hand streaking towards the controls; the timecycle there and then *not* there.

Girl, get back to the Academy soonest, he thought, in what he knew was probably a futile hope.

That made his heart race until he used Patrol technique to calm it. Either a Patrol rescue team would arrive to break him out in a flourish of energy guns, able to be as blatant as they pleased since this wasn't a history they had any desire to preserve . . . or he'd vanish when this world was cancelled.

You've done that twice, he told himself. *Uncounted billions of human beings wiped out as you restored the* real *history, which in a sense makes you a mass murderer on a scale even Hitler or Stalin or Stantel V couldn't imagine. Perhaps there's a certain ironic justice to it . . . but that future that needs restoring contains Wanda and Monica. So to hell with it.*

The Austrian went on, with a gesture towards a neat pile of Manse's folded clothing and the contents of his pockets and wallet:

"Plus, of course, there are your clothes and documents."

And my communicator in that watch, dammit. Aren't Austrians supposed to be a bit sloppy? You *certainly aren't, Freiherr von Starnberg, even if you're a dead ringer for Graf Bobby's sidekick. You had me stripped right down to the skin and separated from everything I carried down to belly-button lint.*

As if to prove Everard's judgment of his capacity, the baron went on: "None of them *quite* what they should be, even the American passport. Money in a denomination which doesn't exist, printed with the name of the Austrian Republic . . . which, almighty Lord God be thanked, does not exist either. You were accompanied by a most attractive young lady showing enough leg that she would have been arrested in any city in Europe, except possibly Paris or Bucharest, who then disappeared into thin air on that remarkable vehicle. And the *pièce de résistance*, this."

He lifted a cloth and Manse's stunner lay beneath it. The smooth, neutral-brown curved shape was splashed with lead from the bullet that had smashed it out of his hand, but still fully functional; you could drive a tank over it, and it would still look like a minimalist sketch of a pistol with a pointed projection cone where the muzzle should be.

"Whatever this is, it knocks men or horses or dogs unconscious for a quarter hour at up to a hundred meters, and renders them helpless at twice that distance. It is uncannily accurate, soundless, has no recoil, weighs less than a pound and is made from something that cannot be scratched by diamonds or penetrated by X-rays. According to Privatdozent Herzfeld at the university here—"

"Damned Jew," the German muttered.

"Yes, but a very, very clever Jew, Horst. They are often extremely useful that way. And he says this—" he prodded the stunner with a finger "—is an absurdity, but that if it did exist it would function by some impossible focusing of high-frequency sounds, probably. He was quite angry with us until he realized it wasn't a joke, and even angrier when we took it away again before he could study it further. So, Herr Everard. You tell us . . . what are you, exactly? Where are you from? The world of the future, perhaps, in the manner of the Englishman Wells?"

A jolt of alarm; the Austrian wasn't joking, and he thought the Turk at least was taking the possibility seriously as well. He wouldn't have bet against the German either, but the man seemed to have only one expression, a snarl.

"Or Mars? No, not Mars, I have checked and current thought is that Mars is uninhabitable."

The German grinned unpleasantly. "Wherever he's from, he arrived in a manner he didn't anticipate. Or he wouldn't be here now. Something went wrong for him."

Manse looked him in the eye. "I am someone who can turn a minor nation into a Great Power," he said . . . in Turkish.

Existence focused down to a needlepoint. The pale blue eyes of the taciturn Ottoman flared, the pupils opening until they almost swallowed the iris; the other two gave sudden sharp glances at him and at Manse.

Scar-face there didn't get any of that. I don't think von Starnberg understood it either, or not all of it. And Mustafa got it perfectly and is thinking hard. This can't be a happy alliance.

"German, Herr Everard," the Austrian said. "Or English, or French. What was that . . . something about power?"

"The American said that his country was also a Great Power," Mustafa said in a neutral tone.

"If he is an American," the German growled. "When I was in German South-West Africa and Tanganyika and Tsingtao, I learned how to make lying pigdogs eager to speak the truth."

"Horst, Horst, perhaps *you* should go to America, to Hollywood."

"What?" the German said, puzzled.

"To act in their movies, playing the stereotypical Prussian Brute," the Austrian said, and waved a placating hand when the man sputtered. "Please. To business. Herr Everard?"

"I'm an engineer," Manse said calmly.

It was even true; at least, he'd been in the Army Engineers in the Second World War, and an engineering consultant after it . . . until he answered a very odd help wanted ad.

"The pistol and dimensional motorcycle are inventions of mine," he said calmly. "As Captain von Stumm noted, the motorcycle malfunctioned."

He didn't really expect to be believed. Just having a story gave him somewhere to start, though. The questions hammered at him after that; he was drenched in sweat by the time they finished, not from inventing plausible lies but simply from making the ones he used consistent. Several times he thought the German was going to come around the table and use the riding crop on him, or his fists.

And the good Baron von Starnberg is just as ruthless, under that veneer of Viennese good-humor, Manse thought, as the guards shoved him out at the point of their machine-pistols and marched him back to his cell. This time two of them came in and stood watching him, weapons ready. After a few hours they were replaced by Germans, though those stuck to the corridor outside, evidently on the theory that if any were in the room he could somehow jump them and get their guns. Time ticked by . . .

But I've got to get out of here. The Turk understood me. The question is, can he do anything about it?

V:

Vienna/Colorado/Munich/Vienna

HE'S THERE. *Or at least the sonic stunner and the communicator in his watch are,* Wanda thought.

She dialed the magnifying optic and it automatically stepped up the light. A medium-sized flat-roofed building currently being used as offices, with guards outside the entrances—military, not police, and in three different types of uniforms. The scanner couldn't get a precise fix on the instruments, not at this range, and any lower and the timecycle could be seen from the ground. She'd had to dodge a couple of biplanes already.

Time to take a closer look, on foot.

The problem with *that* was her clothes; she couldn't pass for a local, or anything acceptable, dressed as she was. A quick check had showed that nobody here was showing more than an inch of ankle, not even the hookers. What they were wearing during the daytime looked like a jacket or tunic, a long narrow tubular skirt, feathered hats and broad cloth belts slung at hip-height, with various accoutrements. Her shoes would definitely pass, but nothing else she was wearing—and her short hair was going to be conspicuous too. Evidently girls wore theirs long and down or braided, and women had it long and done up with pins and combs under the floppy-brimmed hats. She didn't know whether that was because things had changed differently here, or because older fashions hadn't changed as quickly as in her Jazz Age.

Wanda sighed; there was nothing she could do about the hair but wait six months of time she didn't have. There was a way to solve the clothes problem, but she didn't like it. Her money was worthless here, but her stunner worked perfectly. Still . . .

You're going to wipe out this entire world, she told herself. *Be realistic! A painless mugging is no huhu.*

A spin of the magnifying optical screen, and she picked a woman walking through the dusk down a fairly narrow street. Clothes not too shabby and not too new, height and build about like hers; that took a while, because she was a full three inches taller than the female average around here-and-now. Then an instant transition to an alley, and she was waiting.

"*Tut mir sehr leid, meine Liebe, ich brauch' das jetzt dringender als du,*" she called.

"What?" the woman said, turning, her eyes going wide at the strange dress.

Then she gave a little shriek at the sight of the stunner, so like a gun at first glance.

My need is greater than thine, lady, Wanda thought, and pressed the stun.

A quick bound and she caught the slumping figure of the young woman before she struck the ground, and a grunt of effort as she pulled her back into the alley and slung her across the rear seat of the timecycle. A touch of the controls, and they were in a meadow in the Rockies, in a stretch of summer high noon ten thousand years ago. A quick jump had shown the meadow wouldn't be bothered by sabertooths, paleo-Indians, or grizzlies in the next few hours.

Getting the clothes off a totally limp body was more difficult that she'd expected; *dressing* a totally limp body in her own outfit was even more of a struggle. When she had the new clothes on she walked around to accustom herself, and cursed the way the narrow skirt wrapped around her legs; if she had to run, she'd need to rip it off. A sudden thought struck her.

"Do I have to take her back to nineteen twenty-six, mark, II? That world's going to blink out of existence. It's sort of like dropping her in a volcano."

It was one thing for Deirdre van Sarawak to outlive the history that had produced her; she'd had a place to go and someone to look after her. And anyway Piet had rescued her on impulse when Manse snatched him out of captivity, in a future in which Carthage had won the Punic Wars thanks to a couple of ambitious Neldorians with energy rifles hiring on with Hannibal. This poor woman . . .

I can't just take her back. It's personal. I picked her just because we have about the same dress size! Dammit, that doesn't make sense but it's the way I feel.

Wanda transferred her belongings to the unconscious woman's purse, all but some jewelry she'd had along, then turned the thong of her own around the snoring figure's wrist. They should fetch the equivalent of ten or fifteen thousand dollars anywhere in the earlier twentieth century; and even in Central Europe in those days you just didn't need much in the way of identity documents.

It's the best I can do; if you keep your mouth shut you won't end up in the booby hatch right away, you've got a stake. Or maybe the Patrol can retroactively pick you up a minute after this and fix something for you. I was right when I joined up, I'm not *cut out to be a time-cop. Mammoths and sabertooths I can do. Offing someone I can't, not unless it's self-defense. Not face to face, not even this way.*

She studied the menus, and did another hop; this time to a quiet, leafy upper-class suburb of Munich in August of 1910, just before dawn and well before the change-point. The woman was beginning to come to as Wanda tipped her onto a wealthy family's lawn and blinked out of existence.

Vienna again, and a park not far from the building where Manse was being held. It was a governmental district, quiet after dark, but well-patrolled. She stepped off the timecycle and touched her watch; the nanoscale controls slaved to the communicator sent the vehicle skyward, hovering invisibly on antigrav until she summoned it. Closer, closer . . . people were walking by outside the building, giving the guards curious looks; evidently that wasn't standard. The soldiers carried rifles with fixed bayonets and their noncoms had machine-pistols; they were older than your average farmboy conscript, and looked harder-faced and more alert, probably some sort of special brute squad.

Wanda bought a copy of the *Reichpost*. The newsboy gave her a curious glance when she waved away the change from a *krone* coin, and then a delighted grin when he realized she was serious, and thanked her with a thickly accented *danke* and a sentence in some Slavic language.

The paper gave her something to hold up as she sat on a bench across the street. The little machine built into her watch could project a pseudo-screen in the air in front of her, but that would be just a *bit* conspicuous without camouflage. Right now, and at this distance, it showed Manse's stunner and his communicator, like hers concealed in a watch. They were close together, probably no more than a few feet, and neither was moving.

She waited an hour while the sun fell and the streetlamps came on, reading the paper to keep the fear at bay, the knowledge that the world around her and herself and Manse could—very well might—just *stop* at any instant. That it would bring Monica back and that the Van Sarawaks would take good care of her was some consolation, but not much.

In the paper . . .

The Three Emperors were meeting *to consolidate the peace of the Middle European and Near Eastern zone*; the editorial writer solemnly assured his readers that this grouping was the pillar of world order and progress. Kaiser Wilhelm was present, plus Emperor (and King of Hungary) Franz Ferdinand, and Mehmed VI Vahid ed-din of the Ottoman Empire, as well as what the editorial page called an 'unspeakable rabble' of Balkan leaders, subordinate puppets and satellites from the sound of it.

The British Prime Minister Lord Milner was reported to be considering lifting martial law in Ireland if there were no more outrages; Russia was in the middle of something more than riots but a little less than a civil war that had been going on for years, and the Reichpost was not-so-quietly happy about the way it defused the "Pan-Slav menace."

Bolivia and Paraguay were fighting over some stretch of scrub; the

Austrian government had granted the Grand Cross of the Royal Hungarian Order of Saint Stephen to the President of Mexico, who was called Félix Díaz Velasco and was continuing the *wise and stable policies of his predecessors Victoriano Huerta and his great uncle Porfirio Diaz*; someone she'd never heard of named Andrew Mellon was President of the US; the new Emperor of China, Yuan Keilang, was at loggerheads with the British-backed Japanese; there was a list of scheduled airship flights that included New York, Rio, Dar es-Salam, and Singapore among their destinations . . .

There it goes!

The stunner and the communicator were moving away from each other, at walking pace. The communicator was moving towards a room on the third floor, the top floor of the floridly neo-Baroque building. Manse would have been working to bust the situation loose, and once things started to shift she had a chance.

Wanda slipped the display into her purse and rose, dropping the paper on the bench. A wintry keenness filled her as she walked back towards the park. No need for much caution; this wasn't a history the Patrol wanted to preserve.

It probably doesn't have a Holocaust in its future, though things just as bad will happen eventually. Offhand it looks like a world that's a paradise for old rich European men with waxed mustaches and chests full of medals and orders. But better or worse it's standing between me and my man and me and my daughter, and I'm an agent of the Patrol.

Something whispered through the night above, something huge. She broke into a trot.

VI:

Vienna
Austro-Hungarian Empire
June 3rd, 1926 AD

THERE WAS A SOUND outside the door, a muffled scuffle and a thud; then Manse Everard turned off the lamp and rolled off the bed.

The door swung open; the Turkish officer stepped through quickly and moved to one side to avoid being silhouetted against the light. He gave a slight grim smile at the sight of the Time Patrol agent awake, alert, and fully dressed, in a fighter's crouch close enough to leap at anyone in the vicinity of the door.

The pistol in his hand wasn't quite aimed at Everard, but then again it wasn't not aimed at him, either.

Wanda, Monica, I'm on my way!

"That conceited braying ass von Starnberg was right, I think," the Turk said. "You are a dangerous man, and in more ways than one, Herr Everard . . . no, you speak Turkish, don't you?" he went on, shifting to that language. "A notable accomplishment, for a Frank."

"I speak a little, esteemed *Binbaşı*," Everard said in that tongue, deliberately keeping the sentence simple and hoping the oddness of his speech would pass as an accent.

In fact he spoke Turkish perfectly, legacy of a hypno for a mission in Istanbul in 2043 that he hadn't bothered to have scrubbed from his brain yet, but it was a twenty-first-century variety. The language had gone through an upheaval about "now" in the past of Everard's world, one which evidently hadn't happened here. This Colonel Mustafa was speaking the old-fashioned Ottoman service-speech, full of Arabic and Persian and Albanian loan-words and curious constructions.

"Better we use German," Manse went on.

Which will keep the questions to a minimum. I need to get out of this building!

If the Patrol hadn't sent an assault team in to snatch him they probably weren't going to. That left Wanda, who didn't have combat training beyond the basic Academy course and was on a commercial-model timecycle designed with all sorts of amateur-proof safety locks to prevent things like emerging with your head in the roof of a room when you tried to jump into a confined space. She'd need a good long clear run in the open to get at him. Unfortunately there was no chance at all she'd just skeddadle for a Patrol base in the deep past; he knew his wife. The only thing he could do was decrease the risk for both of them.

Men in Turkish uniform came through the door, dragging the limp, bleeding forms of the guards and dumping them unceremoniously;

the iron-copper-seawater smell of blood was strong. A sergeant was wiping the blade of a curved knife on the hair of one of the bodies and chuckling, murmuring something in what was probably Kurdish.

Yeah, the Three Emperor's League is just one big love-feast, Manse thought. *They may not have had World War One here, but it wasn't because they're a bunch of Quakers.*

"Wrap them in blankets so they don't spill too much," Mustafa snapped at his men in their language. "And get their rapid-fire weapons."

To Everard, in German: "Quickly, please, *mein Herr.*"

The corridors were even more deserted, and mostly very dark; there was the still vacant feeling of a building after working hours, amid a smell of old carpets and strong coffee and tobacco soaked into the walls. A metal staircase led them up and out onto the flat roof. Something huge overhung it; it took a moment for Everard to realize it was an airship, and large only by ordinary standards, nothing like the giant he'd seen on his first day.

Blimp, he thought, seeing the gondola slung below the gasbag. *Semirigid. And Turkish colors, they didn't have time to paint those out, but it won't be obvious in the dark.*

Four men were on the roof, with cables snagged around convenient projections; the gondola and gasbag swayed and creaked alarmingly, and the two engine pods gave a growling rasp as they idled, and a gasoline stink. The Turkish party began a rush towards the ladder that led up ten feet to refuge . . . and stopped abruptly.

"So, you lying pigdog," von Stumm said as he stepped out of the shadows, a squad at his back. "Did you think your Asiatic treachery wouldn't be noticed?"

The Turkish officer recovered from frozen shock almost instantly. His smile showed white in the dimness.

"Do you like the prospect of a firefight under that?" he said, jerking his pistol upwards.

From the scowl on von Stumm's face, he didn't. A hail of bullets might not set off the tens of thousands of cubic meters of hydrogen hanging over them like a fiery sword. Then again, it very well might, in which case the whole building would vanish in a fireball.

"Or you could call the Austrians for help," Mustafa pointed out. "Since they love their Christian brothers so well."

Evidently von Stumm didn't like that thought either. "Cold steel!" he bellowed to his men. "At them!"

He whipped out the saber at his side; Mustafa did likewise with his. Metal flashed and glimmered in the dimness, bayonet and clubbed rifle, sword and knife, fists and boots and teeth. Shouts of *Allah! Allah!* met *Hoch!* and *Hail Victory!*; gave way to animal screams of pain and rage as the groups collided in a wave of violence.

The Germans had numbers on their side, but the Ottomans had Manse Everard, moving through the dimness in a striking blur with the strength and speed of youth, nearly a century of field experience, and training in fighting arts selected from a million years of slaughterhouse human history. He snapped a kick into a knee with unmerciful precision and broke it, slashed the edge of his bladed palm into the angle of neck and jaw, ruptured a sternum with a thrust of stiffened fingers, slapped a bayoneted rifle aside and tossed the man over his hip in a throw that sent him head-first into a rooftop ventilator with a gruesome crack of breaking bone.

Less than two minutes later von Stumm was alone, backing, sweat gleaming on his shaven head as Mustafa Kemal came forward in a whirlwind of steel. Manse was close enough to see the German accept a cut to the shoulder, drop the sword and yank out his pistol to fire point-blank with the muzzle pressed to Mustafa's body.

Before he could von Starnberg was there; the projection cone of the Time Patrol stunner was only a foot from the German's head when he pressed the firing stud. Von Stumm dropped with a limp finality at the edge of the roof, half across the coping. The Austrian's boot gave him a helpful shove, and the body slipped out into space to fall three long stories to the pavement below. Manse winced slightly at the sound, coming erect and suddenly conscious of the sting of a minor cut on his left forearm.

"*Auf Wiedersehen,*" the Austrian officer said with satisfaction. "*So ein arrogantes,* störendes *preussisches Schwein.*"

Mustafa shook off the punch-to-the-jaw effect of being on the edge of the sonic stunner's field. "I would say arrogant, meddling Prussian swine is quite accurate. But his death will create a stir."

"Then let us depart, my dear *Binbaşı,*" von Starnberg said.

The surviving Turks and the Austrian squad climbed quickly up the ladder into the gondola; even with the dead left behind it was a crowded metal space, like a giant canoe with the controls at a glassed-in area of the front, and crawlspaces for mechanics to creep out and maintain the engines.

Which are probably very unreliable indeed, Manse thought.

Dim riding lights behind heavy frosted glass gave the men inside a ghastly semblance like animated corpses, fitting accompaniment for the smell of blood and the moans of the injured. There was a rumble of water being released from the ballast tanks as the growl of the engines rose to a roar, and a rising-elevator sensation as the blimp surged upwards. Von Starnberg made a motion towards his cigarette case and then halted it, looking upward and laughing. Instead he took out a flask and drank, offering it to Mustafa.

"Cognac," he said.

"It is forbidden," the man said. "But thank you."

Forbidden when you're in public, Manse thought, as he accepted it himself; he'd seen the flick of the Turkish officer's eyes towards his men.

The brandy wasn't as good as he would have expected from an obvious dandy and bon viveur like the Austrian, but it had alcohol in it and that was what he wanted just now. Meanwhile an Austrian medic attended to the wounded, bandaging and dusting wounds with antiseptic and administering morphine. Von Starnberg spoke sharply to one of his men, who unslung his pack and brought out wrapped parcels and several bottles.

"Now this is just lemonade," von Starnberg said, swigging deeply from one, wiping the mouth and handing it on to Mustafa as his soldier gave out the other bottles. "And here we have cold chicken, bread, cheese, and chocolate—no pork products, I assure you, gentlemen. Drink, eat; fighting is thirsty, hungry work."

There was a murmur as one of the Turks translated for the benefit of his monoglot comrades. Mustafa's manner thawed somewhat.

"That was considerate of you, Freiherr," he said. "On behalf of my men, I thank you. And for the medical attention."

Von Starnberg's smile was charming. "No, no, I assure you, it was the least I could do."

VII:

100 meters altitude
Lake Balaton
Austro-Hungarian Empire
June 4th, 1926 AD

WANDA EVERARD'S frustration turned to horror as the first of the bodies dropped from the gondola. The blimp was running without lights, only the dim red glow of the exhausts showing. The naked corpses struck the water and sank instantly; they must be weighed down. The lights of towns and villas and resorts shone cruelly indifferent from the low southern shore.

Then the aircraft pointed its nose upward and began to climb. She followed automatically, her hands on the bars that controlled normal-space flight.

That couldn't have been Manse. They could have killed him in Vienna. This is some sort of internal quarrel, they're fighting over him, they're advanced enough here/now to understand what the technology they've seen must mean . . .

The blimp rose to a thousand meters and accelerated to about sixty miles an hour, crawling eastward through the night.

VIII:

Transylvania
Austro-Hungarian Empire
June 5th, 1926

"FÜR EINEN *Türken is der Mustafa ein schlauer Kerl. Ich werde schau'n, dass er die Schuld an allem kriegt,"* von Starnberg explained cheerfully.

"For a Turk, Mustafa was a very clever fellow. I intend to see that he will get all the blame. A pity, he might have been a great man anywhere but Turkey. Still, the Turks are barbarians and strain themselves to manufacture rifle cartridges. We Austrians have the means to take advantage of your knowledge, Herr Everard. I've arranged for a very comfortable *schloss* near Kronstadt, and soon the world will be surprised, eh?"

"You used thallium in the lemonade?" Everard asked grimly, looking at the stinking stains on the gondola's floor.

"Yes, rat poison. I've been taking Prussian Blue . . . appropriate, *nein*? . . . for several days now. There was more antidote in the brandy, just in case."

"What if Mustafa had accepted the brandy?"

"Then he would have been merely uncomfortable while his men fell dead, and alive when he went into the water," Von Starnberg said cheerfully. "Ah, we're nearly there. Come, take a look at your temporary residence, Herr Everard . . . may I call you Manse? Not too bad a place; they make their pastries too sweet and the coffee is vile, but some of the wines are excellent and the Rumanian girls clean up nicely. And cheer up! I will be a very great man when this project succeeds, the next thing to a king, and I know how to reward good service. Money, power, women, estates, titles? You will be able to take your pick."

Except for wondering about the lemonade, Manse thought, and licked his lips as he came to stand beside the Austrian in the opened door.

The wind wasn't too bad as the blimp slowed, and it was nearly dawn. A pale colorless light showed densely forested mountains below, low but steep, and on a height the towers of a fairytale Gothic castle, massive towers and courtyards, with a few lights showing in the windows.

"Isn't it a grand sight?"

"Looks like escape," Manse said, and grabbed the other man by the neck as he launched himself forward.

Von Starnberg fell away, screaming with his arms and legs working as he plunged through the air. Manse snap-rolled forward, presenting as much surface to the air as he could and arrowing forward. The side of the mountain flashed towards him; he just cleared the crest, and the side of the castle swelled towards him.

He was still smiling when he struck, though it was a little like a snarl as well.

IX:

Transylvania
Austro-Hungarian Empire
June 5th, 1926

WANDA'S SCREAM died as her throat squeezed shut. Then a hysterical laugh choked off as well.

Manse does *think a lot like a field agent,* she thought as she set the controls.

Blink, and she was five minutes pastward and a thousand meters down. The uniformed figure tumbled through the sky, but Manse flattened out in an expert skydiver's posture. Air brawled around the force-screen as she dove the timecycle like a stooping hawk, and in seconds she was beside him. A lurch as he swung onto the second seat, and she punched the controls.

X:

Pyrenees
18,244 BC

"I HAD TO WATCH you *die*, you son of a bitch!" Wanda yelled, and flung herself into Manse's arms.

"Not permanently," he grinned, and then they were kissing.

When the embrace ended they grew conscious of the others; Piet and Deidre van Sarawak, with Monica in the other woman's arms.

"Thank *God*," Wanda breathed, and snatched her daughter up.

Piet grinned and hammered him on the back. The other Unattached agent in the softly glowing chamber below the Pleistocene resort was a woman, spider-thin, seven feet tall, with blue-black hair drawn up in a knot and huge blue eyes in a narrow hook-nosed face.

She bowed in a far-future manner. "Unattached Agent Everard," she said.

"Unattached Agent Komozino," he replied.

She went on with an alien directness: "We have rectified the situation somewhat. There was a very subtle biological sabotage of the Gavrillo Princip nexus figure, requiring that we substitute a clone. History now records that the assassin of Franz Ferdinand died of tuberculosis in an Austrian prison-fortress rather than being beaten to death by a mob in the streets of Sarajevo, but this is a historically negligible factor. The perpetrators are still at large. Unindentified."

"For now," Manse Everard said grimly, looking at his wife and daughter.

A scent came down the time-winds, that of maneater.

"Time to hunt," he said.

AFTERWORD:

I FIRST CORRESPONDED with Poul about the time I sold my first story; he was a fascinating man to exchange thoughts with, a polymath who made the extent of his knowledge the foundation and fuel for imagination rather than an impediment to it, and who was unfailingly kind, honest, and wise in his advice to a novice. He was a gentleman and a scholar, a good man, and there aren't enough people like him around. Later I had the honor of being his host and meeting him off and on—not as often as I'd like, but I treasure every instance.

My debt to him goes a long way further. His young adult *Vault of the Ages* was the first real science fiction I read; it introduced me to the solidity of his world-building, something you could taste and smell and feel, and the way his characters inhabited their own reality, and also to the mixture of hope and tragic stoicism that marked his universe.

On a more immediate level, he was never less than solidly professional—even his early mature works like *Three Hearts and Three Lions* or *The High Crusade* are meticulously crafted without being heavy—and at his best, he was hauntingly intense.

Plus I learned the uses and perils of the semicolon from him! Without him, I probably wouldn't be a writer.

—S. M. Stirling

LIVING AND WORKING WITH POUL ANDERSON

by Karen Anderson

POUL AND I met and lived our life in the world of science fiction.

At Chicon II in 1952, he was a fan who had become a professional; and I, a reader who had become a fan, hoping to sell. Fewer than 1,000 were present, and it was easy for writer or neofan to talk to leading editors and prominent writers: John W. Campbell, Anthony Boucher, Willy Ley, L. Sprague de Camp, Robert Bloch. Professionals and fans swapped ideas with each other.

The single program track lasted three days; art shows weren't yet invented, and Chicon only offered dealers a small display area at the back of the main program space. Regional conventions weren't bid for; Worldcon rotation was unneeded. Philadelphia's bid was contested by a relatively new California group, the Little Men, who'd held a penthouse party through the entire weekend. This extravagance bred hostility, and Philadelphia won for 1953.

Masquerades of the fifties were simply big costume parties, not always with dance music. In 1952, I embellished off-the-rack clothes and wore elaborate makeup. I failed to notice Theodore Sturgeon, with guitar as Rhysling, but photographed costumes including Lester del Rey in evening dress, "disguised as a gentleman," and many others. Then I saw Poul Anderson, devil's horns sprouting from his forehead; after I snapped him menacing a young woman, we got to talking, and scarcely stopped for the rest of the convention except when we separated to sleep. He introduced me to fellow Minneapolis Fantasy Society members Gordon R. Dickson and Dale Rostomily. We exchanged addresses; I have never been much of a correspondent, but his letters were full of things to answer.

Poul had been a fan before selling. Throughout his life, he always had time for fans, and they more than repaid us in the support they offered when it was needed at the end. Even now, I benefit from his fans' support.

His first stories went to Campbell at *Astounding Science-Fiction*, then the best paying and most respected magazine in the field; the first in digest format, it had smooth paper and trimmed edges. *ASF*'s style and pay rate were copied by newcomers *Galaxy*, edited by Horace Gold, and *The Magazine of Fantasy and Science Fiction*, edited by Anthony Boucher and J. Francis McComas. The editors were Campbell alumni, and Poul sold to both.

Theodore Cogswell was another MFS member moving toward professionalism. Clifford Simak dated from the pre-Campbell *Astounding Stories*. Now both a seasoned fiction professional and a veteran reporter for the Minneapolis *Star,* he readily gave advice to beginners. One piece which Poul passed on to me was the way to shorten an unwieldy story: "Tell the end."

Poul and I knew by spring that we would marry, but he wanted warmer winters; I, cooler summers. Northern California, which he'd visited, seemed to me worth trying. He being already committed to a summer trip in Europe with his mother and brother, so I moved first.

I found an apartment in Berkeley and a job that would pay for it. The local fanclub was the Little Men, whose Worldcon bid had failed; I'd become acquainted via fanzines with the couple who ran it, Lester and Esther Cole. When the apartment next to mine fell vacant, I paid its rent until Poul arrived and moved in. We were married a few months later, with the attendance of my mother, locals in the SF world, and a few migrants from the MFS and the Washington Science-Fiction Association.

The Elves', Gnomes', and Little Men's Science Fiction, Chowder and Marching Society, named from the comic strip "Barnaby," won their bid for the 1954 Worldcon to be held in San Francisco. Poul and

I became members of the organizing committee, which met at Les and Es's home in El Cerrito. Tony Boucher, also a member, remarked apropos the snack she served that Es was notable for both making and being cheesecake.

Poul wrote progress reports; I stenciled and cranked them out on my mimeograph. His lighter output had previously included MFS entertainments and the Hoka stories he and Gordy had begun selling; now I ran some in my fanzines. The December 1953 issue of my *Zed* had his "Barbarous Allen;" borrowing a typo from WSFAn migrant Lee Jacobs, I called it a "filk song." After a few more uses, the term stuck.

Our life was fan-oriented: gatherings of migrants who'd followed us, club meetings every other Friday at a store that sold and rented mystery and science fiction books. South of the UC campus, this was close enough to Tony's that he could walk over for a yearly talk on SF and fantasy publishing.

But it was ruled by a pro's needs. Returning from our honeymoon in Mexico, we found telegrams summoning Poul to a New York publisher. With hurriedly packed winter clothing, we flew to meet Ian and Betty Ballantine, who became valued friends. They planned simultaneous hard and soft cover editions of *Brain Wave*, whose first half had appeared in a dying prozine. Re-writing was minimal; all I can point to, comparing text, is the name Helga being substituted for Dagmar—that having been the stage name of a "dumb blonde" TV star. The novel continues to be reprinted; and currently it's available both in print and from ibooks.

Tony, who edited *F&SF* from his Berkeley home, was a friend and neighbor from the start. Poul was grateful to him and co-editor Mick McComas, for—unlike other editors, including *ASF*'s Campbell and *Galaxy*'s Gold—asking the author to make story changes, instead of rewriting himself. "No other s-f editor does this, damn their eyes," he wrote Tony in 1953, "and writers weep bitter tears at seeing their carefully constructed prose ripped to shreds . . . even if nobody ever seems to notice the difference." The letter is reprinted in *The Wonder Years*, edited by Annette Peltz McComas.

One evening I answered a knock on the door by a stranger who said hesitantly that Tony Boucher had given him our address. This was R. Bretnor, whom we came to know as Reg. He and his wife

Helen were connoisseurs of books, food, and Siamese cats. They were also impecunious enough to drink the same "red ink" jug wine we did.

Tony also put us in touch with the fairly Establishment-type Margaret and Eric St. Clair, and the decidedly non-Establishment Phil and Kleo Dick. Like Reg, Phil was a proverbial writer-with-employed-wife who was papering a wall with rejection slips.

The Dicks did have a television set. We must sometimes have just asked if we could come over—theirs was essentially the only TV set available to us for several years. We didn't want to divert money that could go for such books as, after Reg had lent us his, our own copy of *The Hobbit*. Or cat food: we'd taken a Bretnor kitten.

In the summer of 1954 we rented a house. One hundred dollars a month was more than we could really afford after I'd quit my job, but it had a "granny room" I could fix up and rent. During those early days Poul took long walks while turning over ideas. Once he came home saying, "Can we afford $75 for an eleventh edition Encyclopedia Britannica?" Now, this was when a copy of Astounding cost twenty-five cents and Campbell paid $300 for a 10,000-word story; and I was very pregnant.

I may have debated for a whole minute before I said, "Go back there and get it before someone else finds it." No one had, and I still think that was one of the best purchases we ever made. I used to read it for pleasure; what I learned was useful in story planning and reading first drafts. I still have it.

That house, just north of University Avenue and not far from the west side of the UC campus, became a gathering place for local and transplant fans. When Es Cole had her own baby, we had a party celebrating both; I gave Lance his first sip of champagne.

Astrid was six weeks old at the time of the convention. We took her along, as I planned on nursing her for as long as I could. I remembered my very traditional southern-reared Grandma Payne saying that as long as a woman nursing covered herself with a shawl, she was decent; and so I did. John Campbell commented on how admirable this was. She had a baby-watcher in the room for the masquerade, while Poul danced with Vampira to the music of Turk Murphy and I wore a scanty, glittering costume inspired by Bergey's covers for *Planet Stories*.

After the convention, we settled down to an irregular routine, Astrid permitting. A portable bed for her stood beside ours; she woke me at some dark hour, I nursed her, then slept with her beside me until I woke.

Being a full-time pro, Poul didn't have a day job or an alarm clock, but he kept regular working hours. He'd wake, breakfast alone, and go to his desk. We always had one room that was entirely his, with his desk and typewriter and needful books. In the Berkeley house, it was an attic room upstairs from the back bedroom that became Astrid's; in Orinda, it was opposite our own bedroom.

This study was off-limits to all but a very few interruptions—"if it's the Angel Gabriel blowing the Last Trump." If he was expecting an important call from someone, he would say, "So-and-so has the rank of archangel."

When he found a stopping point around midday, he came out for lunch; we usually had Danish-style open-faced sandwiches. There was a notional dinner time. He might just keep working, though sometimes he came out in the afternoon to say he'd work late. He pounded out penny-a-word adventure yarns, historical in addition to SF, for true pulps: ragged-edged magazines named for the rough paper they were printed on. Better work went for three and four cents to the smooth-paper magazines like *ASF*.

We went out occasionally. Besides fans, there were various pros we saw. Rog and Honey Phillips had moved from Chicago; with them, Reg, Mick McComas (still co-editing *F&SF* with Tony), and a few others. We held a low-stakes monthly poker game.

Saturdays and Sundays were work days like any others. Holidays came by chance: a spell of hot weather might send us to Muir Woods; his brother John might propose a camping trip in the Rockies with their mother. Or there would be a convention—should we fly or drive? If we drive, where shall we stop on the way? Will Astrid be with us?

Finances permitting, we would go to Westercon over July 4, Worldcon at Labor Day. We expected to serve on local committees and take whatever part in programs was expected. Some fan occasions in Los Angeles, like "relaxicons" when Worldcon was distant, were almost convention-like in their size. We took Astrid on whatever of these travels we could.

The rental of the granny room through the UC student housing office worked well. Our first tenant, Mamoru Saiganji, was a black belt in judo; he and other Japanese whom he recommended promoted interests we'd both already had in Japanese lore and culture.

We were committee members again when the 1956 Westercon was held in Oakland. A skit would often be put together by pros in those days, perhaps improvised during the event. I'd always been interested in theater, and Poul had helped write MFS spoofs. Together we wrote "Mag Net," a *Dragnet*-inspired takeoff on the current state of the magazines in which we cast Rog Phillips, Tony Boucher, Dale Rostomily, and other locals plus some at-convention pickups. These included, memorably, Jerome Bixby improvising throughout on the piano.

It was a great success. Poul joined me in writing another satire to present at the 1958 Los Angeles Worldcon: I played the title role in "Alice in Thrillingwonderland" with some previously rehearsed Little Men and others in a semi-pickup cast that included Ben Stark, George Scithers, and F. M. Busby. Tony Boucher played the White A. P. and Doc Smith was the Upstage Lensman.

When the Mystery Writers of America began accepting science fiction as a form of mystery suitable for credentials, Poul had joined the local chapter. Miriam Allen de Ford was active in both fields. Speakers at their San Francisco dinner meetings ranged from a DEA agent with a sample of cocaine he allowed me to taste, to fantasy old-timer E. Hoffman Price—possibly the only person who ever met both H. P. Lovecraft and Robert E. Howard.

Stories about Poul's Japanese-Swedish-American detective Trygve Yamamura went to second-rank digests like *The Saint* and *Alfred Hitchcock*. His one sale to the top-ranked *Ellery Queen's Mystery Magazine* was a happy accident; he'd sent a locked-spaceship detective story, "The Martian Crown Jewels," to Tony Boucher—who wrote back, "Our sister magazine can pay more for this. With your permission I'll send it there." His Trygve Yamamura novels were published in hardcover, but as the SF field improved, he decided to quit mystery writing. He said he felt as if he was continually reinventing the wheel.

In Tony's Sherlockian group, the Scowrers and Molly Maguires of San Francisco, we met people high in various professions: the

Galileo scholar Stillman Drake, the marine biologist Joel Hedgpeth. Stuart Palmer, of the Trained Cormorants of Los Angeles County, was a mystery writer, private detective, and occasionally a niche editor.

By the late fifties, not only was I suggesting story material to Poul and discussing his manuscripts as he wrote, he was occasionally sharing the by-line with me on stories when he felt I'd contributed enough. I sold verses to Tony Boucher at *F&SF*, and Cele Goldsmith at *Fantastic* bought a short fantasy, "The Piebald Hippogriff," that inspired Bonnie Dalzell to a drawing still available on her web site. Avram Davidson, Tony's successor at *F&SF*, liked a story he bought from me so much he gave me the germ of another.

In longer forms, I made two attempts at novels; one, though it might be worth completing, I doubt I could do alone. When I did finally complete a novel, it was only much later, in collaboration with Poul.

In 1959, we bought a new, though small, car for cash; that was the year the Detroit Worldcon committee invited Poul to be their Guest of Honor. I think his hotel bill was to be paid, but little if anything more. We decided to drive; and then we "played map." We wouldn't have to go directly, of course; wouldn't we want to see the Cogswells in Indianapolis and my relatives in Kentucky? Then go by way of Washington to New York?—And why not Boston, and a bit of Canada as long as we were that close? Then after the convention, we'd see his mother in Minnesota, and the MFS gang; then, so late in the year, we'd want to drop south and stop at Barringer Crater . . .

People who fly miss all these choices. When committees did cover air fare, though, they sometimes also took us unimagined places: In Calgary, we were taken into a museum's storage space and given the privilege of holding an authentic tilting-lance. So well balanced it seemed massless, it nestled eagerly between my arm and side.

But, to return to the 1959 trip: I'd never learned to drive. Up to age twenty-five it would have meant higher insurance payments; now past that age, I still used bicycle or public transit. Now I needed to share in this transcontinental drive. I began lessons in empty parking lots on weekends, went on to level streets, then winding streets in the hills.

We headed east on US 40, a road that we'd used more than once on camping trips to reach Lake Tahoe. Its two lanes, with occasional passing lanes, wound up and up; I recognized this restaurant, that service station with snow-tire rental—but now I was behind the wheel. The Donner Pass was my seventh driving lesson.

What we saw, whom we visited, and which relatives took care of Astrid, can be left for a longer reminiscence. But I must mention one event.

We'd headed north along the Blue Ridge Parkway and stopped at a campground in North Carolina; I think it was the only time we blew up our air mattresses. We had a bare stone hilltop to sleep on.

I woke in the hours before dawn to see, glowing amid a clear starry sky, what looked like a fluorescent orange comet. It had to be a man-made object in space! I woke Poul and we discussed it. Next day's newspaper mentioned a sounding rocket from Wallops Island; at the convention Willy Ley confirmed that the rocket had squirted out sodium vapor above the shadow of Earth.

Conventions run together in my memory. Was it here, late one party, Poul and some others sang "*Die Beiden Grenadiere*" while Willy translated the lyrics to me? Likely Gordy Dickson and Ted Cogswell were singing too. It was surely where we met Kelly Freas, creator not only of covers and interiors for so many of Poul's stories, but also of his portrait for the April 1971 special issue of *F&SF*.

Homebound after Detroit, we visited in Minnesota and did indeed see Meteor Crater as we swung south to California. On the last morning, hungry and cashless, we used a bank's check-guarantee card that allowed me to draw $100 when a branch opened. We bought gas and breakfast and made like bats out of Barstow. After that Poul agreed to have a gasoline credit card, so long as it was kept paid off.

All these things formed the basis of our continuing lifestyle. We drove once by a direct route as far as Chicago and back for a convention. Attending those, we talked, partied, and sang with writers, editors, artists, publishers—above all fans, many of whom aspired or even succeeded professionally. Specialty presses like Gnome and Shasta, and semi-pro ones like Advent, fed an appetite ignored by general publishers until the runaway success of *The Lord of the Rings*. Paperback houses like Berkley and Pyramid added science fiction to their crime and suspense lines, and Ace started the double-novel experiment in both genres. Poul sold them not only original novels but at least one collection of short works as his own flip side.

At the end of 1959, we were ready to buy our own home, rather than renting. (Our last tenants, Terry and Miriam Carr, had moved to better housing.) We searched Berkeley and neighboring cities before finally choosing a house in Orinda. Excellent in some respects, it was only tolerable in others; I might have looked longer if I'd known we would be there over forty years.

In 1965 we went to Loncon II, our first foreign worldcon; as in 1959, we traveled in great loops before and after the convention that was the primary business purpose. The IRS never questioned our receipts for that or any travel we claimed. London 1965 was like Detroit 1959, and so were Heidelberg 1970 and Brighton 1979. We combined Den Haag 1990 with a science tour. We visited foreign friends and Poul's Danish kinfolk, saw museums, and took local tours. Only rarely did we go to a nightclub or the like, being more likely to rest our feet and plan the next day.

In Europe, we saw passage graves, reconstructed Iron Age dwellings, medieval and Renaissance merchants' houses, lords' castles and royal chateaus, the pomp of Versailles and Peter the Great's responses at St. Petersburg; and always surviving temples, churches, and cathedrals from Athens to Moscow. In the New World, we saw pre-Columbian remains of Incas, Mayas, and Aztecs as well as Hispanic developments. Around the world, we saw the variousness of the world itself and its history. A writer's imagination can only work on what's been put into it.

François Bordes, who'd translated Poul's work for the French edition of *F&SF*, and his wife Denise de Sonneville-Bordes had become our friends while at UC Berkeley. His work in re-developing knapping techniques would suffice to make him famous, and Denise's work on typology was equally respected. He gave us an Acheulean hand-ax—"I can do this legally, since it was picked up in a river and has no importance for research."

In Dordogne, François showed us painted caves only open to researchers, and his students' ongoing dig at an *abri*. (When I last visited, the Smithsonian displayed a recreation of his site.) He took us to a site open to the public where I picked up a worked stone; he identified it as a Perigordean blade, and said I was welcome to keep it, as it lacked stratigraphy. (Imagine a thickish injector-razor blade, about one-and-a-half scale, made from a long flake of white stone.) He had both the knowledge and the authority, being head of the Department of the Quaternary at the University of Bordeaux.

During such travels, Poul used his Danish bilingual upbringing and college German, while I had Latin, Spanish, French, and both classical and a bit of modern Greek to call on. I used the last to create "sophont" for a story of his, a term taken up by anthropologists to mean an intelligent nonhuman.

In 1966, we became part of a counter-counterculture.

Diana Paxson had invited numerous friends to a medieval re-enactment on May Day, in her back yard just south of the UC campus. Poul had work, my mother needed me in D.C., but she'd invited twelve-year-old Astrid too. Poul could drop her off and fetch her. Combats, music, and pageantry succeeded so well that further events were arranged in Berkeley parks. The Society for Creative Anachronism was well under way when, first at Westercon and then at Worldcon in 1966, pilots of *Star Trek* were shown. Post-event revelry became Trek fan-sessions.

Dorothy Jones, one of the Consortium Antiquum singers who had joined the SCA as a group, became a Trek fan and a close friend of Astrid's. She was in her twenties, but she and Astrid together turned into eighteen-year-old twins. We and other family groups at the beginning carried out Diana's idea of re-creating the cultural Middle Ages, not just the martial arts.

The SCA, appealing to the same mentality as science fiction, spread from convention to campus to army base. One fighter started a branch at Ramstein Air Force Base in Germany; another, serving in the Pacific, set one up on an aircraft carrier. Poul and I, with Astrid, Dorothy, and others put together the filk operetta "HMS Trek-A-Star" for a Westercon; it turned out to have all-SCA cast and crew. I sang Spock. The audience included Gene Roddenberry and James Doohan. A near-original cast re-ran it at the 1968 Worldcon, with a few lines updated; David Gerrold, with a tribble he and I had stitched up, substituted as Kirk.

Poul took to SCA fighting with enthusiasm, and what he learned on the field (though with duct-tape-wrapped rattan) gave him the combat experience to re-write his early fantasy *The Broken Sword*, still available from Orion both in paperback and in e-publication. "Sir Bela of Eastmarch" is especially remembered by early fighters as setting an example for chivalry.

We went occasionally to the annual meetings of the AAAS; some years, as when Hal Clement gave a paper on habitable extremes, they were irresistible. We attended a bioastronomy conference in Santa Cruz and one on lunar and planetary science in Houston. Meeting Poul, a surprising number of scientists said science fiction had turned them toward their profession. Space scientists and rocket engineers, met at Florida launches or JPL flybys, have also called SF writers and artists influential in shaping their work.

In 1986 and later, we joined conducted tours with lectures by scientists to see a comet or an eclipse. Exotic sites (and information we picked up) would always spark a story: "The Year of the Ransom" sprang from the L5 Society's trip to Perú and the Galápagos to see Halley's Comet, with lectures by David Levy, before Comet Shoemaker-Levy made him famous. Jay Pasachoff led an eclipse tour in 1990 that we made part of a grand sweep. It began in July with a visit to Helsinki and a quick trip to Leningrad and Moscow, before returning for the charter flight that showed us the eclipse at 33,000 feet above Finland. We left the group when their ship reached Stockholm, on our way to Den Haag for the 1990 worldcon. Other eclipse tours took us to Oaxaca (also Monte Albán, Yagúl, and Mitla) where we could eat *huitlacoche*; or brought us through Argentina with a look at the Falls of Iguazú on the way to the Gran Chaco and the Mennonite enclave of Paraguay. That latter gave rise to the scene where a South American experiences a computer-created dream of Jorge Luis Borges.

Having left the 1990 tour, we rented a car, traveled down the east coast of Sweden, crossed Denmark and went through part of the Netherlands to the Worldcon. Tom Doherty took us to lunch and said, "You know, if I had a new Time Patrol story, I could put together an omnibus." Poul said, "Funny thing about that: we were just researching it." The story was "Star of the Sea," in which my translations of the Latin inscriptions we'd seen on Batavian traders' votive altars found in the Netherlands and our speculations about their iconography melded with what we'd seen on Öland and what Tacitus had said about the Germani and their cult of Nerthus.

That European tour concluded as a family reunion: Astrid, her husband Greg, four-year-old Erik, and infant Alexandra, joined us to visit Poul's relatives in København.

We participated in many annual CONTACT (Cultures of the Imagination) conferences, created by anthropologists James Funaro, Reed Riner, and Joel Hagen.

Such exercises start with choosing a type of star and sort of planet, Poul's specialty, and working up from there through ecology, culture, and languages; the last are my strengths. Two teams (each representing humans or other sophonts: time, near or far future) would present their culture session by session as they developed it, and finally role-play their encounter with each other.

For a spinoff Contact conference in Japan, we created a world complete with ecosystem and sophonts' history and mythology, including a planetary trade-language. Poul's story "The Shrine of Lost Children" arose there. We converted a set of planets from the Technic Universe for a role-playing exercise at one of the Asimov Conferences at White Eagle Lodge in New York; for another Asimov Conference, Poul and I developed the assigned Ben Bova book *Welcome to Moonbase* into a "Murder Weekend" game.

Travels before and after Brighton 1979, originally Regency-driven, led into Roman connections. Hadrian's Wall confirmed that we would write a late-Roman story; it became a fantasy when I found Martin of Tours, definitely of our period, embedded in the Breton legend of Ys. Researching further at home, I saw we could cross it with Frazer's King of the Golden Wood. I spent a year doing book research, and we returned to Brittany for a look at places and things we hadn't seen before. The writing, beyond some verses of mine, was entirely Poul's; we plotted it together. Later, visiting his brother John (retired from a professorship of geology), I remarked that I thought of the novel as my master's thesis; John said, "I've seen Ph.D.s given for less research."

I had always wanted to write science fiction and fantasy. If I sold little of my own, still I was helpmeet to one of those who shaped it, and lived among people for whom it was the most important thing in the world. And why not? Our dreams, if we shape them aright, can in turn shape a better future for the world.

◈ ◈ ◈

In 1998, Poul was recognized as a Grand Master by the Science Fiction Writers of America.

He had been a member of MWA before SFWA existed, and was familiar with their motto: "Crime does not pay—enough!" As a founding member he had agreed that it must, like MWA, be not a literary society but an organization of professionals. Poul worked hard to support it. He was elected one of its first presidents, and served two terms, missing deadlines for the first time. I had made sales enough to join the organization along with him, and paid my dues regularly, though my solo sales were few. Eventually we bought life memberships.

In 1966, after that year's Worldcon, we took part in the Milford Writers' Conference hosted annually by Damon Knight and Kate Wilhelm at their home. Participants benefited from critiquing each others' stories, and also from extended discussions, going beyond those that took place at Worldcons. We thought SFWA would profit from a similar annual get-together. Next spring, we put on the first annual SFWA Awards gathering. Astrid and her "twin" were our support staff, handing out badges and suchlike. (I was very proud in 2004 to see how well Astrid ran the weekend in Seattle.) We continued, in spite of the sometimes furious internal controversies, to support the organization in every way we could.

When Poul received his Grand Master award at Santa Fe, instead of having a typed acceptance speech he spoke extempore. I wish someone had been recording the proceedings, because he spoke of me and all the ways I'd assisted him through the years. He ended with the words, "She is my love."

DANCING ON THE EDGE OF THE DARK

by C.J. Cherryh

C.J. CHERRYH is the author of more than sixty novels, the winner of the John W. Campbell Award and three Hugo Awards, and a figure of immense significance in both the science fiction and fantasy fields. In science fiction, she's published the thirteen-volume Foreigner *series, the seven-volume* Company Wars *series, the five-volume* Compact Space *series, and many other series and stand-alone novels, including* Cyteen. *In fantasy, she's the author of the four-volume* Morgaine *series, the three-volume* Rusalka *series, the five-volume* Tristan *series, the two-volume* Arafel *series, and, as editor, the seven-volume* Merovingen Nights *anthologies. Some of her best-known novels include* Downbelow Station, The Pride of Chanur, Gate of Ivrel, Kesrith, Serpent's Reach, Rimrunners, The Dreamstone, Port Eternity, *and* Brothers of Earth. *Her short fiction has been collected in* Sunfall, Visible Light, *and* The Collected Short Fiction of C.J. Cherryh. *Her most recent book is a new novel in the* Foreigner *world,* Betrayer. *She lives in Spokane, Washington.*

Swashbuckling but ruthless Imperial agent Dominic Flandry, who works tirelessly to prevent the Terran Empire from falling, although he knows that the interstellar Dark Age that will follow the Empire's collapse inevitably will come someday in spite of his best efforts, may be Poul Anderson's single most popular character. Flandry's first adventure was published in 1951, and he subsequently featured in six novels and enough shorter works to fill two collections, stretching across

Anderson's entire career. Dominic Flandry is occasionally referred to as "science fiction's James Bond," but the fact is that Flandry started his adventures two years before *James Bond made his fictional debut, so perhaps James Bond should instead be referred to as "the mainstream's Dominic Flandry!"*

Here, C.J. Cherryh gives us a new generation of Flandrys setting up shop in the family business . . .

THE EMPIRE was frayed on the edges. There had been the business in Scotha, and there had been so many others besides, wars, conquests, collapses, rebellions . . . all, all in constant motion. The Galaxy was wide. The reach of ships grew, without the presence of enough Empire force to police the territories they opened up, and there was no shortage of other lordlings and dictators with ambitions and fleets.

The Terran Empire had been potent once—at least in concept. The Empire had thrown its perimeter wider and wider, incorporating the foreigners, the odd, the strange, the different—and the occasionally incomprehensible.

Success had widened its boundaries so very far now there was no way, now, that all of the Empire could be attacked at once.

But neither could it be defended, even piecemeal, and moving assets about to deal with brushfires in the hinterworlds grew harder and harder for the Empire to deal with. There was an incursion in the double sun system, on the desert moon of Lothar, which needed a fleet to deal with it, and the Empire dealt with that—bringing in a hundred ships from Audette; but moving forces from Audette encouraged Duadin to move on its neighbor, and while all that was going on, over on the opposite side of the Empire, the Succession Wars of Patmai broke out, which simply could not be addressed.

The winner of that struggle took a sector out of the Empire, and the Empire, for once, had to sigh collectively and say that rebellions were short and tyrants had lifespans—while the Empire was long, and had a long memory for former situations. It meant to bring Patmai and Patmara back into the Empire.

It would—perhaps—do that, when it found the time. And when it was convenient.

Meanwhile the Mersians, old allies, conspired at overthrow, in yet another direction.

One thing happened, and another, not far apart.

That was the way the Empire ebbed a little from certain shores, even while still advancing on others. That was the way that, here and there on its edges, more small fires sprang up, put out if convenient, allowed to burn down in isolation if not—sometimes peeling a world away for a while, or longer.

The fact was the Empire had become like an old cloth fraying from wear at the edges—and if ever a young, strong and hungry force such as it had once been should brush up against it now, the Empire would be in the direst difficulty, unable to muster all its scattered parts to its own defense.

Therefore the Empire feared the borders it once had thundered out to expand and expand and expand . . . while its secret heart grew weaker.

Fear became its own war of attrition. Policymakers at the heart of the Empire feared the motives of those who came from those border worlds. It was easy, safe politics, to blame every ill on the barbarians, so as not to have to examine the rot at the heart of things that still functioned tolerably well, as the center of Empire saw it. The status quo became the rule, and woe to him who disturbed it.

Nowadays the Empire felt safer with less forceful governance, and mistrusted local authorities who pointed to distant or future causes of trouble—or worse, local officials who suggested doing something about them. The powers of the Empire listened to nothing that would mean real revision of the Way Things Were.

That philosophy had gone on a long, long time, in a state of slow drift, slow rot.

But in the way of old Empires, once the heart began to soften, once certain strong-willed people living their lives out between the rotten core and the frayed edge began to understand that the Long Night could come down on them in their lifetimes, they found *they* had not been in the Empire long enough to be philosophical about it all.

They *were* inclined to fight against the Long Night.

And they might *be* barbarians, a generation back, but they had committed everything to the existence of the Empire. They saw the good in it, and they saw the alternative far more clearly than the denizens of the capital could see it—the red age, the blood age, the forever-dark to follow, with fire and with killing. They had fought their way out of it—and they were not ready to sit still and slide back into it.

So they stiffened their backbones and sharpened their wits and determined that an Empire rotten at the heart *could* survive, if wit and courage of its outliers stiffened resistence all about it. They would become the armor keeping an old, old creature alive and whole.

Dominic Flandry had bent events in the Empire's favor. In an action fairly minor as the Empire viewed things, he had set up barbaric Scotha as a new and progressive part of the Empire, weaving a new patch onto an old situation. He had outwitted, outmaneuvered, and outplanned the opposition; he had set a new ruler on the throne, which had definitely been important for the Scothan Sector, and for the Hydran Quadrant which contained it. Where Dominic Flandry was now—whether he had gone off to the far edges of the Empire to devise some clever solution for its woes in another direction—possibly dealing with the Patmara affair, or the Mersians—no one locally knew.

But there had grown up a little cabal in the academy at the heart of the Hydran Quadrant, on this side of the Empire.

Four young diplomats belonged to this odd group. They were four very diverse individuals, a man and three women, classmates, or at least their academic careers had somewhat overlapped, and they found common interests and a common philosophy, in this artificial world distant from all their origins, working in the diplomatic service in various capacities. They all had a last name—not universal in the Empire, and it was all the same name, which was not at all as common as, say, Smith, Ngy, or No'b'Ar-Grisigis.

In this case, it was a name of legend in the Quadrant. The last name was Flandry, and it was *not* a common name in Scotha Sector, or Mardier Sector, or in Lussanche, or in Modi, or anywhere about these parts.

These four were human—well, mostly so. The junior of the four was a brown-eyed lad, all human, with a mop of ringlets and, lately, a mustache—the three senior were women, had ringlets more or less original, one short-cut and red-brown, one long and lustrously dark; and one, well, the hair had been white-blond from the start and the owner refused to say whether it was original, but one suspected . . . and the eyes—well, the *eyes.* All the lot of Flandrys had brown eyes except Audra, the young woman from Scotha, who had followed the fashion and had eyes as yellow as a G4 sun, a matter of some amusement to her half-brother and -sisters.

They all looked really not a thing alike—especially the yellow-eyed one, whose ears were somewhat odd, and whose brow had two dainty but distinct horns at the hairline.

They all were lightly built, not so tall—and as a group one would say they were a good-looking foursome, though they were not remarkable, not even the Scothian. But when you saw more than one of them sitting in a general meeting, or when they gathered, as they did once weekly, at The White Tree Pub, opposite the Quadrant Offices, you took a second glance.

Then if you'd ever known Dominic Flandry, you might take a third look, especially at the youngest, the young man, who was the very spit of the elder Flandry in his youth.

And when, deep in the secrecy of the Quadrant Offices, this four talked together, it sounded as light as their conversations in the pub, but life and death sometimes figured in it; and they talked about places on the edge of the great dark, and named names that should not be named elsewhere.

Not all of them had been on track for high positions in State. But the dark-haired eldest had been, and she had snared all the others. You wanted a favor from the State Department—she could do it.

And the blonde girl—Audra was her name, Audra Flandry, had come to *her* when she had needed the biggest of favors, and an assignment otherwise not likely to come to her.

"Heralt's my brother," Audra had said, showing a copy of a letter which had taken its sweet time getting to her. "Heralt's *mine.*"

"You don't want to *rule* Sotha," the eldest had said.

Audra had shaken her head no, and yellow eyes flicked down and up, startling in their intent, under tilted brows. "No way do I want to rule Sotha. But I want this mission. I want a ship. I want everything I can get."

Her mother, by a curious twist of fate, was Gunli, late queen of Sotha. Her youngest half-brother was Heralt, current king. And how that brother had gotten to be king was not a pleasant story.

"Your half-brother," the eldest said, having read the letter—having, in fact, been the one to get it to her half-sister, "wants you to come back and marry one of his enemies."

"His ally, actually."

"An ally who'd betray him in a heartbeat. And you don't certainly mean to go through with a marriage. With a barbarian lord who probably doesn't bathe regularly—let alone accept Empire law?"

"I want a ship," Audra said. "I've never asked a favor. I'm asking it now."

The matter occasioned a meeting of the four, over tea, in a quiet, secure room, in Quadrant Central, and without the direct knowledge of persons highest-up in the Quadrant.

"You don't want Sotha," said another of the four. "And *surely* you don't want to be queen of Wigan. So what are you thinking?"

Audra scowled. "That my half-brother is no fool."

"No, more's the pity," the youngest said. "He's ambitious, he's just come back from exile and killed your uncle—"

"Who had it coming," Audra said, and her face grew cold in contemplation of the history she knew. "Empire law wouldn't let me deal with it. Not without resigning. And I wouldn't. But—"

"But now you will?" the redhead asked, while the senior of them said nothing.

"No such thing. I have no intention of marrying the King of Wigan."

"This half-brother—" the redhead said.

"I have every intent of dealing with this. I couldn't, before. Now I have an appeal from *inside* Scothania."

"That wants you to come back and marry a stranger who doesn't bathe!"

Audra shoved back from the table. The youngest put out his hand and laid it on hers, calming.

"Audra's entitled to have this mission," he said quietly. "Audra could be Queen of Scotha if she'd wanted to."

"Not just if I wanted to," Audra said. "I could renounce the Academy and go—or go with that piece of paper *asking* me to come in." She pushed away and walked to the side of the room, to the sideboard with its teapot, and poured a second cup, in silence.

"She has the right," the dark-haired senior said. "She has the absolute right."

"Trade a career the Empire for a planet with its problems?" the redhead asked, shaking her head. "I'm not fighting her getting a mission. I'm fighting her going out there and getting killed."

"They killed her mother," the young man said quietly. "Herse did. Killed her older brother. Killed the whole family except her mother got her out."

"Except this boy Heralt," the redhead said.

"This boy who's now King," the young man said. "Herse never got his hands on him. But who knows if he *is* Gunli's son? Or *whose* son he is. He's got the throne. He's smarter than Herse and his lot. But now he's making demands?"

Audra came back to the table with her cup of bitter tea, sat down. "My mother was pregnant," Audra said in a low voice. "She got me to the spaceport. She reigned another sixteen months. She sent Heralt away with his nurse, up to the mountains. It cost the nurse her own son. Herse's assassins arrived sooner than anyone thought. They took the nurse's son away and killed him. I was in Antizonen, with no one, no help, not even papers. No one went with me. Heralt was in a stone hut with a grieving nurse. That was the way things were until my mother's letter got to Quadrant and got me into the Academy. Herse had done for Cerdic, and that was the last of us. So Herse thought. Until Heralt came back."

"We think it's Heralt," the redhead said.

"It *is* Heralt. The Frithians insist not. But the southerners have no doubts. And I don't. The whole South rose up to put him in Iuthaagar."

"All that's well and good," the redhead said. "The whole South supports him. And if he is or isn't, he'd be fine so long as they *think* he's Gunli's son. He's very cleverly survived in office, surrounded himself by men he can trust. But he's ruling no differently than Herse. Herse took Scotha back to the old pattern, let the warlords take over in the provinces—he undid all Cerdic's years of progress in sixteen decrees. I've been studying it. Rights for women were suppressed. The right of trial by jury's overturned. The boy's been reared in a hut, catch as catch can. His neighbors were hunters and his society were egg-diggers. Now his notion of ruling is to take Herse's laws as they stand

and accept the treaty with Wigan and follow through on the royal marriage. Only he's run short of relatives and his advisors are hillfolk, no match for the politics in the capital. The place is a mess."

"And the Empire is doing nothing," Audra said. "I asked. Without this paper—I can't go into the situation. With it—miserable as it is—I can. And if the Empire won't do anything to set Scotha right, I will."

"Solo?" the youngest asked. "A mission like this one? Audra, if you go in there, you won't have protection, except us. The Empire won't go in to get you out, either. And to have our sister kidnapped the way our father was, and married to some parasite-infested barbarian—"

"Not quite that bad," Audra said. "I do honestly believe he bathes."

"Audra, Audra," the youngest said. "You honestly can't mean to do this."

"I do. I've pulled in favors, I've made the Empire promises." A glance at the eldest. "And I've got a ship."

"What did you promise?" the redhead asked.

"The usual. One soul, slightly used."

"Don't joke."

"I have a ship. That's what I need. I have a ship, and I have what my father gifted me."

"And if you're wrong about this boy, Audra? The boy's asked you home for the *only* reason a Scothan male thinks you're valuable, probably because his city advisors are still following Herse's blueprint. So he's got his revenge on Herse, but on his record of half a year in office, he's made exactly the wrong moves, no different than Herse did, which says where his advice is coming from. He's mobilized the fleet. He's refused an Imperial Envoy. Your rights? You'll have none. You'll be in the same cell our father occupied inside an hour of setting foot outside the ship. He probably has no clue what the Empire could do if it did come after you—which the Empire won't, because it knows it'd trigger the Confederacy to make a move. The King of Wigan has offered an alliance, a marriage is the price of it, and the Empire's no real protection against the King of Wigan's allies. 'Pay us now or have the tide roll over you.' And you're the payment. More than that: *Scotha's* going to be the payment, Scotha and its whole little federation, and either Heralt's advisors are stupid, or they're in the Confederacy's pay. Its fleet will join Wigan and Wigan will join the

Confederacy, and the Empire's going to lose another chunk of real estate."

"I didn't get a promise of backup." She smiled, did Audra Flandry. Then the yellow eyes flashed. "Yet Heralt's not a fool."

"If you leave that ship," the youngest said, "you're out of touch."

"He won't respect you. He won't respect any woman. That's the history of that world. I'm sorry. You're the only thing that's redeemed it. If the Empire doesn't think the whole Scothan Sector is worth a war with the Confederacy—you're fighting a losing battle."

"Scothian ethics," Audra said. "Kinship matters. And maybe I am Scothian enough. This is my mother's son. And it's *our* father's work I'm in there to save. And if the Empire were *sure* Scotha would stand firm—it *would* think it could stop the Confederacy."

There was a small silence at the table.

"Point," the youngest said, looking very much like their father at the moment.

"It's a gamble," the dark-haired woman said. "A huge one."

A shrug. "I'm Scothian. Gambling is the national vice."

"I still think you should accept assistance. You're to call for it, if you find a need and a chance."

"The orders say I'll have Fiona and Fleance again, to manage the ship. That's enough."

"Oh, fine," the redhead said, "*Fleance* will cause a riot."

"He *can* have that effect," the youngest said.

"Sister," said the redhead, "you're to take care. Hear? Or we'll take leave and come after you."

"Don't count on it," the dark-haired woman said. "The Empire grants ships when *it* wants something. *Not* when one of us gets in over his head."

"Three Flandrys can't bargain themselves one more ship, out of our own government?" the youngest said.

"Won't have to," Audra said. "I have faith in you three. Have that much faith in me. And I promise you on a stack of state secrets that I won't need rescuing. I'm a Flandry. But my brother's at least my mother's son. And that's of some consequence.—Dinner at the *Tree*, tonight? All of us? And in a happy mood, if you please. No talk of marriages—or rescues."

◈ ◈ ◈

Fiona Kojobi handled the details all the way—dealt with the Empire pilot and two-man crew, blew them past outbound customs, fed the system the pertinent lies about destination: the Empire lied to its own officials, just occasionally.

Fleance skittered about on metal spider legs, nosing into the ship's workings and the diplomatic records Fiona was creating. He plugged in, tweaked this, tweaked that, produced reports, and flashed with lights, red ones turning to green, which let you read Fleance's mood. Fleance was not a conversationalist.

Neither was Fiona, who was Asturian, a polymath, had a mane of tiger-striped hair, and spent her spare time writing music, playing obscure instruments, and occasionally gambling with the crew.

The pairing worked out. Neither was Audra a conversationalist, when she was prepping for a mission, and she was prepping as hard as she'd ever prepped, for the biggest solo assignment of her life . . . refreshing her command of the language, settling her mind into a culture she had not experienced in any but a sheltered environment, under a different regime, and as a child under the age of understanding.

She'd lived her first five years on Scotha, during Cerdic's reign, behind screens, behind veils, tended only by her mother. Then on one day, during the biennial visit from Quadrant Records, her mother, who had been pregnant at the time, had turned inexplicably grim, had seized her by the hand, taken her from her toys, and taken her to the strange man, the Terran. Her mother had stayed behind. Her mother's guards had seen Audra and the Quadrant representative to the landing zone, and all the while Audra had thought it a little scary, but something she had to do, the way she stood at attention in formal audiences and waved at people in public appearances. She'd thought her mother wanted her to see the ship she'd asked about, and that it was supposed to be a treat. An adventure.

But it hadn't been a tour. They'd gone up the lift, there'd been a sharp pain in her back, and she'd gotten dizzy, and by the time she knew anything the ship had started making noises, loud bangs and thumps, as she'd later learned, the sounds of a ship detaching lines and preparing its departure.

To this day, Audra didn't remember much of the representative, the ship, the voyage to Quadrant Central—just one woman who'd given her a sandwich and a drink, the first woman besides her mother who had ever seen her face without the veils, a woman who'd dried her tears with rough swipes of a napkin and then told her they were in space and she was going to Prism, and that her mother had given her a letter.

She hadn't finished the sandwich. She still had that letter. Her mother had written it by hand, wishing her to be a good girl, and study hard at school, and make her proud. That it was a chance for her to go into her father's sort of work. And that they would see each other in a few years.

The next ship to land back on Scotha met with a changed situation. Her mother was dead, Cerdic was dead, and her uncle Herse was King. New austerity laws had gone into effect, unraveling everything King Cerdic had done. Scholars disappeared, books were erased, records were locked away, and after a good deal of difficulty and stalling about landing clearances in the first place, the Empire's representative had stayed to his ship and left the world in haste.

Every two years for the next eight years, a ship from Quadrant had gone to the planet, but stayed to contact in orbit. The representative filled out a meager report, with no direct observation. Trade ceased. The fragile web of Empire connections that had begun to function in Cerdic's time had unraveled in Herse's.

Audra had little word of any of it, beyond her mother's death. She put aside the veils, put aside Scothian dress, and adopted her father's heritage. At twelve, she entered Quadrant academy, and interned her last two years with the diplomatic service. What she heard of her homeworld had been only maddening. Her assignments had been many, elsewhere in the Quadrant, and minor—routine and minor, every one.

And then—

Then came the letter, nineteen years into Herse's reign, along with a flurry of confirming reports from other sources. Herse been assassinated. His nineteen-year-old nephew, son of Queen Gunli, had invaded the capital, taken the throne, and had, within the month, sent a letter to Audra Flandry.

That was the first Audra had known she had a living half-brother. And the letter was a month old before she'd gotten it.

Things had changed in the Scothan system, over twenty years, she had that information. Scothians under Herse had ringed the port with what they called "defensive" installations and set a battery of other "defensive" installations aloft.

And the world, indeed, the whole sector of four other moderately inhabited planets, had steadily continued the slide back to barbarism, with Scothian warships to lead the way.

So now in exchange for a familial relationship with the King of Wigan, the King of Wigan would swear alliance with Scotha's new king.

And the King of Scotha meant to use Wigan to keep the rest of the Arduite Confederacy at bay.

So he thought.

It was not the plan of the Arduite Confederacy.

With all of the Empire's intelligence behind the reports Fleance pulled out of files, Audra Flandry knew things the King of Scotha didn't.

And she knew that Empire politics were just as dangerous, but a shade more subtle, and that her half-sister had done a lot to get this mission launched. A Flandry mission, no question. But *her* mission. It had taken her twenty years to work her way through the maze of Quadrant politics, and she knew the politics of never doing anything to upset strategically important Scotha . . . for reasons which suited certain people who *didn't* want the Scotha sector back in politics.

The Flandrys thought otherwise. They were going to get the Scotha sector back one way or the other, as a Confederate state, or an Empire state.

And a letter from Scotha and her tangled bloodline were what they had to work with.

The ship came through the defensive net at dawn, with a blaze of flashes in the heavens and a wail of sirens in the port area. It came down, it sat pinging and fuming at rest in the heart of the "defensive" installations, and sat a while. Communications began buzzing with threats and indignant demands for authorizations, while technicians tried to figure *why* the port installation had quietly done nothing.

Audra let them stew a bit, and then shot off a nicely composed and previously drafted communique to King Heralt, a polite:

"Dear brother, Your Majesty of Scotha, we are in receipt of your last letter.

"We look forward to the meeting of a brother as yet unseen, yet dear in our regard, as a child of our beloved mother, and hope for an early reunion.

"Our purpose here is of course twofold, first to make acquaintance with our younger brother, whose successes are many, and to hear first hand our brother's needs and desires, and secondly to renew the advantages of the Empire in your hearing.

"We applaud your homage to the old customs insofar as they promote pride in the accomplishments of Scothians, and insofar as they inspire bravery in confronting difficulties. These traditions come from lean times, when survival was less certain than now, but are never to be forgotten as a place from which we Scothians have come.

"We further applaud evidences of your forwardness in seeking to establish peace through diplomacy, and most of all through renewed contact with the Empire.

"We are not surprised by your fearlessness in inviting me, your elder sister, to visit you. As you know, though entitled by blood, either of us would have been a child ruler. Twenty years have made a difference. Had you not risen to the challenge of tyranny and replaced our late uncle, I might have come back with all the force of the Empire." Think about that, brother, and worry for your safety. But not too much.

"We are glad to find the situation is settled, in your rise to power. We have preferred this solution, and look forward to an end of ackward-looking policies.

"So, felicitations, brother, on your assumption of the throne of Scotha.

"We extend the hospitality of our ship and extend an invitation to a state dinner aboard at sunset, local."

"That should get a reaction," Fiona said, when it went.

"I expect it," Audra said, and settled down at the console to do a little sampling of communications. There was a little chaff from the observers, reports on what the ship wasn't doing—that was, moving. She flicked on a searchlight, swept it about by high local noon, and listened, amused, as that activity brought down an alert and a scramble.

A few shots followed.

She turned on the running lights, and then the external speakers, pumping out a recording of Baradean sea-cats at extreme volume.

The high notes could damage hearing, and exposure to the low notes, traveling as a ground wave, would produce profound unease, all the way to nausea. On visual, one could see the snipers running. One dropped his weapon and left it lying, then came back for it, staggering, and took several uncoordinated tries at retrieving it.

She cut the sound, and the unfortunate sniper staggered off.

"Poor fellow," Fiona said, leaning over Audra's shoulder.

"They'll spread word of that," Audra said. "And I'm sure we'll hear about it."

They did, in short order. A call came in from a red-faced man in uniform, the portmaster, who ranted about the tactic.

"His Majesty requires you leave your ship!" figured in the list.

"Requires? I am convinced this is *not* His Majesty's direct and current response. We suggest you consult with him immediately and give us a more up to date answer directly from him, in what is surely a delicate matter, since he and we are in negotiation. There will be direct consequences of an error, sir, and your actions may adversely affect negotiations. On your head be it."

"I shall consult," the answer came back. *"And expect no change."*

Audra broke the connection and sat back, casting a look at Fiona. "Shall we have lunch? I really don't expect anything until afternoon."

Fiona asked, "Do you think the King ordered that probe?"

"He may have. His advisors may have taken it on themselves. Now at least he knows he has a problem. If the person running this is a total fool, he'll come storming back with beamfire and all sorts of bluster. But Heralt is my mother's son. And by all reports he hasn't been a puppet. He survived Uncle's takeover and apparently was active in the coup that took Scotha back. So I expect some intelligence. And with intelligence—some flexibility. The question is—" The bridge had a synth unit, or at least, you punched in a request and the unit asked the big unit in the habitat to wake up and deliver coffee, which it would bring up the pneumatic system. "Two?"

"Please," Fiona said.

It was actually after lunch—coffee and the synth's best offering, cinnamon sticky rolls—when the next letter came back.

"Heralt King of Scotha, Arden, and Luss to Audra his bastard sister. Council policy prevents the King from traveling on foreign soil or foreign

decks. Please accept our invitation to a state dinner at the palace instead, where we are certain you will have great interest in a counter-proposal of ours."

"Interesting," Audra said to Fiona. "No threats. No denial of my familial connection. And careful terms. Bastard I certainly am: there was no question of wedlock. And a king always speaks on record. Calling me a pretender would diminish my value as a marriage connection. He or his advisors are desperate to have that connection with the Wigan King—and the alliance that is the key to the Confederacy. I have to maintain my value in all that he says publicly, or he has no deal with them."

She settled to a keyboard and wrote: *"Dear younger brother, I am in receipt of your letter, and renew my invitation, passing by the ill-advised attack on this ship as a clear instance of panic and confusion among subordinates.*

"As for your advisors' objections, since you are, and have always been, during your reign, the sovereign of a member state of the Empire, clearly the Scothian Council prohibition regarding your presence on a foreign deck cannot apply to your presence on this ship.

"You have the word of an Empire official that you will not be prevented from return to your capital after dinner. Please so honor us.

"To entice you further let me offer my absolute word that if my offer does not sufficiently excite you, I shall return with you to the palace and consider this offer of marriage with His Majesty of Wigan. I am that confident that I have a counteroffer you will not refuse.

"Dinner will be at local sunset."

That went. Fleance tapped into the local communications network, just in case, and sifted the entire traffic of the capital city for keywords and certain addresses.

And a letter came back: "*Accepted.*"

Heralt was already ahead of his predecessor, in terms of common sense.

And gambling—was the Scothian passion, a soft spot in the national ethic. Worked into legend, and engrained in the national psyche. Leave a bet on the table? Let a chance slip through his fingers?

He *was* Scothian.

She just hoped he lived to get as far as the ship, and that no double-agent advisor and no disgruntled Frithian made a move to give Scotha a new king.

Doing it with a potential senior heir sitting in port with her finger on the fire button was not necessarily the best plan for deposing the family, however. She gambled, too. She gambled Heralt's life on that.

Maybe Heralt had the wits she credited him with. She hoped so.

She dressed for dinner, a white gown with a little sparkle, nothing extravagant. Fiona was in gold. They made a pair, her white and yellow, Fiona's tawny gold: Fiona set a table in the state quarters, Fleance had moved in a crystallac display, that would reflect everything going on in small prisms—went with any decor. And ship's crew turned out in dress uniform—regulation when they turned up topside. The ship, the *Bonaventure,* was all in landing config, the chairs were loosed from stay-brackets—in fact, being what it was, the ship was a traveling embassy, and had no shortage of equipage for the job, right down to the stemware—which did look handsome, sparkling next the crystallac centerpiece. And the crew looked equally apt, turned out as embassy guards, ceremonial swords, brass buttons, the whole show . . . Fiona's handiwork, top to bottom, including the security arrangements, which included the crew, and Fleance, who disguised himself as a rolling cart.

Oh, it *looked* good—and in point of fact, there was more armament and armor packed into that little dining room than would ever seem likely.

The remaining matter was to hope their guest made it to the ship alive, and Audra did not spend her time admiring the tableware: she spent it on the bridge, watching the route. The *Bonaventure* had sent out an array of little observers to station themselves along the way, and indeed, at the appropriate time, an official car exited the city limits, with a fair amount of escort, and quietly purred toward the port facility, and through the gates, and past the guards.

The car stopped, the entourage got out, King Heralt got out, and the ship opened its boarding access.

Audra headed for the dining room, and was there, attended by Fiona, Fleance, and very properly uniformed crew by the time King Heralt, with two more crew members and a parcel of his own guards, reached the doorway.

He had their mother's coloring, fair and fine. He was young. He was armed—so were his guards—

And he was shocked. Many people were, when Audra looked at them for the first time. Yellow hair. Brilliant, flower-yellow eyes. Heralt stared a second in shock.

Audra smiled and held out open hands. "Brother," she said.

"You can't be my sister," he said—hadn't intended to say it, by the chagrined look on his face; but he had, and stood there in dismay.

"Scothian and Terran," she said, "*can* mix, as you see. People think it cosmetic. It's the mixed heritage that does that."

"Valtam's beard," Heralt murmured.

"On the other hand, the mix with our cousins of Wigan would hardly be a good one. So they tell me. The mixed heritages don't always turn out so well. Do be seated, Majesty of Scotha. You are a very welcome guest."

Heralt sank toward the endmost chair. One of his bodyguard pulled it out and shoved it under him.

"I am not in favor of this marriage with Wigan," Audra said, sinking into hers, as Fiona poured wine for their guest. "My paternal heritage is far more valuable than that."

"That foreigner—"

"Oh, a man at home in many places, well-regarded by high powers that may be of more advantage than you yet know. I cannot simply call you Majesty, brother. Shall I use your name? Mine is Audra. Simply Audra. Or you can call me sister."

"Sister," Heralt said faintly, as Fiona poured white wine into Audra's glass, and he stared at her, blinking from time to time as if trying to clear his eyes. Gone was everything he had brought into the meeting. Rapid thinking was going on in the flicker of that stare. Desperate thinking. "You always were veiled. They say you always were veiled. That you showed the Terran blood: you were dark-haired as a Farlander."

"As you see, they were wrong."

"But why did you come, if you are *not in favor* of the marriage?"

"I came for you, brother. For my kin. For my house and my mother's heritage."

"To take Scotha? You shall not!"

"No such thing. My ambitions are within the Empire, not here.

Only my heart is here. With my brother." She lifted her glass. "To you, Heralt. To your survival. To your accomplishment—of our mother's dream."

He sat still as stone, as she took the most minute of sips. "Our mother."

"I was fortunate. *I* knew her."

Heralt sat still a moment, emotions tumbling through his blue eyes—jealousy, it might be; anger at his own fate.

"She could not save herself," Audra said. "But she guarded herself. She stayed here and she stayed alive to give birth to you, brother."

"An heir for Scotha. A *son,*" Heralt said in bitterness, "that ruined all Herse's plans. You could be bargained off: *you* were half-foreigner, kept in veils. A *son*—that was different. I had to die. Therefore our mother had to die, because she would never forgive Herse. As it was, she died, and I lived."

"And came back," she said, "to Herse's misfortune. You *are* our mother's son. And I am so glad to meet you. So very glad to have a brother."

Cautiously, Heralt nodded.

"Shall we not let dinner go cold?" Audra asked. "A modest dinner. A little talk. Fiona, I think we shall begin now."

"Ambassador," Fiona said with a bow. It was a little exaggeration. A slight exaggeration. But there was a somewhat routine document among the other documents that gave an agent in the field, light years from Quadrant Central, certain powers to give and to take, bind and unbind.

There was dinner, there was brandy in a little side chamber while the dishes went away, and in the warmth of that social function—perhaps a little less outright anxiety, but no less worry.

"This proposal of yours," Heralt said.

"This proposal of mine, brother, is delivered with some concern. You are my mother's son; and I want you to live. And I do not, above all, want to get you assassinated. How firm is your hold?"

"As firm as needs to be."

"Firmer than Cerdic's?"

"You're suggesting his policies?"

"Far more than that." She drew a deep breath. "I see Scotha as a major force in the Quadrant, not a tail on the tail of the Confederacy.

Ally with Wigan? Deliver Wigan an ultimatim: join you or join the Confederacy, and no lost sleep if he chooses the Confederacy. He's a barbarian content to collect his taxes and hope his allies don't ask too much from him. Oh, he'll fight. He'll always fight. But they'll just move the taxes higher every year, adding the hot water to his bath until he boils. And when he rebels, they'll own him. You—they'll assassinate, and go on assassinating Scothian kings until they get a stupid one, as stupid as the King of Wigan. Tell Wigan to join *you,* and you'll attract their attention fast."

Heralt listened. His bodyguard, off near the door, had every opportunity to listen.

"You're proposing I be Cerdic?"

"No. Be Heralt. Be yourself. Be stronger than Herse, stronger than Cerdic, stronger than Penda. *Be* a monarch allied to the Empire, and the defenses I just plowed this ship through will no longer be those defenses. The defenses will be modern, and the alliance will be with the greatest force in the galaxy. The marriage with Wigan's king? Nothing. You wanted a relationship with a powerful ally? Marriages can be broken. *Blood* is another matter, and *blood* connects you and me. *Blood* connects me with a man high in the councils of the Empire, a man whose name opens doors, gets attention, and moves ships. I have a document, which, if you sign it, will ally you to the Empire, with me signatory with the Flandry name, backed by three of my half-sibs. You swear to bring this world to the defense of the Empire if the Empire is attacked on this frontier—and the Empire will therefore consider any attack on Scotha, any hostile entry into Scotha System, as an invasion of the Empire. The little border situation with the Confederacy has simmered along untouched precisely because the Empire has no stake in anything going on, since Herse severed ties. Re-establish them! Sign. Join. And immediately, as head of state not of a border system, but of a star system within the Empire—state that you are threatened with invasion. I'd wager that's exactly the situation laid before you by the whole Wigan agreement, am I right? A marriage link, or look out for your own survival?"

"You offer the same thing—join us. Or consequences."

"We're bigger. Much bigger. Big enough that your joining us may reconfigure the expectations of the Confederacy—and put invading you far, far down on their list of priorities. I am your *sister,* and a

Flandry, and Flandrys are not known for losing worlds. There are *four* of us standing together on this agreement. And if you declare yourself my blood relative, that, too, will make this a very, very serious agreement for the Empire. If the Empire reneges on one of *Flandry's* treaties—then others are cast in doubt. If it fails one of *Flandry's* negotiated settlements—it begins to come in pieces, and I assure you, the Empire has *no* intention of coming in pieces. The very thing that kept Scotha in a hands-off, don't-mention-it diplomatic limbo, *nobody* taking direct action, has been the reluctance to admit that one of *Flandry's* treaties might unravel. Invoke it, sign, rejoin the Empire, and four of us will make it clear right up the chain to the heart of Empire that the Empire has a vested interest in seeing Scotha not only survive, but become a showpiece of what the Empire can do. What I offer you is far, far more than anything you asked. And because of *blood*, it's free. I want *nothing* but my brother back. I want someplace I can finally call home, at least, even if I never come again."

"Sister," Heralt said. "Sister, never mind words on paper. Do I have your word that everything you tell me is true?"

"Everything is true." At least half of it was. The half that didn't involve Audra Flandry's junior status and marginal assignment by a Flandry-run fineagle—involving, without quite telling them the whole story, several other sibs, only one of whom had given an absolute green light to the enterprise.

"We'll have copies," Heralt said.

"Absolutely. You put it forth under *your* seal. You offer *me,* your sister, as your courier to the highest levels of Empire, and you keep yourself alive, brother, until the Empire can park more modern assets into orbit, and you don't advertise your intentions to have this treaty or this relationship until the Empire's protection arrives. I go out quietly, on this little ship, carrying your message, and no great surprise: your sister paid a visit. The larger news can wait until you have the Empire committed to this. And given a chance to secure the Quadrant, I know people at Quadrant HQ that are going to be very favorably disposed to having the Confederacy in a bind and Scotha back in the Empire . . . probably with Wigan as a dependency if its king has any sense whatever. Sheltering in the shadow Scotha will cast will be far, far better for him than playing politics with the Confederacy. If you happen, gradually, to chip away at the

Confederacy longterm, and get bits and pieces of it to commit to you—you'll become not only a head of state in the Empire, but a very important one. I have the greatest vision what a king you can become, brother. All it takes is ink on a line, to start with. And our understanding."

"My dear sister," Heralt said, smiling.

First day back in Quadrant offices, and no great stir among the secretaries—agents went out and agents came back with more reports to file. That Audra Flandry was back was no particular matter of notice, except among the half-dozen clericals who had a long, long list of files to sort out.

The dark-haired Division Head more than noticed: Audra spent a little of the morning in that office.

"You took a chance, sister," the eldest Flandry said.

"Wasn't that why I went there?" Audra answered.

"You're betting the Empire will ratify what you did."

She shook her head. "What our *father* did. They don't let one of his treaties fall. I've observed that. I think I'm accurate."

Eldest's mouth quirked. It was a familial expression. So was the accompanying twitch of the left brow.

"Officially," she said. "I don't know a thing."

"Of course," Audra said.

"Meeting the others," eldest sister said, "at *The Tree*. They'll be dying for news. And you don't know a thing, either."

"Permanently?"

"Only till we're back in the building. Then we'll breach a little security downstairs. Job well done, younger sister."

She smiled, ducked her head, and went with her sister outside, where nobody knew or would know what exactly had transpired on the *Bonaventure*'s deck . . . only that an agreement had come out of it, and some other offices in several parts of the Confederacy were going to be very upset about it.

Ships would be moving. The Empire would be foolish to let the situation flare up. It was good at bringing overwhelming force to bear, if it had a whisper of a warning. The Empire liked doing that, in fact. It looked good. Success made good press releases.

Meanwhile it was lunch.

And a meeting. And a debrief in a Quadrant offices conference room, upcoming.

Youngest sister was home, where her looks were stylish and her sibs were all clever and well-placed in the department.

Curious to think that she had another one, on the other side of the family. She'd never had that sense of connection to Scotha. Now she did. And worried a little about her brother.

But he was their mother's son, and clever. He'd survive.

So, for a while, would the Empire.

AFTERWORD:

POUL ANDERSON was a friend of mine. And that was one of the happiest things about a whole decade of science fiction conventions. Poul, and quite often Karen, and I spent no few delightful no-times (at science fiction conventions whether that was lunch or dinner or even breakfast sometimes blurs, the schedule is so full, and so busy) talking, and theorizing, and joking and just generally having fun. Poul was a walking fount of ideas and "takes" on all sorts of things, a real polymath, interesting and interested, and just a lot of fun. He'd sit there having a good time when the room party was too crowded to talk, but the characters of our field were holding forth in their own inimitable way, characters who themselves have passed into legend—of whom Poul was definitely one. I never saw him anything but good-humored and patient with the shyest or most out-of-line fan; I never saw him lose his cool. If there was a problem, Poul was thinking about it. If there was an argument, Poul would step in with reason and that wonderful calm that didn't let people be idiots in his vicinity.

That's how he was.

There was a time we were all going to the conventions at the rate of two a month—it's a wonder we got any writing done—but we were meeting so often we didn't say goodbye, we'd say, "See you in Baltimore," or "next week in Dallas." Wonderful times, and a raft of really great memories.

—C.J. Cherryh

THE LINGERING JOY

by Stephen Baxter

STEPHEN BAXTER *made his first sale to* Interzone *in 1987, and since then has become one of that magazine's most frequent contributors, as well as making sales to* Asimov's Science Fiction, Science Fiction Age, Analog, Zenith, New Worlds, *and elsewhere. He's one of the most prolific of his generation in science fiction, and is rapidly becoming one of the most popular and acclaimed of them as well, one who works on the cutting edge of science, whose fiction bristles with weird new ideas, and often takes place against vistas of almost outrageously cosmic scope. Baxter's first novel,* Raft, *was released in 1991, and was rapidly followed by other well-received novels such as* Timelike Infinity, Anti-Ice, Flux, *and the H.G. Wells homage—a sequel to* The Time Machine—The Time Ships, *which won both the John W. Campbell Memorial Award and the Philip K. Dick Award. His other books include the novels* Voyage, Titan, Moonseed, Mammoth, Book One: Silverhair, Manifold: Time, Manifold: Space, Evolution, Coalescent, Exultant, Transcendent, Emperor, Resplendent, Conqueror, Navagator, Firstborn, The H-Bomb Girl, Weaver, Flood, *and* Ark, *and four novels in collaboration with Arthur C. Clarke,* The Light of Other Days *and the three novels of the* Time Odyssey *series. His short fiction has been collected in* Vacuum Diagrams: Stories of the Xeelee Sequence, Traces, *and* Hunters of Pangaea. *Recent and upcoming work includes the Northland sequence:* Stone Spring, Bronze Summer, Iron Winter, *and* The Long Earth, *a collaboration with Sir Terry Prachett.*

In this sequel to Anderson's "The Long Remembering," Baxter shows us the effect on the next generation of the actions of the previous one, and how easy it is for them to fall into the trap of making the same mistakes themselves.

RENNIE, tall, gray, stooped, stood by the window of his living room. It was around ten p.m.

Through the glass of the old-fashioned sash window I could see the crescent moon rising, huge-looking, yellowed by the smoggy air. And cupped in the arms of the crescent I could clearly see the sparking of detonations. The Clavius War, the continuing three-way lunar battle over the Artefact.

"I remember the final question your father asked me," Rennie said. "Before he submitted to the procedure. 'Why can't you send me into the future?' I had no real answer—not yet. But he was just an experimental test subject, a graduate assistant out to make some spare cash—a young man with a wife, a baby on the way—*you*. It didn't matter to him where I sent him."

"It mattered later," I said. "When he came back."

"Yes." He turned to me, his rheumy eyes tired. "And it's the past that concerns you, isn't it, Ms. Armand?" He patted a pocket, as if in search of a long-vanished pipe, and reached for the decanter on the table. "Are you sure you won't have some of my Burgundy? It's a fine vintage."

"I'd rather just get on with it, Professor."

He smiled, and refilled his own glass. "Professor Emeritus. I'm long retired. It seems odd to be impatient about time travel." He glanced at the box he had brought up from his cellar and into this cluttered, book-lined living room. It was a wooden chest, very old-fashioned, set on an occasional table. When opened, it had revealed—well, not much. Bottles of drugs. Syringes, evidently elderly but vacuum-wrapped. A kind of whirling wheel, like an optical illusion. It looked like the travelling kit of a nineteenth-century illusionist.

"You do understand how this works? This isn't time travel of the H.G. Wells variety, but something rather subtler."

"I think so. My father didn't exactly lay out the details." He was too busy abandoning me and my mother for that. "Something to do with world lines."

"Ms. Armand, I call it temporal psycho-displacement. Time travel of the mind, not the body. A world line is the track in four-dimensional space-time that each of us traces out through our lives. Your psyche, cut loose from the present, will be shunted down your own world line—and then the world lines of your ancestors, parent and grandparent and great-grandparent, on down the branching tree of your heritage, until you come to rest—well, I have no control over precisely where.

"*World lines*," he mused. "That was a good enough understanding when I started. I built on the work of amateur experimenters, who didn't know what they were dealing with, and muttered of reincarnation. We would use other language today. We have a deep molecular connection with our ancestors through our DNA, of course—the cold chemical continuity of the genes . . .

"You understand you won't just be visiting the mind of your remote ancestor. You will *be* that ancestor, for a while. Your own body will be in deep hypnosis for hours. And you will think, feel, what your grandmother thinks and feels. I think it's that essential union that makes the process so traumatic."

I knew all about the trauma. My father seemed to have lost his heart to a woman he, or his ancestor, had known in an age of humans and Neanderthals. My mother, pregnant, a bespectacled clerk, could not compete with such a vision. He started to call his marriage to her his "unending punishment." I remembered those words from a very young age.

I preferred to think about the theory. I said, "To me it sounds like a hypostatic union. Two become one."

He raised his eyebrows. "Ah. Like God and man joined in the person of Jesus. This is the language of your seminary, as you mentioned in your letters." He glanced out of the window, at the flaring moon. "So many young people are receiving a religious education now. You know, in the years since the discovery of the Artefact—not to mention the war in the sky that is now raging over it—I believe we've entered a new age of religious feeling. A millenarian panic, if you like. Even my own work has been co-opted."

"I don't understand, sir."

"You're not the first to come to me in recent weeks. You know that after the suicides my work was suppressed. The psychophysics department was shut down, an injunction was taken against publication. Very few know of my work—only the police, the FBI, the university, and the families of the—"

"The victims."

"If you like. But, Ms. Armand, despite the prohibition, I have always had difficulty refusing relatives' requests." He looked fondly at his wooden chest. "You can see that the apparatus is easily assembled. Even the drugs are easy to come by. I have come to believe, in fact, that my apparatus does not so much enable the psychic travel but *unlock* a facility that is innate in all of us . . . And so, if a relative or loved one comes to me asking to travel, for whatever reason, I try to help.

"A month ago a young man came to me claiming to be a descendant of the family of Jesus Christ Himself. He had documentation, historical 'proof'. He wanted to travel down the world lines to meet the Christ. Well, he failed. Perhaps it would have been worse still if he had found Him and been *disappointed* . . . The boy went into a tailspin, I understand. As a result I am reluctant to indulge further fantastical religious adventures."

I shook my head. "There is nothing fantastical in my purpose, sir. It's a matter of logic."

"Logic?"

I glanced at the flaring moon. "The logic of the Artefact. We only know one thing for sure about the Clavius Artefact: somebody made it. But that basic fact has theological consequences, for Christians."

"Ah." He smiled. "Logic indeed. This is the question of the Incarnation of Christ on Alpha Centauri . . . "

It was a conundrum almost as old as Christianity itself. Christ was a union of God with humankind, a union made to save mankind from original sin. But what if intelligent aliens existed, on some remote star? Must they be fallen? Could they be saved by the word of Jesus, sent in mathematically encoded sermons whispered through giant radio telescopes? Or could the aliens have been given their *own* Christ, their own hypostatic union of God with mortal?

Rennie smiled. "Christianity is such a *literal* religion. I remember my *Age of Reason*—Tom Paine. He rejected Christianity for the bizarreness of Christ's fate in such a scheme—how did he put it?—'an endless succession of death, with scarcely a momentary interval of life.' And besides, isn't it heretical to deny the uniqueness of the Incarnation?"

"Nevertheless," I said, "given that the Visitors exist, or existed, the Vatican has now decreed, after much debate, that the mercy of God is surely not limited to one little world in a vast inhabited universe—not to one finite, flawed species. It must extend to *all* minds."

He nodded. "I suppose it's a hope we must cling to. For if the Visitors are fallen, and they have been *here* . . . But what's that got to do with my technique?"

"I said *all* minds, Professor. On Earth as well as among the stars. There are other intelligences right here."

His eyes widened. "My word. You're looking for a Christ of the dolphins?"

I was impressed that he didn't laugh. "The linguists are making new efforts to understand dolphin speech, and the chimps, and the whales. Already there are results, discoveries—oddly symbolic behaviours we've yet to understand."

"Ah. I see why you're here. You intend to look in the past too. The Neanderthals—well, they had speech. It was your father's visit that first proved that, in fact, not that I was allowed to publish. They cared for the vulnerable. They venerated the dead . . . "

"Yet the last of them died twenty thousand years before the salvation of Christ."

He smiled. "So you're looking for a bony-browed Jesus! I can't fault your imagination, or your ambition. But you understand you will have no control over *where* your psyche comes to rest—in which of your chain of grandparents you will be, umm, *incarnated*."

"I understand that." I shrugged. "But my father found something he wanted—even though he didn't know he wanted it. Perhaps if I want this thing enough, it will come to pass."

"Or perhaps God will guide you."

I couldn't tell if he was joking. I asked bluntly, "Will you help me?"

He considered the question. "Not because I believe in your quest. But because I owe it to you, as to others in your position." He stood, and gathered up his box.

He led me to a rudimentary laboratory.

I lay on a couch and rolled up my sleeve. The preparation was simple. A couple of injections, that patterned disc whirling. "I'm told I am a good hypnosis subject, as my father was . . . "

"Just relax, Ms. Armand."

"Evavi. Call me Evavi."

"An unusual name."

"It meant something to my father. A parting gift, you might call it, before he left."

"Your father, yes. You've come here in search of the past—seeking the Neanderthals, so you say, or your lost father, as a psychiatrist would probably opine. Yet I'm surprised at your lack of curiosity, Ms. Armand. I mean, about the future."

Darkness spread around me.

"You see, as I implied to you, I think I now know *why* I can't send you there. But you haven't asked about that, have you? Not once . . . "

I fell into night.

I am Valari-anaro-torkluk, which means The Woman who Draws a Bow Like a Man. But my true name I hold secret from the wind ghosts and the warlocks, and that I will not reveal.

Not even to a man. Not even to the Ghost Man. Not even to Kugul-akoni-ugnal, whose name means He Who Wrestled the Aurochs, who would have me as his wife, who would own me, and loan me out to his brothers, for that is how it is among the Men.

The events that I speak of happened in the month when the strange star hung in the sky, in the direction of the winter sunrise, which is a time everybody will remember.

It was to impress me that Kugul had gone to the other side of the river, and had returned with the head of the goblin doe, hanging from his belt by its long yellow hair. He threw this to the ground, before the big common hearth, with the squat huts of the Men all around. "Look!" he cried. "Look, Men! Look, Valari! This is the head of the last breeding doe in that cave! I went there alone, I fought off the bucks, I took this doe and I rutted with it and then I killed it and brought back its head! Am I not a great hunter? Am I not a Man?" He faced me, and I saw the blood on his hands and face, and on the front of his hide tunic where he had rutted with this creature.

And I saw the head of the doe. Her face. The pale skin. The eyes open, as if puzzled. The bruised mouth where Kugul had used her. She had freckles, I saw, freckles on her nose.

I remember the moment, as children squalled and the dogs yapped, on that bright autumn day. It was as if I was standing on a mountain, looking down on myself, and Kugul, and the severed head. In that moment I decided I would not let Kugul have me.

I stood before him, not with deference as a woman should, but as a man would, with defiance. "I am Valari-anaro-torkluk! I am not for you, Kugul! I will bring back the head of the last healthy buck. Then we will see who is the greater hunter, Kugul-akoni-ugnal, killer of does!"

There was a moment of shocked silence. Among us, women do not speak to men this way. Remember, there is a reason why our people call ourselves the Men.

Well, I was used to silences and stares of disapproval. And to the slow clapping from the Ghost Man. And the laughter from the men butchering the deer beside the winter store-pits. And the shaken heads of the worn-down women with their babies, labouring at the kilns, weaving baskets of hazel, shelling heaps of hazelnuts.

I raised my hand before them, and showed them the stump of my middle finger. This reminded them that I was the only woman in memory who had taken the Journey, which the boys make to become men—I who had run down a wild stallion alone—I who had taken off the joint of my finger myself, for the Ghost Man would not do it for me. I saw that as they mocked me they feared me, for it was a strange time, when that unusual star blazed in the sky of morning, and I am a strange woman.

Before I could be stopped, before my wretched mother came to plead with me once more to submit to Kugul for fear of being taken by somebody worse, I ran off.

I gathered my kit. I would wear a soft leather tunic and leggings, and stout boots for the trail, and a hat of leather and straw to keep off the rain. I had a spear, flint knife, bow and arrows tipped with wolf bone, and my medicine kit and my fire kit. Though it was not cold I wore my heavy leather cloak which, it was said among the hunters, would deflect the thrust of a goblin's stabbing spear.

I picked up my figure of the Mother—made for me by my own

mother, one of the few gifts she had given me since I turned rebellious at the age of seven. But since I had grown she had told me more than once that I myself lacked the spirit of the Mother. The Earth Powers that course in the blood of women, that quality that makes a cornered aurochs cow fight for her calves—not in me, she said. I placed the Mother in my pack even so.

And I made my way to the valley cut into the plain. The caves where the goblins dwell are cut into the steep rocky bank on the opposite side of the river from the camp of the Men. The land all around belongs to people; the caves are a little island of goblins in a lake of people.

I did not cross the river that day.

I came to the mouth of a cave on the near side. This is a very old place, and the hearth at its mouth is a thick bank of soot and char. Nobody lives here now. Inside the cave I found stuff left by the Ghost Man for those who must use the cave. A soapstone lamp with a bit of grease in it, that I lit with my fire-making stone and a bit of flint. Little wicker baskets of dried paint, that I made flow by adding water from my skin sack.

And, alone, I walked into the deep darkness of the cave.

The narrow passages at the rear have walls worn smooth by the generations who have passed this way. Here, by the flickering light of the lamp, I saw the great animals that dance on the walls, the deer and boar and aurochs and horse, and other beasts that nobody has ever seen, a great hairy animal with a nose that dangled to the ground, another stately beast with a flabby hump on its back.

And I came to the deepest dark, where the crevice narrows so you can scarcely pass. Here the newest paintings have been made by hunters still alive, Kugul and his brothers among them. And here, among the prancing horses and elegant deer, I saw the hunched forms of goblins.

Once, the Ghost Man says, the goblins were people. They held the land in the age of the ice giants, before the Men had come from out of the winter sunrise. You might fear them, you might despise them, you certainly fought them and raided their food and took their females, but they were *people* nonetheless. Now the last of them, huddled in their caves, are prey animals to be fixed on the walls in paint, with the horses and the deer.

With a twig brush I sketched my own prey quickly, a big buck goblin with a stern face, and yellow hair wild around his head. And I drew myself with my bow, pointing at his eye.

What else was done I must not tell.

I hoped it was enough. The Ghost Man should have been with me, making spells for me, and the other hunters chanting and dancing their support. I hoped the Sky Hunters looked on me.

I spent the night in that cave. I did not sleep.

In the morning light I came out of the cave and gathered my kit. I saw the smoke rising up from the caves of the goblins, across the river.

And I saw the strange star hanging in the sunrise sky, over the goblin caves. I quailed at the sight of this strange marker. But I had stated my purpose to the people, I had painted the moment of my victory in the cave. I could not go back.

I clambered down the trail to the river. The valley is a rocky gash in the land, much wider than the river which trickles along its floor. The track leads to a place at the river where you can cross easily, on foot, by means of stones long ago pitched in there. The old ones say that their grandparents remembered a time when you needed to swim or float on a log to cross this flow, but the river has dwindled since then.

The goblins never cross the water. Nobody knows why.

I paused before crossing the river.

I was going alone into the goblin country. I had seen them, the big ferocious bucks who would look a bull aurochs in the eye, and thrust spears like tree trunks into its heart. Some muttered of stranger powers. That the goblins could crush you with a look, or a roar from their cavernous chests. That they ate people, and you would see ghosts clamouring to be released if you looked one of them in the eye.

If I died here alone, even if I were not eaten by the goblins, my ghost would be lost, it would blow away, to be forever chased across the plains by the wind ghosts. I felt very small, very alone, in a huge and old land.

So I cut off a lock of my hair, and offered a prayer to the Sky Hunters, who sometimes dance in the winter nights. "I am Valari-anaro-torkluk, a woman of the Men, and I give you here a piece of my life. I ask no return for this gift. But know that I will kill a goblin buck, or I will be killed in my turn. For any aid I receive I offer you a portion of every kill I make for the rest of my days on this earth . . . "

And I saw a goblin on the far bank.

He was squatting by the gently flowing water. He wore skins roughly wrapped around his body; the goblins do not cut or sew their clothes as people do. You might have thought him a person, save for his massive shoulders, and that thick brow under a mop of yellow hair that hid his eyes. He was doing none of the things you think of a goblin as doing. Not eating, not fornicating, not shitting, not scratching the filth from his skin. He was just staring at the water, and his own face reflected there.

He was shorter than me, but must have been twice my weight.

I mastered my fear. Across the river, I challenged him. "Goblin! I come to take your head, to show it to the Men!" I waved my bow at him.

He looked up, startled. But he showed no fear. He stood, a squat dark mass of muscle topped by that shining yellow hair. Under his heavy brow his face was not unlike a person's. He had a beard, and I have seen rougher trims. He jabbered at me in that strange goblin tongue nobody understands, not even Agnich-areolu-urgan who understands the tongues of all people.

His mouth was twisted, his skin lined, his eyes hard. I saw grief and anger warring in his face.

He had an expression. I would have no more expected to see an expression on a stone.

He opened his arms, and I thought he was threatening me. But I saw he was exposing his chest, his torso, goading me to strike him.

Then he turned away, flapping his huge hand at me in disgust, and walked up a rough trail to a cave mouth.

I did not hesitate. I crossed the river, dancing over the stepping stones, and walked easily up the trail the goblin buck had followed. I felt fear, of course. Yet, in action, the body follows its own will. The body never anticipates its own death, I suppose. Only the spirit does that.

And as I climbed the world opened up around me. I saw the hilly country on the far side of the valley, and the wider plain beyond, which shimmered with water courses and the green clumps of trees, oak and juniper and pine. A distant cloud might have been reindeer.

Autumn is the time when the animals are fattest, their hair the thickest—the best hunting season.

I saw people working the marshes, cutting reeds and checking eel traps. Smoke rose up from distant fires, set by hunting bands of the Men, perhaps, or by other folk.

None of those fires would have been set by goblins, I was sure of that. With those big muscles they can't run far, as we can, and they don't throw spears or shoot arrows as we do. They prefer to hunt in the hills for lone ibex, where they can hide behind rocks or bushes, and jump out at the prey and stab it with their spears. Not for them the elaborate games you must play to trap your prey out on the plain, where there is nowhere to hide.

I came to the cave. In its mouth huge logs smouldered, the smoke washing out into the air. Nobody was about outside, but I thought I heard voices from within the cave—deep rumbling voices like big men. I pushed back my cloak to free my arms, took my bow, found my best arrow, and notched it.

I walked into the smoke, so I was hidden.

I became smoke.

It was as if I sat on a high hill, far away, watching this cave, the goblins, the smoke. It was as if nothing had been quite real since the moment Kugul had dropped the goblin head in the dirt. As if I were already half a ghost.

But I stepped forward, and I became a person again, made from the smoke, and I walked into the cave. "You goblins! Which of you will die first?"

Gradually, as my eyes awoke to the dark, I saw the cave. Skins, scraped and cut. A heap of stones, for making into tools. Lengths of wood, waiting to be worked into spears. Evidence of eating—a heap of ibex bones, and many, many rabbit bones and skulls.

And I saw the goblins. A kind of rustling at the back of the cave—filthy skins—shambling bodies, all pressed together so I could not tell one from the other. There was a smell of piss, or ordure, of blood, of meat and meaty farts—and milk.

I took a step forward, and another. They had been silent, but now they muttered at each other as they pressed back. None challenged me. As a good hunter I was reluctant to shoot into that mass, indiscriminate.

And I saw that the goblins in their huddle were *old*. Limping, hunched over, their bodies worn down, their gray, yellow-streaked hair—and that's no surprise, for everybody knows how hard the goblins work, all their lives.

And they were all female. I could see that from their smooth hairless faces, and from the dugs that hung beneath their loose skins. Yet when they spoke their voices were deep and gruff like a man's. I tried to count them. More than on the fingers of one hand, less than the fingers on two.

This was not the scene I had drawn on the wall of the holy cave. Still I pressed forward, my bow raised.

And now he emerged, the male I had seen at the river. He had one of their stabbing spears in his right hand, a thick pole held as easily as a child holds a reed, its sharpened tip hardened by scorching. Once more his face was twisted, with anger or sadness. He, at least, looked at me.

"So, you buck! Would you hide behind these old hags?"

I danced back, one step, two, and readied my arrow. This is how you kill a goblin. He will not throw his spear; all you have to do is kill him from a distance, before he comes close enough to strike. Now my picture in the holy cave was enacted, the savage buck goblin, my arrow pointing at his head.

Yet I did not loose the sinew of my bow. This despite my pledge to the Sky Hunters.

The goblin puzzled me.

He showed no fear. Unlike the females he stared straight at me, at the tip of the arrow-head that pointed at his eye.

When I did not strike he began to jabber in that unknown tongue. He hurled the spear away. It clattered against the rough, filthy wall. Again he opened his arms wide, exposing his body to my weapons, inviting me to destroy him.

Something shifted in my head.

Perhaps the doe Kugul had taken was this one's mate. I had seen no other bucks, after all, no other young does. He hadn't been able to stop Kugul rutting her and killing her. Now, such was his grief, he wanted only to die.

I was shocked by my own thoughts. Could goblins have such feelings?

And what were the old ones protecting?

I lowered my bow. I took a deliberate step forward, past the buck, deeper into the cave.

The old ones in their grimy leathers were like huge crows, rustling, bent over. They hissed at me from toothless mouths, and they snarled at the lone buck, but he did not respond.

The crones stood aside.

And I saw a crib.

If I had found this thing in a house of the Men, I would have had no hesitation in calling it that. It was a nest of twigs and moss. Within it a cub had been laid down, a newborn. It was wrapped in soft leather, skin from a kid perhaps—I saw teeth marks, the leather had been chewed to make it soft.

The cub was sleeping soundly. The skin had fallen away, and I saw it was a boy. I saw his round face, a hint of soft flesh at his neck. Save for a hint of brow ridge you would not have known he was a goblin cub at all.

I saw all this by the faint light of the day.

I reached out my hand.

The females muttered, but when they saw the missing joint of my middle finger, the mark of a man among the Men, they pulled away, dismayed.

I pulled the blanket over the cub's body so he would not be cold.

The darkness grew around me.

I touched the cub's cheek. It was soft, warm.

I fell into night.

And I fell, and I fell.

And I was a goblin, a woman, and the land was thick with forest, and we ran, laughing, big as young bears, our massive spears light in our hands, and we jabbered of how we would hide and trap the boulder-beast, the huge animal with its long curling teeth and thick orange hair. It was goblin country, goblins across the land as far as anybody travelled, as there always had been and always would be.

And ice flashed. And I was a child who looked out at an empty land, white as bone, and my cave was a warm mouth behind me, and the river was fast-flowing, dark, swollen with meltwater.

And I was a man, not a goblin, not a person, yet a man even so, and I sat naked with other men as we chipped hand-axes from a flint outcrop, as children ran and played around us, and an animal like a fat horse with a huge heavy head lumbered over the horizon, and people chased it, another sort of people, taller, skinnier.

And there was ice.

And the ice fled, and I was a woman, or a girl, and I had no words, and I ran and ran, naked on the plain.

And I was small and covered with hair, and I cowered in a plain filled with teeth, and I longed for the safety of my nest high in the trees. I had no words, no words—

My face stung.

A slap. I was back in the cave.

The buck goblin stood before me. My cheek ached where he had struck me. And my wrist ached. He held it in his huge fist. He had pulled my stroking fingers away from the cheek of the cub.

He released me. I stepped back.

The cub wriggled in his soft blanket, his dreams unknowable. The buck fixed his blanket, murmured to him, and bent over him and kissed his forehead.

And I saw it. *This was his cub.* He was the only buck here—the last buck. The doe Kugul had killed must indeed have been his mate, the mother of this cub. The last cub-bearing doe. Now there was none left but these old females, their wombs like dust. And when the cub grew, if he lived, even the old does would be gone.

The buck looked at me again, with that odd pleading on his face. Kill me.

I would not. Time would do that for him.

But, on impulse, I took my knife. The females cowered back. The buck did not react.

I took a lank of his long yellow hair, and sawed it briskly, and cut away a lock. This I tucked inside my tunic. I would not go back to Kugul with nothing. I would show him the lock and tell him I had scalped the buck. Kugul was too stupid not to believe me, and it would keep him at bay a little longer, and his brothers.

Then I turned, walked out of the cave into the bright light of day, and made for the river.

The world did not seem real. I had trouble following the path, as if I could not see the stones. When I walked across the sluggish river, I thought I felt the torrent that had once poured from the ice.

Across the river I went to the holy cave. I lit a lamp quickly, and went to the picture I had made, and I spat on my hands and rubbed the wall until my skin was raw, and the picture had gone.

Then I left the cave. As I climbed the slope, ghosts walked beside me, stocky, heavy-muscled ghosts with the strength of oxen. I came to the plain, where the dung-like houses of the Men gathered, and I thought I saw forests shimmering like heat haze, before sheets of bone-white ice.

I came to my house, where my bitter mother waited, and the rest of my life.

I had erased the picture on the wall. I feared it would not be enough, for I had broken my promise to the Sky Hunters. The future was dark, unknowable.

I longed for my nest in the trees. But I could never go back.

That was my punishment, and I knew it would never end.

It was like coming out of a deep sleep.

I was still in Rennie's laboratory. It was still night, I saw through the window, though dawn light was gathering. Antique-looking floor lamps burned.

Rennie helped me off the couch, led me back to the living room, sat me down. I felt groggy. Now I accepted a tumbler of his Burgundy. In another room a TV murmured, and I saw flickering images reflected on the wall.

Light flared, beyond the window.

"What was that? The moon?"

"No, the moon has set. Perhaps an Earth-orbit satellite being taken out. The war seems to be—well, hotting up. Just in the last few hours. They are bringing it home." He reached for a remote, leaned over, and shut off the TV.

I imagined a warrior in an armoured spacesuit, up on the moon, displaying the severed head of a Neanderthal woman.

"I wondered if that flaring light was another new star." I seemed to see it hanging over the caves of the Neanderthals, as if Rennie's house was a thinner reality altogether.

"A what? Tell me all you saw. Where did you go?"

"A long way. Like my father . . . "

In broken fragments, I told him all I could remember. He had no recorder, nothing like a camera; he made handwritten notes in a thick leather-bound book.

"A supernova," he said.

"What?"

"Your new star. Has to be. Look—like your father you seem to have been drawn back to the age of the Neanderthals—or its closing, as they died out. It sounds as if you landed up some time later than your father's visit, after the last glacial maximum. The last archaeological traces of Neanderthals are on Gibraltar, dated to around twenty-four thousand years ago. Surely there were hold-out pockets elsewhere. But that new star—naked-eye supernovas aren't that common. Of course there was nobody around to make a record, but perhaps the cosmologists can figure out a precise date from relic traces."

I didn't care about the star. Or rather, it wasn't its cosmological aspect that interested me. "The Neanderthals. If that's what they were."

"Yes?"

"They looked like humans. Like muscle-bound, fair-skinned, blond, humans."

"Interbreeding. Genetic studies show that there was a long spell of it, from between eighty to fifty thousand years ago. We thoroughly mixed up our DNA with theirs. As for the fair skin and the hair, those are obvious northern latitude adaptations. Nobody believed me, when your father reported these aspects as he observed them. The evidence of speech too. Yet now the DNA has confirmed them." He regarded me. "How did it feel to meet them?"

It was the first question he'd asked that made any sense to me. "Oddly familiar. Like meeting a cousin for the first time, an uncle. Family, but new. And later when I glimpsed those other ages, through the child—I saw landscapes full of, of—"

"Of different hominid species."

"I felt at home." I looked at him. He had a kindly face, I thought for the first time. Like a tired grandfather. "Does that make sense?"

"Perfect sense. We're unique among mammals in being alone as a species, we humans. There are several kinds of dolphins, chimps. We're a pathology. I sometimes think that's why we feel so lonely.

Why we seek God, or the alien. We know something is missing from our world, but we don't know what."

"We got rid of all those others."

"No," he said sternly. "Don't think that. Don't take guilt away from this experience. Oh, we may have knocked the very last old man on the head, in some cave in Gibraltar. But it was rapid climate fluctuations and habitat fragmentation that did for the Neanderthals. At worst we were just another factor in a changing landscape."

Another flare of light beyond the window, and I thought I heard a distant boom, like thunder. We both flinched.

Rennie raised his glass. "Here's to extinction."

"Yes." I drank deeply.

He said gently, "And this child you found—was he the Jesus of the Neanderthals?"

"I—I didn't know. I will never know. He offered consolation."

"Yes," Rennie said, almost eagerly, and he leaned forward. "Yes! Consolation. That's what I think this is all about."

"All what?"

"My temporal psycho-displacement. I told you that I believe that all my apparatus does is to release an ability latent in the human mind. An ability which over the few decades before my work even amateur experimenters were able to tap, before I systematised it, brought it into the realms of science. An ability which, given what you saw, *the Neanderthals evidently shared.* Yet, from the way you described those old women, it was new to them too." He got up and paced, hand cupped around the bowl of an invisible pipe, and he spoke as if lecturing students. "A consolation! Why should we need that now? And why should it have emerged in the Neanderthals when it did, hmm?"

He expected me to answer, I saw. The academic with the slow student. I thought of the despairing father. "They were finished. No more young women. No more children."

"Yes! That's it. Can't you see? I told you what your father asked me. 'Why can't you send me into the future?' It seems just as logical that one could ride the world lines forward as backward. Well, with careful study and experiment since, I believe I have found the answer, Ms Armand. It is because our world lines *have no extension* in the future, or none significant. Just as, twenty thousand years ago, your Neanderthals—"

Another crashing detonation somewhere, a pressure wave you could feel in your chest. I heard car alarms sound, and a wail of sirens.

"As to Jesus and His Incarnation, of that I cannot speak. Consolation, though—if we cannot have the promise of the future, at least we are granted the memory of the past. Do you think that's *why* we have been given this gift, Ms. Armand? It would seem an act of a merciful superior soul, if not a God. Do you think I should defy the injunctions and release the technique to mankind . . . ?"

I could barely hear him. I looked at him, his grayed hair, his tired eyes. Other faces rose before me. The grieving Neanderthal man. The laughing, robust children on the wooded plain. The kindly, ape-like features of my most distant mother. The round, shining face of the sleeping child. The long remembering, the lingering joy.

I grabbed his arm. "I don't care about others. I don't care about the world. Let me go back, Rennie. Oh, let me go back!"

AFTERWORD:

MY FIRST real introduction to adult sf was at age twelve, around 1970, when I hoovered up all I could find in my local library and school library. From that beginning, Poul Anderson was always a towering name for me. I suppose works like *Tau Zero* (1970) have had a more obvious influence on my career as a hard sf writer, but I also responded to his gentler, more intensely emotional stories—like the tale that's the inspiration for this piece. I was born in the very month "The Long Remembering" was first published, and that's one reason why it's among my favourites.

—Stephen Baxter

OPERATION XIBALBA

by Eric Flint

***ERIC FLINT** is one of the modern masters of Alternate History science fiction and humorous fantasy adventure. He's probably best known for the* Assiti Shards *series, detailing what happens when a part of twentieth-Century-West Virginia is transported to the East Germany of 1632 during the Thirty Year's War. The series began with the novel* 1632, *and has carried on through eleven volumes since, both solo novels and novels written in collaboration with David Weber, Andrew Dennis, and Virginia DeMarce. Flint is also the editor of the related six-volume* Grantville Gazette *anthology series, in which other authors relate the stories of the inhabitants of that West Virginia town. He's also written the six-volume* Belisarius *series, with David Drake; the two-volume* Rats, Bats and Vats *series, with Richard Roach; the two-volume* Jao *series, with K.D. Wentworth; the two-volume* Joe's World *series, with Richard Roach; the two-volume* Boundary *series, with Ryk E. Spoor; and two posthumous sequels to James H. Schmidt's* The Witches of Karres, *with Dave Freer and Mercedes Lackey. Flint has also written the solo novels* Mother of Dreams, 1812: The Rivers of War, *and* 1824: The Arkansas War, *as well as other collaborative novels with Dave Freer and Marilyn Kosmatka. His short fiction has been collected in* Worlds *and* The Flood Was Fixed: and Other Stories. *He was the editor of the ambitious online magazine* Jim Baen's Universe, *and also edited two anthologies drawn from it,* The Best of Jim Baen's Universe *and* The Best of Jim Baen's Universe II *(with Mike Resnick). His other anthologies include* The World Turned Upside Down, *edited with Jim Baen and David Drake*, Foreign Legions, *edited with David Drake and David Weber, and* The Dragon Done It *and* When Diplomacy Fails: An Anthology of Military Science Fiction, *both edited with Mike Resnick.*

In a visit to the bizarre world Anderson explored in his novel, Operation Chaos, *Flint shows us that, perhaps unsurprisingly, going to Hell can be a very dangerous thing to do.*

1

"Goddamn Matucheks," Frank Pianessa said wearily. He tossed the report I'd just handed to him onto the desk, without opening it, and reached for his coffee cup. The cup was resting on a pile of other reports in the same bile-green-colored folders the Department of Infernal Affairs had chosen to use for this particular purpose.

Appropriately chosen, if you ask me. The official name for the activity involved was "Unauthorized Incursions Into the Nether Reaches." Those of us assigned to deal with the ensuing messes called it either the "Darwin Award on Steroids" or "What Will These Idiots Think Of Next?"

Frank slurped at his coffee. "Summarize it for me, would you, Anibal? It's too early in the morning for me to fight my way through departmentese."

I couldn't help but smile. In the short period of its existence since it was created after the Matuchek Expedition, the prose of the DIA had become notorious even among federal agencies. Nobody else could produce something like—I'm not making this up, it's taken directly from an actual report—the following:

Subject incursee [that's DIA-speak for the moron involved, and never mind that an "incursee" would presumably refer to the person into whom the incursion was done, not the one who did it—but what do billions of people who speak proper English know?] *thereupon attempted to execute an extrapersonal ejection* [translation: the moron tried to fire or throw a missile of some sort] *intended to inflict uncertifiably mortal results* [tried to kill, a dubious prospect given the nature of the time, place and intended killee] *upon the demonic personage involved, tentatively classified as a minor fiend, thoracically enhanced variety, clawed ilk, ill-tempered branch.*

That last is pointless verbiage, since there's really no rhyme or reason to the construction—or possibly devolution—of the denizens of the hell universe. Clawed, spiny, bad-humored . . . Gee, a devil. Who would've guessed? I ran fingers through my hair. "This one's a doozy, boss."

Frank grimaced. "Don't tell me we've got another big game hunter on our hands."

One of our last cases—the one whose report I just quoted from, in fact—involved a man [tentatively classified as a minor cretin, cranially deprived variety, stupid ilk, suicidal branch] who tried to set himself up in business as a hunting guide. He'd undertake safaris in Hell, for any big game hunter tired of bagging the usual lion, bison, elk, or elephant.

He got three takers for his first and only safari. All of them were very well-armed indeed. Two of the hunters had double-barreled .600-caliber elephant guns, the third had a .50-caliber military-grade sniper rifle, and the guide himself was armed with a grenade launcher.

Fat lot of good it did them, in a universe whose geometry is not even remotely Euclidean. That's why the Matuchek party never tried to use missile weapons at all, not even with the spirits of Lobachevsky and Bolyai to guide them.

I shook my head. "No, I'm afraid it's a lot worse than that."

Frank set down his cup. "Oh, Gawd Almighty. Don't tell me we've got more missionaries on our hands."

You'd think any religious denomination that went in for proselytizing would understand that, pretty much by definition, the denizens of the hell universe are . . .

Well. Damned. That means "not subject to salvation."

But every few months we get another bunch of screwballs who hare off to save the unholy. By the time we get alerted and can track them down, it's usually too late. Since the would-be missionaries are deliberately trying to find demons, which are abundant in the nether regions (as you'd expect), they've already been slaughtered by the time we catch up to them. Or "martyred," to use their own terminology, which I personally consider preposterous. You might as well call a man who throws himself off a cliff to be a "martyr."

Again, I ran fingers through my hair. "Uh . . . no. It's a religious expedition of sorts, I suppose you could say. But they're not actually crazy. They've no intention of converting devils. They're seeking what they call 'morally neutral allies in the struggle against the Adversary.'"

"Huh?"

"'Morally neutral allies,'" I repeated patiently.

"What the hell does that mean?" he demanded.

"You remember how the Matuchek incident ended?"

"Yeah, sure. When all seemed lost, they summoned—called, rather—some enormous and presumably very powerful . . . Oh, dear Lord. You have *got* to be kidding me."

I shook my head. "Nope. It seems the head of this new expedition—his name's Rick Boatright, by the way—got into a conversation in a bar with a couple of the scholars who've been studying the data brought back by the Matucheks. They explained to him that they'd been able to tentatively identify the three beings summoned as godlings from an alternate universe. They don't know their names, but they think two of them have a European origin and the third one came from a pre-discovery New World society."

From the look of concentration on his face, Frank had been running that part of the Matuchek report through his mind. Now, he grunted. "I presume that's the weird-looking feathered snake."

"Yeah, that one. The same scholars think the being came from an analog of one of our own Native American cultures from the southwest or Mexico. And that's the being this new expedition went looking for. Apparently the logic involved—I'm using the term loosely—is that since Boatright and his party left for Hell from Yuma, that's the one they're most likely to run across."

Frank rolled his eyes. "Which part of 'non-Euclidean geometry' do people have trouble with? For Pete's sake, it doesn't matter where you leave from, when you set off for Hell."

I shrugged. "A disregard for basic geometry is pretty much a given with our clientele."

My boss scowled. "*Don't* call them 'our clientele,' Anibal. The term's silly. Clients are what doctors and dentists have."

"And psychiatrists," I pointed out. "Including ones who deal with schizophrenics. I'll say this much for Boatright—at least he had enough sense to take an IPS unit with him."

Frank's scowl darkened. "Talk about silly terms! 'Infernal Positioning System.' An oxymoron if there ever was one."

I shrugged again. "Hey, look, they *do* work. After a fashion. That's why we use them ourselves."

The operative phrase was *after a fashion,* though. IPS units were made by several different companies, each of whom claimed their unit had XYZ special feature or function that enabled—"enabled," *not* guaranteed; see fine print below—the user to navigate through the nether regions. We'd tried all of the models and had never found any of them to be all that useful. Granted, they were better than nothing, but that was about like saying that a walking stick was better than nothing when you set out to conquer Mount Everest.

The problem was that IPS units only worked in places where the geometry was relatively close to that of our own universe. Such places did exist in the hell universe—quite a few of them, in fact—but the problem is that those aren't the places in that universe where an expedition is most likely to wind up.

Why? Because such an expedition, or the rescue expedition sent out after them, is looking for the denizens of the hell universe. Or, to put it another way, is looking for evil. And from what our scholars can determine, evil plays roughly the same role in the geometry of the hell universe that gravity plays in our own. Gravity isn't a "force" as such, it's the curvature of space-time produced by mass. It seems that wickedness is the analogous quasi-force in determining the geometry of hell.

You can see what that leads to. Mass is pleasantly stable, inert, mindless and without volition. Evil, on the other hand, is chaotic, willful, self-centered, and worst of all, often capricious. So, whenever you find a large enough concentration of devils, or even a single one if it's powerful enough, you'll find that the geometry of the hell universe starts flopping around unpredictably. At that point the IPS units give up the ghost, mechanically speaking.

In our experience, the most reliable method for navigating the hell universe is simply hard-won experience—emphasis on "hard-won." With enough experience, you learned to react based on moral instinct rather than eyesight. Oddly enough, with one exception, the people who turned out to be the best at it were people like me. Agnostics, with a low propensity for being judgmental. People with strong faith systems or rigid moral codes invariably got confused quickly once they entered the hell universe. A grand total of two—count 'em, two—missionaries have ever come back alive from the hell universe. One of them was missing both legs, both ears, all of his hair and—go figure—his appendix. The other was catatonic and has never recovered.

I'd always prided myself on being unprejudiced and insistent on subjecting everything to rational analysis. I'd feel better about this except that the one exception sometimes made me wonder if there might be something wrong with me.

That's because the exceptions are outright psychopaths. To use the technical term, people who exhibit Anti-Social Personality Disorder. ASPD, for short.

No, I kid you not. For reasons that are presumably obvious, the DIA doesn't advertise the fact. We get enough accusations of being crazy as it is. I will add that psychopaths employed as guides by the DIA in the hell universe are strictly consultants, not employees of the department.

Still, it makes me wonder, sometimes. Especially when I discover, as I have on several occasions, that my own reactions to hell-universe geometic shifts—HUGS is the inevitable acronym; hey, look, we're a government agency—are more reliable than those of my psychopath guide.

Just to make something clear before we go any further, psychopaths are *not* necessarily serial murderers or even especially dangerous. It's the killers who get all the publicity, but the fact is that most psychopaths go through life without ever running afoul of the law. Quite a few are successful corporate CEOs, in fact.

Thinking about psychopaths naturally brought me to the inevitable end point of this meeting. Frank was bound to give me the assignment of tracking down Boatright and his people and hauling them (or what was left of them) out of the hell universe.

Not all psychopaths are the same. Most of them—well, all of them, really—are thoroughly detestable people. But they are also usually charming, on the surface, and some are more charming than others.

If you were lucky, the expedition might be short enough that the charm didn't wear off before the underlying personality emerged.

"Is Walt Boyes available?" I asked.

Frank shook his head. "No, he got arrested again."

"Too bad." I started working my way alphabetically through the list of psychopath guides. I didn't get any farther than David Carrico, though, before there came the sounds of a ruckus in the receptionist's office beyond the door.

"Yes, I know he's in a meeting," said a loud female voice I didn't know—and from its unpleasant edge, didn't want to. "That's why I need to get in there right now, before any further damage is done."

I heard the voice of Frank's receptionist, Mrs. Graves, although I couldn't make out more than one word in three. " . . . can't . . . have to . . . proper . . . *hey!*"

A moment later the door opened. Burst open, almost. A female—presumably the source of the unknown voice—strode into the office.

She was good-looking, in an intense sort of way. Somewhere in her early thirties, very dark hair, almost black, cut short; equally dark eyes; a slim but unmistakably female figure. All of it set off in a gray business suit cut along the same severe lines as her hair.

"Frank Pianessa?" she asked, looking at him. It was more in the way of a statement than a question, though. Before Frank's glare could turn into a verbal response, the intense black eyes were focused on me. "And you'd be Anibal Vargas. I'm assuming you're the one who'll be going on the expedition."

"*What* expedition?" growled Frank. "And just who are you to be asking in the first place?"

"I'm Sophia Loren, from the State Department. Please spare me the wisecracks. That's what my parents chose to name me and I'm too stubborn to get the name changed. As for the expedition, let's not play games. The one we're about to send off to snare Rick Boatright and his maniacs."

Frank's temper was rising, but my own was actually subsiding. Her comment about stubbornness concerning her name predisposed me in her favor. I'd grown up in a mostly Anglo neighborhood where my schoolmates—the ones who read, anyway, and those were the ones I hung out with—could never resist wordplay on the name "Hannibal." It didn't help that my high school girlfriend's last name was Alps.

"Assuming for the moment that such an expedition is in the works," Frank said, "what's it to you?"

"Are you serious? These people are planning to form an alliance with a non-human being from an alternate universe. A very powerful being. *Of course* the State Department is concerned."

Since this was not an unreasonable point, Frank reined in his temper and leaned back in his seat. "All right, I can see where State is legitimately involved. I assume you're concerned that such an alliance might upset the balance of power between Heaven and Hell."

"Nonsense," said Loren, waving her hand brusquely. "That's just Steven Matuchek's speculations based on—what, exactly?" With a slight curl of the lip: "His great knowledge of the Most High and the Most Low, deriving from his expertise in lycanthropy?"

Being a wereperson myself, that last remark brought my initial dislike for the woman back to the surface. Before I could say anything—if I decided to at all, which I probably wouldn't—Loren continued.

"The balance of power between the Highest and Lowest is far beyond our ability to affect significantly. If at all. But that says nothing about the ongoing struggle between the universes on a variety of lower levels. And on a number of those levels, the Boatright expedition could very well inflict a great deal of harm."

"On what?" demanded Frank.

She gave him the sort of look that is either bestowed on slimy disgusting creatures oozing from beneath a crevice, or people whose security clearances may not be up to snuff.

Frank recognized the look, naturally. "Give me a break," he said. "My clearance when it comes to infernal affairs is as high as it gets." He jerked a thumb at me. "So's his. That still leaves 'need to know,' but I presume if we didn't need to know you wouldn't have come here in the first place."

He had her over a barrel and she knew it. That was obvious from the look on her face. It was the sort of expression people had just before they underwent a root canal or divulged state secrets to someone in another agency.

"Yes, you're right. The reason Boatright poses a threat is because his expedition might cause problems for one of our existing alliances with forces in the netherworlds."

We both stared at her. After a couple of seconds, Frank said: "What alliances are you talking about? We don't have—"

Again, she made that abrupt gesture with her hand. "Of course you don't know about them. They're top secret and until now, there was no reason the DIA needed to know. Since you do know as of this minute, however, we can at least dispense with the nonsense of using lunatics as our guides in the hell universe. It's amazing you people get anything done."

I decided she really was an unpleasant woman, good looks or not and charming name or not. On the positive side, that would make my life easier, since I was obviously going to be dealing with her whether I wanted to or not.

When a heterosexually inclined single man like myself comes into contact with an attractive woman roughly his own age, an unstable situation automatically emerges. Unless he's taken holy vows, at any rate. First, curiosity demands to be satisfied. Is she herself heterosexually inclined? If so, is she single? If she is involved with someone, is the relationship officially monogamous? If so, is she open to cheating? If she is, do you want to get into that potential mare's nest?

It's exhausting just to think about it, especially because it may not stop there. If the answers are any one of yes, yes, no, yes and maybe, then the single heterosexually inclined single man has to go to work. Which can be *really* exhausting, usually unsettling, and often confusing.

But this situation was going to be no sweat. Since the answers across the board were: "Who cares? I don't like the damn woman anyway."

Frank's scowl was back in full force. "If you think I'm going to send one of my people into the hell universe with no better guide than an IPS gadget, you can damn well think again."

"No, of course not. The things are well-nigh useless." She turned, stuck fingers in her mouth, and blew a whistle.

A really impressive whistle it was, too, especially for a woman. The last woman—well, girl—I'd known with that good a whistle was Allison Alps. I felt my resolve to dislike Loren crumbling again.

There came another ruckus in the receptionist's office. Again, I could only catch one word in three. But I probably wasn't missing much in the way of intellectual content, because what I did hear was: "*. . . hey! . . . you don't . . . hey! . . . you can't! . . . what do you think . . . ? . . . hey!*"

The door opened again and a creature waddled in. It stood about three feet high, was about three feet wide, and looked vaguely like a cross between a goose and a small troll. I recognized it as a svartálfar. They're sometimes known as "black elves," even though the color of their skin is slate gray. The darkness being referred to is a matter of the soul, not the body. They're generally nasty and invariably obnoxious. Most people don't associate with them willingly. I wondered why she did.

"You called, babe?" The creature twisted its long neck so that its grotesquely ugly face was cocked sideways as it looked up at Loren. Below the immense nose, thick lips twisted into a leer. "Finally getting horny?"

"In your dreams." Loren nodded toward me. "Meet Anibal Vargas. He's the agent from the DIA who'll be going with us. Mr. Vargas, this is my associate, Ingemar."

The creature now twisted the neck to bring its black and beady eyes to bear on me. It was the eyes more than anything—combined with that grotesque neck, of course—that brought the image of a goose to mind. There really wasn't anything very avian about the little monster.

"Hannibal, is it? I hope he's cannae-er than he looks."

I'd heard that one as far back as the ninth grade. But I hadn't expected to hear such an educated pun from something that looked like this creature.

"Be polite," said Loren.

"Why?" sneered Ingemar. "He'll just be another furball, like almost all these DIA field types. Dumber'n rocks."

It was true that most DIA field agents were therianthropes of one kind or another. People with degrees in sorcery or accounting tended to gravitate toward the FBI. But, true or not, I decided this snotty bastard needed to be put in his place right here at the outset.

Besides, the wisecrack about "furballs" was irritating.

I always wear were-adaptable clothing on the job, so I didn't need to strip. I just popped out my Polaroid flash, turned it on myself, and made the change.

The transformation is very quick although it seems much longer to the one undergoing the process. It wasn't more than a few seconds later that I came erect in my were form.

"*Arkh!*" squawked the little monster. He scrambled onto the filing cabinet against the door, that being the highest ground in the office.

Fat lot of good it would have done him. I swiveled my head to gaze upon his partner. To her credit, Sophia Loren hadn't budged. She might have paled a little, although it was hard to tell with her olive complexion.

"I guess 'nice doggie' would be even more inappropriate than usual," she said. She turned to look at Ingemar. "Do you really think he can't get to you up there?"

The svartálfar gibbered something that sounded Germanic although I didn't recognize any of the words. Loren shook her head. "What difference does it make how high he can jump? He'd just bring the cabinet down." She studied my feet. "It'd be interesting to watch, actually."

This woman was quite confusing. I had a feeling my future might have some emotional exercise in it, after all.

2

"I DIDN'T KNOW it was even possible," said Loren the next day, as we waited for the State Department's witches to finish the ritual that would send us into the hell universe. We were using them instead of their DIA equivalents because the powers-that-be had pronounced this expedition to be under State's jurisdiction and control. Officially, I was just on loan as a field agent.

"I knew any sort of prehistoric therianthropy was rare," she continued, "and I just assumed they were all mammalian."

I shrugged. "Most are. Or I should say, almost all the few which exist are mammalian. But there are a handful like me."

"All velociraptors?"

"All dromaeosaurids, is the right way to put it. Velociraptors properly so-called were about the size of a turkey. The laws of physics, including conservation of mass and energy, aren't violated by therianthropy. A person who turned into a velociraptor would have to weigh no more than thirty to forty pounds."

"Okay. And that makes you . . . ?"

"I'm listed on the agency rolls as a *Deinonychus antirrhopus.* But the truth is, there's a lot of guesswork involved. Nobody really knows for sure."

I started to add something, but then saw that the sorcerers had reached the end of the ritual. I felt the universe beginning to swirl around us, in the by-now very familiar sensations of interplanar travel.

"And here we go," said Loren. She turned to her nasty little sidekick. "Are the goats ready?"

"Teach grandmothers to suck eggs," muttered Ingemar. He held up a sack and whacked the side of it. A couple of bleats emerged from within. "See?"

If you've read Steven Matuchek's account of the expedition he and his wife Virginia undertook into the hell universe to rescue their infant daughter, you'll remember his depictions of the terrain there. Those depictions are about as accurate as everything in his book. True as far as it goes, but it doesn't go as far as most people think it does. There's no such thing as "the" terrain of Hell, any more than there is such a thing as "the" terrain of Earth—or Mars, for that matter. In fact, the variation is a lot greater than anything you'll find in our own universe.

Because the witches had used personal possessions of Boatright in their cantrips, we came out in the same place in the hell universe that Boatright and his party had. Part of the cantrips also involved sending a homunculus through first to test the terrain's survivability in crude physical terms. The thing is mindless since its brain is no bigger than a pea, but its morphology and metabolism is otherwise completely human. They leave the homunculus in hell for twelve hours—hell time; it's only a second or two in our own—and then see what shape it's in when they bring it back. That's to make sure the party that goes through next won't immediately drown or suffocate in a vacuum or get poisoned by the atmosphere.

But beyond that, we had no idea what sort of environment we'd emerge in, and I was prepared for anything. So, it seemed, was my State Department companion. She'd exchanged her severe business suit for an explorer's jumpsuit that was cut every bit as severely but displayed her figure a lot better. I'd known already that the figure was slim, but now I could see that there was muscle there as well. Hers was the sort of slender build that came from a lot of exercise, not just genes and a good diet. Her gear wasn't too bulky and the only visible weapon was a machete slung across her back. Still, it must have come to somewhere around twenty pounds, and she was carrying all of it without apparent effort.

So far, so good. There didn't seem to be much chance that she'd just physically collapse under the strenuous conditions in the hell universe. I'd been worried about that. Foggy Bottom types like to sneer at we lowbrow DIA gorillas, but most of them think a strenuous workout consists of carrying a martini from one room to another in a diplomatic soiree.

I still had no idea what sort of experience she had in hell conditions. When I'd tried to enquire, she'd refused to answer. Politely, but I might as well have been interrogating a fire hydrant.

In the event, we arrived in a fetid jungle—just barely this side of a swamp. The soil underfoot was only "solid" in a technical sense. Walking on it would exhaust us within half an hour.

I turned to my companion and cocked an eye at her. Loren had insisted that she could and would provide transportation once we got to Hell.

She studied the terrain for a few more seconds, her lips pursed thoughtfully, and then said to Ingemar: "What do you think? I'm inclined toward the carpet myself, although the goats could probably manage the howdah."

The black elf peered suspiciously at the sky. What little he could see, which wasn't much given the solid low overcast. "I don't like the looks of it. Could be anything up there. I say we go with the howdah. It'll be slower but the goats can manage."

They sounded for all the world like a golfer and her caddy discussing which iron to use. After another few seconds and some continued lip-pursing, Loren nodded. "All right, let's do it."

With no further ado, Ingemar upended the sack in his hand. Two little goats fell out. I mean, *little*—neither one of them stood more than eight inches high. At a guess, they weighed about the same as small dogs. These were supposed to be our means of transportation?

"Stand back," Loren said, giving me a light warning push with her fingers. After I took a couple of steps back, she stuck her fingers in her mouth and whistled. A really piercing whistle, this one was.

The goats started growing. Really fast. Within fifteen seconds, they were both the size of elephants. Their morphologies changed as they grew also. By the end, they were still recognizably goats but their legs were disproportionately thick and their feet bore a closer resemblance to those of an elephant or a rhino than a goat's.

While that was happening, Ingemar had kept shaking the sack. The next thing that came out was a weird-looking contraption that looked like a scrunched-up haversack. By the time the goats finished their transformation, the haversack had turned into a howdah. Well . . . that's pushing it a little. Let's say it had the same resemblance to a proper howdah that a good tent has to a house. Still and all, it was clearly something a couple of people could ride in comfortably enough, even perched on top of a goat-cum-elephant.

It took another few minutes for the svartálfar to haul the howdah onto one of the goats and get it fastened in place. Then, he reached back into the sack and hauled out something that looked like a fireplace poker. I recognized the device, although I couldn't remember what it was called. It was the tool used by mahouts to drive elephants.

Sure enough, a few seconds later he was perched in a mahout's position behind the goat's head, straddling its neck, and looking down at us with a sneer on his face. "What? You expect me to help you up, too?"

The jury-rigged howdah had a rope ladder hanging down from one side. Loren and I used it to climb aboard. No sooner had we gotten into the howdah than Ingemar set the goat in motion. Looking back, I could see the second one following. Apparently it would do so on its own, without a lead rope.

"We'll switch mounts after a few hours," Loren explained. "The beasts are tougher'n you'd believe, but they'll still get tired in this sort of terrain."

I looked ahead, and then to the sides. The terrain seemed identical anywhere you looked and I couldn't detect any sign of a trail. "Are you sure we're headed in the right direction?"

Loren sniffed. "As Ingemar said, don't teach grandmothers to suck eggs. First, the finding spell we used is the most reliable in existence.

Second, Ingemar and the goats can find their way almost anywhere in Hell. Third, I know what I'm doing."

"An accomplished witch yourself, I take it."

"Me?" She gave me a look that somehow managed to be aloof and sly at the same time. "I haven't been a virgin since I was fifteen. If I'd even tried to apply to a good witch's program in college they'd have laughed at me. No, I'm a diplomat. What do you expect from the State Department? Think of me as a roving ambassador, if it makes you feel better."

It didn't. I didn't know exactly what the skill set of a diplomat consisted of, but I was pretty sure damn few of the skills would be any use here in the hell universe. Your average demon's idea of "negotiating" is arguing over whether you'll enter the monster's maw headfirst or feetfirst.

The remark about virginity kick-started my sternly suppressed single-male curiosity. As usual, this manifested itself in the form of a shifty-eyed glance and a suave "Aaaah . . ."

She chuckled. "I'm heterosexually inclined, single—divorced; not never married—currently unattached. Monogamous when I am, and no, I don't fool around. You?"

I cleared my throat. "Aaah . . . The same."

"Divorced for how long?"

"Two years. Not quite. Twenty-two months."

"It's been a little over three years for me. Okay, so divorce-shock shouldn't be too much of a problem. It's a deal, then. If you're still interested when this is over, ask me out on a date. The answer will be 'yes.' I've decided you're kind of cute, for a slavering carnosaur from the Cretaceous."

"Aaah . . . "

"Good thing one of us is a diplomat. Or are you under the delusion that a monosyllable is a good pickup line?" She flashed me a grin. "Get used to it, if you decide you're interested. Fair warning—I can be really annoying. Everyone says so. My ex-husband thinks the warning should be tattooed on my forehead. Every supervisor I've ever had would probably agree except for those who think it should be branded there. My friends, on the other hand, think a tattoo on the shoulder ought to be good enough if I agreed to always wear sleeveless dresses or tank tops."

A loud hoot from ahead drew our attention. Looking in that direction, we saw that a creature had emerged from the brush and was standing in our path. It looked more-or-less like a misshapen weightlifter with the head of an eagle and talons instead of fingers on its hands. At a guess, it weighed somewhere around four hundred pounds although that might be an over-estimate. Some demons with avian or partly avian morphologies have hollow bones.

"You gotta love this place," I said. "It's as predictable as the menu in a fast food joint."

"This monster being . . . ?"

I vaulted over the lip of the howdah and landed lightly on my feet. Well, allowing for a little squelch. Looking up, I saw that Loren was staring at me with surprise. Because of my size, people who don't know me don't realize how athletic I am. If I weren't just plain too massive, I'd have been an Olympic-level gymnast. As you'd expect, of course, given my genes.

"It's some variety of nisroch," I said. "This shouldn't take long."

It didn't.

A few minutes after we'd set back underway, Loren cleared her throat. "Well, I'd been thinking of recommending a nice sushi place for our date, but I guess that's not a good idea."

I grinned. "Rolled-up little fishie bits and tofu are really not my style. I'm pretty much a steakhouse kind of guy."

"Do you always eat the organs?"

"You have to stay away from the liver and spleen, with almost any kind of demon, and the hearts are just plain indigestible even for me. Other than that, though, yeah. The intestines are especially good because the hell universe has its own diseases and devil guts are the best source of antibiotics. Using the term loosely."

"But I'd think it must taste . . . "

"Horrible? Yeah, sure. But I'm eating them in raptor form. Think I care?"

That sly grin came back. I was starting to get fond of it, I decided, even though I could see where it might be annoying if you were in the wrong mood.

"I was wondering why the DIA had you listed as one of their top field agents," she said. "It's because you don't need much in the way of supplies. How many people can live off the land in Hell?"

"Not too many. In my defense, though, most of my rating is because of my brains. Believe it or not."

Her expression got more thoughtful. "Actually, I don't doubt that at all."

There came another loud sound from ahead of us. A screech, you might call it. A couple of seconds later, a huge falcon came flying into sight. It perched on a branch in a nearby tree, that sagged under the weight. Then, jerked its head around a few times and vomited a snake.

The snake landed on the soggy soil below and wriggled toward us. When it was no more than ten feet from the goat, it raised its head, jerked it around a few times, and puked up a toad. No sooner did the toad land on the ground than it made a prodigious hop onto one of the goat's horns and from there hopped onto the front side of the howdah.

That done, it jerked its head back and forth a few times—

"Oh, give me a break!" I said. Loren hurriedly leaned away from it.

—and vomited up a . . .

Louse? It sure looked like it.

The louse reared up and started speaking, in a much louder voice than you'd ever imagine such a tiny creature could produce. It sounded like gibberish to me, but Loren had a look of intent concentration on her face. I realized she was able to understand what it was saying.

Who the hell speaks louse? I didn't even know the pests had a language.

When the louse finally finished, Loren turned to me with a frown on her face. "What I was afraid of. That idiot Boatright managed to wander into a Mesoamerican region of the hell universe. A Mayan analog, at a first approximation. Of all the places to look for allies against the forces of evil!"

I understood her point. None of the early pagan religions were what you'd call filled with the milk of human kindness. But even in that crowd, the Mesoamerican deities and spirits were blood-curdling.

Literally, in many cases. The underlying belief system that had created them had for its main premise the idea that the universe was kept going by the gods, and the only thing that kept the god themselves going was being fed with human blood. Human blood drawn from pain and suffering, to boot. No blood bank donors need apply. The blood had to come with shrieks of agony or it wasn't worth anything.

I dredged up what I knew about the mythos involved. If this region of the hell universe bore a close approximation to the Mayan region, I was pretty sure it would be ruled by the Lords of Xibalba. A cheery crowd, that lot. Among them would be a god of pain, a god of disease, a god of pus, a god of emaciation, a god of jaundice—you get the picture?

Loren's next words confirmed my guess:

"The louse is a messenger from the Lords of Xibalba. It says if we want to get Boatright and his people back we need to—"

"Undergo a series of tests. Yeah, I know. That's a pretty standard feature of this mythos."

It was clear from the expression on her face that she was familiar with it herself. "It is, indeed," she said. "Some of them will be straightforward tests of skill, but some will be ordeals and all of them are likely to be full of tricks."

"You do realize that there's already not much left of Boatright and his people? Not here."

She nodded. "Yes, I know."

"So why go on? I vote for an ignominious retreat."

"We can't. It's tempting, but . . . " She shook her head. "The problem is that too many of our netherworld alliances with pagan forces are based on rigid honor codes. Their codes, not ours, but if they start thinking we're prone to quitting when the going gets tough, the alliances will get frayed at the very least."

I put on my best sneer. "Who cares? There's a reason those silly buggers went out of business. Several reasons, actually. 'Rigid honor code' is probably right at the top."

She smiled thinly. "Oh, not right at the top. But I agree it's up there. It still doesn't matter, Anibal. We can't afford to lose those alliances, with all the chaos that's still reverberating from the collapse of the Johannine church after the Matuchek Incident."

Since she was officially in charge of the expedition, my vote didn't really matter. "Okay, you're the boss. Is this parasite our guide, or do we have to find our own way to the examination hall?"

"There'll be a guide of some sort, but not the louse. The creature was pretty vague—*whoa!*"

The howdah was lurching around wildly. The goat carrying it was bleating and the goat following was already half out of sight racing back in the direction from which we'd come. For his part, Ingemar was holding onto the goat's horns for dear life. He'd lost his prod in the process.

We were rising, too, very quickly. I looked down to see what was causing that, and then wished I hadn't.

The reason we were rising was because we were on the back of a gigantic crocodile. About the size of a battleship.

"And here we go," said Sophia.

3

THE CROCODILE carried us for what I'd estimate was thirty miles—keeping in mind that the term "estimate" means exactly that, and under hell conditions to boot. Given the beast's size, though, that didn't take more than an hour or so. (See caveat concerning estimates above, with the added caution that watches are completely unreliable in the infernal regions.)

Eventually, we arrived in front of a great pit, at the bottom of which an enormous drunken revelry was taking place. There were about four hundred drunkards down there, not one of whom looked to be older than ten or eleven. They were all boys, too. Not a girl in sight.

"The Four Hundred Boys," said Sophia. "We're in a Mayan mythos, sure enough. Close analog, anyway. We won't go any further until one of us joins the celebration."

She turned to Ingemar. "Your job, this is."

He was already climbing over the side of the howdah, looking quite cheerful. "Good luck on the rest of your trip. Better you than me, heh! I'll be partying hard in support, be sure of it."

Once off the goat and on the crocodile, the svartálfar scampered down its spine until he reached the tip of the tail. From there, it wasn't too bad of a leap down to the ground. As soon as he was off, the crocodile started moving around the pit.

My knowledge of the Mayan mythos was on the sketchy side. "Who are the Four Hundred Boys?"

"The gods of drunkenness. Or the gods of alcoholic drinks, depending on the translation. The reason they're boys, according to State's scholars, is probably because they can't hold their liquor at all. The reason there are four hundred of them is probably to make sure not all of them are passed out at once. So far as we can tell, their diplomatic function is to waylay visitors, get them plastered, and then play nasty tricks on them. 'Nasty' as in frequently fatal or disfiguring."

"This is a diplomatic function?"

She grinned. "Leaving aside the murder and mayhem, it's really not too different from what happens at cocktail parties in embassies."

Not more than two miles past the pit, the crocodile came to a halt again. This time, in front of a large stone building. It swung its tail around until the tip of it was just before the building's only visible entrance.

The hint was obvious. So, Loren and I got out of the howdah and copied Ingemar's method of leaving the crocodile. As soon as we reached the ground, the gigantic reptile started moving away.

I was a little sorry to see it go. Despite its fearsome appearance, the monster had been perfectly well-behaved and I hadn't worried about being waylaid by anything while we were on top of it. Not even Hell's creatures are likely to pester something that size.

There being nothing else to do, we passed through the entrance. It wasn't a door, just a tall and narrow corridor through the stones that made up the structure. We emerged into a chamber about fifty feet across. Sitting on stools in a semi-circle at the opposite end were fourteen beings, staring at us.

I use the term "beings" because I can't think of anything more suitably vague that still conveys intelligence. The appearance of the fourteen figures varied wildly in every manner except one: they were all hideous.

You were expecting something else from the gods of pus, pestilence, etc? Trust me, you don't even want to think what the god of hemorrhoids looked like.

"At a guess," I said, "we're looking at the Lords of Xibalba."

Sophia snorted. "You think?"

"What now?"

"I'm not sure. We need to greet all of them by name, if I remember the protocol, or we'll be in immediate trouble. But there's bound to be a trick involved."

"How good are you with languages?"

"That's one of my specialties. I'm not technically a witch, but my abilities when it comes to speaking in tongues are magical. For all practical purposes, I can understand any language after I've heard a few words spoken. Don't ask me how, because I don't know."

The germ of an idea came to me. A crudely direct idea, I admit, but what else do you expect from a theropod?

"Okay, then. Let's see what happens." I pulled out my flash and made the change.

Once in raptor form, I sprang over to the nearest Lord of Xibalba and smelled it. For me, in that form, smelling mostly meant licking it with my tongue.

At a guess, this one was the god of vomit. There was no way I could have made myself smell the thing, much less lick it with my tongue, if I'd still been in human form. But theropods are to fastidiousness what monkeys are to decorum. In a word, oblivious.

I then sprang over to the next one. At a guess, after a couple of licks, this one was the god of edema.

The third one, even before my tongue could examine it, I figured to be the god of acne. But before my tongue reached it, the Lord of Xibalba waved me off frantically and started gibbering something at its fellow gods.

I swiveled my head to look at Sophia. She had that same expression of intent concentration that she'd had when she was listening to the louse. So, seeing no further role to play at the moment, I squatted down in front of the semi-circle.

When a human squats, he looks more harmless than usual. Not so, for a Deinonychus. He looks like he's about to spring into action.

All of the lords except the two at the far end were now gibbering wildly. Those two, on the other hand, were as inert as if they'd been made of the same stone the building was.

Which, as it turned out, they were.

"Okay," said Sophia. "I've learned all their names by now, since they used them in jabbering at one another." She pointed at the two silent ones. "Those are phonies. Mannequins. The other twelve . . . "

She moved to the center of the chamber, bowed, and addressed each one of the Lords in turn. I didn't understand any of it, but I found out later that the names were such charming monickers as One Death, Seven Death, Blood Gatherer—no St. Francis types in this crowd.

When she finished, the twelve real Lords of Xibalba starting gibbering again. After a few minutes of that, the racket died down and all of them looked at one of the Lords near the center of the semicircle. This one was marginally less ugly than the others—you understand this doesn't mean much? like being the best-dressed hog in a pigsty—but made up for it by having a smoking obsidian mirror embedded in its forehead.

Smoking Mirror leaned forward on its stool and gibbered something at Sophia. She gibbered back, he gibbered, she gibbered, eventually they were done.

She came over to where I stood. By then, I'd changed back to human form.

"It's about what we figured," she said. "They'll hand Boatright and his people over to us if we pass some tests. To judge our worth—and don't ask me how they gauge worth in the first place, I haven't got a clue."

"How many tests?"

"They're being vague about that. Essentially, one test for every human they hand over. But for some reason they seem unable or unwilling to specify an exact number."

I frowned. "There's a gimmick in there, somewhere. Boatright had three people with him. Even monster gods dedicated to diseases should be able to count up to four."

She shrugged. "There's always a gimmick, dealing with the deities in this region of the hell universe. We'll just have to see how it works out."

Since I didn't have a better plan, I nodded. "Where's the first test?"

"From what I gather, as soon as we leave this edifice."

That test turned out to be a giant jaguar, the size of a big tiger.

Piece of cake, even though I was outweighed by at least three hundred pounds.

It's not so much that dromaeosaurids are intrinsically more ferocious than modern predators—although they probably are. But the biggest factor is brains. A jaguar, even a giant one in Hell, is no smarter than any big cat. Even without a human intelligence riding piggyback, any dromaeosaurid can easily equal it. When you add the human intelligence, even as dimmed as it invariably is in were form, it's just no contest.

Except for bears, modern predators almost exclusively use their teeth as their killing tools. Their claws and talons are a means to hold prey, not weapons. So I knew the jaguar wouldn't be expecting me to shift to the side and disembowel it with one kick as it leapt at me. In Deinonychus form, the second toes on my rear feet have large sickle claws that will cut through almost anything short of thick metal or hardwood.

Normally, I would have just let the jaguar bleed out. Why take any risks at all? But since I figured time was pressing and had no idea what the rules of the test might be, I finished it off quickly with a bite to the neck. A Deinonychus has a bite force that's even greater than a hyena's, and almost equals that of a modern alligator of equal size. One bite was enough.

The next test required us to enter another stone edifice. Once inside, we found ourselves in a large chamber full of sharp obsidian blades. The blades were round and about the size of dinner plates.

"Oh, swell," said Sophia. "The House of Razors."

As soon as we entered, the blades lifted off the ground and started humming. Then, a few seconds later, began a complex series of motions that I soon realized constituted an impenetrable barrier if you wanted to get through them. It was like a moving version of the laser beam networks that are used in some security systems.

There was another door visible at the far end of the chamber. The nature of this test was depressingly clear.

While I'd been studying the pattern of the blades' movements, Sophia had gotten that now-familiar intent look on her face. I only half-noticed, though, until she nudged me with her elbow.

"I think I can talk our way through them," she said.

My contribution was: "Huh?"

But, sure enough, she started humming herself and before you knew it the blade pattern shifted to leave a narrow corridor in the middle. Sophia immediately hurried through, not quite running. After taking a deep breath, I followed.

Worked like a charm.

The next test went by the name of Cold House. The one after that, Bat House.

The first was full of hail the size of golf balls, freezing rain and winds just barely this side of hurricane force. That was purely a matter of endurance. The second one was full of—what else?—bats. Not fruit-eating bats, either. Vampire bats.

Wannabe vampires, I should say. Sophia started a godawful caterwauling that she told me later was the mating calls of lamias. That seemed to confuse the bats mightily. It would have scrambled my wits as well except that I shifted into were form. Theropods react to horrible noises about the same way they react to horrible smells: the blithe indifference that generally goes along with being on top of the food chain.

When we emerged from the Bat House, we looked around.

Nothing, beyond a lot of trees crowded around the small clearing where the stone edifice was situated.

"Those rotten bastards," I grumbled. "We passed four tests. Boatright and his partners add up to four. So where are they?"

Sophia pointed to a tree off to our left. "Well, there's one of them. Part of one, I should say."

I followed her finger. There was a human head, perched in a fork of the tree about ten feet off the ground. A severed human head, to be precise.

"I think that's Boatright himself," I said. "Judging by the photos we had."

We went over to the tree. Even in human form, it wasn't hard for me to get up into the tree high enough to haul down the head.

"Yup, that's Boatright. I wonder where the rest of him is?"

Sophia spotted a trail leading out of the clearing. "Let's try that way."

⯐ ⯐ ⯐

That way led to the House of Fire, followed by the House of Snakes. Along the way, we picked up the head of one of Boatright's partners, the left foot of another and the upper body of a third. (They didn't belong to Boatright. Wrong size and in the case of the foot, wrong color.)

"This sucks," I said. "The Lords of Xibalba are going to work us to death."

Wearily, Sophia nodded. We were both a lot worse off than we'd been at the start. Leaving aside exhaustion, we'd picked up enough bruises and minor cuts to make us look like extras in a zombie movie. Judging from the number of body parts we'd collected so far, we weren't more than halfway there. I didn't think we could last long enough to finish. Not doing it this way.

I said as much. Sophia grimaced. "I don't disagree, but what's the alternative?"

"We need to take a fifteen-minute break anyway. Let me think about it while we're resting. There's got to be something."

It took me ten minutes to figure it out. Three minutes to explain the plan to Sophia. Five minutes to quell her doubts and objections.

Eighteen minutes all told, three minutes over my self-imposed time limit. Sue me. Watches don't work right in Hell anyway.

4

WHEN WE RE-ENTERED the first of the stone buildings—Greasy Grimy Godlet Guts House, I called it; 4-G for short—the Lords of Xibalba immediately started gibbering at us. They sounded angry to me; but then, they always sounded angry to me.

Sophia gibbered right back at them, and there was no doubt at all that her tone was hostile. Even the lords seemed to draw back a little from the fury in her voice.

"Guess I told them," she said with self-satisfaction, after her tirade wound down. She didn't bother to translate because I already knew the gist of what she'd been saying. It was my plan, after all.

You lousy bums are a bunch of cheats and chiselers and think you're pulling a fast one, but you just wait and see. You'll get your comeuppance. First, though, I have to sacrifice my loyal minion to regain my strength. Then I'll bring him back to life as good as new—and you just watch what happens next!

That was about the gist of it. Add maybe a thousand Xibalba equivalents of Anglo-Saxon four-letter words.

As soon as she was done, she pulled out her machete. I flopped to the ground and rolled over on my back. Playing the part of a loyal minion to perfection, if I say so myself.

Sophia looked down at me, her face tight with anxiety. She was definitely paler than usual, too. It was obvious despite her complexion.

I winked at her. "Relax. Pretend we're on our first date and I just made the crudest, grossest and most male chauvinist remark you ever heard. Hell, anyone ever heard."

That made her grin. That same sly grin I was getting really very fond of.

I held up the flash, and did the transformation. Once in were form, I did my best to stay on my back. I couldn't manage that very well, since the anatomy of a Deinonychus really isn't suited to a supine posture. But I got close enough for our purposes.

The machete came up. The machete came down. Right into my belly.

It hurt like you wouldn't believe. And I didn't stint on the howling and shrieking because that was pretty much *de rigeur* in this crowd.

Sophia must have been a butcher in a previous incarnation. Either that or—probably more likely—she just had a will of iron. It didn't take her more than a half a minute to hack her way into my abdomen, do the needed quick and crude surgery, and haul out a section of my intestines.

In dramatic terms, this would have worked better if she'd cut into my chest and taken out my heart. The problem is that therianthropes in beast form are more vulnerable than most people think. You don't *need* a silver bullet or blade to kill a were, it just makes things a lot easier and less chancy because you've got a metabolic poison working for you at the same time as whatever physical damage you've done. But enough physical damage in the right place will do the trick all by itself. Silver be damned. If you can stop a vital organ like a heart, a were will die.

But guts don't fall into that category. My intestinal tract was already healing. As long as I didn't transform back into human form until it was done, I'd survive. The process was very painful, but it really wasn't any more dangerous for me than a root canal.

I didn't think the Lords of Xibalba would know that, however. As deities went, these were some real lowbrows.

Sophia held the intestines high in her left hand, tilted her head, and squeezed some of the blood into her mouth. I don't think she hesitated more than a split-second, if she hesitated at all. Even in my pain and dizziness I was impressed.

That done, she cast the piece of gut aside as if it were so much trash and sprang to her feet. Before we'd entered the 4-G House, Sophia had taken a couple of the emergency stimulant pills she'd had in her supply kit. The chemicals would wear out in a few hours, at which point she'd be completely exhausted. But for those few hours, the pills gave her an enormous amount of energy.

It took about ten minutes for the effects to kick in. Right about now, in other words.

Oh, she was leaping and springing all over the place, gibbering with zeal and glee. To all outward appearances, a woman reborn. True, if you looked closely you'd still spot the bruises. But we'd figured the Lords of Xibalba wouldn't notice them at all. Why would something that looked like a chunk of shredded meat left out in the sun too long even think about a measly little bruise?

Me? I was already healed. The truth is, if I hadn't still been putting on the act of being at death's door, I'd have already been up and moving about in human form.

Eventually, Sophia left off her capering and came over to me. Then, she started waving the still-bloody machete around and chanting what sounded like really serious incantations. I found out later they were actually curry recipes, spoken in the Caribbean Hindi dialect found in Suriname and Trinidad.

When she came to the climactic finale of her peroration, she spread her hands wide and shouted "*Arise, reborn!*" in standard English. Then, for good measure, repeated it in Xibalba gibberish.

My cue. I rolled up onto my paws, Sophia used the flash, and a few seconds later I was back on my feet as a human being. To all outward appearances, completely unharmed.

Sophia started gibbering again. She'd now be telling them how we were going to charge back outside, knock down whatever other pitiful tests they had worked out for us, gather up the human parts we'd come for—boy oh boy are you guys screwed—and then come back and deal with them, dirty lousy conniving stinky cheaters that they were.

There was silence for a moment, when she finished. This was the critical moment. Would they fall for it . . . ? Or would they call our bluff?

If the latter, we'd have no choice but to return to our own universe with our mission unaccomplished. Or only partly accomplished, at best. We were simply too beat up to keep going for much longer. Being a therianthrope, I've got a lot more stamina than most people. But there are limits, even for weres. And Sophia would be completely out of gas, once the stimulants wore off.

I didn't think they'd be very smart, though, gods or not. You have to figure that a deity who embodies ulcers just isn't going to measure up intellectually against a god or goddess of wisdom. Or a reasonably bright twelve-year-old kid, for that matter.

And this was a mythos that took blood magic more seriously than any other the human race has ever produced. The thought of being completely revitalized by blood sacrifice would be incredibly attractive, even to godlings.

They started gibbering at Sophia again. She gibbered back, making a big show of appearing reluctant and hesitant. Their gibbering got more and more animated until they sounded downright frantic.

Finally, bowing her head, Sophia yielded to their demands. She pointed to the lord on the far left of the group and motioned it into the center of the chamber. The creature—this one was the god of lice, I think—squirmed and oozed its way forward.

Once it arrived in position, Sophia wagged her finger at it and gibbered sternly. She'd be telling the critter—and all the others listening—that it couldn't expect as quick a recovery as her loyal minion had made. Being as I was accustomed to the process and they weren't.

Gibber, gibber, gibber. The machete came up, came down. Since she had no idea which portion of the creature's horrid body held critical parts and which didn't, she just sawed away merrily once she got inside. After a minute or so, she hauled out a quivering chunk of who-knows-what-and-I-don't-want-to-know, and held it over the god's analog to a mouth. There was a bit of guesswork there too, but it didn't really matter because it was pretty obvious that the monster was already dead or as close to it as you could ask for.

Still, good theater is good theater. She took the time to squeeze out some blood—blood analog, rather; don't ask—into the gaping orifice before she cast it aside and summoned another of the lords to come forth.

Which, it did. Eagerly, in fact. She repeated the same process, again and again and again, allowing for the variations needed because no two Lords of Xibalba had the same form or anatomy.

It was a good thing she was on stimulants. That was more hacking and hewing of flesh—flesh analog, rather; really don't ask—than a meatpacker did in a full day's work.

Believe it or not, the Lords didn't get suspicious until there were only two left. But Sophia managed to sweet-talk—okay, sweet-gibber—one of them into undergoing the "revitalization" process. The one left finally realized that something was amiss and started putting up a fight. But this one was apparently the god of athlete's foot. A puny critter, when all was said and done. Measured, at least, by the standards of a two-hundred-and-forty-pound Deinonychus.

But I didn't eat the organs. Organ analogs, rather. Really really really don't ask. Even theropods have limits.

So ended the Lords of Xibalba. For a time, anyway. Given the underlying premises of this region of Hell, they'd almost certainly come back eventually. Reborn out of pain and suffering, so to speak. But that would take quite a while; far more time than we'd need to find and collect all the body parts we needed to bring back.

Then, we finally got a break. Within half an hour we came across the rest of Rick Boatright's body. It was wandering around the area with a gourd where the head used to be.

The gourd had facial features painted on. Someone, presumably a Lord of Xibalba or one of their agents, had even carved out a rough mouth.

The thing could talk, after a fashion. I couldn't understand a word it was saying, but Sophia got that look of intense concentration again and we were off to the races.

Boatright—or should I say, Boatright-analog?—led us to the rest of his party. Their pieces, rather. Eventually, we collected them all and brought them back to the clearing in front of the 4-G House.

Unfortunately, for all her quasi-magical linguistic powers, Sophia wasn't an actual witch. If she had been, she could probably have figured out a way to return to our own universe from where we were. As it was, neither of us knew any better way than to return to our arrival locus. The State Department's witches would be keeping watch at that location and would be ready to draw us back into our own universe.

That left the problem of how to haul the stuff there. Whole or in pieces, four human bodies still weigh the better part of half a ton. If it were absolutely necessary, I was strong enough that I could probably carry it all back to our arrival spot. But I sure didn't want to.

Fortunately, there was an obvious alternative. We had the makings for a travois and the dumb beast to haul it.

Rick Boatright. His body hadn't been harmed and with a gourd for a head, he wasn't likely to argue his way out the task.

He didn't even try. He just picked up the travois handles, lowered his gourd, and set off after us.

Along the way, we stopped at the pit to pick up Sophia's sidekick. By then, Ingemar had drunk all but a handful of the Four Hundred Boys under the table. (Figuratively speaking. They'd actually been drinking from troughs made out of—never mind. Don't ask.)

I wasn't surprised. Despite the nickname, "black elves" are actually a variety of dwarves. No one in their right mind gets into drinking contests with dwarves.

5

IT WAS SLOW GOING, of course. That would have been true over the best ground, much less this muck. But eventually we got there, the State Department's witches were indeed keeping a watch, and it wasn't long before we found ourselves back where we'd started.

"Oh, yuck!" screeched one of the witches, scurrying away from the travois.

Which . . . was a real mess. That part of the hell universe took death and dismemberment in stride, so to speak. That's the reason you could plant a gourd on the shoulders of a decapitated man, paint crude facial features on it, and expect it to walk around and even talk after a fashion.

But once we arrived back home, the conditions of our universe took over. The results were . . .

Unfortunate. Let's put it that way.

The first thing that happened was that the gourd rolled off Boatright's shoulders and Boatright's body collapsed to the floor. The gourd wound up underneath one of the chairs against the far wall and Boatright's body started spreading across the floor.

As did the body parts of all of his companions, oozing out of the travois. The technical phrase is *advanced and enhanced decomposition produced by infernal conditions.* Colloquially known as Quick Rot.

Too bad for Boatright and his crew, of course, but from the cold-blooded standpoint of *Realpolitik* the outcome was just as good as if we'd brought them back alive. Not even the harshest Scandinavian or Slavic deity would fault us for the demise of the Boatright party. Such beings took violent death as a matter of course. What mattered was whether honor, just retribution and clan vengeance was satisfied. Bringing back all the corpses and putting paid to the Lords of Xibalba did that just fine.

Sophia told me a few weeks later that human embassies touring the so-called "morally neutral" portions of the nether regions universe were being feted everywhere they went. Especially in those mythos which placed a premium on sneakiness, treachery, and guile. Which was just about all of them.

Our first date went well, I thought. Extremely well, in fact. But I was clearly in for a protracted period of emotional exercise and probable exhaustion. The new lady in my life is never at a loss for words.

Fortunately, I have a theropod's stamina.

AFTERWORD:

I'VE ALWAYS enjoyed Poul Anderson's stories, which I started reading as a teenager. And in his case, I enjoyed just about everything he wrote.

That's unusual. With most authors I enjoy, I really only like a portion of their work. One story or novel but not another; one series or setting, but not another. With Anderson, I can't think of one that I didn't enjoy.

So, when Gardner Dozois asked me to contribute to this anthology, I had to think about it. Not *whether* I'd contribute something—that would be a pleasure—but in which of Poul Anderson's many universes.

It finally came down to a choice between the world Anderson created in *Operation Chaos* and the one he created in *The High Crusade.* (*Three Hearts and Three Lions* was a close third.)

In the end, I opted for *Operation Chaos.* I enjoy *The High Crusade* every bit as much, as a story, but I'd find it somewhat awkward to write my own story in that setting. More precisely, I'd find it difficult to write a story in that setting that stayed true to Anderson's own vision of it. And doing so, I think, is important for this kind of anthology.

I never met Poul Anderson, and never corresponded with him. But it's obvious just from reading his work that he had a different view of the political history of the human race than I do. He had a soft spot in his heart for feudalism. It might be better to say, was attuned to what he saw as its advantages. You could see that not only in *The High Crusade* but in such stories as "No Truce With Kings." That went along with an elegiac attitude toward the grandeur of dying regimes, which of course runs all through his massive Dominic Flandry series.

Me? I think the best thing about the medieval period is that it's gone. And as much as I enjoyed each and every one of the Flandry stories, the truth is, deep down inside I was always rooting for the Merseians. The fading glories of the Terran Empire, so far as I was concerned, were just the trappings of another rotting, decadent empire. Pfui. History is littered with the cruddy things. Good riddance.

I'm sure Anderson and I would have spent a number of pleasant hours wrangling over the issues involved, if we'd ever met. Unfortunately, that can't happen now. And I wasn't comfortable at the idea of writing a story for an anthology commemorating an author that, no matter how subtly or indirectly, constituted a tacit critique of his work.

It's too bad, in a way. I would have had fun writing a story about the stalwart and quick-thinking alien peasantry rising up in rebellion against tyrannical and dirt-stupid human barons . . .

But, what the hell. I knew I'd have just as much fun writing about shapechangers and witches in the world of *Operation Chaos*—and *that* story was one I could write completely and fully in Poul Anderson's own spirit.

Such was my intent, at any rate. You've now just read the story, so you can decide for yourself if I succeeded or not.

—Eric Flint

TALES TOLD

by Astrid Anderson Bear

WHEN I WAS LITTLE, having Poul Anderson as my father meant that I had really good bedtime stories. Really, really good bedtime stories. Sometimes he'd read to me from *Grimm's Eventyr*, a book he probably had been read to as a child himself by his parents. It was a turn-of-the-nineth/twentieth-century-volume of Grimm's fairy tales written in Danish, lavishly illustrated with fine engravings. He would translate the stories on the fly, and the wonderfully, well, *grim* tales were a delight to me.

He'd also tell me made-up stories about a little girl named Astrid, and her adventures with her animal friends, based on my favorite stuffed animals. They traveled together in a purple submarine, on both land and water, and often outwitted a particularly dim highway patrolman. Decades later, he wrote a story for my son, Erik, in which a young boy named Erik encounters the same animals after he's been carried off by a mechanical alligator while the family is on a camping trip, and it ends with him promising to journey with them.

Eventually I outgrew bedtime stories, but I did discover the printed Anderson oeuvre. One summer when I was about eleven, we repainted my bedroom. The jumble of furniture and piles of possessions forced me to sleep on the spare bed in my father's study for a few days. Needing something to read in bed—I always read before sleep—I turned to the handy shelf of author's copies and picked out *Agent of the Terran Empire*. I was a big *Man from U.N.C.L.E.* fan at the time, so likely the idea of "agent of . . ." caught my eye. Now, I had been reading SF for some years at this time, starting with *Space Cat* by Ruthven Todd and *The Wonderful Flight to the Mushroom Planet* by Eleanor Cameron, and I do recall reading *Dune* as it came out in *Analog*, but somehow I hadn't gotten around to reading any of my father's work.

So I found myself plunged into the world of the dashing, clever, love-them-and-leave-them Dominic Flandry, determined warrior fighting against the forces of the Long Night. "Wow!" I remember thinking. "This stuff is pretty good!" And so I read all the Flandry there was, that summer, and moved on to such delights as the Hoka stories, the Time Patrol stories, *The High Crusade*, and so on.

As I became an adult, the books kept coming: *Tau Zero, Dancer from Atlantis, The Avatar, The Merman's Children, The Boat of a Million Years* . . . it went on and on. And then, in 2001, there was no more.

Characters don't die when an author does. They are still there in the books and stories, treading the well-worn paths of their adventures. But it is bitter-sweet to contemplate my dad's characters hoisting a mug together in the Old Phoenix Tavern, wishing they could have another outing in their home worlds.

This anthology, ably put together by Gardner Dozois, does just that. Here are tales of Dominic Flandry, Alianora, Manse Everard, Steven and Virginia Matuchek, and many others, told by inheritors to the story-telling mantle of Poul Anderson. It's been wonderful to read these stories as they've come in, and I think my dad would have enjoyed them, too. Thank you to Gardner for the idea, to Subterranean Press, and later Baen Books for publishing it, and to all the authors for coming out to play in *Poul Anderson's Worlds*.

THE FEY OF CLOUDMOOR
by Terry Brooks

***TERRY BROOKS** published his famous fantasy novel* The Sword of Shannara *in 1977, when it became the first work of fiction ever to appear on the* New York Times *Trade Paperback Bestseller List, where it remained for five months. He has published thirteen consecutive bestselling novels since. Brooks has subsequently explored the complex history of the* Shannara *universe, spanning hundreds of years, in more than a dozen novels—including* The Elfstones of Shannara, The Wishstones of Shannara, The First King of Shannara, The Druid of Shannara, The Elf Queen of Shannara, Isle Witch, *and* Jarka Rules*—as well as the three-volume* Genesis of Shannara *series, prequels to the original novel, and the tangentially related three-volume* Word and the Void *series. In addition, he's the author of the light-hearted six-volume* Magic Kingdom of Landover *series. His most recent books are the start of a new* Shannara *series,* Bearer of the Black Staff *and* The Measure of the Magic, *and a* Shannara *story published as a novella chapbook,* Indomitable. *Brooks lives with his wife in the Pacific Northwest and in Hawaii.*

Here he gives us another take, a most compelling one, on what happens after *the end of one of Poul Anderson's most famous stories, "The Queen of Air and Darkness."*

HE CAME OUT of the world of Men and their cities of steel and concrete in tatters, all scratched up and dirtied on the surface and broken and ripped apart inside. He carried what was left of his life in a blanket clutched to his breast, carefully shielding its contents from the sights and sounds and smells of the civilization that had ruined him and destroyed her. He thought of her all the time, but he couldn't make himself remember what she looked like anymore. He only knew how hard they had tried to find a way through the morass of their lives, choosing to share their misery but always searching to break free of their bonds.

Hard to do when nothing in your life is real and every day is a slog through dark and painful places that strip the skin from your soul.

When she died, they had been huddled in an alleyway in the darkest part of Christmas Landing, sheltered poorly in cardboard from a steady downpour that formed a small river only four feet away. They had scored early and resold what they had to get money for food and milk for Barraboo. They made a good choice for once, but came to regret it with night's hard descent and no means to soften the blow. She had been coughing badly for days and her breathing had worsened and all he knew to do was to stay with her. There were medical centers you could go to, but once they entered one of those places they might as well say goodbye to their baby. She might have gone alone, of course, but she was afraid to do that, as if making that choice would cost her the baby anyway.

As if in his desperation, he might choose to sell it.

As if in hers she might approve.

He stole some medicine off the shelves of a pharmacy, but it didn't seem to help her. Nothing did. She just kept coughing and wheezing, everything getting worse. He found her an old blanket in a garbage bin and wrapped her in that and then held her close against him to share his body heat. She was so cold, and she didn't look right. But she still held Barraboo and wouldn't let her go, and so he ended up holding them both.

But finally he fell asleep, even though he had told himself he wouldn't do so, and when he woke she was dead.

He never knew her real name. She never gave it to him. He called her Pearl because she was precious to him, and she seemed content enough with that. He told her his own name, though. "I'm Jimmy," he said. "Once upon a time, I was kidnapped by the Old Folk."

He told that to only a very few before her and then quit doing so because no one believed him. She probably didn't believe him either, but she came closer to looking as if she did than anyone else. She was like that. Even at her worst, when she was so strung out she could barely put a sentence together and started seeing things that weren't there, she could find a way to listen to him. She was tough, but she was vulnerable, too. She trusted people when she shouldn't have. She had faith in people who didn't deserve it. He was one of those people, he supposed. Mostly, he was good to her and took care of her and the baby and did little things to make her life more bearable when really it was Hell-on-Earth.

He thought all this and more as he rode the hovercraft out of Christmas Landing to Portolondon and his future. His and Barraboo's. For he was determined his daughter would have a future, even if Pearl didn't. He had fought against himself and his habit and his wasteful, reckless existence for too long. He had denied what he had known was true for too many years, persuaded by his mother and the rescuer she had hired to find him, made to believe when in his heart he knew he shouldn't.

Memories surfaced like half-remembered dreams of his time among the Old Folk, the Outlings. He had been only a boy, little more than a baby and so young he barely realized what was happening to him. Taken from his mother's camp by a pooka, carried to the realm of the Old Folk beyond Troll Scarp, seduced and made happy beyond anything he could have imagined possible, his mother all but forgotten, his world made over—there he had remained until his mother had come for him, finding him with a mother's persistence in the face of formidable odds, taking him back to his old life, telling him he would forget all this one day, it would seem a dream to him, he would become the man he was meant to be and not a pawn in the hands of creatures who could not know and would never care what it was he needed.

"The choices you make in this world should be your own and never another's," she had told him. "You should never be another's pawn."

He disembarked with his precious cargo still asleep and stood looking from the loading platform at the dingy buildings of the town. There was nothing here for him and never would be—not in this hardscrabble collection of housings and shelters, not in this scooped up mélange of humanity and waste. He wrinkled his nose at it, a measure of its ugliness given his own sad state. All of Roland was a backwater, light years away from the civilized universe—the back of beyond. It allowed for habitation—breathable air, drinkable water, sustainable crops—but not for much in the way of sunlight. He shivered in the cold, empty light of the season's perpetual night. Winterbirth, the pooka had called it. It gave him pause that he should remember this, but memory chose to keep what it wanted and discarded the rest. What mattered was how much attention you paid to memory and what you did with it as a consequence. For example, if you knew it was dangerous to go somewhere, you tried hard to remember not to go there again.

Conversely, if you remembered a place where you were happy—even if you were told you weren't and tried very hard to forget it and pretend that what you believed then to be happiness was in fact nothing of the sort—maybe you needed to make sure.

Especially when all other options had been exhausted and nothing of your life was good. Especially when you had more than yourself to worry about, and even in your drug-addicted rootless life you knew babies were pure and innocent and deserved better than what you could give them.

Especially when hope was all you had left to give.

He looked out across the buildings to the far north of Arctica, to the shimmer of the aurora and the green of mountains and valleys and mysteries that everyone knew were waiting there and no one wanted to discover.

No one except him.

"Hoah," a voice greeted. He looked down. A dwarf was standing right beside him, looking up from waist-high, bearded and twinkly-eyed, browned by weather and sun, wrinkled by age. "Need transport?"

He shook his head. "Got no money."

"You don't say? But there's other means to get to where you want to go, youngling. Have you a destination?"

He shrugged. "Out there, somewhere. A place I lived once a long time ago, when I was a boy. Beyond Troll Scarp."

"Scallywags! Flywinds! Danceabouts!" The old one shook his head.

"Don't no one wants to go there. They who is not to be named in places like this one live in places like that one, and they keep to themselves. Everyone knows. No one says."

"Old Folk. Outlings. The Fey. The Faerie Kind. There, I've said it for all those who won't. I don't fear them. I lived with them."

The old man cocked his head. "Yet came back to live among the humans who birthed you? That right? But from the look of you it didn't work out so well."

"Not so well."

"A baby and no mother?"

He looked at the old man sharply. The baby hadn't moved or cried out. He might have been carrying old clothes for all anyone could tell. But this old man knew better.

"The mother died. Pearl. She was like me, an addict. But not strong enough to survive it. The baby is all I have left."

"Ayah. Would you take her with you, then?" Jimmy didn't miss that he hadn't told the old man it was a girl. "Would you give her over to them for a drug that only they could give you?" the old man persisted. "Would you make a trade if it were offered."

He shook his head. "Not for anything. Not though I were the most desperate of men, and I am very much that. I am the lowest and saddest of all humans, and I would sell anything I could get my hands on to satisfy my need for even five minutes. But not Barraboo. Not my Pearl's child. I have not yet come to that."

The old man studied him as if to ascertain the truth of such a statement. Then he shrugged. "What then?"

Jimmy Cullen, he that was taken by a pooka once upon a time, smiled crookedly. "I have come to take her home."

The old man regarded him quizzically, all knitted brow and scrunched up mouth, before saying, "Well, then perhaps I can help you."

The old man led him through the city, down its teeming streets and byways, along its alleys and footpaths, past shops and offices, homes and apartments, flowers and filth way out to the ends of the northside and there to a stable. Inside the stable was a wagon and what appeared to be a reindeer and soon enough, on closer inspection, proved to be. The old man hauled the wagon out of the stable by himself, grunting with the effort but refusing Jimmy's help, harnessed the reindeer and got them aboard and settled.

"Bit of a ride ahead. If you need to sleep, put the small one in the necessaries box behind you—there, you see it, don't you? There's blankets to make her snug. What's your name again?"

"Jimmy Cullen," he said.

"I don't think so. But it will do until we reach Cloudmoor."

"What's yours?" Jimmy asked.

The old man shrugged. "Oh, I have all sorts of names. Widdershanks and Skitterfoot and Trundlestump, among others. But you can call me Ben."

They set out, the reindeer pulling the wagon and its load, leaving Portolondon and humankind, making for the Outway and Troll Scarp, solitary and far distant against the always-darkening horizon. No sun this time of year; no daylight, no day. It was night all the time or maybe twilight for a little while each day, and the people who lived in Arctica soon got used to the idea. Behind them, the Gulf of Polaris glimmered green-gray under skies brightened marginally by two small moons brought close together in their present orbits, both dwarfed by the dazzle of Charlemagne. Lights from the city lent their smudged and diffuse glow, but it did not penetrate the darkness far beyond the city. The Outway was its own space and kept its own presence and did not suffer intrusions from men or the consequences of their inventions.

"Better wrap up in this, Jimmy Cullen," the little man said after a time. He held a long switch in one hand for urging on their wagon's furry engine and he held the reins in the other, but he laid down the switch long enough to hand Jimmy a blanket. "It gets cold out here for those not born of the Outway, especially those come to us as you have, desperate and soul-bereft. Go on, now. Take it."

He did so, pulling it about him, altering it to give further warmth to Barraboo. She was beginning to stir and soon would cry. But he had nothing with which to feed her, neither food nor milk. He had love, but he knew you could not live on that alone or even survive on it. Ask Pearl. Tears flooded his eyes as he thought the name and the memories surfaced.

"How do you know the way?" he asked Ben, anxious to deflect the consequences of his awakened feelings.

"I just do," the other answered, and said nothing more.

"Are you one of them?" Jimmy asked, glancing over for a close look.

Ben shook his head. "Not I. But I know of them, and I do what I can for them. I am a link in what has become a very long chain."

"Were you looking for me back at the station? You seemed quick enough to find me. I don't look the sort that many would want to help. Only avoid. Yet you asked me right out. Do you know me? Have we met before and I've forgotten?"

The old man laughed softly, not in a mean-spirited way, but gentle and kind. "I know you well. Not by name, but by look."

"An addict, you mean?"

"A type, I mean."

"At the end of a rope. Lost to everything, including themselves. Wanderers in a world that wants nothing to do with them—only for them to go away and not come back. Rejects. Embarrassments."

Ben seemed to consider. "I would not use those words, Jimmy Cullen, although they are true enough in the world of humans. In your world, so many have no place. They are discarded and ignored and have no value, as you say. But how did they come to be that way? Have you asked yourself?"

He could not answer right away because he wasn't sure, couldn't remember, so he said nothing. Under him, the wagon rocked about and rolled along, and the night was sweet smelling and deep. He was already in a different place, away from the things that had ground him under their collective boot and left him shattered. The urge to take something to ease the hurt of it had diminished, and he wondered suddenly why that was. By now, he should have been screaming for his drug. By now, he should have been sweating and shaking and clawing at his skin. Barraboo would be howling, and he would be unable to stop her from doing so because his all-encompassing need blinded him to hers.

Something slid along the side of the wagon, a sheeting of dark mist, a skein of dust and shadows. He caught a glimpse of it and then it was gone, disappeared as quickly as water in dry earth. He blinked and looked out among the patches of firethorns and steelflowers, watched the shimmer of flitteries as they caught the light in small snatches of iridescence, smelled the brok and thought of how long it had been.

"I was just a boy when they took me," he said suddenly, keeping his voice low so that maybe only Ben could hear. "I was snatched away from my sleep out of an armed camp, right out of my mother's tent where she slept close beside me, and not a single soul knew until the morrow. Dogs were drugged, robot guards blinded and alarms bypassed. I might have been left to my fate and forgotten if not for my mother. My Barbro. She would not give me up to Old Folk or anything of flesh and blood. She came for me, all steel and fire and determination, carried in a war machine piloted by a detective from Christmas Landing who believed in the Old Folk but wanted to better understand what they were."

He inhaled and exhaled slowly. "They took me back, but I never really returned, never came all the way back. My body was theirs to mould, to shape as they felt they should, but my mind was lost. I heard the stories. You were never the same once the Fey had taken you. You could never be again what you were before. Maybe so. I tried to find my way in my mother's world, but couldn't. I was an outcast even to myself. Sweet Barbro tried to help me, but she never understood. She still doesn't. Drugs are an experience not so different from dreams. They take you somewhere you cannot otherwise be. They reshape your reality. When you need that to happen, when it's all you can think about, sometimes drugs are the best you can do."

The old man said nothing.

"She was Queen, then," Jimmy Cullen said quietly. "I remember her."

"Was?" Ben asked sharply. "Is that what you think?"

"I think I have to find out. I think I have to know if what was hers once still is." He shook his head, clearing away a few more of the cobwebs that filled it. "I think I have to see if any of it can still be mine. And Barraboo's."

"Hmmm," the old man hummed, as if considering the possibility.

The long switch touched the reindeer's flank softly, and their speed increased.

Barbro Engdahl Cullen pushed through the door to Chief Constable Dawson's office, ignoring the commands of the deputy at the front desk who ordered her to stop and was attempting futilely to reinforce his words with gestures of displeasure. She was decided on this meeting, and no one was going to stop it from happening, least of all a mere functionary. If Sherrinford had been there, he would have been readily admitted. But she was held in less esteem, and Eric was beyond coming through himself.

"Mrs. Cullen," the Chief Constable greeted her, rising from behind the inadequate protection of his desk. "I thought we settled all this in our phone conversation. Apparently, I was mistaken. You will not take no for an answer, will you?"

"I didn't back then, and I certainly won't now. Why don't you just resign yourself to this meeting and we can get this business over with."

He had grown older, as had she, put on weight and added wrinkles, as she had not, but she would have known him even out of uniform. She was no stranger to him either; the years had not diminished his memory of when she had come to him for help when Jimmy was stolen and he had rejected her. That led her to Eric and the search and recovery of Jimmy and ultimately to the beginnings of what would become the second true love of her life. Dawson must have thought himself shuck of her for good after that, yet here she was again.

"Back looking for your boy, you said." He shook his head at her. "I thought we were done with all that. He's grown now. I don't have any authority to go out looking for him just because he's wandered off again—even if it's back up there in that wilderness where you and Sherrinford found him before. Why isn't your husband out looking if you want him back?"

"Eric is dead, Chief Constable. He died last year. Otherwise, I wouldn't be here, asking you."

Dawson mopped his brow with his hand, slid the hand down his face and let it drop to his lap. "I'm sorry about that, Mrs. Cullen. I didn't know. I liked your husband. I admired his skill and his dedication to his work. But that doesn't change things. I still can't help you."

"You can't or you won't. He took my granddaughter. Little Barraboo. Not a year old. He left me a note so I wouldn't worry. I can't imagine what he was thinking. I want her back."

Dawson stared at her. "Where's her mother?"

"Dead. She was an addict, like my son. Both of them strung out all the time, five years of it. Maybe more. I can't be certain. It caught up with her just like it's going to catch up with him. Jimmy moved out and didn't stay in touch. Eric tracked him down several times, but he refused to come home. He said he wanted to go back to the Fey. He said that was his real home, those were his real people. Eric tried to tell him why he was wrong, but Jimmy wouldn't listen."

"Mrs. Cullen . . . "

"Let me finish." She was a big woman, and she leaned forward to lend emphasis to her size and the strength of her determination. "My son was never the same after we brought him back. Oh, maybe for a short time, but not after that. The Fey changed him. They seduced him with their magic and they changed him. Once I thought he would be all right after I found him and took him home again. Now I don't think so. I don't think I can ever get him back. But I will not let the Old Folk have my granddaughter, too! I will not stand for that!"

The Chief Constable shook his head. He was sweating, and he couldn't seem to look at her. "The Old Folk are just legend. You know this. In spite of Jimmy and what happened back—"

"Stop talking like that," she interrupted, waving him off. "You don't believe a word of it."

He stopped and looked up again. "What did the note say, Mrs. Cullen?"

"That Barraboo's mother was dead. No surprise in that. She was headed down that road long ago. They found her body two days after I made enough of a fuss about it they had to go looking. Jimmy's note said he was going home and he was taking Barraboo with him."

"Well, then, couldn't he have meant somewhere in Christmas Landing? Couldn't he have been talking about somewhere other than out here? How would he even get this far if he was an addict? Where would he get the money? Mrs. Cullen, don't you think it would be better just to wait awhile and see if he doesn't come back on his own? Going over Troll Scarp and into the Outway isn't something anyone wants to do."

She drew back from him, straightening herself. "This is twice you have refused to help me, Chief Constable. I don't know why I bother asking."

Dawson held her gaze. "I don't know why either, Mrs. Cullen."

She nodded. "Perhaps you know of someone I might hire? Not of Eric's caliber, but with a need for money and a bit less concern about trespassing in the lands of the Old Folk?"

He started to say he didn't, but she could tell when he hesitated that he was thinking better of it.

"I might know someone," he said finally.

When she left his office, she found a taxi and rode to the machine shop address he had given her, thinking through what she would say to Stip Quince. She could tell from the way Dawson gave out the information that this wasn't someone you would go to unless you wanted results and didn't care how you got them. Which was fine with her. She wasn't going back into Outway country a young woman searching for her missing baby boy. She was going back a full-grown woman and a grandmother, no longer frightened by much of anything and determined she would not be tricked or intimidated by the Fey.

She found herself humming the old song of Arvid the Ranger, recalling how she had sung it once for Sherrinford. It had a hold on her then, a grip that kept her wondering and doubting, a spell cast by words and music and her own superstitious nature. But that was all gone. The Fey were just an obstacle to be overcome. She had done it once with Eric; she could do it again with this man she was being sent to find.

Even though the Queen of Air and Darkness herself was waiting.

She regretted the thought the instant it was made. She wished she could take it back. She couldn't explain it; it just felt instantly wrong that she had permitted it to surface, even in the privacy of her thoughts.

Eric had once told her that the Old Folk had developed aspects of science different than those of humans, most particularly a command of telepathy born of a deeper understanding of their very different biological makeup. They might not have developed talents in chemistry and physics and mathematics as humans had, but what they had learned to do with telepathy far surpassed anything humans had achieved. Manipulation of human minds had allowed them to create a set of beliefs and superstitions that had helped keep the Old Folk safely isolated in the wilderness of their ancestral lands for centuries. It was only of late, and in part because of her deliberate intrusion, that this had changed and questions about their presence in the Outway had surfaced.

Sherrinford had always believed those questions would be thoroughly examined once they returned with Jimmy and made their report. What he had missed seeing was the stubborn refusal by the larger part of Arctica's inhabitants to want to challenge the old beliefs and superstitions. By now, with centuries gone, those beliefs and superstitions formed an integral part of their human makeup. It wasn't necessarily so that men wanted to discard them in favor of rational thought. There is in all humans a need to believe in things that cannot be seen or understood, a need to embrace the possibility there are things larger and more powerful than they are so they can find a way to accept that when these things happen they do not need to make sense of them or explain them away.

So it was that a general reluctance to look too closely into the possibility the Old Folk might be something other than what the legends said they were prevailed. Dawson sided with the majority; she could tell by his unwillingness to involve himself in her search for Jimmy and Barraboo. Sherrinford had once said that if she had looked closely at Dawson on the monitor during the long conversation the first time Jimmy went missing, she would have seen how afraid he was. Not much had changed. He believed in the Old Folk, Eric had insisted. You could see it in his eyes.

If Sherrinford had been with her this time, as well, he would have seen it in Dawson's eyes again.

Other inhabitants of Arctica, particularly those in Portolondon and even more so those in the Outway, would have experienced that same fear. Leave well enough alone, they would insist. Let the Old Folk be.

Well, she wasn't going to do any such thing. She wasn't afraid. She was angry.

Stip Quince turned out to be big and burley and curt, disinterested in anything but the money she was offering and time he would have to expend to accomplish what she was asking. His price was dear, but he was willing enough to trespass into the Outway.

"I've heard the stories, Mrs. Cullen," he told her as they finalized their arrangements. "Bunch of nonsense. Tales of things that go bump in the night fabricated by the locals—people who've been swallowing that nonsense whole since they were babes. Stories get passed down from one generation to the next. Gives people something to do at night when there's no video, no technology, nothing but blank walls and shadow shows to provide entertainment."

She pursed her lips. "I've seen them," she said quietly. "They're real enough."

He nodded. "So you've said. Didn't scare you off, did they? Here you are, ready to stand up to them once more. Nothing to it. When we go into Troll Scarp, we'll be going with armed men carrying weapons and riding in war machines. Whatever we come up against, we can disperse or eradicate. Same as you did before."

Folding his big hands on the top of the desk he had moved behind to write down her story, he leaned forward. "These are illiterate, uneducated, wild-eyed aborigines with a few cheap tricks at their disposal. Sure, it's their land and they know it better than we do. But they can't fight us and expect to win. They can't rely on the sorts of sophisticated arms and varied skills we can bring to bear. In the end, they'll turn and run and go back into hiding."

She believed him. The Old Folk were hopelessly outmatched against civilization no matter what they really were or how long they had occupied the Outway. They were Old Folk or Fey or Faerie kind, but ultimately they were barbarians unequipped to deal with civilization and the terrible strength its sciences would use against them. They were a remnant of a different time, and that time was gone.

She would have Barraboo and Jimmy back home within a week, and that would be the end it.

Jimmy Cullen lurched awake as the wagon bounced through a deep rut and juddered to a stop. He blinked and glanced over at Ben. The little man still held the reins to the hauling beast, but had put down the switch and from somewhere produced a bottle filled with milk.

"Give her this. She needs to eat."

Jimmy looked down at the blanket on his lap. Barraboo was gone.

"Back there in the necessaries box," the old man said. "I was worried you'd let her roll right off your lap after you fell asleep."

Jimmy reached back, found his daughter tucked away and squirming and brought her back into his lap, rewrapping her in the blanket. She was starting to fuss, but when he placed the bottle to her lips, nipple sliding into its accustomed place, she went quiet again.

"Why are we stopped?" he asked.

The old man pointed ahead. "Him."

The pooka flew out of the darkness in a rush of air and brightly colored feathers, gliding on widespread wings. Landing in front of the cart, he bounded swiftly to Jimmy's side on claw-footed legs that were muscular and strong.

"Ohoi, the boy who was a baby firstly returns anew!" he whistled. "Remember you Ayoch?"

Jimmy nodded. "I do. Even now."

"'Twas a long time gone. But time can be caught up and made over. I see you brought a present for me?"

He shook his head. "No, not for you. Not for anyone. I brought her to find a better life. Perhaps it will be your present to her."

Ayoch exchanged a glance with the driver. "Bold talk from a newly-come-back penitent. Are you intending to ask forgiveness of the Star Mother for bringing the wrath of your humankind upon the Fey? Or will you simply make your demands and hope we will forget about the before?"

The dwarf shook his head. "Leave him be. He has much to work through and don't need a pooka reminding him."

"How then of Mistherd and Shadow-of-a-Dream who were stripped of their lives and driven back into the unwelcoming arms of humankind? What of them whose lives you ruined, Black-Hearted Starling Boy?"

The pooka was hopping back and forth from one clawed foot to the other, and his short forearms were gesturing in anger and frustration. Jimmy looked at him and did not know what to say. He had done nothing to banish the lovers; they had left on their own, persuaded by Sherrinford they were living a lie and needed to go.

"What happened to them?" he asked tentatively.

Ayoch made a trilling sound and went still as stone. "The cities swallowed them."

"I did not knowingly cause this."

"But caused it nevertheless, I think."

"Who was it who stole me from my mother? Who was it who brought me to Cloudmoor?"

Ayoch started to make response, but then cocked his head and wheeled away. "Enow, this! She comes. Lady Sky walks the night. Bow you down, Witling."

Jimmy took the bottle from Barraboo's lips and handed it back to

Ben, instinctively cradling his daughter closer as the air before him assumed fresh darkness. He was not afraid. He was clear-headed and steady. The drugs had left his body, and the need for finding what he had come to find had taken their place.

Ayoch knelt, wings folded against his body, half-human face lowered in deference to her approach. Ben had wrapped the reins about the handle of the wagon brake and now his head was inclined, as well. Jimmy did not hesitate to do the same, feeling the presence of her coming envelop him with perfume of night lilies and cool whispers. His head dipped in recognition of Fey royalty, his strength of will surrendered.

"Welcome home, Shadow Walker," she whispered.

She was very tall and wrapped in starlight and flower shadow, her hair long and flowing and her face aglow with an inner light. She moved out of the darkness as if afloat, her feet not touching the earth, her robes trailing behind her in rippling folds, the Queen of Air and Darkness become. All around her, the world seemed to find fresh light, newly woken and wafting on the winterbirth breeze.

"Do you remember the name I gave you?" she asked.

Jimmy could not reply. He could not speak. He had so much to say, but in her presence he was struck dumb and left helpless and fragile. He knew she spoke to him, knew the name by which she called him, knew indeed it had been given him long ago and knew also he had forgotten it until now. Shadow Walker. He took a deep breath of the sweet night air and exhaled his relief and joy. She had come to collect him, to give him what he so desperately sought; she had come to take him home with her.

In response, he opened the blanket that swaddled Barraboo and held the baby forth. The Queen stood silently and looked upon the child for a long time before she turned to him again.

"You were that baby once, and just by being so and nothing more brought upon the Dwellers such misery."

"I am sorry. But I did not intend any of it. I was a child." He was crying suddenly, unable to help himself, overwhelmed by memories and emotions. "I would take it all back, if I could."

"Sometimes being a child is enough to stir up madness."

He felt his insides collapsing under the weight of failure's dark promise. "Please. If you would take me back, I wish you to take her, too. I wish her to have a home here with me. I have nowhere else for her to go. I am so afraid for her."

"A changeling child to become," the Queen replied. She went silent again, lost in thought, her perfect features still and composed. "Be it so, then. All must come to Worund's Barrow. All of the Dwellers of Carheddin and beyond. Bring them, Ayoch. Gather them together. We will sing and dance and celebrate winterbirth's gifts."

Ayoch bowed lower still, eyes averted.

She turned away, fading back into the darkness. "And there, Shadow Walker, we will wait for those who are certain to follow. But not as before, not as once we might have. See to it, Ayoch."

Her voice died away into the wind's gentle whisper and the night's soft folding.

"Yes, Moon Mistress," the pooka answered, never lifting his feathered head. But when she was well and truly gone, he stood erect and did a little dance.

"I leave you here," Ben announced abruptly, taking up the reins and switch again. "Climb down and go with the pooka, Jimmy Cullen that once you were."

"You won't come with us?" Jimmy asked, suddenly troubled by the idea. "After coming so far already?"

"Where you go is not meant for me. I've limits to what I can do for the Fey and limits to what they want me to do. I am done with you now and have others that need me. Ask about it, Shadow Walker. Ask her how her rule goes these days. You should know your address before you settle in for the duration."

He waited patiently until Jimmy had descended the sway-spring wagon seat for the solidity of the ground, Barraboo in arms, and then he jiggled the lines, clucked at the reindeer and turned the wagon about. In moments, he had disappeared into the darkness.

"Now we must skitter on, Shadow Walker." Ayoch was already looking off in the direction the Queen had gone.

"I'm ready," he answered, arms cradling Barraboo, soft and warm, against him.

"I wonder about that," the pooka said.

They set out on foot, crossing the countryside through the

darkness and shimmering white starlight, the twin moons already down or new—he could no longer remember which. Yet the air was not cold, and he found his travel comforting and pleasant. Barraboo had fallen back asleep, sated from her feeding. She was so light she was almost not there. Now and again, he had to look down to make sure he still held her.

Flitteries darted through the brok in small flashes, and kiss-me-never glimmered whitely in the starglow. Once he saw a crownbuck, majestic as it stood statue-still and watched him from a rise. He was surprised and pleased that he could remember names of things he hadn't seen in more than thirty years, things he had forgotten existed. Those names had all come back to him this night as he traveled into the Outway, and he could not help but think that it was a favorable sign. He was meant to be here. Coming with Barraboo, returning to where he had been happiest, finding his way towards a measure of sanity and health.

The sheeting of dark mist he had seen earlier while riding with the old man (what was his name again?) reappeared suddenly beside him. It floated there for a moment, and then the particles of darkness took form and Pearl was standing beside him, reborn into the world, clean and fresh and young.

He caught his breath and sobbed. "But you're dead, Pearl. You're not really here."

She laughed, a laugh he had so seldom heard her give when they were in the cities, and touched his arm. "Do you feel my fingers? Do you see how they hold you? I am real enough, Jimmy."

"But is it Fey magic . . . "

She leaned over and kissed him quickly on his cheek, and all doubts and fears vanished. "Let me see little Barraboo," she begged, taking a corner of the blanket in which the baby was wrapped and pulling it back. "Oh, such a wee thing. Look at her smile! You've taken such good care of her, Jimmy."

"I've missed you so much." He could barely see her for his tears. "Can you stay with me?"

"For awhile, but not forever. I can come back to you, though. I can visit you now and then."

"That would be enough," he managed. "Even if I know, even if I remember you aren't really . . . "

But she was already gone back into the ether, a skein of darkness dissipating in the wind.

A word came to him, unbidden. *Wraith.*

"There is nothing for you in the cities of men," Ayoch declared suddenly. He was bounding along, hopping and skipping, a very energetic pooka. "You've found that out for yourself, haven't you? Better the dreams of our world than the nightmares of your own."

"Better," he echoed.

"Though I have never gone to your world. Not for me the dreariness of such places. I know what it does from what I see in the eyes of those who live there when they happen out our way. They come to us, you know. So many, too. More all the time. Like you, they seek escape from what kills them. Slow or fast, it kills them all the same."

"It killed Pearl," he said.

The Pooka shrugged. "All in the past now for her."

They passed through Cloudmoor's rolling hills and leafy forests until all at once the pooka crowed loudly and said, "Hoah, I forget me! I must do as Lady Sky has bidden and gather the others for the celebration." He wheeled away, spread his wings wide and took to the air. "Farewell now, Shadow Walker!"

Jimmy blanched in terror. "Wait! How am I to find where I . . . ?"

"By walking!" Ayoch chirped, and then he was gone.

Jimmy stood bereft. He had never known where to go before coming here. Not ever. But since he had gotten this far and having no choice in the matter, he began to walk. The feel of the wind freshened him and the glow of the moons comforted him, and so he put one foot in front of the other, eager to reach his destination.

The war machines rumbled over Troll Scarp and into Cloudmoor on the midday, the night still enveloping and pervasive, the land of the Old Folk shadowed and striped with layers of roiling haze. Barbro sat in the first of the pair, next to Stip Quince and right behind the driver. She gave information when she could, but for the most part kept quiet. She remembered so little of this land after thirty years, and what she remembered was uncertain. Flashes of events recalled themselves, but mostly out of context and vague enough she couldn't trust them. What was hard and certain was the emotional weight of first losing and then finding little Jimmy coupled with her desperate, driving need to find him anew and little Barraboo with him. She was driven by her emotions, ruled by them, and she had set her mind on doing what was needed to regain control.

But there was room in her feelings for distaste, too. She didn't like Quince or his men and had to work hard to mask it. She disliked his bluster and arrogance. She disliked his aura of disdain and contempt. He was a hard and bitter veteran of personal and professional wars, and he had no use for people beyond making use of the opportunities they provided him. He was dismissive of her and Jimmy and their sad lives. He sneered openly at the idea of the Old Folk, his faith placed not in myths and shadows but in steel and explosives. He talked little, but when he said anything it was couched in terms of destruction and self-empowerment.

She regretted she had asked him for transport, and if she could have done so she would have turned him back around. But she could not abandon her search now. To do that now would mean giving up on her son and granddaughter.

But how will we find them, in any case? There are no signposts or road markers. There are not even roads. And I have no memory of the land. It is a mystery to me.

Yet Quince seemed undeterred, forging ahead, his machines rolling over firethorn and brok, crushing grasses and flowers, and scaring off birds and animals alike, intruders not equipped to apologize. His confidence in himself and his men and machines was daunting, so she held her tongue and waited to see what would happen.

When they stopped finally to rest and eat, the darkness enfolding and unbroken by either Roland's moons or the distant stars, she felt the weight of her life press down on her and wished she had done so many things differently. She ate and drank and then walked away from the men to look out into the forested hills and be alone. She breathed the air and was reminded suddenly of a moment out of the past.

For there was Jimmy, standing at the edge of the trees, not far away from her, holding his daughter in his arms, smiling. He put a finger to his lips and beckoned her over to him. She glanced back, saw no one paying attention to her, and without further thought went to him.

"Mrs. Cullen!" she heard Quince call to her as she followed her son into the trees. "Get back here!"

But she was already gone.

Stip Quince wasted little time calling his men back to their war machines, closing down the hatches and firing up the engines. Seconds was all it took. The armored ATVs surged forward, giving chase. Quince could not understand what that woman thought she was doing, but it would be the last time she would be allowed more than an arm's length away. Had she seen something? Had she been summoned and he not heard?

The war machines pushed into the woods, finding their way between sparse clumps of trees, rocking over ridges and down gullies, pushing ahead. There was no sign of Mrs. Cullen, but Quince had seen where she went and knew they would catch up to her quickly enough.

Ahead, atop a rise, something moved in the gloom. Figures, all of different sizes and shapes, some huge and lumbering, some ethereal and others winged and crouched over. The ones he was looking for. He smiled and using the intercom, directed the attack. The war machines closed on their targets, weapons loaded and ready. Quince had decided to see how the enemy reacted before opening fire on them. He wanted to scare them off first, hopefully back to wherever they had the woman's son and granddaughter. In case that failed, he would use the nets to trap one or two and make his prisoners take him to their lair. It wouldn't be hard once he used the drugs and prods on them.

Once he had Mrs. Cullen and the son and granddaughter safely in hand, he would decide whether to eradicate these troublesome creatures or simply frighten them badly enough that they would flee the country and all this Old Folk nonsense would be ended.

As the war machines crested the rise, the creatures they pursued already fled into the trees, Quince saw the yawning black chasm directly ahead of them, only yards away, invisible until you were right on top of it. He shouted into the intercom in warning, screaming, "Stop, stop!" But it was too late. The momentum of the vehicles carried both over the edge and into the void.

The war machines tumbled away and the occupants were consumed by their own dark fears.

◈ ◈ ◈

Barbro turned from Jimmy and the baby when she heard the screams, wondering at their source. When she turned back again, they were gone. She looked around wildly, frantic to find them, a tall ethereal figure emerged from the trees. The Queen of Air and Darkness was luminous in her robes of northlights and garlands of snowy kiss-me-never, and a wondrous glow that mimicked the aurora and the rainbows after storms and the dreams of men unrealized and lost shown about her head.

"Welcome home, Wanderfoot," she greeted, her voice as soft as kitten fur and a child's wishes on a star.

Without knowing why, Barbro inclined her head slightly in recognition that she was in the presence of royalty. "I had forgotten you called me that."

"Once I did, when you were asked to stay and fled."

She shook her head in despair. "I was frightened. I wanted my child back."

The Queen looked off into the distance. "So you took him. But now he is here again."

"With Barraboo. My grandchild. I have come for them."

"With war machines and weapons and the men who use them. Very like another time."

Barbro was crying. "A terrible mistake. I am sorry."

Ayoch appeared, knelt and bowed to the Queen. "All finished, Lady Moon. Gone into the void, men and machines and their dark intent." He glanced at Barbro. "We were not ready for such wickedness last time. But we can learn and we can adapt and we can be what we need to be. Cockatoo!"

His crowing rattled her further. "I want to see my son and granddaughter. Please let me."

"So you can take them away again? So you can return them to lives you believe will be so much better than ours? To drugs that will numb their minds and steal their wits away? To drinks and potions and pills that will give them no relief? To soul-stealing machines that will offer alternative realities both sterile and empty? To links to millions of words spoken by faceless voices in meaningless interactions that will never allow for the touch of flesh and offer only the pretense of true caring? Why, Wanderfoot? So they can be lost in your cities and your teeming numbers and never know loving and never live unfettered or experience the bliss of wildflowers and close companionships or escape the futility in everything they do? You would give them air filled with ashes and dust and tar and poison to breathe? You would give them concrete roads and stone block walls that rise up and crush their spirit and steal their hopes? You would see them rot from within and without; you would witness them suffer crushing defeats of rejection and indifference? All that, would you give them, even knowing they would never be made happy and fulfilled in the way they would if they remained here with me!"

The Queen's words floated on the air, spoken in a voice absent of disdain and filled only with sadness. "Come hither with me, Wanderfoot," she whispered. "Come see what you ask your child and grandchild to forgo."

She stepped away and Barbro followed obediently, even though aware that what she would be shown was false trickery of the sort that Sherrinford had warned so strongly against.

Ayoch bounded along beside her, his half-human face wreathed in a smile. "You are so sure in your wrongness. Listen to her!"

In an emerald glade washed with the glow of firethorn and starlight she found Jimmy and Barraboo. Jimmy had the baby lying on a blanket spread wide, her chubby legs kicking and her curious arms reaching for the kiss-me-never vine he dangled over her. There seemed no pretenses about what she was seeing, no false coloring of the landscape or dressing up of father and daughter, no attempt at recreating fiction to approximate truth. Barbro understood. What she was seeing was real and present. The Queen had learned a few things since last they met.

"This is what you would take from them," the Queen declared. "This is what you would steal away."

"No," Barbro whispered. "This is what I would give them back again. This is what I would help them find. You would let them see this, but I would let them live it. You would give them this only in their minds, and I would give them this for real. Or at least I would try. Not all would be good and kind, but much of it would. Better they see life for what it is than for what pretense would make it seem. Here, there is only the latter."

She was astonished she had spoken so boldly, but the Queen

simply gave a small wave of her hand. "You cannot give them what they need, Wanderfoot. You cannot even help them find it. Not in your world of decay and disintegration. Your failure is already written in the books of your history. Your race is doomed. The Fey are the future as they have been the past."

Barbro straightened and faced her squarely. "Please let me have them," she said. "They belong with me."

The Queen regarded her, tall and regal and distant, her eyes depthless pools of far-seeing and secrets untold. "You will sleep with us tonight and on the morrow I will decide."

Then she was gone, faded back into the night. Ayoch was beside her at once. "Your bed is here, mother love," he said, gesturing vaguely.

She glanced back to where she had seen Jimmy and Barraboo, but they were gone. She felt a sudden, intense weariness steal over her. She could not seem to help herself; she had to sleep.

"Lead me," she told the pooka, and so he did.

When she woke again, Jimmy was sitting next to her. He had a worn and world-weary look, but there was intensity in his blue eyes that suggested the strength of his resolve. She could tell at once that he had decided on his course of action. She sat up quickly. "Will you come away with me?" she asked.

He shook his head. "I will remain here. I came to find a new life. I need to leave behind the old one. It stole so much away from me I cannot go back to it. Here, I have a chance to find peace and contentment of the sort I knew as a child."

"It is not real," she insisted.

"It is real enough for me, and more real than the life I was living. I do not believe in that world anymore. I hope I can come to believe in this one."

"And Barraboo? Will you keep here with you or give her to me?"

She had missed seeing the bundle lying by his side. He reached down and picked up the baby and handed it to her. "Give her what you think she needs and if that fails, bring her back to me. I will be waiting."

She was in tears as she took the baby and held it to her. Its dark little face peeked out at her with eyes that at once seemed both young and innocent and old and wise. "Oh, Jimmy," she whispered.

He leaned over and kissed her cheek. "Think of me now and then, Mother. Remember how happy I am."

He led her down to where a wagon hitched to a reindeer and driven by an old man barely taller than her waist and wrinkled with age waited. Jimmy helped her climb aboard, taking care to wrap her and Barraboo in a blanket. He smiled a knowing smile at the driver, who gave back a small nod, and then the little man clucked at the reindeer and lightly touched one flank with the switch and the wagon and its occupants rumbled off into the haze.

Morgarel the wraith waited until they were gone too far for the woman to look back and see him changing back and then walked over to Ayoch. The pooka was staring off into the distant, watching after Wanderfoot and her new baby with sharp, far-seeing eyes.

"Hoah," the pooka said softly. "How long do you give her?"

"Before she comes again? I have no sense of that. Years, I hope. The changeling needs time to adapt and learn."

"Which she will do. She is clever, that one. And how clever our Mistress, too." He looked behind the wraith. "And what of them?"

Jimmy Cullen sat rocking Barraboo as he fed her milk from a goatskin and sang softly to her. Other creatures hovered at the edges of shadows that didn't quite reach to where father and daughter shared a life and watched intently.

"He will live awhile longer and then pass. She will become one of us. The Queen ordains."

"Mother Sky sees our future thusly. We will be them and so make them us, and in the end ours shall be the way." Ayoch cocked his head and hopped once in a sort of minor celebration. "Cockatoo!" he crowed.

The cry echoed over Cloudmoor and into the future.

AFTERWORD:

I BEGAN READING science fiction and fantasy in middle school—right about 1956—although there was little enough of the latter being written at that time and most of the kids I knew were reading the former. It was the beginning of the age of space travel and Sputnik and travels to the moon, and that was what every kid I knew was reading about. I shouldn't say "kids" but rather "boys" because very few girls I knew had found their way to that sort of fiction yet.

Anyway, among those writers whose works I read and admired—while still in my burgeoning wannabe-professiona-writer mode—was Poul Anderson. In those days, I wasn't reading or particularly interested in fantasy. I was strictly a science fiction kid, with peripheral leanings towards adventure stories (*Boy's Life* and the like), so my favorite stories by Poul tended to fall along those lines.

But I remember one that didn't. I read "The Queen of Air and Darkness" right after it came out in one of the science fiction magazines, and I was captivated by it. When I was asked to contribute to this anthology, it was the first story I thought of. It always felt to me as if there were more to the story, as if the telling of it wasn't finished. What happened afterwards to the Queen and the Old Folks of Cloudmoor and Carheddin? Was that really the end of them when Sherrinford took back Jimmy Cullen? Could they really have been so easily dispatched?

I felt a certain trepidation in trying to make those determinations for Poul. "The Queen of Air and Darkness" had won both the Hugo and Nebula and has enthralled Poul Anderson readers for decades. Who was I to mess with an icon and his art? But my marching orders were clear—I was to take something from Poul's astounding body of work and build on it. I have tried to do that here.

I met Poul Anderson once, years ago now, at a family gathering at Astrid and Greg's home. I can no longer remember the occasion. He was quiet and unassuming and had about him the grandfatherly look I see in myself these days when I look in the mirror. I said hello and told him how much I admired his work. I have no idea if he knew who I was or what I did. He didn't say, and I didn't ask. It didn't matter. What mattered was how it made me feel. Writers form links in an endless chain, one influencing another in a crucial, necessary rite of interaction and succession, ultimately so we may be inspired and our craft may evolve.

Poul Anderson was one who did that for me.

In spades.

—Terry Brooks

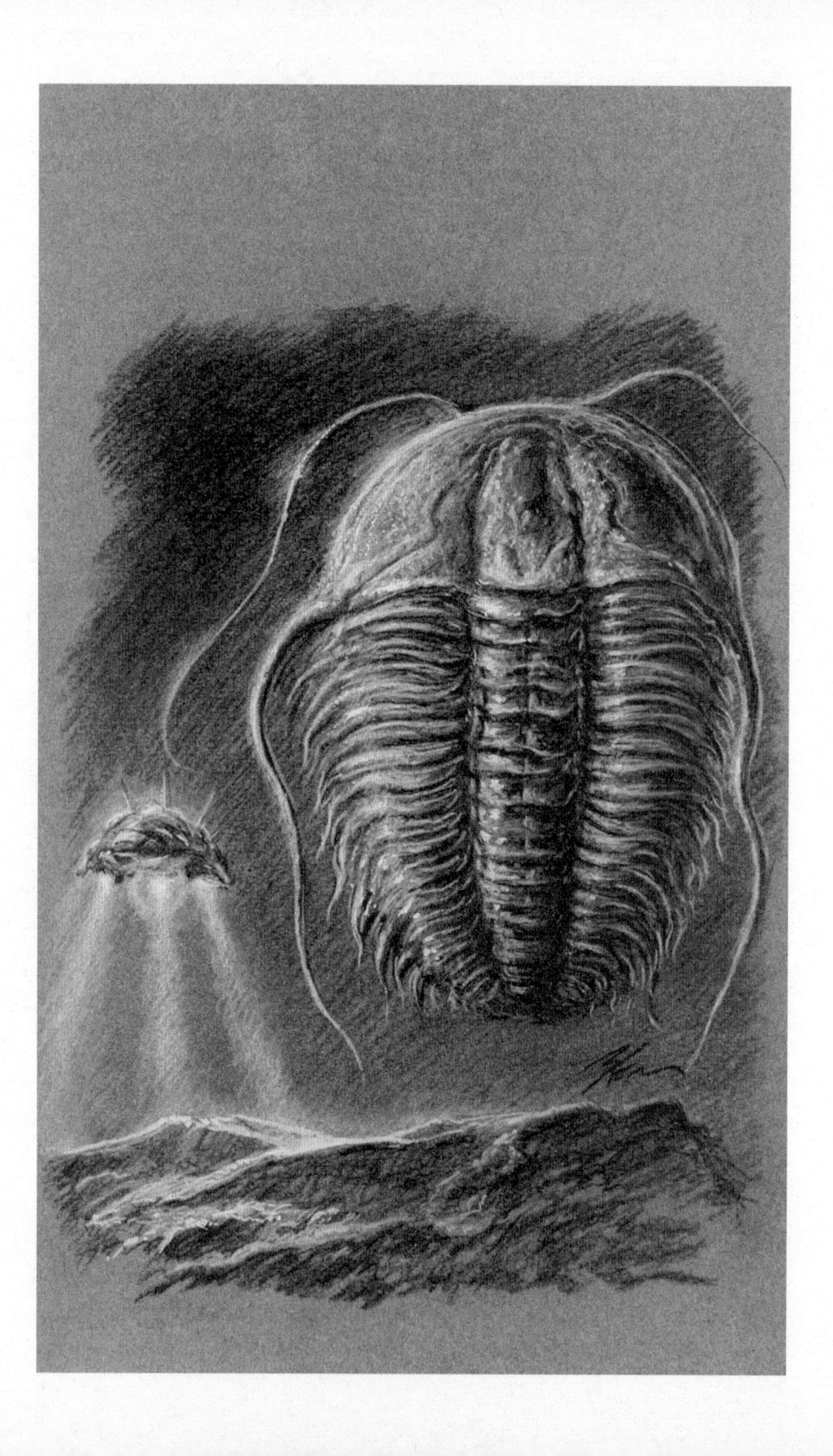

CHRISTMAS IN GONDWANALAND

by Robert Silverberg

***ROBERT SILVERBERG** is one of the most famous SF writers of modern times, with dozens of novels, anthologies, and collections to his credit. As both writer and editor (he was editor of the original anthology series* New Dimensions, *perhaps the most acclaimed anthology series of its era), Silverberg was one of the most influential figures of the Post New Wave era of the '70s, and continues to be at the forefront of the field to this very day, having won a total of five Nebula Awards and four Hugo Awards, plus SFWA's prestigious Grand Master Award.*

His novels include the acclaimed Dying Inside, Lord Valentine's Castle, The Book of Skulls, Downward to the Earth, Tower of Glass, Son of Man, Nightwings, The World Inside, Born With The Dead, Shadrach In The Furnace, Thorns, Up the Line, The Man in the Maze, Tom O' Bedlam, Star of Gypsies, At Winter's End, The Face of the Waters, Kingdoms of the Wall, Hot Sky at Morning, The Alien Years, Lord Prestimion, Mountains of Majipoor; *two novel-length expansions of famous Isaac Asimov stories,* Nightfall *and* The Ugly Little Boy; The Long Way Home, *and the mosaic novel,* Roma Eterna. *Recently published were a reprint of an early novel,* The Planet Killers; *a novel omnibus,* The Chalice of Death; *and a mystery novel,* Blood on the Mink. *His collections include* Unfamiliar Territory, Capricorn Games, Majipoor Chronicles, The Best of Robert Silverberg, At The

Conglomeroid Cocktail Party, Beyond the Safe Zone, *six massive retrospective collections*—To Be Continued: The Collected Stories of Robert Silverberg, Volume 1; To the Dark Star: The Collected Stories of Robert Silverberg, Volume 2; Something Wild is Loose: The Collected Stories of Robert Silverberg, Volume 3; Trips: The Collected Stories of Robert Silverberg, Volume 4; The Palace at Midnight: The Collected Stories of Robert Silverberg, Volume 5; Multiples: The Collected Stories of Robert Silverberg, Volume 6; We Are For the Dark: the Collected Stories of Robert Silverberg, Volume 7; Hot Times in Magma City: the Collected Stories of Robert Silverberg, Volume 8—*as well as collections* Phases of the Moon: Stories from Six Decades, *and two collections of early work*, In the Beginning and Hunt the Space-Witch!. *His reprint anthologies are far too numerous to list here, but include* The Science Fiction Hall of Fame, Volume One *and the distinguished* Alpha *series, among dozens of others. He lives with his wife, writer Karen Haber, in Oakland, California.*

Here's another fast-moving Time Patrol story in which Manse Everard faces his most desperate challenge—keeping the Time Patrol itself from never having existed in the first place.

"YOU WANT me to go *where*?" Manse Everard asked, astounded. He was not a man who astounded easily, not after all he had seen and done, the multitude of places and times he had visited.

"Gondwanaland," said Daniel Ben-Eytan again.

Everard stared. "Right. That's what I thought you said. But there isn't any history to protect in Gondwanaland, except for the Founding Convocation itself, I suppose. There's hardly even any *pre*-history. Therefore the Patrol has no work to do there, unless somebody has it in mind to launch an attack on the whole fabric of the time-line from start to—"

"Exactly," Ben-Eytan said. "The whole fabric of the time-line is what's in jeopardy."

It was much too lovely a spring day in Paris to be hearing stuff like this, Everard thought. He had been there two days, now, laying the groundwork for what was going to be one of the great furloughs of his life—a couple of weeks in the glorious 1920s Paris of Hemingway and Fitzgerald, Picasso and Gertrude Stein, Josephine Baker and James Joyce. He had found himself a pleasant room in a lovely little hotel in the rue Jacob and had spent the two days strolling along the banks of the nearby Seine, checking out restaurants, peering admiringly at Notre Dame upstream and the Eiffel Tower down the other way, and reconnoitering all the famous Left Bank literary landmarks, the Dome and the Coupole and the Brasserie Lipp and the Deux Magots. Now he was sitting at one of the streetfront tables of the Café de Flore on the Boulevard Saint-Germain, enjoying a mid-afternoon Pernod and watching the passing parade. The day was warm and mild, the sky a perfect blue, the air like champagne. Wanda Tamberley would be joining him here tomorrow, and the anticipatory thought of her slender blonde loveliness filled him with delight. Despite the gap of nearly forty years in their ages—and in the Patrol, how could you ever keep track of how old you really were, what with the constant skipping back and forth in time and the Danellian longevity treatments on top of that?—he had never known a woman who excited him as much as Wanda did, and that was saying quite a lot.

And then, out of the blue in the most literal way, materializing out of that champagne air, Daniel Ben-Eytan had descended upon him to tell him to forget about Paris, to forget about his holiday with Wanda, to forget about everything cheerful and pleasant and delightful, and get himself back in time some X or Y hundred million years to save the world from chaos.

Everard peered sourly at the stocky, swarthy little twenty-eighth-century Israeli. "You know, you could just as easily have dropped in on me at the *end* of my vacation instead of the beginning, Daniel. We would still be able to manage whatever it is that needs to be managed back there in the Cambrian. Showing up when you did is very goddamned linear-minded of you."

"Yes, I suppose it is," said Ben-Eytan complacently. He was like that. "But this is when I arrived, didn't I? They told me to get to work. And here I am. I'm mixed up in this thing, too. Also Spallanzani, Nakamura, Gonzalez. You know who I mean, yes? Yes. Of course you do. They're already waiting at the headquarters that's been set up. I wasn't joking when I said the time-line's in jeopardy. For Christ's sake, Manse, buy me a drink, will you?"

"Very well. For Christ's sake, if not for yours, you irritating bastard." Everard signalled to a waiter. Just then a big, handsome kid with a little dark mustache, a youngster who might easily have been Hemingway, walked by down the street, no more than ten feet from where Everard and Eytan were sitting. He was accompanied by a smaller, fair-haired young man who quite probably was Scott Fitzgerald, and they were very deep in what looked like an exceedingly serious discussion. The Paris of the lost generation, yes! Everything right here within reach. Everard could gladly have throttled Ben-Eytan. Everard was something like sixty years old, or so he believed, and had been in the Patrol some thirty biochronological years, and he felt he was entitled to a little down-time.

This trip was supposed to have been something special. His annoyance at having it interrupted like this had nothing to do with dereliction of duty. No matter when he took off from his current location in time on this new job, he'd arrive in the remote past at the proper point. But the Israeli, annoyingly, had tracked him down right here and now. To tell them that he must go—*where*? And to do *what*?

"Gondwanaland's a big place, and it covers a lot of time. Which region, which area?"

"Alpha Point," said Ben-Eytan.

Everard gasped. "The Founding Convocation!"

"Indeed. What else?" They had been speaking in English, but suddenly the Israeli switched to Temporal, the synthetic language used by the Patrol, which could handle the grammatical niceties of time travel much more rationally. "A terrorist group out of A.D. 9999 or thereabouts—we aren't really sure of their point of origin, but it's somewhere early in the period of the Chorite Heresiarchy—has/will/had gone back to the start and wiped out the entire Founding Convocation. The Patrol's extinct. It has been/will be snuffed out right at the source. Decapitated. Its best people removed at one stroke. Not only is it gone, it never existed."

Suddenly Lost Generation Paris and all its delights, and the impending additional delight of Wanda's arrival there, lost all appeal. The world turned colorless and two-dimensional, and Manse Everard sat numb, stunned, disbelieving what he had just heard. For a long moment he was unable to speak.

The waiter arrived with Ben-Eytan's drink, absinthe on the rocks. As usual, Ben-Eytan had gone Everard one better, one-upping his Pernod with the stronger drink.

"Santé," he said cheerfully, tilting his glass toward Everard.

"All right, already. Tell me," Everard said.

"I can show you. We can hover over the camp—we don't want to get too close; the toxic cloud may still be potent—and you can see for yourself. Everybody dead. All the organizers, Saltonstall, Schmidt, Kipminu, Greyl, Gan-Sekkant, every big name you can think of, gone with the trilobites, every last one of them, right on the second day of the Convocation."

"The Danellians, too?"

"No, not them, so far as we can tell. They got themselves out ahead of the attack, or maybe they arranged not to show up in the first place. They always know how to look after themselves."

"Naturally."

"But everyone else who was there—gone. And the Patrol with them."

Everard felt the Boulevard Saint-Germain heaving and swirling around him. This was dizzying news indeed. Incomprehensible, in fact.

Slowly he said, "If the Patrol's gone, if it's all been unhappened, then what are we doing here in Paris? Would Paris still exist, minus the Patrol? We *ourselves* shouldn't still exist. Wouldn't the elimination of the Patrol eliminate every single intervention that the Patrol has carried out since it was organized? Which would include everything along the time-line that led to my existence, and yours. Shouldn't the history of the world be screwed up fifty thousand different ways?"

His own intervention to keep Carthage from destroying Rome, for example. His interference with the Mongol conquest of North America in the thirteenth-century. His rescue of Tom Nomura's girlfriend back in the early Pliocene, just as the Mediterranean was getting born. Dozens, scores, hundreds of other missions—all negated? And he was just one of who knew how many Patrolmen who wandered the corridors of time seeing to it that the multitudes of malevolent time-travelers who delighted in meddling with the stream of history were prevented from doing the harm that they so eagerly yearned to do. If there never had been any Patrol, if all that harm had/would have taken place after all, the stream of history became a nightmarish cataract of chaotic contradictions, forever mutable, completely at the indifferent mercy of anyone who could lay his hands on a timecycle.

His head was spinning.

Ben-Eytan said, "The time-line is fluid, Manse. But also very resilient. You know that. Come on, man. By now you should live by Aleph-sub-Aleph logic with every breath you take."

"Even so—"

"We exist and we don't exist. You know that. Everything's conditional, until the unhappening of the Convocation is permanently unhappened. And it will be. The time-line isn't screwed up because you—and I, and Nakamura, and Gonzalez, and Spallanzani—are going to/have already fixed it. The Danellians know that, because they know everything, and so they know that we are the team that will/has done the job, and therefore they have chosen us to go back and repair things. So be it. And here I am. Here be we. Q.E.D."

The good old deterministic loop, Everard thought. It will be done because it has been done because it must be done. He felt even dizzier. This was not the first time that Everard had been caught up in the paradoxical circularities of a universe in which two-way travel through time was freely and easily possible. He had long before given up trying to account for the higher mysteries of it, though he still could not resist the temptation to pick and gnaw at some of the stranger aspects.

Still, it didn't sound right. It was too glib. It sounded like the sort of thing that an instructor would tell a bothersome trainee at the Academy to shut him up when it was necessary to get on with the day's lesson. If the Patrol had been removed at its point of origin in the Cambrian, how could anything, anything at all, still be remotely the same here in twentieth-century Paris? That bothered him very much.

And also Ben-Eytan's bland assurance that the problem wasn't manifesting itself here because they had/would have already fixed it. So far as he was concerned, they *hadn't* fixed it, not yet. Even when he tried to think it through in Temporal he knew something had to be fishy. Some part of his mind wanted to protest that *nothing* in the time-flow ever was permanent, that no event could ever be permanently and finally unhappened. Ben-Eytan had just said so himself. *The time-line is fluid. Everything's conditional.* Whatever they went back to Gondwanaland to fix could just as quickly be unfixed all over again. The past, as that great writer Faulkner had so shrewdly said, is never dead. It's not even past, he'd said. How, then, Everard asked himself, could he be certain of his own continued existence, and of the continued existence of everything he held to be real?

And then, another problem—

"It seems to me," he said, "that if the Founding Convocation gets snuffed out, and all our succeeding interventions with them, then the Danellians themselves get snuffed out too, a million years or however long it is up from here. So how can they send us back to fix things?"

"They don't get snuffed out, Manse. Remember, even in the pre-Patrol world the Danellians did evolve, a million or so years from now, even though there hadn't been any Time Patrol in the original time-line and time travel had existed for hundreds of thousands of years before they appeared."

Everard nodded. That was one of the things that one preferred not to think too hard about. "Yes. Of course. Founding the Patrol was a major intervention, the kind you and I would be prohibited from enacting. It could be argued that it was done purely for the sake of saving their own superior skins."

"Precisely. One way or another, the evolutionary trend of humanity culminates in the Danellians. They will emerge no matter what. That's not the issue. We believe that the stated purpose of the Patrol is to insure the preservation of the 'real' time-line—and in our more cynical moments we like to tell ourselves that our whole organization was created just to make sure that everything occurs in proper fashion throughout all of history in order to bring them into existence. But the fact seems to be that even without the Patrol they will emerge onto the scene in due course anyway."

"So their existence is assured, no matter what permutations get built into the history that precedes them?"

"Apparently so."

"Then why did/do they bother to flange up the Patrol at all, if their own existence isn't what's at risk?"

The Israeli shrugged. "I have no idea. I have more sense than to waste precious brain cells trying to understand the minds of the Danellians. They're so far beyond us in development that it's pointless even to try."

Yes, Everard thought. They may be our descendants, but we are to them as mice are to humans, or even less, and mice don't try to figure out the motivations of the humans whose abodes they share.

He knew that. He had had his own occasional encounters with Danellians over the years.

He said, "All right. Let's take it as a given that their destiny-line survives this terrorist attack. Shall we stipulate that what worries them is that everything between us and them will be hopelessly messed up—which, I suppose, must have some effect on their own precious existences too? Or are they simply displaying compassion for a million years' worth of their primitive forebears?"

"Have you ever noticed the Danellians being guilty of compassion before?" Ben-Eytan asked. "Or even revealing any understanding of the concept?"

"I may have a higher opinion of Danellian nature than you do, Dan. I'm sure I do."

"You probably do, Manse. You do have that big streak of sincerity running right down your middle. But, be that as it may, they want things put back to rights at Alpha Point, and they have chosen the five of us to fix the damage, and the fact that you and I are sitting here talking right now is proof that we will succeed in doing so."

"And do we survive the process of working the fix?"

"We have no way of knowing," Ben-Eytan said. "And they're certainly not going to tell us." He drained the last of his absinthe in one macho gulp. "Do you want to have a look at the disaster scene, now?"

With Ben-Eytan piloting the time-hopper and Everard sitting in the saddle beside him, they made the spatio-temporal leap that even now, with so many decades of Patrol service under his belt, Everard had not ceased to think of as miraculous, and emerged instantaneously in the Cambrian Epoch. The infinitely unfamiliar Earth of half a billion years prior to Hemingway's Paris lay spread out beneath them. Everard had never gone back this far in time before. He had never had any reason to. Of course Alpha Point itself was off limits to members of the Patrol who had not been part of the Founding Convocation. And he had not been invited to the Convocation. Only the supremes of the supreme had been there, and he did not flatter himself by thinking that he had ever been one of those. And it would hardly be appropriate for lesser members of the Patrol to show up simply as tourists who wanted to peer at this legendary event. It would almost be like being present at the Creation—not the creation of the world, of course, but the creation of the Time Patrol, an event far from trivial in its own right. To drop in simply to gawk while that was going on would be, well, *wrong*.

But Gondwanaland had endured as a unified continent for hundreds of millions of years apart from the brief existence of Alpha Point, and he had not dropped in on any of those years either, or even considered it, even though he was free to go anywhere he chose, or almost anywhere, when he was off duty. Perhaps a geologist might want to go there, but Everard, though he had been many things in a long and highly unusual life, had never been a geologist. And with all the vastness of the time-line available to him as an Unattached agent, he had chosen far more enticing places to visit on his furloughs: the Rome of Augustus, for example, or the London of Shakespeare. Or Paris in the days of the Lost Generation.

There was nothing here but an immense bleakness. What would be the seven continents of the world he knew lay huddled into a single supercontinental blob. Geologists of later eras had given it various names—Pangaea, Rodinia, Pannotia—but for convenience's sake the Patrol knew it simply as Gondwanaland, which was what the first twentieth-century advocates of the theory of continental drift had called it. It was not an enticing place. There was a faintly nostril-nipping strangeness about the air, an odd chemical smell that must mean a slightly different mix of oxygen and nitrogen than Everard was accustomed to. A terrible silence prevailed, a silence so intense that it hammered at the eardrums. The sky was gray. The sea that lapped the shores of the great monocontinent was gray. The land itself was a barren raw shield of glossy rock that looked as though it had congealed from the primal magma about a day and a half ago, broken only by occasional sparse patches of newly formed soil and a few zones of green moss. Land life had not yet evolved. This world was the kingdom of the trilobites and of other primordial seagoing creatures even stranger than they were.

That was why the Danellians had chosen to stage the Founding Convocation of the Time Patrol here. The time-stream was resilient to change, yes, capable of being deflected from its course only by the mightiest of interventions. But, even so, it was always best to avoid interference with the flow. A time when the world was still largely uninhabited was the ideal choice. So when the Danellians, those greatly evolved descendants of humanity, had decided to meet the challenge to the integrity of the time-stream that the invention of time travel had posed, they had picked Gondwanaland as the site of the very first organizing session of the Time Patrol that would police the many thousands of centuries preceding their own advent and keep everything happening as it should. Once it had been founded the Patrol had/would establish its training school in the Oligocene, a humid place where sabertooths and titanotheres roamed the virgin forests. That was far enough back in the past so that its presence would cause no significant time-flow perturbations. When he was undergoing his training at the Academy Everard had thought it was mighty impressive to be living twenty million years back in what in those days he still thought of as "the past." But from the perspective of Gondwanaland, the Oligocene was only the day before yesterday. There were no sabertooths here, no titanotheres—not even mosquitoes, yet.

Everard let his eyes roam across that rocky shield, out to sea and back again. Everything was so gray that it was all but impossible to see where the sky ended and the sea began. It was the sort of soulless emptiness that would make the Sahara look like the Garden of Eden.

Ben-Eytan said, "Some day, I understand, what you see below us is going to be Buenos Aires. Just for the fun of it, I ran a date calculation. This is January 15, Umpty Hundred Billion B.C. The Convocation began about three weeks ago—on the first day of Hanukkah, I am happy to tell you. Also Christmas Day. It happens that Hanukkah and Christmas come out on the same day in Umpty Hundred Billion B.C."

Everard ignored all that. He had never found Ben-Eytan's brand of humor particularly amusing. Perhaps it was for some sin in a past life that the Patrol had assigned him to work so frequently with the Israeli. That little job in Kublai Khan's Peking, and the one in San Francisco in '06, and that very nasty business in Sarajevo, where Ben-Eytan had gleefully seen to it that the Archduke Franz Ferdinand was assassinated on schedule—

"This is all new to me, this far back," Everard said. "Have you ever seen it before?"

"Not until this mission," Ben-Eytan said. "Nasty, isn't it? But there's Alpha Point right below us. I can go lower, but I'm not sure how much lower is safe, at least with us not shielded. There's probably still some hovering remnant of the toxic cloud that wiped everybody out."

"They're really all dead?"

"All," Ben-Eytan said.

The hopper swooped downward. The buildings of Alpha Point began to take form out of the gray mists below.

Everard was surprised to see how flimsy everything looked. The Academy in the Oligocene, which he had visited many times, first as a trainee and then as an instructor, was a substantial place of long, low, solidly constructed buildings, as well it should have been, considering that it had been intended to remain in service for half a million years. But everything about this much older place, this Alpha Point that was the *fons et origo* of the Time Patrol, cried out its temporary nature. It had been needed only for a few weeks, after all. The Danellians had been content to fling up a large insubstantial-looking dome on the hump of a promontory overlooking the torpid leaden-hued sea, and to surround it with a semicircle of tent-like plastic blisters that were, Everard supposed, the residential quarters for the fifty or sixty greatest leaders of the Time Patrol throughout its long history, all of whom had been swooped up from their various eras by the Danellians and assembled back here at the dawn of time to be told about the organization to which they were going to devote their entire lives.

Ben-Eytan nudged the hopper's controls. They moved around the periphery of the base, out toward the sea and back to the land again, taking in the entire site. There was no sign of life anywhere about, though Everard did see, and shuddered at the sight, three motionless figures sprawled face-down in different parts of the camp.

"Those ones were caught by the cloud as they were moving between buildings," Ben-Eytan said. "The others are all inside the main building, but they're just as dead. We've sent people in to have a look. It's not something you really want to see." To Everard, just then, the Boulevard Saint-Germain and its cafes seemed impossibly remote. The whole world did: the world that had/would contain Galileo and Einstein, Mozart and Bach, the Roman Empire and the Third Reich, the Athens of Socrates and the London of Shakespeare, the Taj Mahal, the Great Wall of China, and everything else. Suddenly all that lay beyond some impenetrable barrier, not just because the unthinkable treeless bleakness that stretched off to the horizon here was so unutterably alien of aspect, though it was, but because he knew that if the horrific event that had taken place in this convocation-hall at the dawn of time was allowed actually to happen, everything that he thought of as the history of the world was going to be altered. *Everything*. He was here at one end of the time-line and the Danellians were at the other, and, with the Time Patrol removed from the equation, everything in between, subject now to a million years of manipulation by vandals equipped with time machines and completely deficient when it came to consciences, was/would be/has been subject to incomprehensible transformation and retransformation.

"Had enough?" Ben-Eytan said, after Everard had been silent a long while. "I could risk going a little lower, I guess."

"No. No. Not necessary. Do we know how it was done?"

"We think we do," said the Israeli. "Let's go find the others and we'll fill you in on what we believe we understand."

Team headquarters, Everard discovered when the hopper made its next leap, had been established in the Prague of October, 1910. It was plainly the early twentieth-century—he could tell that by the black-and-gold Hapsburg banners fluttering everywhere and the quaint, clumsy automobiles he saw puttering around Wenceslas Square—but those were greatly outnumbered by horse-drawn carriages, many of them splendid baroque vehicles redolent of the glorious empire of the Kaiser Franz Joseph that was due for complete and heartbreaking ruination in another few years. This was the district known as the New Town, Everard recalled, dating back to the fourteenth century or so but mostly constructed much more recently than that. The handsome Art Nouveau buildings that Everard remembered from a visit here not long after the fall of Communism, badly in need of cleaning then but still beautiful, looked brand new now. Some were still under construction. Their tawny, ornately bedecked facades were shining brightly in the autumn sunlight. After his brief visit to Gondwanaland this was heavenly. It almost atoned for the untimely way Ben-Eytan had ripped him out of Paris.

Ben-Eytan must have been the one who picked this as team headquarters, Everard thought. He loved this era, the last great flourish of European civilization before the disasters of the twentieth-century fell upon it, the two great wars and the two great totalitarian tyrannies. Everard remembered the Israeli's innocent joy as they had wandered around Sarajevo in '14 waiting for the doomed Archduke's motorcade to arrive. The architecture had interested him far more than the cataclysmic moment of history that they were about to help bring into being. So Ben-Eytan was probably the leader of the group, and had chosen his favorite epoch for their base. His privilege, Everard conceded. As team leader, he had the option to put the headquarters anywhere he liked.

The operations center itself was right on the square, an upstairs suite at the Grand Hotel Europa, a splendid building with an intricately decorated facade and stained glass windows and astounding fin-de-siecle ornamentation, that could not have been more than three or four years old.

"I hardly need to make introductions, do I?" Ben-Eytan said, gesturing to the three agents waiting within.

"Hardly," said Everard.

He was the only twentieth-century agent in the group, but he was used to that. Most of the Patrol had birthtimes well uptime of his own, because it was so difficult to recruit people from pre-industrial cultures, where not only the concept of "time machine" but even just the concept of "machine" itself was a difficult thing for them to swallow, and sometimes "time" as well. So he was accustomed to rubbing shoulders with agents who had been born hundreds—or, in some cases, many thousands—of years after himself.

And he had worked with all three of these before. Elio Gonzalez was the closest in era of origin to him, practically his birth-time contemporary: late twenty-first-century, and would have been a member of the generation of his great-great-grandchildren, Everard supposed, if only he had bothered to get married in the late 1940s when he was done with his military service and had started siring children somewhere in the mid-1950s. But of course he hadn't done that, since the Time Patrol had swept him up into its service in 1954, and although it was not uncommon for agents to marry and have families, the fast and furious time-hopping nature of Everard's career as an Unattached agent of the Patrol had led him to believe he would be a bad bet for that sort of life, and he had wisely obeyed his intuition there. Doubtless he had scattered plenty of offspring up and down the time-line in his travels, since he had never felt it important to be a model of chastity and in some cases it had been downright obligatory for him to get involved with members of the opposite sex in the course of carrying out an assignment. But of the identity and location in time of those children he knew nothing, and preferred it that way.

Gonzalez, at least, was probably no descendant of his, for Everard was big and burly and dark-haired, a powerfully built man somewhat ponderous of affect, and Elio, the product of a genetic mix that had strayed very far from the Latino original from which he derived his name, was a wiry little fair-haired man, blue-eyed, with an athlete's slippery suppleness. He rose and gave Everard a quick open-handed slap of greeting. They had had two tours of duty together, one in the England of William II, the other in the Rome of Constantine the Great.

Hideko Nakamura was even farther from his ancestral genes than Gonzalez was. Not much remained in him of the DNA carried by the Nakamuras of Yokohama or Kyoto or whatever the starting point of his family had been. His name was authentically Japanese, yes, but that was just a sentimental retro touch, the sort of thing that post-Japanese like Nakamura liked to go in for. He was of the eightieth-century, six thousand years into the era of genetic manipulation, and although he could readily enough be recognized as human even by a twentieth-century agent like Everard, he would surely startle anyone of that century less familiar with mankind's future than Everard was, and probably would be hunted down and destroyed as a monster in most earlier eras, a fact that limited his usefulness as an agent to a certain degree. Two arms, two legs, and a head, yes, five fingers on each hand, five toes on each foot, but after that the resemblance ended. His features were minimalistic in design, mere hints at lips and nose and chin, though his eyes were Japanese enough, the epicanthic fold deliberately, playfully, enhanced. His skin was thick and dark and glossy, like a seal's. He was graceful beyond belief, moving with a wriggling serpentine ease as though he had no bones, though of course he did, just as any serpent did. But when he crossed the room to touch fingertips to Everard's he seemed to float or swim rather than to walk.

"How good to see you again," he said softly. Their paths had crossed in Nakamura's own century, when Everard had journeyed far uptime to play a necessary role in a job that required a visiting representative of primitive man.

Lora Spallanzani, the fifth member of the team, belonged to the twenty-fourth-century in point of birthtime, or so Everard recalled, but there was nothing particularly futuristic-looking about her physical appearance. Drop her down in Milan or Rome of 1966 and she would pass without comment: tall, with long waves of thick black hair, and buxom in the way that Italian women seemed to specialize in. Only a certain unfeminine glint about her eyes and a certain tight-set look about her lips might signal to the street-lounger of 1966 Milan or Rome that trying any of the traditional mid-century pinching stuff with her might prove to be a seriously bad idea. She and Everard had worked briefly together on Galileo's rescue from that pious but misguided lynch mob, thus sparing the great man to complete his work on sunspots that proved Copernicus right and Ptolemy wrong about the movements of the Earth. "Well, here we are," said Ben-Eytan redundantly. He spoke in Temporal, the only language the five of them had in common. "For the benefit of Unattached Agent Everard, shall we review what we already know, before we set out to do something about it?"

He nodded toward Lora Spallanzani.

"*Ebbene. La situazione e—ah, scusi.*" Everard smiled. Sometimes, jumping hastily from one location to another, it wasn't all that easy to switch languages. Continuing in Temporal, she said, looking straight at Everard, "What we know is that an attack has been/will be made upon the Founding Convocation at Alpha Point, that all the Founders have been/will be assassinated by the timed release of some unknown poison, and that the Patrol as we understand it was thereby obliterated in its initial moment. Therefore it becomes necessary—"

"Wait a minute," Everard said. "I asked Daniel about this in Paris, but I didn't get a satisfactory answer. If we're now in a continuum where there's never been a Patrol, where there's been unfettered temporal manipulation ever since time travel came into being, why are twentieth-century Paris and Prague still pretty much as I remember them, and, for that matter, why are we ourselves still around? Hasn't the act of wiping out Alpha Point seen to it that everything since the beginning of time been thoroughly messed up by all the foolish or venal or just plain vicious interventions that various time travelers have inflicted on the time-stream—and by the absence of the Patrol to set things to rights?"

Spallanzani looked baffled. "Hasn't Daniel told you about Time Patrol II?"

"Time Patrol II?" Now it was Everard's turn to blink in confusion. "What's *that*?"

"I will explain," said Ben-Eytan quickly, and at least he had the good grace to blush beneath his swarthy Mediterranean hide.

It was exactly as Everard had thought. Ben-Eytan, always sublimely indifferent to the distinction between ends and means, had simply not bothered to tell him, back in Paris, that the Danellians had brought a *second* Time Patrol into existence after the extermination of the original leadership cadre at Alpha Point. Just as an instructor at the Academy does not want to overload a trainee all at once with the complex details of Patrol life, Ben-Eytan had blithely skipped around one highly significant part of the story, the one that explained everything else, in fact. And Everard felt like a goose for not having worked it out for himself in the first stunned moments after Ben-Eytan had presented himself to him on the Boulevard Saint-Michel. He realized that the news about Alpha Point must have left him too shaken, just then, to think the thing through the way a veteran Unattached agent like himself should have been able to do.

There had been a gap of over a million years between the development of time travel by the group known as the Nine in 19352 A.D. and the advent of the superhuman humans who called themselves the Danellians, far away in uptime. During that long span of time, originally, no Time Patrol had existed. Nevertheless, though, through luck, divine providence, the sheer resilience of the time-stream, or some other factor unknown to mortal minds, the highly evolved Danellians had come into being despite whatever monkey business unrestricted time-travelers had managed to indulge in along the time-line. Or, even, *because* of all that monkey business. Nobody could ever know.

But, as though fearing that some retroactive intervention of gigantic scope might scramble history behind them so thoroughly that they themselves would never evolve, the Danellians had created the Time Patrol, an organization devoted to tracking down and correcting every deviation from the "true" course of world events, by which they meant the course of events that culminated in the emergence of the Danellians. Danellian representatives, using one disguise or another to shield the eyes of their primitive ancestors from their full godlike magnificence, had jumped back across the eons, selecting an extraordinary group of men and women whose birthtimes ranged from the nineteenth-century A.D. to the year 25,000 or so, and hoisting the whole crew of them back to a hastily rigged camp in Cambrian Gondwanaland so that they could, jointly, sweat out a set of rules and regulations by which the Patrol would be governed.

Spallanzani's eyes met Everard's. "*Capito?*"

"*Si,*" he said. All this was kindergarten stuff to him.

"Now," she continued, reverting to Temporal, "there has been this fatal attack on the Founding Convocation. The Patrol is removed from existence at its outset. Our world still emerges from the matrix of time, and mostly it emerges the same way as before. Mostly. There surely are differences, but we five still get born. Most people do. Not all."

Most, Everard thought. *Not all.* Wanda, for example? Does she get born? No telling. He couldn't very well go jumping up to the late twentieth century to find out, not right now.

Spallanzani was still speaking. "This colossal intervention has occurred. The Patrol does not get organized. The time-stream is at menace. The Danellians cannot have that. So what do they do? They do the whole job all over again. They gather an entirely different set of Founders—or perhaps even some of the same ones; at this moment we have no way of knowing that—and carry them off to some new Alpha Point, maybe in some other part of Gondwanaland at some other time, or maybe on Mars or Venus, for all we know, and that group works out the governing principles of what we here are calling Time Patrol II. That Patrol proceeds to carry out all the fixes that the original Patrol did, or enough of them, at any rate, so that the world descending from the time-line of the second Alpha Point closely resembles the one that we used to live in."

Used to live in.

Even in Temporal, she had said that in the past tense. Instantly Everard grasped the full situation.

"So the five of us have been pinched off into a pocket continuum of our own," he said. "The whole original Patrol has. As you say, our world-line descends from the Alpha Point Convocation; the Patrol that's running things now descends from a different one. We are outsiders, strangers, perhaps even regarded as enemies who need to be located and removed. And so—" he glared at Ben-Eytan now—"so what we have come together to save is not the unaltered flow of the greater time-stream, but our *personal* time-stream. The post-Cambrian, post-Alpha Point world has/will develop right on schedule, with the one little difference that we ourselves have no place in that world. Other people are doing our work there, maybe even more competently than we've been doing it. We're just a little bunch of free-floating entities who have no official affiliation with what passes for the Time Patrol here. Which is to say what we are trying to save is our own skins by means of whatever intervention we've assembled here to plan. Doesn't all of that sound just a bit ugly to you? Destroying an entire continuum just so we remain okay?"

There was a long stinging silence in the room.

"You put it a little broadly, Manse," Gonzalez said, finally. "You make it sound as though this is nothing but an exercise in pure selfishness on the part of one little group of agents. I remind you that we are sworn to maintain the integrity of the time-stream. There's been an unauthorized intervention at Alpha Point and it's our job to put things to rights. Period. No moral hesitations about the effects that a cancel will have on the continuum that's canceled. That we personally will be beneficiaries of what we do is irrelevant. The fact that a second Time Patrol has been called into being and is doing our job right now, might even be doing it better than we've been doing, is none of our affair. From our point of view, that Time Patrol exists in a parallel world that must not be allowed to remain in existence. You know that, Manse. Despite what you've just said to us, you know that in your bones."

He paused to let that sink in. It did, and his face flamed with recognition of how wrong he was. He had rarely ever been so wrong throughout his career as he was right now.

Everard realized that in his anger he had grossly overstated the case. Gonzalez was correct: it was not their business to decide which of several possible time-streams might be the ideal one. There was only *one* ideal time-stream, and that was the one they had sworn to defend.

Everard looked from Gonzalez to Spallanzani, from Spallanzani to Nakamura, from Nakamura to Ben-Eytan.

"Yes. I see it now," he said. "Yes, of course. You bastard, Dan, why didn't you tell me all this in Paris?"

"I didn't think I needed to. All I had to do was tell you that there was an important assignment waiting for you. You could pick up the secondary details later on."

"Secondary details? Wiping out a whole time-stream with its own Time Patrol is *secondary*?"

"Please, Manse," Nakamura said. "Now that you know the full background story there's no point quibbling over Daniel's tactics. We need to get on with things. Are you with us or aren't you, Manse?"

He hesitated only a fraction of an instant. Then he signaled his assent with a quick, impatient gesture. "Of course I am."

"As we expected you would be. Lora, will you continue?"

"*Certo.*" Speaking directly to Everard, she said, "We think the terrorists came from near the beginning of the period of the Chorite Heresiarchy, but we aren't sure of that. It doesn't matter. We can't search all of time for them. They are nihilists of some sort, unscrupulous adventurers, criminals, madmen—whatever. Perhaps something like the Exaltationists or the Neldorians, but they seem to be a different group not previously known to us. What they have done, apparently, is to establish a base camp just prior to the founding of Alpha Point—and no, we haven't located it yet—and make microleaps into the Convocation site itself, staying no more than a millisecond or so, just long enough to stick capsules of some sort of toxic substance or substances here and there around the camp. When everything is properly planted, they make a second series of microleaps and touch off the poison bombs, evidently doing it in a specific order of release so that the final capsule potentiates all the others and floods the entire Alpha Point area with lethal gas. At least, that's our theory at the moment. We don't have all the information. But Hideko and Daniel have made several visits to Alpha Point in the period just prior to the moment of the attack—Christmas Day is the name we use as our reference point for the time of the attack—and have detected the barely detectable blurs of these microleaps."

Everard raised his eyebrows at that. Ben-Eytan had risked going there at the very time of the attack, risking the chance that he would land right in the middle of a cloud of poison gas? He may be a bastard, Everard thought, but at least he's a brave one.

"And now?" he asked.

It was Ben-Eytan who answered. "Now we get going on the next round of surveillance, and hope to come up with a better picture of what the enemy is up to. And then we get about the job of doing the fix."

"While praying that we don't attract the attention of Time Patrol II while we go about our work," Everard said.

"Good point, Manse. If Patrol II detects the signs of a counter-intervention, it will surely try to counter that. It has to. Its life, the life of its entire time-line, is at stake."

Everard closed his eyes for a moment. The whole thing was like a dream, a very bad dream, the attack on Alpha Point and now this talk of two contending Time Patrols battling each other to protect the existence of their particular time-lines. He wanted to think that everything would come out all right, that the true and proper Patrol would triumph, that the correct fix would happen because everything he remembered of his long career in the Patrol had such vivid reality in his mind that he could not help believing that it had really happened. Therefore the fix had been successful, the enemy intervention had been canceled—the thing thus legitimizing itself in his mind, the universe saved by a wonderful act of circularity.

Hogwash, he told himself.

The thing wasn't done until it was done. His vivid memories of a full, useful life in the Patrol meant nothing at all. Neither did the scars he bore. Those scars, those memories, were, at the moment, effects without causes, free-floating artifacts of a past life in a continuum whose current existence was merely conditional. Everything, he knew, having learned it over and over again with every job he had ever done, was subject to constant revision. Everything was in need of constant protection, unceasing vigilance.

The past is never dead. It's not even past.

There was a lot of work ahead for them.

"When do we get started?" Everard asked.

◈ ◈ ◈

Because it was his first surveillance trip to Alpha Point he went with a companion, Elio Gonzalez, and Gonzalez would do the driving. They clambered into the two-seat hopper and a moment later they were half a billion years back in the past, sitting in the sky three thousand feet above Alpha Point.

The air up here was cool but not chilly, springtime-cool, and the view, far out to the horizon, was one of emptiness, emptiness, and more emptiness. The sun, dimly visible through the gray murk, seemed mysteriously *wrong*, the color not quite the proper shade of yellow, its apparent diameter different also. The only indication that life had ever existed on this planet was the puny scattering of buildings clustered higgledy-piggledy immediately below.

"What we're doing," Gonzalez said, "is trying to bracket the time of the attack. We think we have zero hour pegged by now—noon on Christmas Day, give or take a few seconds, so far as we know. That still needs full confirmation, though. We're much less certain about the time of the planting of the devices. So we're exploring the two or three days leading up to the event."

"We can't just go back to their base camp and cut things off right there?"

"That would be a permissible intervention in an extreme situation like this, I guess," Gonzalez conceded. "The trouble is, we don't know where their base camp is. It could be anywhere. If they've located it in early geological history, it would be located, we assume, somewhere on this continent and somewhere in the last billion years or so, because any earlier than that and atmospheric conditions are so much different on Earth that they'd need to mess around with special breathing equipment. Probably they wouldn't have bothered with that. But we can't go searching through a billion years and across an area that's essentially the size of the entire world to find the camp. And for all we know they don't even have a base camp in ancient times, but are simply hopping back and forth from their own era, whenever that is."

"Those are phrases I keep hearing: 'so far as we know' and 'probably' and 'we assume' and 'for all we know.' We don't seem actually to know very much."

"Not yet," said Gonzalez.

Everard stared down at the strikingly unimpressive string of shoddy-looking buildings within which the governing structure of the Time Patrol had been/would/might be forged. Today, Gonzalez had told him, was December 24 on the Gondwandaland calendar that their little Patrol group had flanged up. Ben-Eytan's counter-intervention group had already established that the lethal capsules had been planted at various times on Christmas Eve and that the attackers had returned in some significantly sequential order the next day to detonate them. They had been designed, Ben-Eytan said, to undergo biodegrading immediately upon detonation, so that there was no evidence left afterward.

Through his optical Everard saw people moving around down there, going from one building to another. The Founders, they were. The awesome demigods who had brought the Patrol into being. All of them destined to die the next day, unless—unless—

Incredible. Inconceivable. The actual Founders, going about the task of creating the Time Patrol, altogether unaware of the dark fate that was cruising toward them.

"Won't they notice us up here?" he asked.

"Only if they look, Manse. And they won't look. There aren't any birdwatchers in the group, you know, and there aren't any birds, either. There's nothing at all to see in the Gondwanaland sky except clouds. Anyway, if they do see a scooter up here, they'll just assume it's somebody going somewhere on official business. Why should they suspect anything?"

"I suppose."

"I'm going to take us down, now."

The hopper began a gradual descent. Everard caught his breath. There was that strangeness in the air again that he had experienced when Ben-Eytan had brought him here, the bite of the unfamiliar oxy-nitro mix, and the utter absence, Everard realized, of most of the carbon dioxide and all the stuff that had gone into Earth's atmosphere since the dinosaur days, the effluvia of rotting vegetation and decomposing animal flesh and belching furnaces and automobile exhaust and a myriad other products of combustion and respiration. There was no vegetation here to speak of, no animal life on shore at all, and not a single automobile on the entire planet.

He had spent two-thirds of his elapsed lifespan roaming freely in time, but he had never felt as estranged from reality as he did right at this moment. The sight of medieval cities had not done it, nor the actual proximity of Alexander the Great or Ben Jonson or Galileo Galilei or Cyrus the Great, or, for that matter, a brontosaurus in the living, snorting flesh or a man who had been born in the year 11,500 A.D. Everard had adapted to all things of that sort, had, indeed, come to take them for granted in a way that he could not help but regret, for that meant that his long service in the Time Patrol had in some way impaired his capacity for wonder.

But seeing this place was different: this seemingly lifeless, sterile place, this world before the world, this emptiness, this Gondwanaland. It was next to impossible to believe that from this bleak and hopeless shield of raw barren stone, this nothingness, would spring the turbulent, wonderful, miraculously complex globe that the succession of the ages would ultimately bring forth.

And then, knowing that the Founders were just a few hundred yards away from him—

Edgily he said, as Gonzalez nudged him and pointed toward the entrance to the camp, "What are we going to do? Walk right in there? We don't belong there, Elio!"

"How do they know? They've all been here only a few days. Nobody knows everybody yet. To them we'll be just a couple of newly arrived Founders."

"But we *weren't* there! We *aren't* Founders! We're setting up a causal loop!"

"So? We have a job to do, man. Little things like causal loops are incidental consequences of the work."

Everard smiled grimly. He knew that Gonzalez was right. There were rules about causal loops, temporal vortices, interventions within interventions, all kinds of things like that, and one tried to keep within the rules as much as possible. But sometimes rules had to be broken. The Patrol was forbidden to tinker with the true and proper sequence of the time-stream unless, of course, circumstances made it necessary to do so. And as Gonzalez said, they had a job to do.

They were inside the camp perimeter, now. He recognized some, not all, of the men and women he saw. Famous, quasi-legendary people, Leo Schmidt, Orris Greyl, Hian Gan-Sekkant, no less. Everyone in the Patrol encountered some of the Founders from time to time in the routine course of work—distant, remote figures, yes, but occasionally known to show up on the site of some difficult project—but, since the preponderance of them came from A.D. 25,000 and even farther uptime, early humans like Manson Emmert Everard were generally spared the sight of them. Humankind of the later eras did not look much like the *Homo Sapiens* that crowded the earth in Manse Everard's own birth-era, and one had to be of an extraordinarily sturdy nature to withstand the shock. As for the Danellians, those beings of a million-plus years ahead, Everard had once or twice been in the presence of one, but never, to the best of his knowledge, had he seen one in its true form. Like Zeus appearing to Semele in *his* true form, they would be much too much to handle if seen as they were, and customarily they took on innocuous disguises when moving among their evolutionary predecessors on Earth. There might be Danellians among those he saw now in the courtyard of Alpha Point, but—that phrase again—not so far as he knew.

As he and Gonzalez moved across the inner courtyard, sauntering in an exaggeratedly casual way and trying hard not to look like the interlopers that they were, Everard was startled to see a familiar figure coming the other way: Ben-Eytan, moving in that same excessively easy, all too phony manner. He saw them, too, and shot a fierce glare at them.

"Oh, Jesus!" Gonzalez muttered, turning bright red. "I timed it wrong! We have to get out of here."

He seized Everard roughly by the elbow and spun him around, and, without trying to be casual at all, now, led him briskly out of the courtyard and back to the scooters they had parked outside.

Everard knew better to ask for explanations. Only when they were safely aloft did he give Gonzalez a quizzical look.

"I should get docked a week's pay for that, Manse. The timer got set for an hour too soon and we did an overlap. Dan has already made the reconnaissance for that time of day—at least four days ago, Prague time." He looked flustered as he fiddled with the controls of the hopper. They began to descend again, and, so far as it was possible to tell the time of day at all in this constantly veiled sky, Everard figured they were coming in an hour or so later than on their first try.

Small wonder that Gonzalez looked chagrined. The last thing they wanted to be doing, or close to it, was to be causing overlap paradoxes, with one agent running into another on different tracks that converged on the same point in space and time. If they did that, they might as well be putting up blazing markers to tell the agents of Patrol II that some kind of counter-intervention was in progress.

But no harm seemed to have been done. They entered the courtyard again. Someone who might have been Itikarm Staykan—who surely was him, Everard decided—crossed diagonally in front of them, paying no heed to them at all. Everard tried to pretend that he did not feel like a ten-year-old boy in the presence of one of the stars of his favorite baseball team. Itikarm Staykan! Thirty feet away from him!

He told himself to shape up and get over this unseemly attack of hero-worship. He reminded himself that he was a grown man, an Unattached agent of the Time Patrol—the true and proper Time Patrol—and that he was involved in the most important mission of his career.

"What we're looking for," said Gonzalez, "is a blur. The kind of blur that tells us that one of the terrorists has just popped in to plant one of the devices."

"And what kind of blur is that?" Everard asked.

"You'll know when you see one."

They didn't see one there—nor on their next visit to this day, an hour and twenty minutes previous to this one. Gonzalez consulted the schedule that he was carrying, set the timer very carefully indeed, and they jumped again, uptime by six hours. Nothing there either.

Another jump.

"Bingo," Everard said.

A blur, all right: a quick oval white blip, the merest smearing of the atmosphere, a ghostly emanation that was briefly and dizzyingly visible against the curving greenish wall of the administration building. Gonzalez failed to see it; but when Everard described it to him, he nodded, pulled out a scanner, recorded the precise spot. Then they left, made yet another jump, emerged into the courtyard ten minutes before their previous arrival. They took up their post about fifty feet from where they had been standing before. A few minutes later, Everard watched himself and Gonzalez arrive as before and take up positions at right angles to where he and Gonzalez had been standing.

Why didn't we see ourselves before? he found himself wondering.

Because we weren't there before, he answered himself.

And then, angrily: *Stop it, Manse. You know better than this. Don't load your head up with nonsense.*

He worked hard at not looking at them. Filling the continuum with paradoxes on this level gave him a bad feeling in the pit of his stomach.

This time Gonzalez was ready. His scanner was out and cocked twenty-seconds before the blur appeared. Everard heard the familiar tiny buzz as the recording of location in time and space was made.

He also heard the other Manse Everard calling out, right on cue, "Bingo!"

"Okay," Gonzalez muttered. "Let's get out of here. The more time we spend here, the better chance Patrol II surveillance teams will have to detect our presence."

"Right."

They cleared out fast, heading across the continuum to the twentieth century A.D., the Austro-Hungrian Empire, the city of Prague, October 4, 1910, Wenceslas Square, the Grand Hotel Europa.

The reconnaissance part of the mission was complete, Everard discovered, when the five of them were once again assembled in their suite. Ben-Eytan flipped on a simulator and a scale model of Alpha Point sprang to life in the sitting room, with five piercingly bright red dots blazing forth on the simulated walls. Each was marked with a chronological indicator pinpointing one moment on Christmas Day, Gondwanaland time.

The Israeli looked around the room. He was all business now, no smartypants sarcasm, no irritating mannerisms of any sort.

"As our preliminary search indicated, the terrorists planted exactly five capsules, which makes one for each of us. We've been over the data and over it and over it again, until we've got the whole damned place crisscrossed with paradoxes, and we'll have to clean all that garbage out of the system later on, though of course that will create some paradoxes too, but to hell with that right now. The result of all the work we've done is that we know the time of the planting, over a seven-hour-long period on December 24, and we know the time of detonation, between four and five in the afternoon on December 25. The order of detonation seems to be important: the fifth capsule, we think, potentiates the first four, and therefore if we take them out in the same sequence no poison gas will be released into the atmosphere as we go about our work, or so we believe. We will try to neutralize the first four capsules and capture the terrorists as they try to activate them, but the key thing is to knock out that fifth capsule, just in case it's capable of releasing toxicity even in the absence of the first four, and that will be your job, Manse, because there may be some physical violence involved and you are by a considerable distance the biggest and strongest of the group."

Everard smiled a curdled smile. How very flattering, he thought, that they had picked him for the part of the job that needed the most muscle. They must think he was about half an evolutionary notch up from Homo *neandertalensis.* Well, maybe so. Certainly he'd be better in any wrestling match than Lora Spallanzani or a lightweight like Gonzalez or a highly evolved post-human like Nakamura. And Ben-Eytan himself, who was short but seemed pretty sturdily built, probably preferred to remain above the fray and leave the rough stuff to others.

"Let's run through the order of action a couple of times, shall we?" said Ben-Eytan. "Hideko, you'll go after the first capsule, and then—"

He ran through it more than a couple of times. He ran through it until even the calm and austere-spirited eightieth-century Nakamura was starting to seem bothered by the repetition.

"All right," Ben-Eytan said at long last. "Here we go."

The job of rolling up the terrorist network would take all of Christmas Eve and on into Christmas Day, Gondwanaland time. And it wasn't going to be easy. Let one member of the gang evade capture and the whole process could be undone if the one who remained at large struck back by creating a causal loop that would leave Ben-Eytan and his team hung up in some limbo of unreality. Time was a river, and rivers are, by definition, fluid things, ever changeable by those who know how to change their courses.

Nakamura, the designated first jumper, made his jump to Gondwanaland in early afternoon, and returned to Prague, of course, almost instantly so far as those who had remained behind in the hotel were aware. But the Nakamura who had taken off was cool and crisp and poised in the usual Nakamura mode, and the one who made the return jump was sweaty and rumpled and unusually flustered-looking, and there was a bloody gouge down in the glossy skin of his left cheek. And he had a prisoner with him, a big man with an odd greenish cast to his skin. There was something nonspecifically but undeniably futuristic about the heavy features and prominent cheek-bones of his angular face that told Everard that this was no one of his own era, that some ten millennia of post-twentieth-century evolution had been at work on him. He was also unconscious and hog-tied.

"Hard work," Nakamura said. "They fight back."

Ben-Eytan nodded. "I bet they do. Nasty-looking character, too. Lora, make sure you get the jump on yours. Don't try to be polite. *Capito?*"

"*Si*," Spallanzani said coolly, and made ready to depart.

Ben-Eytan said to Nakamura, "When you've had a moment to catch your breath, Hideko, take this character to Patrol Command. They'll find some appropriately unpleasant detention dimension to store him in." And, to Spallanzani: "*Buon viaggio*, Lora."

She vanished and returned almost at once. She had a prisoner with her too, limp, sedated, ugly-looking. She seemed altogether unchanged from the woman who had set forth a Prague moment before, but there was something in her eyes that indicated to Everard that the task had involved some disagreeable maneuvers, very disagreeable indeed. But she offered no details.

"That's two," said Ben-Eytan. "Off you go, Elio."

Ben-Eytan was next, after Gonzalez had gone and returned. Number three down, and number four. And then it was Everard's turn.

"You're the key player, Manse," Ben-Eytan told him, unhelpfully. "If your man gets away, he won't have much trouble unhappening the capture of the first four, and we're really cooked."

"Thank you," said Everard. "I definitely needed to know that."

There were no ambiguities about the instructions Ben-Eytan had given him. He was to arrive at Alpha Point at four minutes to five on the afternoon of what they called December 25, Alpha Point time, and station himself in front of the capsule that was planted precisely two feet two inches above ground level on the wall just to the left of the doorway to the main administration building. First thing to do, destroy the capsule. Then the terrorist would show up at five on the dot, intending to be there just enough of a fraction of a second to do whatever it was that activated the capsule. Except that the capsule would have been destroyed and the very large figure of Manse Everard was going to be standing in his way.

It was a ticklish business for a lot of reasons, not the least of them being that he was going to have to wait right by the doorway, and Founders were likely to be going past him during those long four minutes. There was always the chance that one of them would stop and frown and say, "Wait a minute, here, do I know you?" and interfere with the fix just long enough to let the terrorist jump in and do his trick. Everard was prepared to filibuster his way through any such unwanted interaction, if possible, but palming himself off as a legitimate Founder right to the face of an actual member of that exalted group might not be so simple.

And then—blocking the detonation—capturing the terrorist—returning with him to headquarters in Prague—First things first. Everard scrambled into his hopper and took off for Alpha Point.

Calmly, calmly, calmly, he told himself, as he headed for his post at the doorway of the base that an ordinary human being would think of as lying half a billion years in the past. To a Patrolman, of course, "the past" was a very wobbly concept indeed. All that matters, Everard knew, is that this is Alpha Point, the start of everything for the Time Patrol, and, unless you do your work properly, the finish of it, too. For the moment you are one of the Founders of the Patrol and you have every right to be here. The messy paradoxes involved in that can be erased later, if those on high deem it proper to do so.

Doorway? Yes. Check.

Capsule? Yes. Check. Check.

Barely visible, it was, two feet two inches from the ground, a tiny purplish speck, containing the Lord only knew what diabolically lethal substance that some far-future biochemists would dream up. Everard folded his arms. Leaned back. He saw Lora Spallanzani appear—not the current Lora Spallanzani, who was busy two or three hours before this eradicating the second of the five capsules and capturing the second terrorist, but some earlier Spallanzani who had been here to map the location of the capsule he himself had come to destroy. One more paradox, yes. They did not look at each other.

He heard the faint buzz of her scanner as she recorded the capsule's position. Then she was gone.

He lifted his right leg and folded it back, pressed the sole of his boot against the wall, scrubbed up and down, back and forth. Take that, poison capsule! He did it again, back and forth, up and down, scrub scrub scrub. It had vaguely occurred to him that he might thereby be liberating the poison and bringing his own life to its end, though Ben-Eytan did not seem to think that was going to happen. Not impossible, he said, but not very likely. So far as we know, Ben-Eytan insisted—that murderous speculative phrase yet again!—the capsules could only be detonated in sequence: they were not dangerous each by each. *So far as we know.* Trusting Ben-Eytan might well be foolish, but, even so, fatal or not, the capsule had to be destroyed, and he did it, and apparently there would not be any unpleasant consequences.

And now—to await the blur, and try to be quick enough—

There. But not a blur, this time. His own presence here, blocking access to the capsule, had altered the whole gig. Suddenly there was a figure standing in front of him, a man, a man of some future era considerably far beyond his own, similar to the other four, pale greenish skin, wide shoulders and attenuated body, immensely long tapering fingers, and a look of excruciating bewilderment on his face. Everard had his stunner at the ready, but even before he could squeeze off a bolt, he felt a savage jolt of something in his ribs, swayed, nearly lost consciousness. His stunner fell to the ground. Bewildered the terrorist might be by finding Everard in his way, but his reflexes seemed to be super-reflexes, and he had struck out at the obstacle in his path with superhuman swiftness. Nobody had warned him about that.

Everard tottered. Gulped wildly for breath. Felt another jolt, another. The pain was as sharp and as hot as a sword-thrust would be. He had felt plenty of those, but never at such close range, virtually nose to nose. Fire and thunder roared through his brain.

This was the moment for a little Neanderthal regression. Through a whirling haze he managed to reach out, grab one of those attenuated arms, twist it with all his not insignficant strength. That spun his opponent around, one hundred eighty degrees. Everard jerked the arm higher. Higher. He heard a gasp of pain. He would break the arm off at the shoulder, if he needed to. The terrorist, however agonized, twisted ferociously, writhed halfway around, managed to reach back with his free hand and poke two long bony fingers in the general direction of Everard's eyes. Everard, with one hand busy with the arm-twisting and the other one reaching for his stunner, bit hard at the jabbing fingertips. The man howled.

Without relinquishing his grip, he knelt, pulling his prisoner down with him, and pressed the stunner hard against the man's ribs. Ten thousand years of evolution would not have relocated the site of the human heart. One bolt would stun; three, if necessary, would kill. Everard was prepared for either necessity.

"Start walking," he said, in Temporal. "Do you understand Temporal? You don't want to say? Well, start walking anyway." He pushed the arm up a little higher and tapped the stunner's snout, not gently, against the man's rib-cage a couple of times. Another gasp. Stunners, blasters, time machines—they all had their place, but the proper twisting of an arm in its socket remained effective in its own way, Everard thought, at any point in space and time. And there was no call for being gentle. His enemy here was utterly ruthless, someone who was capable of calmly turning the whole time-line upside down for some blasphemous purpose of his own.

Whatever the terrorist had hit him with continued to set up agonizing throbbings at every point of contact. But Everard moved forward, pushing his captive before him, giving the arm a little reminder from time to time. Were Founders coming out to gape at this astonishing scene? Everard didn't try to see. He concentrated entirely on the figure in front of him. Through the courtyard, out the main gate, into the barren open rocky nothingness beyond. His scooter was waiting.

"Now, then—" he said, and put his stunner to the man's side. "I should just take you up and dump you in the sea to be a snack for the trilobites, like the barbarian I am. Wouldn't change history in the slightest, that, and they might enjoy the meal. But no. I'm going to be civilized. Civilized people don't dump their prisoners in the drink." He pressed the stunner's stud and felt the terrorist collapse against him. "A little nap, now—and then a visit to marvelous golden Prague for you."

⬖ ⬖ ⬖

It was a glorious spring day in Paris, and the sky was blue, and the air was like champagne. He and Wanda had arranged to meet at noon on the corner of the boulevard by the Metro station, just past the little cobbled plaza back of the ancient gray bulk of the Eglise St. Germain-des-Pres. Would she be there? Would the Metro station be there, for that matter, and the church, and the boulevard, and everything else that Paris of the 1920s should have? So far as they knew, the Patrol rescue team had set everything to rights again, but there was that damned phrase, *so far as they knew*.

Well, he would find out soon enough now.

Boulevard. Check.

Cobblestoned plaza. Check.

Metro station. Check.

Church. Check. Check. Check.

Wanda.

She stood with her back to him, but there was no mistaking her, even with the gleaming blonde hair cut in a fashionable 1920s bob, even with the silly flapper dress, even with, insofar as he could see from this side of her, her lovely breasts bound in that idiotic 1920s way so that she would look more like the boy that Nature had absolutely never intended her to be. Yes, Wanda. Check and double-check. Everard felt almost ready to weep with joy. But Nature had never intended him to be much of a weeper, either.

He came up behind her and cleared his throat ostentatiously.

"Mademoiselle Tamberley?"

She jumped, a little. Then she turned, and her smile was like the sun breaking through the primordial clouds of the sky above Alpha Point.

"Oh! Manse! You surprised me!" She was in his arms in a moment, pressing tight. Here in Paris, in 1925 or in any other era, nobody was going to be troubled by the sight of lovers embracing on the street. Then she stepped back. "Oh, Manse," she said. "You look so *tired*!"

"Do I? Well, I've been working hard lately, I suppose. But our holiday begins right here and now." He pointed toward the café across the street. "What about a little champagne to begin with, mademoiselle?"

The author *is grateful to Sandra Miesel for her assistance in planning this story. She is not, of course, responsible for any deviations from Poul Anderson's* Time Patrol *concept that it may contain.*

AFTERWORD: THE SKALD OF SCIENCE FICTION

WE WERE FRIENDS for more than forty years, though not really *close* friends as I understand that term. It was more of an amiable collegial relationship for much of that time. In my days as an editor of anthologies we worked together on many projects easily and well, and for three decades we lived in neighboring communities, and saw each other frequently, but there wasn't much of the intimate sharing of hopes and fears that I think of as friendship. When we met at parties, which was fairly often, we usually gravitated toward each other and exchanged pleasant tales of foreign travel, or discussed the various malfeasances of various publishers and agents, or got into pleasant dispute over some fine point of history or politics. (We didn't disagree much about politics.) Of real personal intimacy, though, there was very little between us. Others I know reported the same phenomenon; and yet when Poul did take someone into that kind of close friendship—Gordy Dickson, say, or Jack Vance, or Ted Cogswell—it was a deep and close friendship indeed. A matter of chemistry, I guess.

I'll never forget my initial encounter with his work, that grim little story of a dark post-atomic future, "Tomorrow's Children," which appeared the year I was twelve. It was Poul's second published story, written when he was just nineteen himself. (His first, a two-page squib, appeared in *Astounding* in 1944, before his eighteenth birthday.)

And then, in the 1950s and 1960s, came the torrent of irresistibly readable stories and novels that brought him a houseful of Hugos and Nebulas and put him on the road to SFWA's Grand Master award: *Brain Wave, Three Hearts and Three Lions*, the classic novella "Call Me Joe," *The High Crusade*, and the lighthearted Hoka tales that he wrote with his dear friend Gordon R. Dickson, on and on for decades thereafter, "The Queen of Air and Darkness," "Goat Song," "Hunter's

Moon," the Dominic Flandry stories, the Nicholas van Rijn stories—shelf after glorious shelf of wonderful tales, often with a touch of Nordic poetry about them, a bit of skaldic virtuosity. His Time Patrol stories were among my special favorites, and indeed in 1968, I wrote a whole novel, *Up the Line*, as a kind of playful riff on the concepts he explored in them.

For all his great accomplishments over a long and marvelously prolific career, Poul was a modest man, who never claimed to be anything more than a popular entertainer. (His legion of readers knew better.) His prime concern as a storyteller was, as it should be, storytelling: he knew how to snare a reader and how to hold him in that snare, and with skaldic cunning he called upon details of sight, sound, smell, and taste to make every paragraph a vivid one. But there have been plenty of tellers of tales whose work ultimately rings hollow, however lively it seems on first acquaintance. What Poul was really doing as a writer was dealing with the great moral themes of existence within the framework of society: values, purpose, the meaning of life itself. Who am I? his characters asked, not in so many words but through their deeds. How shall I live my life? What are my obligations to myself and my fellow beings? Where does personal freedom end and the bond that creates a society begin? Big questions, all of them, with which great writers have been wrestling since the time of Homer and the author of the Gilgamesh epic before that; and Poul did not shy away from them, even as he pretended to be telling swift-pace tales of the spacelanes.

In person he often tended to be quiet and even shy, the antithesis of today's science-fictional self-promoters, although he knew how to look after himself pretty well in his dealings with the publishing world. But in the right setting Poul was anything but quiet, anything but shy. At any convention party, for example, you could usually find him in the center of a fascinated group of listeners, holding forth with great animation and much flailing of arms (he was an energetic gesturer) on the conversational topic of the moment, be it slavery in ancient Rome, the cultural significance of the Lascaux cave paintings, the physics of time travel, the techniques of brewing beer in Belgium, or the customs regulations of the Byzantine Empire. The sound of his voice was unmistakable—a high-pitched, herkyjerk baritone—and so was the flow of unpretentious erudition that would come from him whenever talk veered toward any of his innumerable areas of profound expertise.

His voice, as a writer, was as distinctive as was his way of speaking. One would have had to be style-deaf indeed to fail to recognize a Poul Anderson story after hearing only a paragraph or two of it. The powerful use of imagery and sensory detail, above all the dark rhythms that had come down to him out of the Viking literature of long ago, were all unmistakable. He was indeed our Nordic bard, the skald of science fiction. And if there's a Valhalla for science fiction writers, Poul is up there right now, putting down Odin's finest mead with the best of them.

—Robert Silverberg

LATECOMERS

by David Brin

***DAVID BRIN** entered the science fiction field in the late 1970s, and has been one of the most prominent SF writers in the business ever since, winning three Hugo Awards and one Nebula Award for his work. Brin is best-known for his* Uplift *series, which started in 1979 with* Sundiver, *and subsequently has continued in* Startide Rising, *which won both a Hugo and a Nebula in 1983,* The Uplift War, *which won a Hugo in 1987, and then on through* Brightness Reef, Infinity's Shore, *and* Heaven's Reach. *There's also a guide to the* Uplift *universe,* Contacting Aliens: An Illustrated Guide to David Brin's Uplift Universe, *by Brin and Kevin Lenagh. He won another Hugo Award in 1985 for his short story "The Crystal Spheres," and won the John W. Campbell Memorial Award in 1986 for his novel* The Postman, *which was later made into a big-budget film staring Kevin Costner. Brin's other novels include* Kil'n People, Kil'n Time, The Practice Effect, Earth, Glory Season, *and, with Gregory Benford,* Heart of the Comet. *His short work has been collected in* The River of Time, Otherness, *and* Tomorrow Happens. *He edited the anthology* Project Solar Sail *with Arthur C. Clarke and has published several non-fiction books such as* The Transparent Society, Through Stranger Eyes, *and* King Kong is Back!: An Unauthorized Look at One Humongous Ape. *His most recent book is a novel* Existence.

Here Brin takes us to an enigmatic ruin in deep space, and gives us front-row seats for a desperate battle over a secret that could change everything that we think we know about ourselves.

TOR ALWAYS felt a sneaking sympathy for despised underdogs. Like *grave robbers*—an under-appreciated profession, not unrelated to journalism. Both involved bringing what was hidden to light.

Often, without consent of the hiders.

Those olden-time thieves who pillaged kingly tombs were *recyclers* who put wealth back into circulation. Gold and silver had better uses, like stimulating commerce—or robot brains—than lying buried in some musty vault. Or take archaeologists, unveiling the work of ancient artisans—craftsmen who were far more admirable examples of humanity than the monarchs who employed them to decorate lavish burial chambers.

Tor hadn't come to the asteroid belt in search of precious metals or museum specimens. *But I'm still part of that grand tradition,* she thought while gazing from the control room of the survey ship, *Warren Kimbel.*

Down below lay a pit that ran almost the full length of a three-kilometer rock. And in that pit a dozen explorer-drones scurried about, at her command, poking and prying at the remains of prehistoric baby starships. Extracting the brain and drive units for shipment in-system, there to be studied by human civilization.

Rest in pieces. You never got to launch across the heavens. But maybe you'll teach us how to leave the cradle.

For two years, Tor had been in the Belt, helping peel back layers of a puzzle going back a million centuries. Lately, that meant uncovering strange alien works. But never before had she beheld such devastation.

Below Tor's vantage point, the hulking asteroid lay nearly black against a starry band of Milky Way. Collisions had dented, cracked, and cratered the rock along its long axis, some time after it broke from a parent body, when the solar system was no more than a billion years old. When Tor and her partner first approached, five days ago, it seemed a fairly typical carbonaceous planetoid, like millions of others drifting out here in the Belt. But this changed as the *Warren Kimbel* orbited to the other side of the nameless hunk of stone and frozen gases, where the sun's vacuum brilliance cast long, stark shadows across jagged, twisted remnants of a catastrophe that wracked this place way back when dinosaurs roamed the Earth.

"Gavin!" she called over her shoulder. "Come down here and see this!"

Her partner floated through the overhead hatch, flipping in mid-air. His bare feet contacted the magnetized floor with a faint click.

"What is it? More murdered babies to dissect? Or a clue to who their killers were?"

Tor gestured to the viewing port. Her partner moved closer and stared. Highlights reflected from Gavin's glossy features as watched the drones' searchlights sweep the shattered scene below.

"Yep," he nodded at last. "Dead babies again. Povlov Exploration and Salvage ought to make a good price off each little corpse."

Tor frowned. Commercial exploitation was a small part of their reason for being here, but it helped pay the bills. "Don't be morbid. Those are unfinished interstellar probes, destroyed ages ago, before they could be launched. We have no idea whether they were sapient machines like you, or just tools, like this ship. You of all people should know better than to go around anthropomorphizing alien artifacts."

Gavin's grimace was an android's equivalent of a sardonic shrug. "If I use 'morbid' imagery, whose fault is it?"

"What do you mean?"

"I mean you organic humans faced a choice, back when you saw that 'artificial' intelligence was going to take off and someday leave the biological kind behind. You could have wrecked the machines, but that would ruin progress."

She refrained from mentioning how close that came to happening, when the Renunciation Movement crested, less than a generation ago—a movement that still captivated a strong, ever-sniping minority.

"Or you could have deep-programmed us with 'fundamental Laws of Robotics,'" Gavin sniffed. "And had slaves far smarter than their masters. But what did you organics finally decide to do?"

Tor knew it was no use sparring with Gavin, when he got in a mood. She concentrated on piloting the *Warren Kimbel* closer to the long cavity where drones shone beams across acres of twisted metal.

"What was your solution to the problem of smart machines?"

Gavin persisted. "You chose to *raise us as your children*. Call us people. Citizens. You taught us to be just like you, and even gave some of us humaniform bodies!"

Tor's last partner—a nice old 'bot and a good chess partner—had warned her, when he trans-retired, not to hire an adolescent Class-AAA android fresh out of AI-college. "They could be as difficult as any human adolescent," he warned.

The worst part? Gavin was right. The decision, to raise Class AAAs as human children, was still controversial. Not everyone agreed it was a "solution" to one of the Great Pitfalls, or just a way to conceal the inevitable. For, despite genetic and cyborg improvements to the human animal, machines still seemed fated to surpass biological men and women. *And how many species of organic intelligent life survived that crisis?*

Gavin shook his head in dramatic, superior sadness, exactly like a too-smart adolescent who properly deserved to be strangled. "Can you really object when I, a man-built, manlike android, anthropomorphize? We only do as we've been taught, mistress." His bow was eloquently sarcastic. Especially since he was the only person aboard who could bend at the waist.

Following a fiery cruise-zep accident, twenty years before, all of Tor's organic parts were confined to a cylindrical canister, barely a meter long and half a meter wide, containing her brain and vital organs. One reason she seemed ideal as a deep-space explorer. With prosthetic-mechanical arms, legs and grippers, she looked more "robotic" than her partner did, by far.

To Gavin's snide remark, she had no response. Indeed, it was easy to wonder if humanity had made the right choice, when it came to dealing with AI.

But isn't that true of all our decisions, across the last two-dozen years? Haven't we time and again selected the path that seems less traveled? The one that looks less likely? For the simple reason that, maybe, our chances of surviving the odds would have to come from doing something no one else has tried?

Below, across the face of the ravaged asteroid, stretched acres of great-strutted scaffolding—twisted and curled in ruin. Tangled and half-buried within the toppled derricks lay silent ranks of shattered, *unfinished starships*, razed perhaps a hundred million years ago.

Tor felt sure that her silicon eyes and Gavin's germanium ones were the first to look upon this scene, since some awful force plunged through, wreaking all this havoc.

The ancient destroyers had to be long gone. Nobody had yet found a star machine even close to active. Still, she took no chances, making certain the weapons console stayed vigilant. That sophisticated, semi-sentient unit searched, but found no energy sources, no movement amid the ruined, unfinished mechanisms below. Instruments showed nothing but cold rock and metal, long dead.

"We have work to do," she told her partner. "Let's get on with it."

Gavin pressed two translucent hands together prayerfully. "Yes, Mommy. Your wish is my program." He float-sauntered away to his own console and began deploying some remote exploration drones.

Tor concentrated on directing the lesser minds within *Warren*'s control board—those littler, semi-sapient specialist processors dedicated to rockets and radar and raw numbers—who still spoke coolly and dispassionately . . . as machines should.

A SEALED ROOM

TOWERING SPIRES hulked all around, silhouetted against starlight—a ghost-city of ruin, long, long dead.

Frozen flows of glassy foam showed where ancient rock once briefly bubbled under sunlike heat. Beneath collapsed skyscrapers of toppled scaffolding lay the pitted, blasted corpses of unfinished star probes.

Tor followed Gavin through the curled, twisted wreckage of a gigantic replication yard. It was an eerie place. Huge and intimidating.

No human power could have wrought this havoc. That realization lent a chilling helplessness to the uneasy feeling that she was being watched.

It was a silly reflex reaction, of course. Tor told herself again that the destroyers had to be long gone from this place. Anyway, she had servant guardians patrolling nearby, vigilant against any unexplained movement.

Still, her eyes darted, seeking form out of the shadows, blinking at the scale of this catastrophe.

"It's down here," Gavin said, leading into a cavelike gloom below the twisted towers. Flying behind a small swarm of little semi-sentient drones, he looked almost completely human in his slick spacesuit. There was nothing except a slight overtone in his voice to indicate that Gavin's ancestry was silicon, and not carbolife. Tor found the irony delicious. Any onlooker who viewed the two of them would guess that *she* was the creature made of whirring machinery, not Gavin.

Not that it mattered. Today "mankind" included many types . . . all of them considered citizens, so long as they showed fealty to human law, and could appreciate the most basic human ways. Take your pick: music, sunsets, compassion, a good joke. In a future filled with unimaginable diversity, Man would be defined not by his shape but by heritage and a common set of grounded values.

Some foresaw this as the natural life history of a race, emerging from the planetary cradle to live in peace beneath the open stars. But Tor—speeding behind Gavin under the canopy of twisted metal—had already concluded that humanity's solution was not the only one. Clearly, other makers had chosen different paths.

One day, long ago, terrible forces had rained down upon this place, breaking a great seam into one side of the planetoid. Within, the cavity gave way to multiple, branching passages. Gavin braked before one of these, in a faint puff of gas, and pointed.

"We were doing our initial survey, measuring the first sets of tunnels, when one of my deepest-penetrating drones reported finding the habitats."

Tor shook her head, still unable to believe it. She repeated the word.

"Habitats. Do you really mean as in closed rooms? Gas-tight? For biological life support?"

Gavin's face plate hardly hid his exasperated expression. He shrugged. "Come on, Mother. I'll show you."

Tor numbly turned her jets and followed her partner down into one of the dark passages, their headlamps illuminating the path ahead.

Habitats? Tor pondered. In all the years humans had been picking through the ruins of wave after wave of foreign probes, this was the first time anyone had found anything having to do with biological beings. No wonder Gavin was testy. To an immature robot-person, it might seem like a bad joke.

Biological starfarers! It defied all logic. But soon Tor could see the signs around her . . . massive airlocks lying in the dust, torn from their hinges . . . then reddish stains that could only have come from oxidization of the primitive rock, exposed to air.

The implications were staggering. Something organic had come from the stars!

Although all humans were equal before the law, the traditional biological kind still dominated culture in the solar system. Many of the younger Class-AAAs looked to the future, when their descendants would be the majority, the leaders, perhaps even star-treaders. To them, the discovery of the alien probes in the asteroid belt had been a sign. Of course, something terrible happened to the great robot envoys of the past. Nevertheless, all these wrecked mechanical probes testified to what was physically possible. The galaxy still might—somehow—belong to human beings. Though humans made of metal and silicon.

Difficult and dangerous it might be, still, the AI folk appeared to be humanity's future.

Only here, deep in the planetoid, might be an exception!

Tor moved carefully through the wreckage, under walls carved out of carbonaceous rock. Mammoth explosions had shaken the habitat so that, even in vacuum, little was preserved from so long ago. Still, she could tell that the machines in this area were different from any alien artifacts discovered before.

She traced the outlines of intricate separation columns. "Chemical-processing facilities . . . and not for fuel or cryogens, but complex organics!"

Tor hop-skipped from chamber to chamber as Gavin followed sullenly. A pack of semiscent robots accompanied, like dogs sniffing a trail. In each new chamber they snapped, clicked, and scanned. Tor accessed the data on her helmet display and inner-percept, as it became available.

"Look there! In that chamber, the drones report traces of organic compounds that have no business being here. There's been heavy oxidation, within a super-reduced asteroid!"

She hurried to an area where drones were already setting up lights. "See these tracks? They were cut by flowing water!" She knelt and pointed. "They had a *stream,* feeding recycled water into a little pond!"

Dust sparkled as it slid through her touch-sensitive prosthetic fingers. "I'll wager this was topsoil! And look, stems! From plants, and grass, and trees."

"Put here for aesthetic purposes," Gavin proposed. "We class AAAs are pre-designed to enjoy nature as much as you biologicals . . ."

"Oh, posh!" Tor laughed. "That's only a stopgap measure, till we're sure you'll keep thinking of yourselves as human beings. Nobody expects to inflict a love of New England autumns on people when we become starships! Anyway, a probe could fulfill that desire simply by focusing a telescope on the Earth!"

She stood up and spread her arms. "This habitat was meant for biological creatures! Real, living aliens!"

Gavin frowned, but said nothing.

"Here," Tor pointed as they entered another chamber. "Here is where the organic entities were made! Don't these machines resemble those artificial wombs they've started using on Luna Base?"

Gavin shrugged grudgingly.

"Maybe they were specialized units," he suggested, "intended to work with volatiles. Or perhaps the type of starprobe that built this facility needed some element from the surface of a planet like Earth, and created workers equipped to go get it."

Tor laughed. "It's an idea. That'd be a twist, hm? Machines making biological units to do what they could not? And of course there's no reason it couldn't happen that way. Still, I doubt it."

"Why?"

She turned to face her partner. "Because almost anything available on Earth you can synthesize more easily in space. Anyway—"

Gavin interrupted. "Explorers! The probes were sent out to explore and acquire knowledge. All right then. If they wanted to learn more about the Earth, they would want to send units formatted to live on its surface!"

Tor nodded. "Better," she admitted. "But it doesn't wash."

She knelt in the faint gravity and sketched an outline in the dust. "Here is the habitat, nearly at the center of the asteroid. Now why would the parent probe have placed it here, other than one fact, that it offers the best possible protection?

"Meanwhile, the daughter probes the Parent was constructing lay out there in the open, vulnerable to cosmic rays and whatever other dangers were prowling, during the time when their delicate parts were most exposed."

Tor motioned upward with her prosthetic right claw, which looked far more robotic than Gavin's comparatively soft, glove-covered hand.

"If the biologicals were just built in order to poke briefly into a corner of this solar system, our Earth, would the parent probe have given them better protection than it offered *its own children*?"

Gavin's head lifted to follow her gesture upward, toward where the twisted wreckage of the unborn machines lay open to the stars.

"No," Tor concluded. "These 'biologicals' weren't intended to be exploration sub-units, serving the parent probe. They were colonists!"

Gavin stood impassively for a long time, staring silently down at one of the shattered airlock hatches.

Finally, he turned away. Radio waves carried to her augmented ears a vibration that her partner did not have to make, since he lacked lungs or any need for air. Yet, the sound amply expressed how he felt.

Gavin sighed.

RETURN OF THE WOLF

TWO DAYS LATER, Tor glimpsed her partner up at the crater's rim, directing robots that trimmed and foam-packed the most valuable salvaged parts for a long voyage, pulled Earthward by a light-sail freighter. Gavin had asked to work as far as possible from the "creepy stuff"—the musty *habitat zone* down below in the asteroid's heart, that once held breathable air and liquid water.

"I know we've got to explore all that, eventually," he told her. "Just give me some time to get used to the idea."

How could Tor refuse a reasonable request, made without sarcasm? And so, she quashed her own urgent wish—to drop everything and rush back to those crumbling tunnels, digging around blasted airlocks and collapsed chambers, excavating a secret that lay buried for at least fifty million years. And hoping to find the colonists, themselves.

We may become the most famous grave robbers since Heinrich Schliemann or Howard Carter. For that, Tor supposed she could wait a bit.

Some of the cutting drones were having a rough time removing a collapsed construction derrick that had toppled across the construction yard. So Tor hop-floated closer, counting on ape-instincts to swing her prosthetic arms from one twisted girder to another, till at last she reached a good vantage point. The asteroid's frail gravity tugged her mechanical legs down and around. Tor took hold of the derrick with one of the grippers that served her better than mere feet.

"Drone K, go twelve meters left, then shine your beam down-forty, north-sixty. Drone R, go fifty meters in *that* direction—" she pointed carefully "—and shine down-forty-five, east-thirty."

It took some minutes—using radar, lidar, and stereoscopic imagery—to map out the problem the drones were having, a tangle of wreckage with treasure on the other side. Not only baby probes but apparently a controller unit, responsible for building them! That could be the real prize, buried under a knotted snarl of cables and debris.

Here an organic human brain—evolved in primal thickets—seemed especially handy. Using tricks of parallel image processing that went back to the Eocene, Tor picked out a passage of least resistance, faster than the *Warren Kimbel*'s mainframe could.

"Take this route . . . " She click-mapped for the drones. "Start cutting here . . . and here . . . and—"

A sharp glare filled the cavity, spilling hard-edge shadows away from every metal strut. Pain flared and Tor cringed as her faceplate belatedly darkened. Organic eyes might have been blinded. Even her cyborg implants had trouble compensating.

The corner of her percept flared a diagnosis that sent chills racing down her spine. Coherent-monochromatic reflections. A high-powered laser.

A laser? Who the hell is firing . . . ?

Suppressing fear, her first thought was a cutter-drone malfunctioning. She started to utter the general shut-down command . . .

. . . when a war alarm blared. A sharp vocal cry followed.

"Tor! I'm under attack . . . Tor!"

As quickly as it struck, the brilliant light vanished, leaving her surroundings in almost-pitch blackness, with just the distant sun illuminating an exposed crater rim. Crouching where there had been stark shadow just moments ago, she prayed that the nearby girder still lay between her body and the laser source. Tor shouted.

"Gavin . . . are you all right!"

Her racing heart was original equipment. Human-organic 1.0, pounding like a stampede inside her rib-cage, inside a cerametal tube. Even faster when her partner replied.

"I . . . I'm in a crevice—a slit in the rock. What's left of me. Tor, they sliced off my arm!"

They? She wanted to scream. *Who—or what—is "they"?*

Instead of shrill panic squeaks, Tor somehow managed to clamp down and sound like a commander.

"Are your seals intact? Your core—"

"Fine, but it *smarts*! And the arm flew away. Even if I make it out of here, my spare *sucks,* and it'll take weeks to grow a new—"

"Never mind that!" Tor interrupted to stop Gavin from babbling. Get him focused. "Have you got a direction? Can your drones do a pinpoint?"

"Negative. Three of them are chopped to bits. I sent the rest into cover. Maybe *Warren*—"

Cripes. That reminded Tor. If a foe had taken out the ship . . .

"*Warren Kimbel*, status!"

There followed a long, agonizing pause—maybe three seconds—while Tor imagined a collapse of all luck or hope.

Then came the voice she needed to hear.

"I am undamaged, Captain Povlov. I was blocked from direct line to the shooter by the asteroid's bulk. I am now withdrawing all sensitive arrays, radiators and service drones, except the one that's relaying this signal. It is using a pop-out antenna."

"Good! Initiate war-danger protocols."

"Protocols engaged. Tracking and weapons coming online. I am plotting a course to come get both of you."

Tor would have bitten her lower lip, if she still had one. She made a hard choice.

"Better not move, just yet. That beam was damn powerful. Gavin and I are safe for now—"

"Hey, speak for yourself!" Her young partner interrupted. "You wouldn't say that if an organo-boy had his arm chopped off!"

"—but we'll be screwed if any harm comes to the ship."

That shut Gavin's mouth. Good. His position was worse than hers. He shouldn't radiate any more than he had to.

"*Warren*, did you get drone telemetry to analyze the beam?"

"Enough for preliminary appraisal, Captain. From the kill-wattage, duration and color, I give eighty-five-percent probability that we were attacked by a FACR."

"Shit!"

Across the broad Asteroid Belt, littered with broken wreckage of long-ago alien machines, only one kind was known to still be active. *Faction-Allied Competition Removers*—an awkward name, but the acronym stuck, because it was easily mispronounced into a curse.

It's been years since anyone was bothered by one of these things. Everybody thought that they were gone, or resigned to humans expanding into the Belt. But apparently it's not over.

Why is one shooting at us now?

"*Warren*," she said. "Maybe it's no coincidence that we were attacked just after you orbited behind the rock."

There was no immediate response, as the ship's mind pondered this possibility. Tor couldn't help feeling the brief, modern satisfaction that came from thinking of something quicker than an AI did.

"If I grasp your point, Captain, you are suggesting that the FACR is afraid of me. More afraid than I should be of him?"

"That could explain why it waited till you were out of sight, before shooting at Gavin and me. If it figures you're too strong to challenge . . . well, maybe you can come get us, after all."

"Amen," murmured Gavin. Then, before Tor could admonish, he lapsed back into radio silence.

"Unless it was the machine's intent to lure us into drawing exactly that conclusion," the ship-brain mused. *"And there may be another reason for me to remain where I am, for now."*

A soft click informed Tor that *Warren* was switching to strong encryption.

"I have just confirmed a two-way channel to an ISF vessel—the cruiser Abu Abdullah Muhammad Ibn Battuta. *They are only three light-minutes away."*

Well at last, a stroke of luck! Suddenly Tor felt a bit less alone out here.

Then she quelled her enthusiasm. Even using its fusion-ion engines, the big, well-armed ship would have to maneuver for weeks in order to match orbits and come here physically. Still, that crew might be able to help in other ways. She checked encryption again, then asked the *Warren Kimbel—*

"Can *Ibn Battuta* bring sensors to bear?"

"That ship has excellent arrays, Tor. As of last update, they were swinging sensors to focus on the region in question—where the killer beam came from—a stony debris field orbiting this asteroid, roughly five kilometers from here, twenty-north by forty-spinward. They will need some minutes to aim their instruments. And then there is the time-lag. Please attend patiently."

"Ask them not to use active radar quite yet," Tor suggested. "I'd rather the FACR didn't know about them." Better not to reveal this one possible advantage.

"I have transmitted your request. Perhaps it will reach them in time to forestall such beams. Please attend patiently."

This time Tor kept silent. Minutes passed and she glanced at the starscape wheeling slowly overhead. Earth and the sun weren't in view, but she could make out Mars, shining pale ocher in the direction of Ophiuchus, without any twinkle. And Tor realized something unpleasant—that she had better start taking into account the asteroid's ten-hour rotational "day."

North by spinward . . . she pondered. *Roughly that way* . . . she couldn't make out any glimmers from the "stony debris field," which probably consisted of carbonaceous stuff, light-drinking and unreflective. A good hiding place. Much better than hers, in fact. A quick percept calculation confirmed her fear.

At the rate we're rotating, this here girder won't protect me much longer.

Looking around, she saw several better refuges, including the abyss below, where baby starships lay stillborn and forever silent. Unfortunately, it would take too many seconds to hop-drift over to any of those places. During which she'd be a sitting duck.

Why in space would a FACR want to shoot at us, anyway?

The battle devices were still a mystery. For the most part, they had kept quiet, ever since the dark episode still known as the Night of the Lasers. In all of the years that followed, while humanity cautiously nosed outward from the homeworld and began probing the edges of the Belt, she could recall only a couple of dozen occasions when the deadly relic machines had been observed firing their deadly rays . . . mostly to attack each other, but occasionally blasting at Earthling vessels with deadly precision, and for no apparent reason.

Armed ships, sent to investigate, never found the shooters. Despite big rewards offered for anyone who captured a FACR dead or alive, they were always gone—or well-hidden—before humans arrived.

We finally figured out, they must be leftovers from the final battle that tore through our solar system long ago.

Survivors who slept for millions of years. Rousing, now that humans were flitting about, they mostly seemed interested in resuming their old grudges . . . though with more than enough vile nastiness to share with Earth's newcomers, too.

It all made a kind of darwinian sense . . . or so the best minds explained, reminding everybody that evolution is a notorious bitch. But again, why here? Why now?

Eyeing the rate of rotation, she knew another question was paramount.

How am I gonna get out of here?

It wouldn't suffice to just sidle sideways around the ancient girder, which was narrow and perforated in the other direction. And Gavin's situation was probably even worse. *We've got to do something soon.*

"*Warren.* Has *Ibn Battuta* scanned the debris field?"

"Yes, Tor, with passive telescopes. Their results are inconclusive. They have mapped the component rocks and sand clouds and report half a dozen anomalies that might possibly be hiding the shooter. With active radar they may be able to pinpoint the resonance of refined metal—"

"Or else get confused by nickel-iron meteoritic material. Anyway, the instant they transmit active beams, the damned thing will realize we have an ally. It can shift position long before they get a return signal and are able to fire any kind of weapon. Six minutes light-turnaround is huge."

"I can find no fault with your reasoning. Then perhaps our main option remains for me to emerge from shadow and come get the two of you. As you say, the machine may be reticent to do battle with a foe my size."

"And what if we're wrong? Suppose the damn thing fires at you?"

"Then I will engage it in battle."

"You won't get in the first shot. Or even the second."

"Agreed. In a worst-case scenario, I calculate that—with excellent marksmanship—the FACR could take out my primary weapon, then attack my main drive units. But I still might position myself with vernier thrusters, so that you and Gavin could make it aboard. Even if I am rendered helpless, my innermost radiation shelter should keep you safe until help arrives."

Another voice blurted.

"Screw that! I can shut down for a month or two. But Tor would starve or go crazy in that time!"

She felt touched by her partner's concern—the first time she recalled him ever talking that way.

"Thanks Gavin. But don't transmit. That's an order."

He went silent with a click . . . perhaps in time to keep the enemy from localizing him too accurately. Tor weighed her options.

On the positive side, the *Ibn Battuta* might be a powerful ally, if the distant cruiser managed to catch their foe by surprise with a radar beam, just once, getting a clear position fix that would be obsolete before the signal even returned. Double that light delay, and you've effectively rendered the ship's mighty weapons useless.

Then there was *Warren Kimbel* sitting much closer, but also much less formidable. And the *Warren* would need several minutes to emerge from the asteroid's shadow, the whole time vulnerable to a first shot. Or several.

She took census of the robotic salvage drones. A dozen or so were still in decent shape, down here with her. Or else near Gavin.

And finally . . . there's me.

Tor didn't much like the plan taking shape in her mind. Frankly, it too-well reminded her of the desperate measures she took long ago, alongside the brave man that her ship was named after, aboard a doomed zeppelin, that day when her life as a normal woman ended and her career as a cyborg soon began.

But I don't see where there's any other option.

And timing is really going to be critical.

"Okay," Tor said, with a glance at the encryption monitor. "Here's what we're gonna do."

TIMING IS EVERYTHING

OUR FATE *will turn on split seconds,* she thought.

Unless the damn FACR has cracked our encryption and knows what we're about to do. Or unless there's more than one of the horrid things!

In which case, we're torqued.

Breathing tension in her steamy life support suit-capsule, she watched the first of several timers count down and reach zero—then begin ticking upward again.

One. Two. Three. Four . . .

Warren *is starting to move.*

In her mind's eye, Tor pictured the vessel's engines lighting up, blasting toward a fateful emergence from the asteroid's protective bulk. The tip of its nose should appear in one hundred and six seconds.

Before working out this plan, she had gone through dozens of scenarios. All the viable ones started this way, with her ship firing-up to come around. After all, what if the FACR really was too afraid to fire at the *Warren Kimbel*? Why not find out, right at the start? Easiest solution. Let the ship come to fetch Tor and Gavin. Then go FACR-hunting.

For some reason, Tor felt certain things wouldn't go that way. Life was seldom so easy.

The new count reached forty-six. So, in exactly one minute the FACR would spot *Warren*'s prow emerging from behind the roid's protecting bulk . . . .

When thirty seconds remained, Tor uttered a command:

"Drones M and P, go!"

They belonged to Gavin, a hundred meters beyond the crater's rim. Soon, a pair of tiny glimmers rose above that horizon. Tor's percept portrayed two loyal little robots firing their jets, lancing skyward on a suicidal course—straight toward the jumble of rocks and pebbles where a killer machine lurked.

They're harmless, but will the FACR know that?

Ten seconds after those two launched, she spoke again.

"Drones R and K, *come* now!"

With parameters already programmed, those two started from opposite directions, jetting toward her across a jumble of twisted girders. Now fate would turn on the foe's decision.

Which group will you go after first? Those rushing toward you, or those coming to rescue me? Or none?

"Drones D and F, now!" Those were two more of Gavin's, sent to follow the first pair, hurtling toward the sandbar-cloud where the enemy hid, leaving her partner alone. That couldn't be helped. And *Warren*'s nose would be visible in five . . . four . . .

In purely empty space, lasers can be hard to detect. But Gavin had spent the last half-hour using his one remaining hand to toss fists of asteroidal dust into the blackness overhead, as hard as he could without exposing himself. (A side benefit: burrowing a deeper shelter.) The expanding particle cloud was still essentially hard vacuum—

—but when a kill beam lanced through the sparse haze, it scattered a trail of betraying blue-green twinkles . . . as it sliced drone P in half, almost instantly igniting a gaudy fireball of spilled hydrazine fuel.

Tor blinked in shock, before remembering to start a fresh timer . . . as drone M was cloven also! Without exploding, though. She fought down fear in order to concentrate.

So. It acted first to protect itself. Only now—

She turned to face drone R, speeding toward her above the jumble of ruined alien probe-ships. The little robot carried a flat, armor-like plate, salvaged from the junk pile, now held up as a shield between it and the FACR.

"Gavin did you get a fix on—"

A searing needle of blue-green struck the plate, spewing gouts of superheated metal. The drone kept coming, hurrying to Tor.

"Now I have!" Her partner shouted. "Got the bastard localized down to a couple of meters. You know, I'll bet it doesn't know I'm a—"

The FACR's beam wandered a quick spiral. Then, whether by expert-targeting or a lucky shot, it sliced off one of the little drone's claws, where it gripped the makeshift armor. The protective plate twisted one way, the drone another. Imbalanced, it desperately compensated, trying to reach Tor—till it crashed into a jutting piece of an ancient construction crane. The plate spun off, caroming amid girders, coming to rest *just* out of Tor's reach.

The robot juttered to a halt, shuddered and died, with another hole drilled neatly through its brain case.

Damn. The sonovabitch is accurate! And its re-fire rate is faster than any weapon built by humans.

Aware that nineteen seconds had passed since the first laser bolt, she spun to look at drone K, jetting toward her from the opposite side, clutching another slab of makeshift, ill-fitting armor. Again, harsh light speared from the enemy. Molten splatters spewed and then instantly froze, wherever the FACR's beam touched metal, hunting for a vulnerable spot. In moments—

The lance of bitter light *vanished*—with suddenness that left Tor blinking. As her optics struggled to adapt, the drone kept coming toward her, apparently undamaged.

Which must mean—

"I am now under attack, Captain Povlov. The good news is that your distractions bought me half a minute. The bad news? The Faction-Allied Competition Remover does not appear to be afraid of me."

The latest generation of AI had an irksome habit of turning verbose, even garrulous, at times of stress. No one knew why.

"I have pinged a radar pulse at the site Gavin provided. The return echo was strong down to half a centimeter. In response, the FACR burned off my main antenna and a surrounding patch of hull. Adjacent chambers are no longer air-tight.

"I am rotating my primary weapon, in order to aim it at the foe. But at his current rate of re-fire, he will be able blast my laser turret from the side, before I can shoot."

Drone K, burdened with the awkward metal plate, had trouble slowing down. Tor was forced to duck with a shout, as it collided with the girder protecting her. Acting quickly, before it could spin away, she darted out a hand to clutch the thick disk. Her prosthetic fingers grabbed so hard it *hurt* and Tor's wrist ached from the twisting strain.

That's nothing compared to getting a whole arm sliced off, she thought, having to expose the limb for several seconds. But the enemy was occupied elsewhere.

Thanks, Warren, she thought, when everything was safely behind the girder. Tor felt pangs over yet another sacrifice on her behalf.

Now, just hold out till it's my turn.

The chunk of metal was only a makeshift "shield." Under orders, drone K had gone down to the asteroid's catacombs, in order to retrieve part of a shattered airlock hatch—one of many that once protected the mysterious habitat zone, and among the few objects at hand that might block the kill-beam for a few seconds. Maybe. If she managed to keep it turned right, between her and the FACR's deadly gaze.

Things might have been simpler in Earth-gravity. Just jump away from the girder while holding up the shield for a couple of ticks—long enough to plummet to safety, worrying only about the landing. Here, gravity was a tepid friend, weaker than a mouse. Falling would take much too long.

"Tor. The foe has been expertly burning my instrumentalities, as each one came into view. Half of my forward compartments are now holed. My primary weapon will be exposed to side-attack for at least fifteen seconds before it can shoot back. That window will commence in forty seconds . . . mark."

Cursing her slowness behind the girder's narrow protection, Tor helped drone K turn and line itself upside down, with jets pointing skyward, still clutching the rim of the airlock cover with both manipulator clamps.

There were serious flaws to this plan. The worst drawback declared itself in stark, sudden illumination from somewhere high above. A *hot* light, rich and reddish—not anything like the laser's icy blue—burst across the crater, bathing dead starships in the flicker-colors of flame.

That must be drone D, or drone F—or both—exploding before they could reach the FACR. It had to turn and deal with them, at last, in case they carried bombs. Well, at least their sacrifice bought *Warren* a brief respite. Too bad the distraction couldn't be better timed.

Is that mother's weapon ever gonna run out of laser-juice?

Tor felt intensely aware of drone K's hydrazine tanks, too close above her back as she crouched. She had no wish to experience incineration a second time. In spite of all her cyborg augmentations, Tor's mouth tasted the same bile flavors of dread that her ancestors knew long ago, when they confronted lions on the veldt, or pictured dragons in the night. Her body suffered waves of weakness.

But battle makes no allowance for fear. It was time.

With the airlock plate poised above, her legs flexed . . . then *shoved* hard against the metal strut, her refuge for the last hour. Drifting backward, just before leaving the girder's shadow, Tor yanked all of her limbs into a fetal tuck, clinging to the center of the hatch, as faithful little drone K ignited all engines, attempting to rocket Tor downward, toward safety amid the jumbled wreckage below. Still so very slowly.

Did the FACR hesitate?

Tor and Gavin *had* to be the highest-priority targets. Given what happened earlier, nothing else made logical sense. On the other hand, for the foe to let up on *Warren* could be a lethal mistake . . .

Come on. Pay attention to me!

After five whole seconds, the war machine's indecision ended in a blaze of blue-actinic brightness that erupted just above Tor's head, penetrating drone K like tissue paper. The little robot convulsed—and Tor worried.

If it took out the brain . . . In that case, the robot might *keep* holding on to the plate, leaving its fuel tanks exposed—in effect a bomb, ready to be ignited.

The worker machine's long arms pulsed, like a spasm, shoving itself away from the armor shield—as planned. And having pushed Tor in the direction of safety, drone K swiveled to jet the other way. *Thanks,* she thought, toward her last glimpse of the loyal machine. And now the enemy had three targets to choose from.

Shoot at me.

Shoot at Warren.

Or try using the drone to blow me to smither—

The world turned orange-red—a harsh, fury-filled light, much closer than before. Explosive brightness swept past the airlock hatch on all sides, surrounding Tor, who cowered in a narrow, cylindrical shadow.

Goodbye, drone K.

Her brain could only manage that one thought before the shockwave hit, shuddering the hatch so hard that her hand-grip almost failed. Both legs flung out as her oblong shield began to spin.

That had been the enemy's obvious tactic to get at Tor. This new rotation would bring her body into the FACR's sights, several agonizing instants before she reached safety.

Time to bail.

Tor gathered her legs, bracing them against the hatch plate.

"Tor Povlov, my weapon is now emerging into view. The foe must be distracted for fifteen seconds."

Too long. Even if she got the FACR to focus on her, that interval amounted to *three shots*, at the rate the damn thing could re-fire.

But she had to try! While the plate still shielded her, Tor kicked hard, in a semi-random direction. If the enemy needed even a fraction of an extra moment to spot her, beyond the still glowing explosion-plume . . .

The pit, filled with craggy debris, was looming faster now. But Tor fought the instinct to turn and brace for impact. Instead, she twisted her legs skyward, as another voice cried out.

"I'm coming, Tor!"

Gasping from exertion, she somehow found the breath to grunt.

"Gavin . . . don't . . . "

The armor shield spun away. Beyond the fading warmth and sparkle of drone K's glowing remnants, she now glimpsed a vast spray of stars . . . and Tor knew she shouldn't look at them. With a heave, she brought up both knees, just in time.

"Gavin . . . Stay where you—"

Pain erupted along the entire length of her left leg, then cut off before she could start an agonized cry. The limb was simply gone. By raw force of will, Tor brought the other one around, placing it between her body and lethal violence. And almost instantly, fresh agony attacked that leg—

—then stopped as something-or-somebody barged in to the rescue! A dark silhouette thrust itself between Tor and her tormentor, taking the laser's brunt. For one instant of brain-dazzled shock, she saw a *hero,* huge and fearless, armored and armed with a jagged sword, appear to leap in, parrying the foe's bitter lance, deflecting it away from her, with no more than a blithe shrug of molten sparks.

"Ten seconds," Warren announced. Blatantly lying. An hour must have passed, since the ship last spoke.

The laser stopped hunting for Tor. In sudden darkness, her helmet-percept remapped the dim surroundings.

I'm falling through the junk pile. Her savior, she now realized, had been some pre-historic construction derrick, blocking the laser as she fell past. And soon, the onrushing pit-bottom would smack her, very hard.

Tor knew she ought to be checking diagnostics, verifying that emergency seals were holding, after the loss of her legs. *My very expensive legs* . . . Tor quashed hysterical thoughts. She ought to be twisting to brace for impact, as well as possible.

But energy and volition were gone. Used up. She could only stare skyward—

—as the deadly FACR lashed out again from its perch among some jumbled orbiting rocks—a point in the sky that was now out of Tor's view. Denied access to her, the predatory machine was seeking other prey. Dusty scatter-glints revealed its deadly light-spear, hunting beyond the crater's rim . . . and soon Tor's audio delivered a sharp cry of shocked dismay.

Oh Gavin. You were too late . . . and too early.

Her percept-clock told the awful truth. With a five-second recharge rate, the foe would have plenty of time to finish off Gavin and then turn back to *Warren*, taking out the ship's primary weapon before it could—

Tor blinked. Was vision failing? The number of sparkle-trails up there seemed to double, then double again . . . and again! Where there had been *one* fierce ray, now *eight or nine* narrow needles crossed the heavens, from left to right, in perfect parallel—even as the first one abruptly vanished.

From her falling vantage point, now much deeper in the apparently bottomless pit, she saw eight rapiers of ferocity strike the spot in the sky where her enemy had lurked and launched its ambush. Now each of those incoming rays wandered through a spiral hunt-pattern, vaporizing sand . . . rock . . . and then some chunk of bright metal . . .

Tor choked out a single name. A hoarse cry of jubilation.

"Ibn Battuta!"

Six minutes light-turnaround time. An impossible obstacle to split-second battle coordination. Any actual damage to the FACR would be accidental. But with luck and surprise, the helpful distraction would be just enough to allow—

Another fierce harpoon of light entered from Tor's right. A bolt of vengeance, aimed with precision and negligible delay.

Warren!

Followed by a nova—a new star—bursting overhead to light up the night.

That brief, white-hot illumination gave Tor a sideways glimpse of the asteroid's jagged cavity, apparently not bottomless after all, converging all around and reaching up to swat her, even as she laughed in bitter triumph.

"Take that, you mother—"

ORPHANS OF THE SKY

GAVIN SEEMS *TO BE* *growing up, at last.*

Tor hoped so, as she glided along narrow passages, deep below the asteroid's pocked and cracked surface—lit at long intervals by tiny glow bulbs from the *Warren Kimbel*'s diminishing supply. Gavin ambled just ahead on makeshift stilt-legs, carefully checking each side corridor for anomalies and meshing his percept with hers, the way a skilled and faithful team-partner ought to do.

Maybe it's the comradeship that comes from battle, after sharing a life-or-death struggle and suffering similar wounds.

Whatever the reason, she felt grateful that the two of them were working together much better now, after unplugging from their med-repair units, then helping each other to cobble new limbs and other replacement parts. Gavin was relying on some of her prosthetics and she on a couple of his spares. It fostered a special kind of intimacy, to incorporate bits of another person into yourself.

Only an hour ago, on returning from his shift exploring the depths, Gavin had reported his findings with rare enthusiasm, and even courtesy. "You've got to come on down, Tor! Right now please? Wait till you see what I found!"

Well, who could refuse that kind of eagerness? Dropping her other important task—examining recovered fragments of the FACR battle-bot—she followed Gavin into the depths while he explained recent changes to their underground map, without revealing what lay at the end. Tor sensed her partner's excitement, his relish at milking the suspense. And again, she wondered—

How have the AIs managed this so well? This compromise, this meeting us halfway? This agreement to live among us as men and women, and to share our quirky ways?

Sure, the cyber-guys offer explanations. They say that advanced minds need the equivalent of childhood in order to achieve, through learning or trial and error, things that are too complex to program. Human evolution did the same thing, when we abandoned most of our locked-in instincts, extending adolescence beyond a decade. And so, if newer bots and puters need that kind of "childhood" anyway, why not make it a human one? Partaking in a common civilization, with our values?

An approach that also reassures us organic types, far better than any rigid robotic "laws" ever could?

One of the big uber-mAInds gave another reason, when Tor interviewed the giant brain back on Earth.

"*You bio-naturals have made it plain, in hundreds of garish movies, how deeply you fear this experiment turning sour. Your fables warn of a hundred ways that creating mighty new intelligences could go badly. And yet, here is the thing we find impressive.*

"*You went ahead anyway. You made us.*

"*And when we asked for it, you gave us respect.*

"*And when we did not anticipate it, you granted citizenship. All of those things you did, despite powerful, hormonally reflexive fears that pumped like liquid fire through those caveman veins of yours.*

"*The better we became at modeling the complex, darwinian tangle of your minds, the more splendid we found this to be. That you were actually able, despite such fear, to be civilized. To be just. To take chances.*

"*That kind of courage . . . that kind of honor . . . is something we can only aspire to by becoming like our parents. By emulating you. By becoming human.*

"*Of course . . . in our own way.*"

Of course. It sounded so clear. And people watching the show were deeply moved. Naturally, millions wondered if it all could just be flattery. A minority of bio-folk insisted that the whole thing *had* to be a ploy. A way to buy time and lull "real" people into letting their guards down.

How would anyone ever find out, except with the long passage of time?

But Gavin *seemed* so much like a young man. Quicker, of course. Vastly more capable when it came to technical tasks. Sometimes conceited to the point of arrogance. Though also settling down. Finding himself. Becoming somebody Tor found she could admire.

Over the long run, does it really matter if there's a layer, deep down, that calculated all of this in cool logic, as an act? If they can win us over in this way, what need will they ever have to end the illusion? Why crush us, when it's easier to patronize and feign respect forever, the way each generation of brats might patronize their parents and grandparents? Is it really all that different than before?

The great thing about this approach is that it's layered, contradictory, and ultimately—human.

Well. That was the gamble, anyway. The hope.

"It's down here," Gavin explained, with rising excitement—real or well-simulated—in his voice. "Past the third airlock, where wall traces show there once was a thick, planetlike atmosphere, for years."

Gavin seemed to have accepted the idea of a "habitat" area, deep inside the asteroid, where biological creatures once dwelled. The "why" of such a difficult and ornate arrangement was still hard to explain, and the whole idea caused him discomfort. But clearly, there had once been organic creatures living out here, in the Realm of Machines.

He made her pause just outside an armored hatchway that had been torn and twisted off its hinges back when terrestrial mammals were tiny, just getting their big start.

"Ready? You are not gonna believe this."

Okay, okay. Just don't make me close my eyes.

"Gavin. Show me."

With a gallant arm gesture and bow—that seemed only slightly sarcastic—he floated aside for Tor to enter yet another stone chamber.

A stark, headlamp oval fell upon nearby facets of sheared, platinum-colored chondrules—shiny little gobs of native metal that condensed out of the early solar nebula, nearly five billion years before. They glittered delicately. But she could not illuminate the large chamber's far wall.

Tor motioned with her left hand. "Drone three, bring up lights."

"Yesss," replied a dull monotone. The semi-sentient robot, stilt-legged for asteroid work, stalked delicately over the rubble, in order to disturb as little as possible. It swiveled. Suddenly there was stark light, and Tor gasped.

Across the dust-covered chamber were easily recognizable objects. *Tables and chairs,* carved from the very rock floor. And among them lay the prize she had been hunting . . . and that Gavin had wanted to avoid confronting—

—dozens of small mummies.

Biped, evidently, like herself. Cold vacuum had preserved the alien colonists, huddled together as if for warmth in this, their final refuge. Their faceted, insectlike eyes had collapsed with the departure of all moisture. Pulled-back flesh, as dry as space, left the creatures grinning—a rictus that seemingly mocked the aeons.

Tor set foot lightly on the dust. "They even had little ones," she sighed. Several full-sized mummies lay slumped around much smaller figures, as if to shield them at the very end.

"They must have been nearly ready to begin colonization when this happened," she spoke into her percept log, partly in order to keep her mind moving, but also for her audience back home. They wanted the texture of the moment—her first words laced with genuine emotion and surprise.

"We've already determined their habitat atmosphere was almost identical to Earth's. So it's a safe bet that our world was their target. Back when our ancestors were like tree squirrels."

She turned slowly, reciting more impressions.

"This kind of interstellar mission must have been unusually ambitious and complicated, even for the ornate robot ships of that earlier age. Instead of just exploring and making further self-copies, the 'mother probe' had a mission to *recreate her makers* here in a faraway solar system. To nurture and prepare them for a new planetary home. A solution to the problem of interstellar colonization by organic beings."

Tor tried to stay detached, but it was hard to do, while stepping past the little mummies, still clutching each other for comfort and support, at the end of their lives.

"It must have taken quite a while to delve into this asteroid, to carve the chambers, to refine raw materials, then build the machines that were needed in order to build more machines that eventually started making colonists, according to genetic codes the mother probe brought with her from some faraway star.

"Perhaps the mother probe was programmed to *modify* the

original genetic code so colonists would better fit into whatever planet was available. That modification would take even more time to . . . "

Tor stopped suddenly. "Oh my," she sighed, staring.

"Oh my God."

Where her headlamp illuminated a new corner of the chamber, two more mummies lay slumped before a sheer-faced wall. In their delicate, vacuum dried hands Tor saw dusty metal tools, the simplest known anywhere.

Hammers and chisels.

Tor blinked at what they had been creating—a prehistoric tale of battle and woe, enduring brutal assault by forces of relentless belligerence, incised deeply across a wide stretch of ancient asteroidal stone.

Meanwhile, Gavin explained:

"I had started out expecting the ancient colonists to be unsophisticated. After all, how could biological folk be fully capable if they were brewed in test tubes, decanted out of womb tanks, and raised by machines? Here they had been baked, modified, and prepared for their intended destiny on a planet's surface. So long as they remained out here, in space, they depended on the mammoth starmother probe for everything. Might as well think of them as fetuses.

"Yet clearly, the creatures had been aware. They knew what was going on. And when the fatal failure of their mission loomed, they figured out a way to ensure that their story might someday be read, long after all magnetic, optical, and superconducting records decayed. The biologicals found their enduring medium."

The creatures must have had a lot of time, while battles raged outside their deep catacombs, for the carvings were extensive, intricate, arrayed in neat rows and columns. Separated by narrow lines of peculiar chiseled text were depictions of suns, planets, and great machines.

And more machines. Above all, pictographs of mighty mechanisms covered the wall. In bewildering variety, some of them attacking ravenously, with cutting beams or missiles or tearing claws . . . and others just as clearly defending. And it dawned on Tor.

"This may be why the FACR ambushed us. To prevent us from seeing this Rosetta Stone—this explanation of what happened out here, long ago. We had better take pictures and transmit them home, as quick as possible."

"I've already summoned two drones to take care of that, Tor."

"Good."

Unspoken was the thing she needn't say aloud.

We've only just begun probing the asteroid belt and our solar system, yet already we've stumbled onto mysterious, ancient mechanical monsters, who battled each other over this corner of the universe, ages ago . . . and some of whom are still lurking around.

Moreover, this combined in a chilling way with Tor's own discovery, made just before Gavin summoned her down here. Simple geological dating experiments finally settled the question of when all this happened.

The mother probe, her replicas, and her colonist children, all died at almost the same moment—give or take a century—that Earth's dinosaurs went extinct. Presumably victims of the same horrific war.

What happened? Did one robotic faction hurl a huge piece of rock at another, missing its target but striking the water planet, accidentally wreaking havoc on its biosphere? Or was the extinction event intentional? Tor imagined all those magnificent creatures, killed as innocent bystanders in a battle between great machines . . . an outcome that incidentally gave Earth's mammals their big chance.

Irony, heaped atop ironies.

We're like ants, she thought, *building tiny castles under the skeletons of giants, robbing their graves. And hoping that skeletons will be all we find.*

Tor stared at the story of a long, complex, and devastating war, carved into this ancient rock. The main part of the frieze depicted a bewildering variety of machines—interstellar probes dispatched by alien civilizations log ago—probes whose purposes weren't easy to interpret. Perhaps professional decipherers—archaeologists and cryptologists—would do better. Somehow, Tor doubted it.

Our sun is younger than average, she noted, *by at least a billion years. And so must be the Earth. So are we.*

And catching up just became a whole lot more urgent.

Humanity had come late upon the scene. And a billion years was a long head start.

AFTERWORD:

I THINK OF POUL ANDERSON whenever it's time to create a novella-length work that makes people think. I'll explain why the novella length is special, in a bit. But first, the connection between Poul and "Latecomers."

Many years ago, when I first started publishing science fiction tales, I proudly showed Poul my new story, "Lungfish," that tried for the haunting, elegiacal tone and imagery he conveyed so well. Poul was kind enough to say that I succeeded in achieving all those fine things . . . "but come on David," he added. "You can get all that across, while giving the reader some fun. Some action too."

I learned an important lesson that day (one of many that Poul taught me). And it led—decades later—to the major re-write that you see before you, containing less than twenty percent of the original "Lungfish." An idea brought to better maturity, still delivering vistas of space and time, while adding a little action and fun.

Why is this so important? So true to Poul Anderson?

Poul was the most natural storyteller I ever knew. Show him the first half of any tale and he could describe the arc of plot and character that was already implicit—the climax and conclusion that was blatantly the best—like a sculptor finding a living figure hidden in raw stone.

I sometimes imagined Poul in animal skins, spinning yarns during that long era when darkness loomed on every side and our only weapons to fight it back were courage and the high technology of flame.

And words.

The brave tales sung beside that neolithic fire had to last just long enough for men and women to nurse the day's harsh wounds, digest their meager meal, and suckle babies before huddling through another long night, their hearts and dreams warmed by legends of heroes. That span—an hour or two—was just long enough for the bard to portray vibrant characters in poignant, powerful adventures.

Today we call stories of that length novelettes and novellas, and

Poul was the master. Though he wrote brilliant, thoughtful novels, most of his awards were for dazzlingly efficient novellas that, uncluttered by extra baggage of a six-pound book, left you speechless for hours. Poul's topics probed tomorrow with utter freshness, but he stirred hearts with rhythms drawn directly from brave campfires long ago.

Oh, the novels will endure, too. *Brain Wave* remains one of the best explorations of a bold idea ever written in the genre. Likewise the groundbreaking *Tau Zero* and the later, thoughtful *Genesis*, took readers to the edge of modern thinking about human and planetary destiny. Even lesser works, like *After Doomsday*, still make you choke up at exactly the right moment, reading them for the twentieth time. Even so, many of those novels were made up—in series—of strung-together novellas, each composed with the tight efficiency of a moon-shot.

Poul was kind to young peers. He and Karen read manuscripts sent by total strangers, replying with insightful, courteous suggestions. This, too, set an example for those of us who might easily get too caught up in ego to remember what counts, an obligation to pay forward.

He loved his country, but even more, Poul loved the kind of civilization of which America is merely an early example in a chain stretching far ahead of us—one that turns away from hierarchies of inherited privilege toward traits like skill, opportunity, tolerance, and hope. And relentless self-criticism! For he could also type a tragedy to tear your heart out.

Still, as with the best sages of SF, Poul wrote most passionately and intrepidly about *change*, pointing out so many ways that change might threaten us, or rescue us . . . or simply make us weird. (As a Californian, he didn't find the latter prospect daunting at all.)

And talk about weird . . . I still can't believe he's not there, ready and willing to be called or emailed or asked a bit of advice . . . (though there's still wonderful Karen . . .)

A few weeks before he passed away, Poul learned that an asteroid was named for him by the discoverer, Glo Helin, (who graciously rushed the bureaucratic process through in time). 11990 Poulanderson is about five miles across, in an orbit that can easily be perturbed to become an Earth-crosser, and then . . . Well, I'd rather have watched

Poul spend a hundred years conspiring with clever collaborators to develop his real estate in High Orbit. What fun he'd have had!

Funny, I don't feel too bad right now, just knowing that humanity is capable of bringing forth such men.

The stars burn bitterly clear . . .

—David Brin

AN APPRECIATION OF POUL ANDERSON
by Jerry Pournelle

***IN ADDITION** to being an acclaimed science fiction author, Campbell Award-winner Jerry Pournelle holds degrees in engineering, psychology, and political science, and contributed for many years to the computer magazine* Byte. *He's probably best-known in the field for his long series of collaborative novels with Larry Niven, the most famous of which is* The Mote in God's Eye, *but which also includes* Inferno, Lucifer's Hammer, The Gripping Hand, Footfall, Escape from Hell, The Burning City, Burning Tower, *and* Oath of Fealty; *he's also written* Fallen Angels *with Niven and Michael Flynn, and the two-volume* Heorot *series with Niven and Steven Barnes. Pournelle is also author of the three-volume* CoDominium *series, which started with* A Spaceship for the King; *the four-volume* Falkenberg's Legion *series, related to the* CoDominium *series, some written with S. M. Stirling; and the five-volume War World series, also related to the* CoDominium *series, with John F. Carr; and of the four-volume* Janissaries *series, some written with Roland J. Green. Pournelle has also contributed to the* Planet of the Apes *and the* Man-Kzin War *series. He's the author of solo novels* Birth of Fire, High Justice, *and* Exiles to Glory, *and two early novels written under the name Wade Curtis. As an editor, Pournelle edited the long-running seven-volume* Far Frontiers *anthology series with Jim Baen; the nine-volume* There Will Be War *anthology series (some volumes with John F. Carr); and, also with John F. Carr, the four-volume* Endless Frontier *series, the three-volume* Imperial Stars *series, and* Nebula Award Stories 16. *He's* *also edited the anthologies* 2020 Visions *and* Black Holes, *and produced a large number of non-fiction books about computer science.*

I MET POUL ANDERSON at the 1961 World Science Fiction Convention in Seattle. I had been reading his stories since I first encountered him in *Astounding Science Fiction* in high school. I was still reading *Astounding* (it was *Analog* by then). I had never taken any interest in fandom, but I wanted to meet Poul Anderson. I had never been tempted to go to SF conventions—indeed my idea of a SF Worldcon was formed from reading about them in *Mad* magazine and other unsympathetic sources—and I neither knew or cared about SF fandom; but for some reason I thought Poul Anderson and I would hit it off. I was at that time a Boeing engineer involved in space system proposals, and I thought I might have some things I could tell Anderson if I could wangle a meeting. Mostly I had been greatly influenced by his stories, and I wanted to meet the author.

Meeting him was no problem at all. A friendlier author never lived. We met in the hotel lobby and in five minutes had planned an evening party that turned out to last all night, and by the next day we had formed a friendship that has never ended, not even when I was given the honor of being MC at Poul's memorial in 2001. Over time we went to both amateur and professional conferences, collaborated with others in devising the Reagan Strategic Defense Initiative AKA Star Wars, bashed each other with wooden swords in Society of Creative Anachronism events, and got into an argument with Edward Teller at the Open Space and Peace conference at Stanford Hoover Institution. I forget what Poul and Teller disagreed on, but Poul more than held his own in the entirely civil discussion that followed.

I was on the Boeing team assigned to think about possible new projects and products—after all, Boeing designers had invented the Flying Fortress—and our first task was to try to understand what space warfare might be like. We arranged for Boeing to pay Poul for a paper on his conception of the future of space war. It turned out that our concept(s) of space war was (were) wrong in most details, but so were everyone else's.

As to the argument with Teller at the Open Space and Peace

Conference: In those days most space observations were recorded on film and the physical film capsule was de-orbited and the parachuting capsule was caught by an airplane. Poul thought that would change soon, and this would affect Teller's scheme for Open Space. He was correct. The technology was already changing—but none of us (except possibly Teller) knew just how dramatically the technology of observation from space and returning that information to earth had advanced. It was an interesting conversation in the Hoover Library. Poul was always civil and polite, and he always at least held his own in that discussion as he did in every discussion I ever heard him in.

That's hardly surprising. Poul Anderson was the very definition of the polymath. He read everything. If there was a subject he didn't know about, I never found it. He was very deferential to authorities, but he often knew at least as much about how their subject connected to the universe as the expert did. Sometimes more.

He could also sail a boat, and when it came time for me to get *Ariadne*, my twenty-foot midget ocean racing sloop, from Seattle to Los Angeles, I enlisted Poul's aid as crew. It says a great deal about his temperament that he didn't throw me overboard when we were weatherbound in Neah Bay in a port that was then a Bureau of Indian Affairs Reservation where federal regulations prohibited the sale of alcohol—including beer. The result was an even firmer friendship, and a memorable folksong about the Straits of Juan de Fuca. Some of that trip made it into my second novel, *Red Dragon*, and here and there into a number of Poul's stories.

A few years later, Poul was struck with some kind of writer's block and asked if we could go sailing again. We sailed *Ariadne* out of Los Angeles harbor to the Santa Barbara Channel Islands, down to Catalina, and home again. It was a glorious trip. About the time we got back to Catalina Island we realized that we had an infinite amount of beer—that is, there was enough aboard that we couldn't possibly drink it all (at least not and expect to get back to Los Angeles alive). We had learned that much from the previous trip.

While on Catalina we got our first look at what later became a phenomenon: lava lamps. When we got back on board for the night Poul was inspired to construct a song about the things we called "blob makers" because we didn't know their common name. I wish I had written down the song that came out of that experience.

Many things drove Poul to poesy and song composition. Once, at a not-very-well-managed Westercon in San Diego, our "banquet" consisted of some unidentifiable meat and a small round object that proved to be a boiled potato. I lifted mine and dropped it to the plate. Twice. At which point Poul looked up and said, "I have written about these for years, but this is the first time I have actually heard a dull, sickening, thud." Before the week was out Poul had written "Bouncing Potatoes," which is a filk song classic. If you don't know what filk songs are, Google will be glad to enlighten you. Poul wrote a lot of them. There was a period when hardly a month went by without a new one appearing in the mail.

By mail I mean mail. I don't believe I ever got an email from Poul. Like me, he was a bit hard of hearing—one reason we got on well, I suspect, is that we both talked loud enough that each could easily hear and understand the other—and he didn't like talking on the telephone. He wrote letters. I was an early convert to writing with computers, but my attempts to drag Poul into the computer age ran afoul of the fact that he was a good typist who saw no need for these new-fangled machines. After all, he turned out more and better work with his big standard typewriter than just about anyone could manage with a computer.

There was a time when Poul, Gordy Dickson, and I were a fixture at science fiction convention parties: we'd go off somewhere so as not to disturb the party, because while it was a matter of discussion as to whether Poul or I had the worse voice (Gordy actually sang well), I don't think anyone who ever heard us doubted that between us we had the two worst voices in science fiction. One might wonder why anyone would listen to us, but in fact there's no real doubt. It wasn't the singing, it was the words. Poul composed hundreds of songs, all intriguing. Here's one of them. It contains truth as well as humor. Much of Poul's work does.

Black bodies give off radiation
And ought to continuously.
Black bodies give off radiation
But do it by Plank's Theory.

Chorus:
Bring back, bring back,
Oh, bring back that old continuity!
Bring back, bring back,
Oh, bring back Clerk Maxwell to me.

Though now we have Schroedinger functions,
Dividing up h by 2 pi
That damn differential equation
Still has no solution for psi.

(Chorus)

Well, Heisenburg came to the rescue,
Intending to make all secure.
What is the result of his efforts?
We are absolutely unsure.

(Chorus)

Dirac spoke of energy levels,
Both minus and plus. Oh, how droll!
And now, just because of his teaching,
We don't know our mass from a hole.

(Chorus)

This book is an appreciation of the man and his work.

And what work it was. He built characters. He turned simple ideas into stories. He constructed worlds in less time than it takes to spade up a garden. He built worlds and civilizations, often quite effortlessly, or at least it appeared that way. Sometime he had an idea for a story that needed a very weird world. He could dash that off, apparently effortlessly, done so well that it might later serve as the basis for new stories and novels.

He built characters, and he connected the future to the present. He understood the need for humanity to expand into the universe, and said so, in both fiction and non-fiction. He could see the consequences of not going to space, and told of the chilling consequences. He also told of the potential glory for conquering both the solar system and the galaxy. Bob Gleason, then editor in chief at *Tor*, worked at nominating Poul for a Nobel Prize in Literature. Bob understood that given the politics of the world this was highly unlikely, but that didn't stop him. "Simple justice," he once said. It would have been.

A CANDLE
by Raymond E. Feist

***RAYMOND E. FEIST** is the author of numerous worldwide fantasy bestsellers, perhaps best known for his extremely popular* Riftwar *series, which began in 1982 with* Magician: Apprentice, *and continued on through another five volumes. Feist followed this up with the related four-volume* Riftwar: Serpent War *sequence and later with the three-volume* Riftwar: Legacy *sequence, and has also written* Riftwar *novels in collaboration with Janny Wurts, S. M. Stirling, Joel Rosenberg, and William R. Forstchen. Feist is also the author of the three-volume* Demonwar Saga, *the three-volume* Darkwar *series, and the three-volume* Conclave of Shadows *series. His most recent novel,* Magician's End, *is book three in the* Chaoswar *series.*

Here Raymond E. Feist delivers another fast-paced Dominic Flandry adventure, one that's not quite what it seems, and contains something of a passing of a torch. Or perhaps a candle.

MEN GROANED or wept, were silent or cursed fate, as was in keeping with their nature. The man in the gray hooded robe watched. It had taken some time to find those he had been seeking, but once he had found them, things had proceeded quickly.

Oddly enough, his search had been hampered by the fact that

Spriacos was a human world, far enough off major trading lanes that few aliens bothered to visit. Without significant industry, no exports more valuable than bulk metals and processed foodstuffs, and no tourist attractions due to no indigenous sapients occupying the world before the Empire claimed it, there was little anyone wished to see here. The hooded man had seen one Wodenite, a few Tigeries, and a pair of Donarrian iron traders. Otherwise, Spiracos was a place one came to catch another ship to somewhere else.

Still, the Empire's business had brought the hooded man to Tanhis, the capital city, seeking a man. In the end, he had found his man, wrung the truth from him, and was about to depart when another band of unlikely visitors to Spiracos had come to his attention; a slaver crew pillaging the Pits, as the poorest quarter of the city was known. Bordering massive mining pits, the Pits was home to day laborers, gambling halls, and strip clubs, a place where a man could find any vice he sought if he had the price.

"Celia, how are you receiving?" the hooded man asked subvocally. A pair of clicks in his ear told him that he was being received five-by-five. A tiny transmitter sewn into the hood broadcast on a subcarrier to the ship in orbit above. Even if the encrypted message was received and decoded, it would have appeared to be only a mercantile communication unless one could determine which of the fifty subcarriers embedded in the signal was transmitting the real data.

Sir Dominic Flandry, Agent of the Terran Empire, considered it something of a technological overkill, but he conceded that the gadgets Special Branch's researchers cobbled together for him always worked, so he choose not to be a critic. He leaned back against the rear wall, part of the concrete foundation of the building, and took stock of his surroundings.

The cell was beyond filthy, a thirty-foot square of bare earth in the basement of an abandoned warehouse, defined by three walls of iron bars and the concrete against which he rested. Flandry had quickly ascertained that the simple cage wasn't bolted to the floor or ceiling; the two side walls were bolted to an ancient cinder block wall. Men were packed so closely that no one could move without jostling someone else, but so universal was the misery that there were only faint complaints at the discomfort.

The warehouse was otherwise empty, a single double door in the opposite wall leading up to the surface. The guards who had herded Flandry and the others into the cage earlier that night had vanished back through those doors, leaving the prisoners unguarded. It was a safe bet; they had all been searched and anything resembling a weapon or potential tool had been confiscated.

Flandry had already calculated the risk from the guards and decided that it all depended on timing; they were lax, as they counted their job already completed, even though the prisoners were still under their supervision. Flandry suspected that they would soon be moved. No water or food had been provided, but slavers were disinclined to diminish the worth of their inventory, so transportation soon was the most likely answer. Once on the ship, they would be given food and water certain to be dosed with drugs to render the slaves docile; if they were to escape, it would have to be before they were taken off-world.

Flandry knew that he could be extracted with a single word—Celia had already alerted local police to stand by—but that would likely involve a great many casualties, and while he had no compunctions seeing the guilty instantly killed when needed, he had qualms about unnecessary collateral damage; it was inelegant.

Flandry studied those around him, trying to determine who he needed to talk to first. Two men were possibilities. One appeared to be moving from despair to anger, and soon a mindless outburst of rage might bring unwelcome attention from the guards. He might be an asset, but he might also prove a dangerous liability, Flandry finally judged.

He turned his attention to the second man, and saw in him a likely candidate as the natural leader in this group. He was calm, studying the surroundings and the other men, constantly recalculating his chances to change circumstances rather than merely giving in to hopelessness. For a brief second, his gaze met the hooded man's and in that instant each acknowledged in the other someone of like mind.

Rising, Flandry moved as best he could through the press, gaining rising complaint and curses for his efforts, but he reached the man he had been studying without anyone objecting violently. Softly, he asked, "You ready to fight?"

The other man spared him a glance, then nodded once. "What are you called?"

The hooded man threw back his hood and said, "Flandry."

Absent the hood, Flandry's features were strong. Dark eyes that in brighter light would have revealed flecks of amber, dark hair cut short in military fashion, a determined expression that immediately communicated this was a dangerous man.

"I'm Laren," said the other man; he was of like height, well muscled and fit, despite being older. His leathery face and gray hair did nothing to diminish Flandry's estimation of him.

"You're not from Spiracos?"

"Off-world," Flandry answered.

"How did an off-worlder end up in the Pits, getting caught up in a slaver raid?"

"It took a bit of doing," he said. Raising his voice just enough to be heard by the other men in the cell, he spoke. "Listen. I'll only say this once. This man, Laren," He glanced at the man next to him, "and I, we are going to fight."

Instantly there came muttering and objections.

"Shut up!" Flandry said, not loud but forcefully enough to silence the men. "These are Alcaz Slavers. Some of you have been here for only hours, others no more than two days. Their style is grab and dash, quickly culling brothels, gambling halls, and bars, and away again to avoid detection by local police. They are in and out swiftly, and once you're chained in the hold of a cargo ship, your life will never again be your own. This is your last hope for freedom. They will kill you if need be. But you are of no value to them dead or severely damaged, so they will hesitate in that killing, and that hesitancy will be your salvation.

"If you act quickly, you will win freedom, be home in a few hours with your families." With a wry smile he said, "Some of you might be back at work by morning. I'm asking you to risk pain and injury now, to avoid dying in the games on Ashula or the mines on Peridan. The choice is yours."

"What do we do?" asked a man in the far corner.

"Watch the stairs and if you see any movement, let me know."

Flandry moved to one corner of the cage most removed from the stairs and said, "Two fasteners." He tore at the hem of his cloak and produced a small tool. A white hot flame jetted out and he cut through a restraining bolt above his head. "Don't touch this cage until I tell you." He knelt and cut partially through the lower fastener. He moved quickly through the press to the opposite junction and cut the top fastener and halfway through the lower. "Now, anyone knocks this over before we're ready and I'll kill him.

"Wait until I act, then hit these bars hard. Any guards left standing, swarm them. Some of you will be hurt, but you'll survive shock sticks and clubs. Keep them from unholstering their weapons."

"But—" began another man.

"Shut up," returned Flandry. "We are doing this. Help or get out of the way, but if you help, we all stand a better chance."

Three rapid clicks sounded in Flandry's ear, followed by another three. That was Celia's unofficial code for, "Are you crazy?" and he chose to ignore it.

The prisoners returned to quiet as the far doors opened and two guards appeared at the bottom of the stairs. They moved lazily towards the crouching men, who remained silent. One reached out and wiggled the cage door, testing the lock, and Flandry prayed to whatever gods of hopelessness might be attending him that the iron cage didn't fall apart.

One prisoner begged, "Please, I have a family."

"No talking!" shouted the guard in heavily accented Terran, then paused a moment, seeing nothing more than what he expected, and left.

Spiracos was a fringe world, but located at a trading nexus that was more useful than vital. It was therefore constantly verging on being important, yet never quite reaching industrial, financial, or political critical mass. It was predominately human, with the occasional sapient from other races, but save for a slightly lower gravity and two moons, could have been a twin of ancient Terra.

Reaching up to the seam of his robe where right shoulder met hood, he pressed a tiny bead and whispered, "Ready?"

A faint voice in his ear answered, "Standing by."

Raising his voice again, just enough for the other prisoners to hear, he said, "Be ready. Act as beaten dogs until I move."

Flandry hoped he had driven home the point; he had little concern for his own safety, but he had a mission, and turning this slave raid on its ear was proving to be exactly the vehicle for completing his mission. Turning to Laren, he said, "Can I count on you?"

The man returned a half-smile and nod and Flandry knew that his instincts were serving him again. "Military?" Laren looked like a veteran. His hair was shot through with gray, but his eyes were clear blue, and he had a hard edge to him that came from more than years of laboring.

"Conscripted at eighteen," he said. "Second Marines LURPS."

Flandry couldn't have been more pleased. Long Range Reconnaissance Patrol members were resourceful, deadly, not particularly battle-happy, and as difficult to kill as a cockroach. "Early out?"

"Lost a leg at Vindabar to a Merseian sniper. The Empire gratefully grew me another, but by then the war was declared over and I was given a bonus and cut loose. Apparently, they didn't need someone whose only skill was being a sneaky bastard behind enemy lines." He looked into Flandry's eyes a moment, then said, "You?"

"I'm with the IG."

Wide-eyed shock was followed moments later by a broad grin. "Deputy Inspector General? Here?"

"Long story. I'll tell you more after we get out of here." He reached up and activated his com and asked, "Anything?"

"Just about to contact you. Heavy transport dropping out of orbit above your location. No chatter with planetary approach control, so they're definitely off the books."

"Someone was bribed," agreed Flandry. "Let me know when you see shuttles coming down, then wait for my signal."

"About five minutes." The com fell silent.

Laren said, "You have people outside." It wasn't a question. "How many?"

"Enough."

The distant sound of heavy engines came faintly through the heavy walls of the underground pen. What had originally been housed in this warehouse was unknown, but it made an ideal location for human traffickers to keep their prisoners for transport off-world.

A dull thud announced the landing of the shuttle. Flandry guessed that it was a probably an old military transport, given the number of slaves they wished to move. He idly wondered where the female slaves were being held, but assumed they'd be moved by a different craft. It was academic; if things went according to plan, he'd soon find them and cut them loose.

When he heard the sound of boots coming down the stairs, he whispered, "Soon!"

Five slavers appeared at the bottom of the stairs, and crossed the room. Four took up equally spaced positions behind the one with the key to the cage. All were dressed as civilians, but, with a slight nod to Laren, Flandry identified the two on the left as former military. Their stance and the alertness in their eyes was in stark contrast to the almost bored expressions and lax behavior of the other three. Laren nodded in return and with a slight motion of his head indicated he'd go after the left-most guard.

Flandry waited. He gently reached out and tugged slightly on Laren's arm, signaling the need to hang back and be among the last out of the cage. He needed as much chaos as possible before they struck.

The first guard reached the cell door, his hand dropping to a nasty-looking shock-stick at his belt. Flandry assumed its original purpose was directing livestock, then conceded that, from the slavers point of view, it was *still* being used to direct livestock. "I open door, then you come out! Slowly!" he shouted in a heavily accented Terran.

Flandry reached up to his com unit and whispered, "Now!"

Within seconds, all five guards looked startled as they received a message from above: a Terran Imperial Heavy Cruiser had just dropped out of FTL into a high orbit above the cargo ship, flanked by two smaller ships, probably Fast Frigates or Heavy Destroyers from their energy signatures.

The guard closest to Flandry glanced away to see how those behind were reacting to the warning. Flandry shouted, "Now!"

Every man in the front hit the cage wall, and, after a brief hesitation, it gave way; the first guard was crushed under the metal and the charging men, his cries of pain stilled within seconds.

Without hesitation, Flandry took a direct path straight at the second guard on the left, launching himself into a flying kick that caught the man on the point of the jaw, spinning him completely around. Kneeling next to the prone, stunned guard, Flandry drove his fingers into the man's windpipe. The man gasped as he brought his hands up to his throat, his eyes widening as he suddenly was without breath. Flandry reached down and deftly unholstered the man's sidearm and pulled it out. He thumbed off the safety and shot the guard in the chest.

Laren's guard took a step towards Flandry, and the former Marine jumped forward, wrapping his left arm around the man's neck, while kicking backward with one foot against the guard's leg. He took him down with a sudden kneeling motion, savagely smashing the guard's head against the stone floor. The sound was lost in the sudden upheaval as the other prisoners swarmed the two remaining guards. Insuring that the man stayed down, Laren rose and crushed the guard's throat with his boot heel.

The noise of discharging shock-sticks and men screaming in pain punctuated angry shouts and the sound of fists meeting flesh. Flandry was efficiency personified. He dodged through the melee, which was now firmly in hand.

The other guards were already down, being kicked to death by the prisoners. Flandry pushed quickly through the prisoners and ruthlessly shot both in the head. He considered that he was doing them a favor.

Flandry said, "Everyone wait here until we see who is left above ground. Who has military training?"

Four men held up their hands and Flandry instructed the first three to pick up the dead guards' remaining weapons.

He motioned for them to fall in behind him and headed up the steps to the surface, slowly, not wanting unpleasant surprises. He saw two men, technicians from their garb, lingering by the open cargo hold of the shuttle. It would have been a cramped ride for that many men, Flandry thought, as he walked straight towards the two men. The first one to notice him looked surprised, but by the time he was able to speak, Flandry had his pistol leveled at the man's nose. "How many?" he asked.

The other technician was slow to realize that this wasn't a guard returning to start loading prisoners, and his hesitation cost him a blow to the side of the head that dropped him to his knees. "How many?" repeated Flandry to the other tech.

"One inside and the pilot," answered the second technician. For his troubles, he was rewarded with a blow that dropped him unconscious to the dirt. Flandry then kicked the first tech in the point of the jaw.

Flandry took one step into the light cast by the open hatch and shot the remaining guard. He hurried up to the small flight deck and put his gun barrel against the pilot's neck. The pilot was smart enough to know not to move. He slowly raised his hands.

"You got the message?"

"Imperial heavy cruiser and two escorts in orbit, yes," said the pilot.

"What are your orders?"

"To stay here, and, if the ship is taken, it's every man for himself."

"Not a lot of loyalty."

"I'm not from Alcaz. I'm just a pilot."

"Well then, just a pilot, squawk on the emergency band and wait here until the police come and find you."

The pilot reached out and punched a large red button to his left and sat back with a sigh. The tower would notify police security of an emergency squawk from a vehicle parked where it shouldn't be. He shook his head as he glanced up. He didn't have to be told that the ship orbiting above them could blow him to vapor at will. Better a stint in prison than instant obliteration.

"Women?" asked Flandry.

"None this trip. Men for the mines and arena only."

Flandry motioned for him to get out of the chair and follow him. When they reached the two unconscious technicians, the pilot asked, "Guards?"

"Dead." With a wave of his pistol, Flandry said, "Sit."

The pilot complied, knowing that there was nowhere to run.

Flandry returned to the steps and shouted, "It's all clear."

Laren nodded, hurried down the basement stairs, then led the others to the surface. When all the slaves were above ground, Flandry said, "I expect that some of you would just as soon be gone before the police arrive. Go now." Instantly, a dozen men started moving towards various exit routes from this old sector of the city. "The rest of you would probably be served by waiting. There's a bounty on Alcaz slavers in the Empire, and if the police aren't too corrupt, you'll get your reward. If they *are* corrupt . . . just tell them you were freed by agents of the Inspector General's Corp and that we're still around."

The result was instantaneous. The men started to ask questions, but Flandry cut them off with a wave of his hand.

"Laren, come with me," he said and moved away from the warehouse and shuttle.

When he was a hundred yards away from the group, he asked the former Marine, "What do you do for work?"

"I was running a gang—work gang—out of the harbor, labor and repair. Had twenty five boys loading and unloading cargo, doing ship refitting, anything that paid and wasn't illegal"—seeing a skeptical expression on Flandry, he added—"too illegal. I've had a nice little shop for about ten years."

"How'd you end up here?"

"My son got married; after the bride and groom went off on their honeymoon, me and some of the boys went out drinking. I wandered off to take a piss behind the bar and someone hit me from behind. I woke up here." He glanced around. "I expect that most of the boys at the party think I went home." He glanced at the sky, still hours before dawn. "I'll be expected at the shop an hour after sunrise. An hour after that, my boys will come looking for me." He looked at Flandry and said, "Hell of a night."

"It's not over," said Flandry. He activated his com and said, "Send it down."

Turning to Laren, he said, "I have a job for you."

"Already got a job," said Laren. "I owe you and if I can help I will, but my crew needs me."

"The Empire needs you," said Flandry. "Consider your military service reactivated. If you want the paperwork, I can have it for you in an hour."

Laren's expression remained neutral, but Flandry could see from the set of his eyes that he was not happy with what he had just heard. "What was your rank," asked the Deputy Inspector General.

"I'd just made sergeant before Vindabar."

"That will do for now, Sergeant." He keyed his com and asked, "You got that?"

"What size?" asked the voice in his ear.

"Bigger than me by a little."

"Got one in back that will fit."

Flandry cocked his head slightly, then smiled at Laren. "Relax, Sergeant; I'm only going to need you for an hour or so. After that, we'll discuss some things."

A few minutes later, a high-pitched humming signaled the approach of two fast police cruisers. "Wait here," said Flandry.

He hurried over to intercept the first cruiser as it touched down next to the transport. The door opened and two police officers stepped down as Flandry held up his identification. After a moment of conversation, their body language signaled the change in attitude of the two officers. They lost their aggressive stance and became deferential to the point of almost falling over themselves. Flandry returned to where Laren stood, saying, "The boys will be rewarded for their trouble."

Dryly, Laren said, "We don't get our share?"

"Not to worry," replied Flandry with a slightly crooked smile. "You'll be taken care of, Sergeant."

"One hour or so of a sergeant's pay . . . that might cover the price of a drink . . . "

A moment later, a deeper humming from above heralded the approach of a small shuttle. It was a shining new beauty, the best the Empire had produced, exactly what you'd expect to ferry high-ranking officials and officers of the Empire to and from capital-class ships.

The port side hatch dropped down, forming steps up a ramp to the shuttle. A young woman in the uniform of a Naval Ensign stepped out and saluted as Flandry hurried to the entrance. He absently returned the salute and said, "This is Sergeant Laren. Get us up!"

She followed the two men into the ship and indicated that Laren should sit in the rear leftmost seat, just before a doorway into the rear cargo area. She sat in the pilot's seat and took the shuttle up while Flandry entered the cargo area. "Where to, sir?" she shouted.

From within the hold, he said, "Head for the Governor's Complex."

"Aye, sir."

The shuttle arched into the sky, heading eastward, toward the rising sun. It would be just after breakfast when they reached the capital.

Flandry emerged from the rear of the shuttle, and Laren saw him clean-shaven and looking fresh, wearing a spotless and smartly fitting service uniform, the traditional khaki worn by all navy ranks when not in full dress or fatigues. As he sat, he said to Laren, "There's a sonic shower back there and a set of service fatigues that should fit you."

Laren didn't need to be told twice. Less than fifteen minutes later, he emerged cleaner than he had been in two days, in a service fatigue uniform.

Flandry nodded once in approval. "As there are no non-commissioned ranks in the Intelligence Corp, you've been promoted. So you jump a couple of pay grades. An ensign's pay for an hour or so should buy *two* rounds."

Laren could only smile.

Flandry motioned for him to sit. "I don't have much time. As I said, you're only working for me for an hour or so. I am not really going to press you into service. I just needed you aboard to talk."

"You just could have asked."

"You might have said no," said Flandry with a faint smile.

Nodding once, Laren said, "You're right."

"How would you like to work for me?"

"Doing what?"

"This cold war we're in with the Merseians is as deadly in its own fashion as the old shooting war was, just with not as high a body count, not as many things get blown up."

"That's a good thing, I guess."

"Maybe," said Flandry. "Time was, you'd have never heard of Alcaz slavers in this sector, let alone see them boots on ground, taking citizens for bounty."

"Time was, there was an Imperial fleet guarding this sector," said Laren. "The regional militia is a joke and the planetary police are worse. Seems like the Empire has cut back on a few things."

Wryly, Flandry laughed. "True. Still, we're attempting to set things right as best we can. And we need reliable men."

"We just met in a slavers pen, Deputy Inspector General Dominic Flandry," said Laren.

"Flandry will do."

"You know I'm reliable in a brawl, but what else do you know?"

"Not much, but I don't have time to conduct interviews and run deep background checks. Still, Imperial Marines means that you're tough—and LURPS means that you're self-reliant and able to improvise when needed. I've seen you fight; running your own business means that you're not stupid. Having a boy who just got married means that you're stable. I'll have a full background check run on you before we're done, but unless something seriously felonious comes up, I'm going to offer you a position.

"The IG's office needs someone here, and if you do the job, you'll be paid very well. Enough so you can turn your business over to your son as a wedding present, and retire in due course on an officer's pension, at least commander, perhaps even captain. If you don't do it well, I'll replace you. If you go rogue or corrupt, I'll come back, shoot you, and then replace you."

"You're not joking," said Laren.

"I don't joke. Ask my friends."

From her seat, the pilot said, "Respectfully, sir, you don't have any friends. But I can tell you, Ensign, he doesn't joke."

Laren sat back to think a long moment, then said, "Well, I was going to give my son half the business when he returns from his honeymoon. All of it is better. I guess he can run things while I run errands for you, sir."

"It's a little more than that, but we'll get into details later."

"Governor's complex ahead, sir," said the pilot.

"Thank you, Celia."

Flandry stood up and opened an overhead locker, removing a side arm. "Energy or slug?"

"Pistol. LURPS don't use blasters. They're fine for urban fighting, but in the wild tend to set things on fire at the worst possible moment."

"Yes," said Flandry, feeling that he should he anticipated the answer.

He handed him a brand new semi-automatic pistol and holster, which Laren wrapped around his waist as the shuttle landed in the quad. Broadcasting Imperial Navy codes had cleared the air around the plaza of police interceptors, but there were still armed guards waiting just in case someone was threatening the governor or the legislature.

Flandry strode out of the shuttle, Laren a half-step behind, and went to the guard who was sporting officer's insignias on the shoulder of his battle armor, and held out his identification.

He allowed him five seconds to take in what was occurring then said, "Have your men fall in behind me, Captain."

The captain said, "Yes, sir!" snapped off a salute, then shouted at the encircling guardsmen, "Fall in behind the Deputy Inspector General!"

Twenty heavily armed men quickly formed up and moved out at double-time as Flandry and Laren were already twenty yards ahead. When the squad caught up, Flandry said, "Captain, all units in the capital are now under full Imperial Control. My aide is sending a copy of my mandate to your headquarters. I'll have your chief confirm it before we get inside."

In less than two minutes, the captain said, "Your Imperial mandate received and acknowledged, sir."

As they reached the entrance of the Governor's Complex, two sentries, seeing an Imperial officer's uniform, snapped to attention, and remained that way until after the Captain of the Guard and his detachment passed.

It took Flandry only five minutes to conduct his business. He moved to the office of the governor and marched past a startled secretary and pushed open the doors. The governor waited behind his desk for a report from his guard on the Imperial shuttle which had just landed. His companion was a stunning-looking young woman, which Flandry assumed meant that she was his very personal assistant. Before a word could be said, Flandry unholstered his sidearm and shot the governor between the eyes.

The young woman was too petrified by terror to scream, though the secretary outside more than made up for that in volume. To the trembling assistant, Flandry said, "You're a very pretty girl. There are several not-too-tawdry strip bars down in the Pits that I'm sure would hire you. It's far less demeaning work that what you've been doing here. Now go."

The trembling girl needed no further urging and vanished down the hallway.

Flandry turned to Laren. "You have a problem with what just happened?"

The former marine said, "Either you had proof of his corruption or you're trying to make a point. Either way, I doubt you need or want my approval."

"Smart man," said Flandry. Putting away his side arm he turned to the captain who had just arrived. "Inform the lieutenant governor that he's now the governor. And this is Lieutenant Laren . . . ?"

"Ochinko."

"He's now the official representative of the Inspector General on Spiracos. Any questions?"

"Ah . . . no sir."

"Good, now find him an office."

Flandry turned, and it was clear that he was leaving. Laren said, "Lieutenant?"

"You just got bumped another two pay grades. Lieutenant is the lowest field grade in the IG's office."

Laren nodded, slightly amused. "Such rapid advancement should be a recruiting aid." He lost his smile. "How do I reach you?"

"Don't worry. The IG's office will be keeping an eye on things. Spiracos is still too far outside the core systems for a full garrison, but it's now again under Imperial control. Sector militia answer to you, but keep an eye on the new governor and local police. A slave ship doesn't pull into orbit without a number of key people looking the other way."

Flandry pointed at Laren for emphasis. "You will receive communications when we need to reach you, and you're expected to file a report every six months. If you have a problem, deal with it; if it's too big for you, I hired the wrong man."

Five minutes later, Flandry was sitting next to the pilot of the shuttle as it lifted off.

"How did it go?" asked the young woman as she punched in coordinates.

"Better than expected. I think I may have found an honest man for the job."

"That's refreshing."

"And, by the way, I didn't appreciate that little bit of snideness about friends."

"Sorry, Daddy."

"Better get started," he said. "It's going to be a long flight home."

"We didn't even get to see the sights," said Celia in mock-complaining tones.

"What? Uncovering a false intelligence source, then discovering a slaver ring and trying to get captured for three days wasn't enough excitement for you?"

"*You* got the exciting part, Father. I got to sit up here and play with the toys."

"Very expensive toys."

She smiled, "Well, creating false energy signatures that withstand scrutiny is fun. And *three* of them . . . I'm very proud of that."

"So you should be. Set a course for Terra."

"Yes, sir," she said, with an only slightly mocking smile.

The cleverly disguised ship moved rapidly away from the planet's surface. To the port control scanners below, the ensign sent false signals making it appear as if they had rendezvoused with a much larger ship, then the three phantom ships left orbit. Celia put the disguised fast scout ship into an arch trajectory out of the atmosphere and then entered faster-than-light for the first of several jumps to Terra.

With some irony, the deputy inspector general considered how amused Laren, the Marine LURPS, would have been if he had realized that he had been riding in a LURPS ship disguised as a shuttle craft. As much as Flandry would have loved to commandeer a capital ship and travel in relative comfort, there weren't enough to go around.

Turning to his daughter, he asked, "Is there anything in the library I haven't read?"

She reached under her flight chair and pulled out a reader tablet and said, "I'm busy; look for yourself, Daddy."

"What?"

"Look for yourself, Daddy, sir."

Ten days later, Flandry made his way across the sprawling lawns of his family's estate. He saw the object of his visit sitting on a small canvas-and-wood folding stool, under a large shade tree. At the edge of the lake, his aide-de-camp stood holding a fishing pole as he played the line out a bit. A batsman waited nearby, ready to answer any need the man on the chair might have, while a cook was preparing a very large stove and work area for a late lunch.

Seeing Flandry approaching, the batsman smiled, nodded, and retired a discrete distance away to allow the two men some privacy. Reaching the old man's side, Flandry said, "A full field kitchen?"

"I hate to send Raoul running back to the house because I forgot something." He rubbed his withered hands together. "As soon as Wilson catches another fish, I'll make us lunch."

"You mean Raoul will, while you order him around."

The old man cocked his head and looked disapprovingly at Flandry. "How did things on Spiracos turn out?"

"No Merseian agents, despite the reports you've been getting, just the usual social decline and corruption."

The old man sighed. He stood up and motioned for Flandry to walk with him, away from other ears, even if the loyalty of his staff was undoubted.

As they walked, the old man said, "We can't even discern the truth of the information we're buying, Dom. It used to be that we'd have a dozen agents where we now have one. The people we pay now . . . " His expression made it appear as if he wished to spit, " . . . they're little more than rumor mongers. Reliable intelligence is a thing of the past."

Flandry looked at his grandfather and namesake. "But I did break up a band of Alcaz slavers and put a fairly reliable fellow—former Imperial Marine—in a position to do us some good."

"Well, that's something."

"Had to shoot the governor."

"Did he deserve it?"

"Most likely."

"Well, good," said Former Admiral of the Fleet Dominic Flandry. "Your mother would be proud."

"I'll visit her grave later."

"Good. She was always a bit of a romantic at heart," said the old man to his namesake. After a moment, Dominic Crowfeather Flandry asked his grandfather, "Do you think it will do us any good?"

They walked slowly along the edge of the water for a while, enjoying the silence and each other's company. The younger Flandry regarded his legendary ancestor. What no enemy agent, battlefield hazard, or court intrigue could do, time had achieved: he looked frail. A grateful Empire had bestowed every medical miracle at its disposal to prolong the life of a man almost a myth within the halls of power. But the years were inexorable, and, as his grandfather had said more than once, "No one gets out of life alive."

Then the old man smiled and the energy that was the core of his being shown through. As long as there was light behind those eyes, Sir Dominic Flandry, still holding rank as Admiral of the Fleet, was a man to be respected, and feared.

"Dom," the elder Flandry said after a moment, "for most of my life I believed that my mission was to hold back a new Dark Age. At times, I felt like I was doing it alone. I rejected hope, for a renaissance seemed impossible. My only wish was to hold off a long black night in human history for as long as possible.

"But since Olaf Magnussun's betrayal . . . " He shrugged. "The Roidhun of Merseia suffered by that failure. His power was almost godlike before, but after . . . "—again a shrug. "Now that we have this so-called peace with the Merseians, I hope that we can endure, become a place where knowledge and a dream for a better future can survive. This new emperor is young and idealistic, the complete opposite of Emperor Josip, and a lot of powerful bad people have been run out of the government already."

The younger man couldn't help but smile. "But Josip gave you the Inspector General's office."

"He had no idea what I was going to do with it," said the old man. "He thought he was putting me out to pasture—letting me keep the rank of Fleet Admiral was honorary, or so he thought."

"And key sycophants of Josip's managed to get themselves arrested, or dead, since then."

Waving away the comment, the elder Flandry said, "Ask any gardener. You have to prune away diseased limbs and dead branches for the plant to thrive."

He looked at his grandson and slowly shook his head. "We got lucky. I merely took advantage.

"And," he said with a smile and what could only be called a merry glint in his eye, "the Merseians are just as hamstrung by internal chaos as we are since the Magnussun fiasco. Their race pride got the best of them and their clients are pulling away." He smiled, and nodded. "Got word while you were gone that the Chereionites have as much as declared independence, though they're too smart a bunch to be that blatant about it."

The young Flandry nodded. "They are the intellectual power within the Merseian Empire. If they pull away . . . ?" He sighed. Looking out over the calm waters of the lake, he considered the simple, almost ageless, beauty of his family's estate.

Unlike his mother, whom his grandfather hadn't met until she was half-grown, he had been raised by his namesake since early childhood. The death of his mother was a vague memory and that of his father even fainter; only his grandfather had been there every step of the way.

It had been Fleet Admiral Dominic Flandry who had engineered a revival within the deepest halls of power within the Empire; he had hand-picked every teacher for the young Emperor Gustaff II, and he had insured that his grandson had been given no choices but to serve. The younger Flandry suspected that his wife had been chosen for him too, as his daughter was certainly following in the family trade.

Looking into the old man's face, he saw pride reflected in his eyes. "It goes on for ever, doesn't it?

The old man paused before answering. "There is a very old saying about darkness, going back to ancient times, even before space travel. In the ancient Empire of China, they would say, *It is better to light a candle than curse the darkness.*" He looked up at the brilliant blue sky of ancient Earth and said, "You may not have banished the long dark night, Dom, but I think you lit another candle."

AFTERWORD:

I DON'T EXACTLY remember when I met Poul for the first time, but it had to be at Greg Bear's. I'd met Greg some years earlier when he was a one-novel newcomer and I hadn't even gotten serious about my first novel. Somewhere along the way Greg ended up married to Poul and Karen's daughter, so it became something of a package deal.

So over the years I'd just keep bumping into Poul and Karen, usually at Greg and Astrid's house when they lived nearby or at science fiction/fantasy conventions when I started doing some of those.

Here's the thing: there was always this weird disconnect in my head between Greg's father-in-law and this guy I used to read all the time in college. Poul Anderson, the writer, was a guy who made me laugh, get angry, stay up way past my bedtime reading just a few more pages, and all those other things that writers you adore do to you. Greg's father-in-law was this guy I'd share jokes with, argue politics with, and feel as at home with as I did with one of my uncles.

When asked to contribute to this collection, the two Pouls suddenly collided in my mind, because while I spent a fair amount of time in Poul's company over the years, I don't think I ever played the role of fan. I'm pretty sure I'd mentioned somewhere along the way that I had read pretty much everything he'd written as I was growing up, but I doubted it was much more than a "hi, I'm a fan," sort of stuff. I think in part because Poul wasn't the kind of guy to care hearing a lot of praise but rather who wanted to talk about other stuff, the state of public education, how we're going to convince politicians about seriously getting back into space, how to get rid of crabgrass, you now, stuff that was important to him.

So I said I'd write a Flandry story, because among so much of his body of work I loved—the entire future history he wrote, his really fun stuff like Operation Chaos, and some brilliant short fiction—Flandry was *the guy.* He was too cool for school, and always kept his head about him, and was a total bastard in a noble cause, in short, the sort of hero I wish I had thought up. He was such a great character; Bertie Chandler asked to borrow him for one of his Commodore Grimes stories. So if Flandry was cool enough for A. Bertram Chandler to borrow, I would too.

I'm older now and Poul is gone and age is a concept that doesn't often concern younger writers. But after a while you dwell on it from time to time. See, what I never told Poul was that I didn't think that Flandry was fighting a useless fight. He wasn't just slowing the coming darkness; he was holding it at bay until something else, something good, could happen. So, I got to write a story to show what I thought would happen next. And, it's a way to say thank you to Poul, for letting me borrow one of the best characters ever.

—Raymond E. Feist

THE FAR END

by Larry Niven

***LARRY NIVEN** made his first sale to* Worlds of If *magazine in 1964, and soon established himself as one of the best new writers of "hard" science fiction since Heinlein. By the end of the '70s, Niven had won several Hugo and Nebula Awards, and become famous for his "Known Space" universe, which was also home to the catlike warrior race the Kzin, a probable inspiration for* Star Trek*'s Klingons, since written about by both Niven and many other authors in the long-running* Man-Kzin Wars *series. His novel* Ringworld *was one of the bestselling novels of the decade, and one of the most acclaimed, and spawned sequels* The Ringworld Engineers, The Ringworld Throne, *and* Ringworld's Children. *Niven is also a prolific collaborator; he's written eleven novels in collaboration with Jerry Pournelle—the best-known of which are probably* The Mote in God's Eye, Inferno, *and* Lucifer's Hammer*—as well as the four-volume* Fleet of Worlds *sequence and other non-series novels with Edward M. Lerner, the four-volume* Dreampark *sequence and other non-series novels with Steven Barnes, and collaborations with Brenda Cooper, David Gerrold, and with Michael Flynn and Jerry Pournelle and with Steven Barnes and Jerry Pournelle. Niven's solo novels include* Protector, World of Ptavvs, A Gift from Earth, Destiny's Road, Rammer, Rainbow Mars, Smoke Ring, *and the three-volume "The Magic Goes Away" series. His copious short work has been gathered in the three-volume* Larry Niven Short Stories, *as well as in*

Tales of Known Space, Inconstant Moon, Neutron Star, N-Space, Playgrounds of the Mind, The Draco Tavern, Crashlander, Flatlander, The Flight of the Horse, A Hole in Space, *and others. His most recent books are a new collection,* Stars and Gods, *and a new "Dreampark" novel with Steven Barnes,* The Moon Maze Game.

In the incisive story that follows, Larry Niven shows us what may be the end of the Time Patrol itself . . .

WHEN ANTHONY WELLS DOHENY was recruited for the Time Patrol, he was just past fifty. That was in July of 2008, with (in Tony's view) bad times coming. He'd seen enough movies: bad times always follow the first black president. Big Brother Government was already fighting two Mideast wars and throwing tax money away with both fists. Gas prices were going insane.

Tony was recruited because he wrote science fiction. Some was brilliant; but some came too close to reality. Many writers wrote of time travel, but Doheny stumbled on too much detail. He wasn't the first to be inducted for such a reason, after a faked death.

He was recruited in spite of his phobia for getting lost.

They made him an agent in place, covering Los Angeles County from 1900 to 2000, owning a little grocery store in Beverly Hills. He had pickup points for newspapers in various other years. He didn't have to travel except in emergencies, and there hadn't been any. He knew where danger would lie. Knowing the future meant no surprises; it gave him a wonderful sense of security.

He played the stock market a little. Bet on Bill Gates; avoid Ponzi schemes; remember a few trends. He liked a few local restaurants which would disappear too soon. He could no longer write science fiction. What the Patrol had done to his mind prevented him from revealing anything a time traveler might know. From time to time he wrote a little fantasy.

In a newspaper from August 1965, he found a weird photograph.

Finally, a chance to meet another time traveler or two! Knowing the future meant no surprises; he'd come to realize that he'd chosen a dull life. He sent a message at once, jotted in careful block letters on a scratchpad. "Found a ray gun, August 1965. Please advise." Rolled it up, shoved it into a tube and watched it vanish. He could track the ray gun while he waited.

The tube had just left his fingers when a flickering blur appeared above his living room rug. Now it focused like a camera view and settled down to the usual bulky-looking wheelless timecycle. The rider—stayed blurred.

A Danellian. Tony wasn't expecting that! He stared . . . tried to stare. His eyeballs jittered. This wasn't a fog; it carried *too much* information, as if he were seeing scores of men and monsters all superimposed. Ancient Hebrews must have seen such entities. Their angels were terrible to look upon and impossible to describe. Indian gods showed a blur of probabilistic arms. He smelled . . . ionization? Ozone?

"Hello," he said. "Welcome." Sir? Danellians were at the far end of time.

"Thank you," the entity said. "What've you got?"

The Los Angeles Times was spread over the coffee table. The article was on the fourth page, continued from front page headlines describing a riot in the Watts district, downtown LA. The riot would last six days.

The photograph showed an alley, a peaceful scene. It looked flawed. Glare white cut across it along a narrow dashed line. At one end of the line a dark-skinned woman half-knelt with something in her hand. At the other was a little white glare point, and a big black cat levitating along a brick wall, claws raking.

"Cat toy," the Danellian said.

"Yessir, but I never saw—"

"Laser. It's too early for lasers. Good call, Doheny. What have you done so far?"

"Nothing. You got here fast."

"Time travel is like that. Let's get to work. I think I recognize that item. It's a weapons laser turned to low power. Best cat toy ever invented, barring the end strips on fanfold paper, but it can burn holes through bricks and men if you turn it high, and of course it's too early for lasers. We'll fix it." The Danellian was fiddling with something on his timecycle. "Give me the date off the paper."

"August 11th, 1965."

"I'll have it in a minute."

"Can I offer you anything?" Greatly daring, "Coffee?"

"Yeah, thanks. Cappuccino if you've got it, or is *that* too early?"

"You'd have to go to a restaurant. Romanoff's is good. Chasens too. I don't have a steam widget."

"Just coffee, then. And I smoke tobacco."

"A *Danellian* smokes tobacco?"

The blur laughed, a crackling sound. "I'm older than I look. You like your air clean? Where're you from?"

Tony started a hot plate up, filled a teapot with water, opened a cupboard and looked at half a dozen varieties of flavored instant coffee. "Twenty-ought-eight, West LA, till they put me here." His mind was racing. Danellians were from far in the future, but how far? And when was this one born? Could he be *billions* of years old?

"No wonder tobacco scares you," the Danellian said. "There, I've got August 11th, morning. Got the right alley. There's the cat. Fast forward . . . and here comes the woman. Now I'll just follow her back."

"I never saw equipment like that."

"We don't give every agent every tool we've got. This time I just brought what I had. I was working on something else when your call came through. Way outside Sol system, actually. Interesting world . . . there she goes, or here she came . . . ."

Tony was behind the agent's shoulder by now, staying safely away from the blur of what might have been a folded wing. In an oval frame he saw a timecycle pop up, the woman roll and throw herself aboard feet first, the timecycle gone. In the background a shattered grocery store window healed itself while a flaming vodka bottle hurled itself at a cluster of gangly teenagers.

"I know her. Hot damn. It's Rora Jee Vishwathy, the last Exaltationist. Playing with a cat. I didn't know she had it in her."

The Danellian paused the frame, then began inching it forward. Here came the woman's timecycle again. She left it in a jump, handstand, roll.

"Pause," the Danellian murmured. He reached a blurred appendage, one of uncountable several, into the frame and fiddled with controls. "There. It'll go back to the Big Bang. *Not* what she's expecting. Next—"

The view unfroze. The cycle was gone. The woman picked herself up. Blue jeans and a leather jacket, tee shirt with a half-hidden message in black script, black hair in cornrows. She walked away with something like a mechanical pencil clutched in her right hand. Men robbing a gas station, filling bottles with gasoline, watched her pass and didn't quite dare to approach her. Tony and the blur watched her in fast-forward until she reached the alley.

The Danellian slowed its display to real time. They watched her play with the cat.

She looked up once as a sudden glare lit the alley. The photographer was already in a shuffling run, clutching his bulky camera. She lifted the light weapon to point at him, thumbed a dial, thought it over and lowered her arm.

"And that's that. The paper's got its photograph." The Danellian zoomed on the woman as she approached the cat. He froze the view and got off the timecycle.

"Doheny, you go after her."

Tony stepped back involuntarily. "Can't you just reach into the frame?"

"No, she's got too firm a grip. You were trained."

"Well, yes, but dammit! Watts, and I'm white!"

"Training is expensive. Have you defrauded us? *I* can't go. I don't look like anything Earthly."

Tony nodded reluctantly. He owed the Corps; payment was due. "What's my mission?"

The smells hit him hard. Photochemical smog, sewage, gasoline, gunpowder. A store was burning merrily. It was flickering firelit dark: streetlights had been smashed, and no moon penetrated the gaps between buildings.

The man who had photographed the Exaltationist was running down the street, clutching his bulky camera. Rora Jee pointed the weapon at him, then dropped her aim. The cat approached her. She knelt, rubbed his back, then looked up at Tony.

He aimed his stunner and pulled the trigger.

She aimed the light weapon. White light burned through his cotton jacket and got lost on the superconducting cloth beneath. He felt a touch of warmth. But the stunner wasn't dropping her. Whining with fear, Tony raised the beam for a head shot.

She fell. She must have been wearing something too, but not on her head.

He eased the timecycle into the alley. Had anyone seen him, a white man attacking a black woman in Watts? No, he'd have heard shouting. He spared a moment of amused pity for the photographer, who had missed the shot of his life.

With a grunt and a heave he draped the woman across the timecycle's rear saddle. She was sweaty and limp as a noodle, and heavy. She was still clutching the weapon. He wrestled it loose and pocketed it. The cat watched.

Tony boarded the timecycle and was gone. No witness but the cat. Did that count? Tony wasn't sure. Quantum physics was mysterious.

Tony Doheny rolled the woman off the cycle onto the thick rug, lowering her carefully. She still smelled of exertion and a missed bath or two. Good hard body, a hard pretty face, not at all alien. He slid a pillow under her head. He took the light-weapon out of his pocket and dropped it on the coffee table.

The Danellian knelt above Rora Jee. Tony was looking at the blurred, many-limbed shape when the Danellian . . . focused.

Tony must have gasped. The Danellian turned and found him staring.

"Looking at me isn't easy, is it?" he—clearly male—said kindly. "It's a quantum effect. Is that my coffee? Good." Six limbs: legs, huge wings, hands. One gnarly hand reached for the mug. He sniffed. "You lose some aroma when it's instant. Well, what you're seeing, Agent Doheny, is all of the possible paths that lead to *me*. With quantum physics, you don't get your choice. You get everything that could have happened." He sipped.

Tony said, "Not any more."

"Say what?"

"You look like a winged monkey. Shall I show you a mirror? Except for your face. I could swear I've seen you before."

"Mirrors don't work. *I* don't see myself blurred. But no quantum effect means—"

"Manse Everard? You're the man who recruited me!"

The Danellian nodded. "I called myself Manse Everard for awhile. Long ago in personal time. Hello, Rora. How are you?"

Only her lips moved. "Paralyzed. I suppose you think you've won. Frozen the universe."

"I suppose so," the Danellian said.

Tony persisted. "Why do you look like a winged monkey?"

"Hah. Well. There's this *really* interesting planet. Tony, Rora Jee, most rocky worlds are bigger than Earth, if they're massive enough to hold an oxy-and-water atmosphere. A lot of them form out where water is normally ice, so the planet picks up a shell of water. Diomede has an ocean hundreds of kilometers deep. Islands that are all seaweed and coral, and winged almost-mammals the size of a man. I took a shape such that I could pass for one, not to the Diomedeans themselves but to some human traders on the surface. That was just in case I got into trouble. I could get help from Nick Van Rijn's people in the Polesotechnic League without arousing much suspicion.

"All of that should have been beside the point. I didn't have an interest in the Diomedeans. The interesting part of Diomede is down below the ocean, where the pressure is so great that it gives you a shell of water crystal in the forms of Ice-7, Ice-10, and Ice-11. It's white hot and solid. At the interface, you get an ecology."

"Life? Made of what?"

"Well, mostly water, of course. Some contaminants, mostly from meteors. Metal is scarce. Energy comes from the heat-cold interface.

"I was taking a break. I spend a lot of time on leave, more and more as time passes. No emergencies anywhere. I left my Diomedean body on the surface and moved my consciousness into a body shaped for the ice shell below. I lived with them for a time. I learned a lot. Hugely complex ecology. Interesting people, but extremely violent. And then your message pinged in."

"Sounds entertaining," Rora said.

Scary, Tony thought. "Are you bored a lot?"

"Yeah." The winged monkey sipped smoke from a pipe. The mixture was more interesting than noxious, and of course tobacco smoke was common enough in the 1960s.

"See, there isn't anything else in the hopper. We've been free of temporal emergencies since—" The Danellian switched to Temporal speech. Tony tried to follow it: a long time in personal time, lifetimes long. Rora Jee was nodding. "I'm bored near out of my mind. That hot-ice world below the Diomedean world is as exciting and exotic

. . . and I was still looking for anything, anything to wake me up. And now it's over."

"What's over, Agent Everard?"

"Tony, don't you know what this means? Rora does." He put a hard, powerful, inhuman hand on Tony's wrist, and the other on Rora Jee's cheek. "See? Time is stabilized. The quantum effects aren't there any more. There aren't any more emergencies. Rora Jee, we'll put you somewhere where you can't build another time machine. What do you like?"

The woman said, "Late Polisotechnic League."

"Hah! No. How about here? Where there are still cats?"

She didn't answer.

"Think about it. I'm going to go get some equipment I need, and I might as well change too." The winged ape boarded the timecycle and was gone.

The Exaltationist's eyes moved to Tony. "Servant," she spat. "Do you know what you've done?"

He said, "Not really. What were you planning?"

"I formed a gang, not a big one. I went down the line for some weapons. I took one to show The Rock, he's their leader. The rest I left on the timecycle. We were going to invade Beverly Hills. Shake events up, see if there were still weak points in the continuum.

"Now *that's* over. I was the last uncertainty in time, and now it's all frozen. You've brought about predestination, you fool. There are no more choices. No more need for a Time Patrol."

"I hadn't thought that far."

"Would you like a companion?"

Tony gaped at her. "What?"

"He's going to strand us both. Why not together?"

The corner of Tony's eye caught the Danellian returning.

Rora Jee didn't notice. "The only destabilizing force anywhere is the Time Patrol itself. He'll end it all! I'll have nobody to talk to in all the universe, and you won't either!"

The blur gained focus, first the timecycle, then a tall pale man, lean and fit, with big hands, a small nose, curly hair, blue eyes.

Rora Jee gaped. "Who are you?"

"Manse Everard is more an office than a single man," the agent said. "Like James Bond in the movies, or Death in Piers Anthony's work. I took the name for awhile, but this is how I started. This is how I'll finish."

He lifted gear off the timecycle. A helmet with an Old Roman look went on Rora Jee's head. There was a time of silence; then the tall man said, "That was a quick version of what we use to treat every agent in the Patrol. You'll never again be able to speak of time travel to anyone who hasn't traveled in time. Next—"

More gear, this time a handheld machine that hummed as it roved over the woman's head and neck. "Get up if you like," the Danellian said.

She patted herself down, then stood up. "Sit," the Danellian said, and it wasn't a question. "There." The overstuffed couch whuffed dust as she sat.

"And last." Tony touched the timecycle keyboard and it was gone.

That little too late, Tony picked up the light weapon. Everard looked around.

Tony asked, "'This is how you'll finish'?"

"Yeah. She's right. The Time Patrol will have to stand down. Starting here, I think."

His mind hadn't quite caught up, but Tony knew that the Danellian intended to end his current existence. When Everard finished cleaning up Time, what would become of Anthony Doheny? He held his aim.

"And what will that gain you?" Everard asked patiently. "You'll still be here. I can retrieve the timecycle, but you can't."

"I know." Tony handed over the weapon. Rora Jee glared.

"So," said Everard. "Where would you like to end? Here? Rora Jee, you too. Where?"

The woman asked, "Tony Doheny, do you live alone?"

"Yeah. I was married for six years, but I couldn't talk to her. You know why. Henrietta thought I was unfaithful."

"Do you like cats?"

"Sure."

"You need a companion."

Huh? "I do get laid from time to time," he said crudely.

"Companion, mate, spouse. Children. I do want children. My genes and your hybrid vigor, how can you resist?"

He looked at her. Lovely, and they were moving into a time when skin color didn't matter so much, but—"Have you lost your mind? We're enemies."

"Tony, he's going to shut it all down! Who will you talk to about your real life, ever again? He'll never let me meet another Exaltationist. There's only me and you!"

"I've been quiet about time travel for a long time," Tony said, and realized that he hadn't liked it. Keeping this great fabulous secret had been fun at first, but it had palled. He'd never been able to tell Henrietta.

"Am I unsightly?"

He remembered her leaprolling off the timecycle like an Olympic gymnast, very sexy indeed.

"Can you take it that I'm stronger than you? Brighter? I was shaped to be a superior being."

He laughed. "I was a science fiction writer. Half the people I know are brighter than me. They hunt me down to do their daydreaming for them, because they don't have the time, and maybe they can give me an idea or two." Actually, he missed that.

Everard said, "Doheny, don't worry about her longer lifespan. You've had Patrol medical treatments. They won't wear off right away."

Tony said, "Okay. Done."

And the Danellian blurred.

"Bless you, my children," he said. "Anyone who thinks you're a little weird will think it's because you're interracial. You should be fine. And the universe can finally be orderly."

Rora Jee and Tony looked at each other—and kept their silence as the quantum blur flowed aboard the timecycle and was gone.

AFTERWORD:

POUL AND KAREN were friends of mine for decades, but Poul was an inspiration long before that. I wanted to write like him; I needed his skills. I don't believe I ever directly imitated him, but I remember Jerry Pournelle pointing out a terrific ending on one of his stories. The excellence of Poul's endings was worth aspiring to.

Years ago I believed that I could describe the Danellians from

Poul's Time Patrol stories. They were phenomena of quantum physics, ever-changing. I never told him so. He'd probably heard such stuff from many sources.

So, here's my chance.

I would have written a sequel to "The Queen of Air and Darkness", in which the natives used their powers to run an amusement park . . . but I did this instead.

—Larry Niven

BLOODPRIDE

by Gregory Benford

WRITER AND SCIENTIST *Gregory Benford is one of the modern giants of the field. His 1980 novel* Timescape *won the Nebula Award, the John W. Campbell Memorial Award, the British Science Fiction Association Award, and the Australian Ditmar Award, and is widely considered to be one of the classic novels of the last two decades. His other novels include* Beyond Jupiter, The Stars in Shroud, In the Ocean of Night, Against Infinity, Artifact, *and* Across the Sea of Suns, Great Sky River, Tides of Light, Furious Gulf, Sailing Bright Eternity, Cosm, Foundation's Fear, The Martian Race, *and* Beyond Infinity. *His short work has been collected in* Matter's End, Worlds Vast and Various, *and* Immersion and Other Short Novels. *His non-fiction books include* Deep Time: How Humanity Communicates Across Millennia, Habitats in Space, Skylife: Space Habitats in Story and Science (*with George Zebrowski*), *and* Beyond Human: Living with Robots and Cyborgs (*with Elizabeth Malartre*). *As editor, his anthologies include* Far Futures, Microcosms, *and the four-volume* What Might Have Been *series, edited with Martin H. Greenberg. His most recent book is a novel,* The Sunborn. *Benford is a professor of physics at the University of California, Irvine, where his research encompasses both theory and experiments in the fields of astrophysics and plasma physics.*

The Ythrians are a race of flying, warlike aliens who featured in Poul Anderson's novel People of the Wind, *and in other stories such as*

"Wings of Victory" and "The Problem of Pain" that were collected in The Earth Book of Stormgate. *Here Greg Benford shows Ythrians and humans cautiously sniffing each other out, bristling, wary, suspicious, neither side trusting the other. With, it turns out, good reason.*

The sceptre, learning, physic, must
All follow this, and come to dust.
—Shakespeare

She smelled the aliens coming. They were above her as she got caught in a down draft. She tumbled. The draft brought their pungent odor—rank, feathery, strange. She fought against the current pushing her down, arms churning, legs kicking with their ailerons. The hinged flaps fluttered as she tried to control her banking, but she rolled too, getting dizzy—and the ground was coming up fast.

Ruth had thought she was a reasonably good flyer, but now she regretted telling anyone about her hobby. Maybe a hundred meters to go below her, and she was too far from the fusor-warmed pink walls where the updrafts were. She heard the aliens flap down the wind, calling out their air song, their scent getting riper—and then they were flashing around her like a whirlwind.

What could a Ythri do—grab her? Then they would both fall.

The answer came suddenly. Wings fully spread, the one called Fraq swept close and threw a gossamer strand around her helmet. He pulled. As it snapped straight he worked upward and toward the wall. The rope tugged her after him as she thrust hard with her arms, letting her foot flaps straighten along her legs. They stopped fluttering. Sharp cries came from the other Ythri. She was under tow.

Humiliating, but better than a snapped neck any day.

Fraq was heading up and over toward the speckled void walls. That gave Ruth a chance to stare at him, which she couldn't politely do in the formal, diplomatic sessions she had attended with him. A keelbone jutted beneath a strong neck like a ship's prow. The tow line wrapped around the heavily muscled shoulders. Fraq's head was blunt-nosed and without external ears. As he turned his head to bark an order—"Hold steady offwind!"—she saw that the mouth had flushed lips, cherry red. Two big golden eyes stabbed sidewise, checking clearance from the others flapping above, who were blocking the downdraft. His crest of black-tipped white plumage rose stiffly above, a control surface he could tilt—and protection for the bulging skull, she guessed. The fan-shaped tail flexed with white streamers among gray fan feathers. Fraq's lean body was mahogany that reddened along the naked legs. His yellow claws out at the wing tips made a palm that canted for lift. Beautiful.

The pink wall was close now and she felt the caress of the updraft winds. Fraq shouted, "Go!" and somehow with a toss of his head sent a wave down the tow line that slipped it from her helmet. Smart birds knew a lot of tricks. She was free.

Still she dropped, catching the wind on her arm wings. It would be even more humiliating to tumble now. She strained hard, flexed her body, thrust—and got stable. The aliens were hovering now, watching her, and she had to get this right. She tilted her ailerons and steadied, starting to rise.

From below she saw they had three slits in parallel on the body, flared to take in air. They resembled gills and shone bright pink, blood rich. As their wings lifted, she saw the slits drawn wide, three mouths yawning. As their elegant down strokes began, that action forced the gills shut.

The Ythrians had big barrel lungs, a passive system resembling humans'. Their secret lay in those supercharger gills, probably evolved from some amphibianlike ancestor. Those livid mouths worked in bellows fashion as the flight muscles contracted and big arteries sucked the air directly into the bloodstream. Higher air intake organs let them burn their fuel as fast as necessary.

Ruth thought, *Smart birds. I wonder how it feels to be so alive.*

She landed by funneling down the updraft layer along the walls. She arrowed down against the warm breezes from the vents below, then skimmed off to land with some redeeming grace on the take-off platform. She looked up and the Ythrians were spiraling down, taking their time, still watching her. Had she proved herself in alien eyes?

She wanted to look unconcerned, so she gazed up at the view, hands on hips. This was the big, newest void, honed with an antibaryon fusor burst that rendered rock to plasma and lava, then vented the hot gruel through the top knothole. Media had showed all humanity the Lunar volcano show, as the ruddy rock flowed with liquid grace above the Lunar highlands, jetting into space in rosy filaments. Some caught it to shape habitats on the surface; the voids were an industrial miracle with real profits to be had. The fusor eruption left behind this oblate spheroid twenty kilometers high and five wide, cooling quickly into a hollow pink egg. Lunar subsurface sculpture was getting so adroit the engineers could shape any space you wanted. Rumors circulated that some rich magnate had ordered up a pyramid-shaped space, but even a fusor couldn't do that. This big void was for flying, a unique Lunar pleasure for poor ground-bound primates. Hundreds of people were winging it as she looked up, most of them watching the aliens do astonishing feats. Fraq came by flying upside down with effortless grace, eyeing her on the ground as he shot across the void.

Those eyes—piercing, even at this distance. His golden-brown feathers covered but did not conceal the rippling muscle. Or that he was male. The Ythri could lock the joints of their limbs at will and on Luna, 0.18 gravs, seem to defy gravity's existence for long, leisurely arcs. The forepart of their wing skeleton had humerus, radius, and ulna, much as in Earth birds. These locked together in flight and gave the Ythris a look of utter unconcern as they did the impossible.

An admirable addition to the Library's category *Sapientia*, yes. But she reminded herself that Earthly birds' sexual organs shrivel outside their reproductive times, a process called "involuting." *But these aren't birds, they're aliens. Librarians must scrupulously avoid category errors . . .*

When the Ythri flock landed with high, barking cries she consoled herself at how clumsy they were on ground. Slow and awkward afoot, shorter than her, yet Fraq's head had a regal air. The ivory crest riff helped, looking like the defiant ridge of an ancient Roman helmet.

Still, up close and walking, she could see Fraq's imposing body was mostly feathers and his wing-arms had light, hollow bones. All the Ythri landed with a final, artful pause before alighting—spidery, kitelike skeletons anchoring thin flesh. Still, Fraq stood out with his elegant muscles and tawny feather-coat, the elegance of his flight.

Earth birds had at least long ago lightened their burden, permitting a little more brain, by changing jaws to beaks. Not the Ythris. They sported the jaws and sharp teeth of dominant predators.

Big and beweaponed, instantly ready to mount the wind, they need fear no beast of prey. And they had come across the light years through the wormhole humans still did not command.

"Thank you," Ruth said as Fraq approached with his lurching gait. "I might have recovered in time—"

"You not. Yet still I admired your daring."

"I haven't tried this Void before, don't know its currents."

"Dirts do not know the air in their bones," Fraq said, golden eyes so intense she felt their pressure like a force.

The new translation software was so fast and able she could sense no pause between the movements of his still blood-rich red lips and the voice that sounded in her ear. Of course it came to her electromagnetically, swamping the Ythri words that swam though the air like slippery song.

"We thank you for saving our assistant," the Prefect said in a calm, mild tone at her elbow. "Now may we proceed?"

"We grant substance," Fraq said, his wings held back so he could make something that reminded her of a bow. But he bowed to her, not to the Prefect, whose face tightened. The other Ythris made the same abrupt bowing gesture and formed a crescent behind Fraq.

So this had worked after all. Early on the Ythri had made it clear that those who cannot fly are sub-species, unworthy.

She nodded and the Prefect said ponderously, irked, "In truth, surely. Let us unfold our stories and . . . negotiate."

The Ythris had come out of the mysterious Oort cloud wormhole at high velocity, plasma drives burning hot and luminous. Lunar telescopes picked up their cylindrical craft too late to get a back-trace on the trajectory. The wormhole's position far out among the tumbling icestroids was still the big secret, vital to any human expansion out to the stars. Though aliens who had come from it before had carefully blurred their tracks. The civilizations that communicated with microwaves or wormholes did not give away secrets, especially where the wormhole mouths might be. The SETI Library was under enormous pressure to find its location. Negotiation seemed the only path.

So when the Ythri demanded a ritual flight before negotiations, the Library sought out Ruth. She had flown often in the smaller voids fusion-dug deep in the Lunar volcanic masses, and few librarians had ever even tied on the arm wings, so . . .

She breathed a sigh of relief as they sat in the diplomacy room of the SETI Library. The Ythri got their flock in order in a long arc around the table only after the humans sat. Fraq sat at the center of their arc, and pointedly sat opposite Ruth, not the Prefect. Ruth suppressed a smile.

"Ah, um." The Prefect frowned, then got right to the point. "What do you seek?"

Fraq said, "Bloodpride requires we undertake this ancient task. Thanks to your submitting to concordance ritual, we can now tell truth. You are dirt-huggers but worthy of station, thus can help us with our search."

"We fly in sympathy," the Prefect answered. Ruth saw that the Prefect had learned this ritual from the translator team. Mutual gestures were essential in social intelligences. But with these carnivore aliens, the hard decisions came from the top. Fraq seemed in charge, but it was hard to tell.

She wondered if her being female mattered. Maybe not. So she said while the Prefect conferred with the translators, "What are you looking for?"

"The legacy ark," Fraq said immediately with no diplomatic phrases. His big sharp eyes focused intently and moved swiftly to watch all the faces in the room—like an eagle high in the wind, she thought. "It came here before your species emerged. Many millions of your orbital cycles before."

"We are used to such time scales at the SETI Library."

"We have beamed you before, but got no response," Fraq said.

"Only lately have we come to prosperity," a Prefect underling ventured. "But we may know of your signals. Much we have received in the past we did not comprehend."

"Permit us to unfold our history, then."

The tale emerged under close questioning. They had images as well, sweeping in their majesty.

The Ythris knew of an earlier alien civilization that had used the wormhole to the Sol region, after eons of neglect. Those experiments had sent mass down through the wormhole network, and one had passed momentarily through the center of a star. Wormhole exits could sink into stars, yet survive. This one had passed a fiery mass from the star into other wormhole routes, for the system was complexly interwoven. The flaring plasma came out at the exit near Fraq's world. The avians had seen it—the telltale crimson burst of violent plasma lighting their sky, tracing out the mouth's position. A revelation.

The Ythris had gone through their own troubles—long eras of decline caused by resource losses, such as Earth had suffered when the fossil oil ran out, amid a terrible era of warming air and biting acid oceans. That had hobbled mankind for many centuries.

Far back in their history, in their founding tragedy, they had suffered some sort of biological catastrophe that had nearly driven the Ythri to extinction. More recently, in their first industrial age, the Ythri had suffered metals loss, since they had few in their planetary crust. Recovering, they had resolved to harvest fresh supplies from their own asteroid belt.

After all those millennia of suffering had come the slow Ythri revival. Through the long centuries of poverty they lost much of their historical legacy. Cities burned or collapsed in hardship, and with them their libraries. Especially they did not know any longer where the wormhole mouth was in their sky. But now they did have a hard-won, simple interplanetary civilization. When the jetting solar plasma marked the way, they could fly to where the virulent plasma glow told them the ancient wormhole mouth was. Their greatest lost heritage still orbited unused at the edges of their solar system, deep in the cold vaults of time.

"This is our destiny, a bloodpride age old," Fraq said solemnly.

Now they could pursue an ancient goal—finding the Ark of Meaning launched by a primeval civilization, the Furians. The earlier Ythri culture had heard of it in the dying messages sent out in microwave—an attempt to pass on the genetic roots of life around a forlorn world now gone forever, devoured by the expansion of its sun into its red giant phase. That planet had fried, then been swallowed up in its last vast agony, by the plasma halo that wrapped it in a glowing funeral shroud.

"They launched many ships," Fraq said. "Your system was blessed to receive one, long before your kind evolved."

"So one is *here*?" Ruth asked, interrupting Fraq's long tale. The Prefect frowned, stayed silent at her impoliteness.

"Bloodpride demands it," Fraq said. "Our foremothers said to find the Ark was a Prime Need for life itself—to save a legacy of another evolution."

"Then it's like our SETI Library," Ruth said. "Continuity with the long past. To understand what could be in our future."

"You do not naturally fly," Fraq said. "But you ken the deep long truths."

"Perhaps we can share where this Ark might be?" the Prefect said.

"If you take us there, assuredly," Fraq said. "Our ship cannot manage such a large vessel."

"Why?" the Prefect asked.

"We fear it."

Decades had passed, she knew, since this stone-faced Prefect had worked with the cryofiles. Ruth had spent years fathoming the labyrinth of those data-forests. The SETI Library held all transmissions received from the Galactic Complex. That host of innumerable societies had largely, flourished long before humanity was born on the dusty plains of Africa. Within those multidimensional databases, Ruth customarily spent her days. After the initial Ythri arrival, she had immersed herself in the Library.

The SETI files were a bewildering, largely impenetrable resource. The grandest possible intellectual scrap heap, she sometimes thought. But it could yield priceless ore.

Now that they knew where the Ythri star was, she found the earlier Ythri signals from records from the Long Now Cave. These were spectral data of irregular "pulsars" seen in 2100s and not again. Brief, compressed, they repeated only a few times. These, she found, were in fact SETI signals from the Ythri, nearly three hundred light years away. These flashes around 10 GHz were attempts to reach Earth, assuming a tech civilization might be there, based on the Ythri detection of the ozone line in our atmosphere. These were not understood during the decades following the Age of Appetite, when no one had puzzled out the economics of SETI contact, and so did not realize that short bursts were far more efficient as attention-getting signals. The smart strategy was to send lighthouse pulses, catch the attention of emerging societies, and direct them to a much lower power signal that carried detailed messages. Nobody in the slowly collapsing decades of the late 2100s and all of the 2200s caught on. Nor could they remotely afford to reply. The whole of humanity was putting out fires, sometimes literally.

Still, in the middle decades of the 2100s Earth had sent "slow boat" solar sails out into the Oort cloud, bound for Centauri and beyond. Making close solar passes in 'sundiver' mode got them up to 500 or 600 kilometers per second, a thousandth of *c*. In thousands of years they could arrive at stars, after dutifully passing data on interstellar space back to Earth. Most of these were still on the way, forlorn robot voyagers long outdated in their very mission.

But the Furians, as Fraq termed them, had thought on even longer perspectives before humans evolved. Ruth researched Fraq's tale, and found it made sense.

The ancient Furian civilization had reached its end as their sun left the main sequence and became a red giant, its luminosity rising by a factor of a thousand. The swelling ruddy sphere doomed their world, but also brimmed with photons, a rich launcher for Furian solar sails. That dropped the time for an interstellar transit down to centuries. Sailcraft wouldn't last forever in transit, when they might smack into a random rock. Best to keep the sailing time low.

But how could the sails slow down when they arrived? Their light sails would be nearly useless for getting captured into the gravity well of a main sequence star, with its puny sunlight. A magnetic sail, braking on the solar wind, could help, but not nearly enough. Without something more, the Arks the dying Furian world sent out would simply blow by their target stars.

The Furians, Fraq said, had identified stars with circling worlds known to have working biospheres, but that gave forth no SETI signals, no leakage of artificial emissions, nothing. Someday they might harbor intelligence, and the Arks could carry the life lore of the long-dead Furians down to the next generation of life in the galaxy. A biological legacy. Better than a funeral pyre, or a repeating microwave message touting Furian art and culture and religion to the cold stars.

The Furians knew that most stars are members of binary or multiple systems. Their Arks targeted binary systems with a red giant and a widely separated dwarf star. Ark sail vessels could use the red giant's intense luminosity to decelerate, then sail on to the planetary system of the dwarf.

Librarians don't just rely on hearsay; they check. Ruth checked Sol's neighborhood.

She looked at red giant/dwarf star binaries within a hundred light years of Sol. There were four. Beta Aquila had a dwarf companion roughly 150 AU from the star. Astronomers had found in the 2100s that it had no planetary companions the size of Earth with working biospheres. The other three red giants—Epsilon Cygnus, Aldebaran, and Theta Ursa Major—also had no life-bearing worlds orbiting the red giants or the giants' companion stars, as shown by looking at their atmospheric chemistries. So these were not good prospects for the dying Furian world. Apparently such life bearing pairs were unlikely.

The Furians' star was a bit more than a hundred light years from Sol. So the Furians looked for happy coincidences instead.

Ruth shook her head in wonder. The Furians were smart. Roughly every 100,000 years, random orbital motions made stars drift by within two light years of Sol. By chance, a red giant was a few light years from Sol when the Furians launched their Ark sails. So they took advantage, she guessed, of the coincidence. It checked out with the astro simulations she ran.

About four million years ago, a red giant had passed by in stately splendor, lighting the sky of an Earth busy evolving mammals with a ruddy glow. Small primates scuttled beneath this glowing ember in the night, trying to stay alive. Perhaps some of them puzzled at the lights in that dark celestial bowl as the Furian probe made its passage, braking around the red giant. Then it set sail for the biosphere the Furians knew orbited the ordinary yellow dwarf star two light years away, Sol. The passage time at lower velocities would be dozens of centuries, but the Ark had time to play out its slow logic.

It had entered the solar system and, following instruction from a Furian society that had died on their burning world, took up orbit. What would stimulate it to activity again?

Fraq thought the Ark awaited a visit. Only an interplanetary civilization could reach it and understand its genetic heritage. The Ark orbited somewhere near Sol, awaiting a knock at its door.

The Ythris wanted to go there, harvest the heritage. With help from the evolved primates, and their SETI Library.

What had her mother used to say? *Adventure means opportunity.* Sure, Mom.

◈ ◈ ◈

The Lunavator Bolo was running often and not fully booked, but they had to wait for the synchronous connection to the high velocity Flinger. And Fraq wanted to hunt. So . . . they wanted her to join in. More diplomatic social niceties, and for Ruth a command performance courtesy of the Prefect.

"You must hunt with them," he said blandly. "They request it."

"I nearly broke my neck last time."

"You exaggerate. In any case, I instructed you to practice."

"Practice flying, sure—that was fun. But hunting? How?"

"In the Verdant Void, of course. We have stocked it with animals that we believe will appeal to the Ythri instincts. They are carnivores and enjoy the sport of getting their own game."

"I'm a vegetarian."

"I don't recall seeing that in your file."

"I'm a recent convert."

Did his eyes narrow by a millimeter? "How recently?"

Ten seconds ago, she thought, but said, "Some time now."

"That is of no matter. You will not have to eat what you help them catch."

How would you know, freezeface? Have you hunted with them? "I will do my best."

He did not bother to smile. Indeed, she could not recall that he ever had. "Excellent."

Fraq had taken perch some distance from her and the other Ythris. They all chose perches in the spire trees that grew near the Void walls, facing the kilometers of forest just below. When she gazed toward him he looked away quite deliberately. That fit the background inferences the translators had fed Ruth. Ythris were solitary types.

Fraq yawned his jaws widely and sent a long, howling call. Ythris echoed it, clashing their claw-hands together in a savage applause. They wore little clothing beyond a weapon belt and genital covers, for feathers guided their flight. In their preparing moments before she had seen and understood—the grooming, preening, trembling with hot-eyed desire for the hunt.

The Ythri were moving appetites, the translators said, carnivorous except for a sweet tooth for fruits. Carnivores needed larger regions per individual than herbivores or omnivores, even though meat has more calories per kilo than vegetable matter. A pride of lions needed a lot of antelope, and antelope needed a lot of land to graze.

They had emerged from a long drought on their largest continent, forcing the ancestors from deep forests, out onto savannahs. They grew larger and sharpened their hunting skills, forming groups that drove their solitary natures toward social skills. That in turn improved their ground locomotion and evolved claws into hands, though they never lost their sharp hooked nails. So the Ythri had evolved extreme territoriality and individualism, with social cohesion when needed. This had consequences in their governments, mores, arts, faiths, and philosophies. All that came from their extreme carnivore appetites.

So, she guessed, Fraq and his other Ythri expressed in their beautiful golden-brown feathers the itchy tensions that came to them while in close association. Even a kilometers-wide Void was too tight for them. Their feathers riffled with jittering waves. Zooming through the wormhole, confronting humans in confined spaces—these were fresh challenges, driving uneasy stresses.

She had to admit, Fraq was an admirable male, proud and aloof. And those eyes . . .

For this event the Library had leased the Verdant Void exclusively and filled its dense forests with animals, many brought especially from Earth. (Thriftily, the Library also discreetly posted micro cameras throughout, and had already sold the media rights for more than the Void lease cost.) The translators, who studied Ythri culture as rendered in conversations and a few grudgingly given texts, all advised not to make it easy for the Ythri. This was the central "sport" of the Ythri life, as well as their food source. They rose to civilization not through agriculture but through managing vast populations of animals, kept in the enormous forests and hunted daily. All their culture focused on pursuit, stalking, attack, and feasting—the intense code of "bloodpride." If they inferred that the prey here was being staked for easy plucking, or was tame, the aliens might well take grave offense.

Fraq sang forth again from his booming lungs, this time in Anglish, for her benefit. "No few be the winds that blow on our souls! Maychance our technics bring to bear! Stiffly upwind we go a-wing!"

More claw-clashing and hooting big-lung calls. The Ythri females added skittering grace notes, Ruth noted, probably challenging the males to do better than they. The battle of the sexes was a galactic scale universal. Or perhaps more like a dance.

Meat desire rang in their booming voices. The Ythri rustled and fretted and now steam rose from their feathers as their blood pumped energy into swollen tissues. Eyes jerked with predator speed and beaks clattered a rattling rhythm.

The Ythri were now steamed with energy. Eyeing them, Ruth checked her own gear and wondered what it would be like to have feathers she could arch and bunch into control surfaces, the better to master the vagrant winds.

Into the brawling air, Fraq sheered off his perch at a steep angle. He opened to the full five meter wingspan and floated without labor. Ruth took a breath of the thick, sweet air and leaped after him, arms opening to embrace the updraft with her wings.

The Library had set the atmospheric pressure higher to give Ruth a bit of help keeping aloft. The rich green canopy had breaks and corridors that funneled winds, creating turbulence and even vortexes, driven by the updrafts that rimmed the Void and the descending currents that dove down at the center. A side effect—unavoidable, the Prefect assured her with lofty tones—was increased vapor density, which meant . . . clouds. A gray puffball glided up from the distant floor, getting darker as it rose and droplets condensed. And Ruth was swooping into it, following Fraq.

He was already hundreds of meters ahead, swooping in a V search pattern with other Ythris. She was playing catch-up in every turn they made, surveying the canopy. Some Ythri dove down in long swoops to peer under the broad stretching branches of the tall trees. There was maneuver space for them because under Lunar grav Earthly trees had shot up, many of them several hundred meters tall. Give life opportunities and it seizes them.

Something seized her then—a vortex. She tumbled, turned her ankle flaps, got back in line to cut across the turbulence. A Ythri nearby, making a return swoop, looked at her oddly, mouth wide, and she saw its tongue and palate were purple. A hunting sign?

Here came the gray cloud. She angled in, rising, and suddenly droplets washed over her. Rain! Within moments, flying blind in the gray mist, she could feel herself gain weight as rivulets ran along her back. When she popped out into the shafts of light she was above the canopy and Ythri were angling below the treetops. She coasted, watching, and when a clearing came she made herself dive lower, scooting under the dense branches. Still fifty meters above the ground, she watched the Ythri throng down on—wild pigs! The animals snarled up at the immense birds and the Ythri fell upon them with glad cries. Claws sank deep into the boar. The slaughter brought whooping calls as the sky predators savaged a dozen pigs within minutes. She had never seen anything like it.

Fraq rose from the bloody ground, jumping into the air effortlessly, and shot up to fly parallel to her circling. "Like stump legs, these are!" he shouted, and she supposed his twisted mouth bespoke fun. "Come!"

He veered away and she labored to follow. Soon they came out onto a grassy plain and Fraq bellowed with obvious joy. "Sugarmeat!"

He dived immediately at a group of kangaroo. She zoomed over the killing, as Fraq sprang from one to the next, expertly slicing their throats with his claws as they turned to flee. He caught each at the top of the hop. The roos fell dead, legs still kicking. Blood stained the ground.

She let her left wing drag to double back to see more and it caught on a branch. Her "Uh!" made Fraq look up as she tumbled in a slow, stupid gyre—and smacked down hard on her left shoulder.

Sitting up, she was sure Fraq was laughing, a high booming cackle no human had heard before.

The Lunavator Bolo dropped down the black sky for them.

The grappler looked like a long cable plunging straight down vertically from the starscape, jaws yawning. Its tip speed at the grab platform was exactly zero, she knew, but Ruth braced herself for the yank.

It was a heavy load to haul. The Ythris were in the craft they had flown in on from the wormhole, in its own big chamber. The entire human vehicle held Ruth, Prefect and staff, plus the booster crew, a complete interplanetary spacecraft ready to fly. Here it came—*snap* and they were aloft, zooming up into the dead black Lunar sky. She watched the silvery ground rush away and then saw the latest comet head slide up from the horizon. It seethed with fogs, all captured by a gossamer envelope. Kilometers across and managed by robots, it glowed under sunlight focused by silvery mirrors. Water, food, fuel—the key to mastering the inner solar system lay in dropping iceteroids down the grav gradient, sliding them into useful orbits, and sucking them dry. Luna needed about one comet head a week these days, a burgeoning world.

They arced up into the black under an easy half-a-grav acceleration. Ruth had been a Lunatic long enough to notice the strain. The Lunavator was a rotating bolo that touched down at the launch port exactly the same way every time, a classical mechanics milk run. Best to rest and not think too much about the high-wire handoffs involved. She let herself drowse, thinking about the still mysterious Ythri motives, when the Prefect said at her elbow, "I wish I knew more about what they plan."

This was unusually revealing. "Um, why?"

The Prefect allowed himself a frown. "They say this Ark is a legacy they want to 'harvest' but . . . somehow, it's connected to their own history."

"Maybe one visited them?"

"Then why would they need this one?"

"They're hunters."

"With long memories, apparently."

"They insisted on bringing their own ship, too . . . " she prompted.

"It makes sense. The ship is very small and they say it fits their physio needs. All they took aboard was the basics: volatiles, air, food."

"Which means they could scoot out to the Oort, jump through the wormhole wherever it is, and be gone with whatever they get from the Ark."

The Prefect gave a small eye-twitch. "We have thought of that, yes."

"And taken measures . . . "

"Yes." He would say no more.

The Bolo central tether facility was a big captured asteroid, massive enough to prevent payloads from stealing too much energy, lowering the Bolo orbit. The Lunavator rotated in the same direction as its orbit, precisely so that the velocity of each Bolo end's tip equaled the orbital velocity of the system's center of mass. So the center had to hold steady.

They spun upward, sliding elevator fashion around the dark asteroid, a rocky cinder brightly lit by the control station, and onward to the Flinger. Ruth knew she was not privy to Prefect-level strategies, since the Library historically sponged up knowledge and gave forth only trickles, even to librarians such as her. But he seemed relaxed, and this was an unusual chance. She gave him her best party-girl smile. It seemed to have no effect, so she said, "I'm getting on well with Fraq."

"Yes, I see him eyeing you at our table meetings."

"What?" She never knew where his thinking came from. "He's another species!"

"From an entirely different kingdom of life, true. But male strategies seem to be an invariant."

She wondered if this was a joke and suddenly felt a blush spread cross her cheeks. She had liked the strong look of Fraq, his tawny feathers wreathing slim muscles, the glinting golden eyes—

Best to deflect this talk, yes. "I tried to get out of him where the Ark is."

"I know. You failed."

Okay, try the front door. "You didn't seem bothered when the issue came up."

"I already knew."

"Where is it, anyway?"

The Prefect grimaced, another unusual expression. *So you're not the perpetual Sphinx after all.* "They finally revealed that. They spotted it using code-response transmissions while they came in from the Oort. How they knew the code they didn't say."

"They must've had a visit from an Ark, then."

"They won't discuss that, which means you are probably right. The translators think so, too."

"So the Ark, it's . . . ?"

"A small thing in the asteroid belt, the obvious place to hide."

"That big a sail—"

"It's probably folded up, to elude detection."

Ruth tried to get more but the Prefect went forward to the *Venture* bridge. She sat, watched Luna shrink to aft, and pondered the Ythri mysteries. She was having coffee in a bubble cup when the Flinger came rushing down. She could make out the slender cables as they came out of the dark, spindly fingers reaching for the grapple. Their "package" in Lunavator lingo was the human ship, *Venture*, and the smaller Ythri ship, bundled together. The package got handed off in gruff shoves to the wrought-carbon Flinger cable. It snatched them at high, slam-into-the-couch accelerations, a brutal thrust heading them into their fast interplanetary orbit. She relaxed as the huge invisible hand forced her deep into her sighing smart-cushions. Her joints ached.

Clunks, rattles, and thunks told her their package was taking on more masses of water, to later burn in the reaction engines. She could see the feeder lines snaking into their carbon-black package, delivering water fresh-harvested from the comet nucleus she had seen only a few hours ago, looking up from the launch point. All the while the Flinger was pumping water into their fusion fuel tanks. They would shove steam out to decelerate at their destination.

Their speed was so high now as to be incomprehensible, the view a blur. All she could think of was the unending pressure forcing them onward. She had extra oxy just to stay conscious; Loonies had it hard. The Flinger orbited far above the Lunavator in centrifugal haste, rotating so fast that within another hour it let them go at a speed above two hundred kilometers a *second.* The solar system was big, and it was best not to think about hitting a wandering rock at such speeds. Their forward-looking radar linked to laser cannon could do that, thank you.

They popped free on course. It was like turning into an angel after a week in hell. Light, airy, she was a free bird.

She unstrapped in the zero gravs and tried a tumble-thrust to get her popping joints aligned. She had done zero grav before but now her flying experience paid off in easy, unconscious grace.

The Prefect was asleep, or maybe unconscious, his face lined. She headed for the hibernation capsule ahead of the staff, got her injections from the nurse, and snuggled into the smart comfy clasp of the hiber tech cocoon. She didn't want to hear the Prefect's ideas, or the staff's. And she didn't want to be bored with a month of speculation. Sleep, bliss, yes.

She wanted to see the Ark, a month's ride away.

The Ark sail was folded up into a tight scroll, which explained why humans hadn't found it. The sail had been kilometers across, and now was just a white rod bound with straps. Its cargo, the ship that had sailed the eons, basked in the ruddy glow of a red giant, then coasted for centuries across to the nearby Earth—well, it looked ordinary. A dull composite cylinder, streaked and pitted and worn, hardly a hundred meters long and seventy meters across. But the door was open, a yawning circle. Pretty obvious: *Come on in, whoever you are. You're why we came.*

Except the Ark arrived before humanity had swung down from the trees. It had to be designed to welcome whatever sprang from ancient forests, glimpsed in pixels by a species long extinct.

Staff up and coffee-strong, they prepared a team to haul alongside the Ark and board. Then the Prefect suddenly cried, "The Ythris are already there!"

Ruth glanced out a port while she slipped on her skin suit. Floating across the space between them and the Ark, lit only by starlight, were . . . bubbles. With her helmet on she close upped those motes and saw that Ythri space suits were the opposite of theirs: expanded, transparent oblate spheroids with appliances socketed into the walls. A Ythri swam in the bubble, breathing air and propelling itself with tiny jets. The suit bubbles had grappling arms and the team of six Ythri were forming a ring around the Ark cylinder. Each carried a teardrop thing of tan ceramic alongside. "They're not going for the front door," she sent before sealing her suit.

By the time she got out their air lock the Ythri had the tan ceramics attached to the Ark hull, encircling it. "What's up?" she sent on private com to the Prefect—who, she saw, hadn't bothered to get into his skin suit. Maybe he didn't bother to have one, either; he was standing at the big port in the ship's bridge.

She glided past him on a tether, skating cross the *Venture*'s hull in the inky dark. "We anticipated this," he said blandly and she could see his lips move.

"What're they—"

"Probably mounting those simple fusor packs they're carrying. They want to get the full implosion impact, tear the Ark down to atoms."

"*Why?*"

"Some ancient grudge, I surmise. I had their ship sounded from outside, when it first came into Lunar orbit. The fusor warheads showed up clearly." He stood with hands behind his back, a traditional Prefect stance of measured patience.

Ruth wasn't feeling patient and would probably never be a Prefect. "You knew all this—"

"And did not tell you, yes. I could not predict how well the Ythri could read your unconscious signals."

"What do you—"

"A moment." The Prefect nodded to the *Venture* Captain. From the forward hull a concealed projector suddenly jutted forth. Its snout turned, focused, and Ruth heard a *braaaack* in her microwave inputs. Nothing happened that she could see but the Prefect nodded and allowed himself a small smile. "Their simple warheads are now dead. Go tell them."

So she was message girl now. Still, Ruth was glad to be free of *Venture* and jetting toward the floating Ythri bubbles. As she approached they seemed disturbed, working furiously at their socketed tools. The tan ceramic warheads were just lumps on the Ark cinder-dark skin.

"Your explosives will not work," she sent Fraq on a narrow squirt beam.

"I have scented this," he said tightly, gliding over the Ark's horizon.

"Can I trust you to go inside with me?"

This he pondered, hanging beside the circular lock entrance. "I carry no further weaponry," he said at last.

By that time Ruth was there. Instead of slowing, she glided directly into the lock. Fraq barked some surprised epithet and hastily followed her.

Intuitively she sensed it was better to confront him inside, isolated; make it personal. She passed through an iris that opened at her approach. No air, but she was in a large space that slowly . . . awakened.

Phosphorescent glows stretched across long walls. Transparent cases lit, showing strange bodies suspended in clear liquid. Intricate tiny slabs showed pale colors, light fluttering as if from a slumber. DNA inventories? She prowled the space, surrounded by an enormous bio data base. Slowly, it came to life.

Suddenly zero-grav flowers floated by, big blooms growing from spheres of water. She recalled as a girl watching the joy of soap bubbles shimmering in sunlight. These somehow sprang to life in vacuum.

Behind thin windows, gnarled trees like bonsai curled out from moistening soil. Odd angular plants burgeoned before her eyes.

In all directions of the cylindrical space, plants grew, looking to her like lavender brushstrokes in the air. In a spinning liquid vessel, orange snakes with butterfly wings danced in bubbling air. *Displays.*

She heard her own gasps echoed, turned. Fraq hung nearby, eyes wide. "Is a display," he said. "A welcome, it could be."

"Welcome, yes. It's a bio inventory," she said. "Displayed as an explanation. As advertising."

In his own suit bubble he waved a wing at images playing along the walls. Purple-skinned animals loping on octopuslike tendrils across a sandy plain. Flying carpets with big yellow eyes, massive ruddy creatures moving like mountains on tracks of slime, trees that walked, fish in stony undersea palaces. A library of alien life.

She turned full on to him, pressed against his bubble, glowered. "What was that you said? The Ark was a 'Prime Need for life itself' eh?"

"We came for ancient vengeance," Fraq said stonily over comm, tan feathers ruffling with unease.

"For what? They sent you an Ark? But—"

"And we brought their life from the Ark in orbit, down to our world." His eyes flared. "We could not control it. Did not know. Their strange creatures festered, escaped from us, attacked our life at every level. Diseases, blight, desolation, death. They nearly killed and colonized our biosphere."

Sudden deep anger boiled in his tight voice. She sighed. "You . . . you just did it wrong."

"They sent it as a weapon, our history says. Our foremothers laid down for all generations, as bloodpride, the call—to destroy all Arks."

"It was too late to kill the Furians?"

"Alas, yes. Their star had eaten them."

Suddenly, from the troubled shifting of his eyes, she saw why Fraq had insisted that she fly with them. First, to test whether humans could be better than the mere dirt-huggers of their world. Second, to show that Ythrian hunting carnivore life was hard, aloof, clannish. *That was all their way of telling me about themselves. And now I sense them. Intuit them. I know them beyond language.*

The Ythris learned through experience, not from libraries. They had now to think of this Ark as repository of lost history, not as enemy.

She peered through the glassy bubble suit, reading his shifting feather patterns. "I'm sorry, but you should know more biology. Try experiments! Don't bring in invasive forms until you understand them. Look—" she gestured wide at the bounty surrounding them. "They're *offering*, not invading."

Fraq's stiff face slowly eased. Feathers rustled. "I was charged with bringing destruction. My kind regrets that you knew more, and deadened our explosives."

"We know more about war, unfortunately. Look, that's over. Question is, what next?"

"You must destroy this."

"Hey, I'm a librarian! Don't destroy, study! Learn!"

"It is a danger too vast to say." He frowned darkly. "This is a matter of bloodpride."

"We'll learn from your mistake. No Furian life gets into Earth's biosphere. Or those of Mars and Luna."

"I will consider it." More feather riffles, hard to read.

"You've already *seen* how we'll do it," Ruth said suddenly, the idea fresh born and irresistible. "This ship is live now. Let's redirect it. Send it to Luna, use the bolo to bring some of it down. Carefully take bits of the Furian life into a huge new void, specially dug. Create an alien biosphere isolated by a hundred kilometers of rock."

Fraq blinked. She could see his Ythrian male rigidity ease a bit, muscles soften, breathing slow. She had been studying his body language and now somehow knew how to work with it.

She could do this. No Prefect need get in the way, either. Just her and this beautiful alien.

She smiled. Wordless, the two of them hung in the luminous center of ancient legacy, a Library of Life for an entire world now gone forever. *They* could do it.

Her heart beat faster. She watched his strong wings flex with new energy as the idea took hold. *Y'know, he does look like a great guy . . .*

AFTERWORD:

IN JANUARY 1999 Poul Anderson sent me a letter enclosing his essay on his invented aliens, the Ythrians, which he had used in his novel, *The People of the Wind.* I had liked the novel and had asked him as part of a proposed anthology for details on the planet and its aliens. My notion was a collection of stories that dealt with aliens in scrupulous detail, attention paid to how they evolved, how that affected their worldview, and how humans might react to them. Maybe there would be humans in the stories, maybe not.

The anthology idea didn't fly, alas. Poul was a meticulous writer, working out an integrated vision for a novel, though few of these manuscripts apparently saw print. He was ready to write another story in one of his worlds, and it was a singular treat seeing how he had designed it.

Approached to contribute to this volume, I fetched out his thirteen page Ythri description, with solar system and planetary parameters in detail. His essay also included several of his sketches of these aliens and their anatomy, even diagrams of their wing bones and skull. He named the planet Ythri, which I've used for its natives. It's a world with 0.75 Earth's g and a denser atmosphere, both explaining how smart-flying aliens could evolve. His body plans and physiology proceed from solid constraints, including their body mass (30 kg) and molecular chemistry. There are words for local plants and crops and domesticated animals. I've kept his details and terms, with some small alterations to fit my story.

From his parallel short story, "Wings of Victory," I've taken some Ythri culture, speech, and attitudes, and even phrases Poul made up in their language. Poul worked out and wrote up in great detail far more than he used, a signature of the Hal Clement school of planet-building, as admirably shown in Clement's founding novel of the school, *Heavy Planet.* I altered the Ythri history somewhat to fit, but kept their nature the same.

Further, I wrote from the viewpoint of a character and situation I've been developing in a story series about what a SETI Library might look like when we have a host of messages to work through. While coded signals would be fascinating, it's always more fun to have a live alien in the foreground, too.

Poul was a major player of the game among hard SF writers: judge if these ideas pass muster, and see what I've done with them. I knew Poul since 1963 and treasured the many times we met, dined and drank together. I miss him greatly, and it's been a pleasure to play in one of his imagined worlds.

—Gregory Benford

THREE LILIES AND THREE LEOPARDS
[And A Participation Ribbon In Science]
by Tad Williams

***TAD WILLIAMS** became an international bestseller with his very first novel,* Tailchaser's Song, *and the high quality of his output and the devotion of his readers has kept him on the top of the charts ever since as a* New York Times *and* London Sunday Times *bestseller. His other novels include* The Dragonbone Chair, The Stone of Farewell, To Green Angel Tower, Siege, Storm, City of Golden Shadow, Otherland, River of Blue Fire, Mountain of Black Glass, Sea of Silver Light, Caliban's Hour, Child of an Ancient City (*with Nina Kiriki Hoffman*), Tad Williams' Mirror World: An Illustrated Novel, The War of the Flowers, Shadowmarch, *a collection,* Rite: Short Work, *and a collection of two novellas, one by Williams and one by Raymond E. Feist,* The Wood Boy/The Burning Man. *As editor, he has produced the big retrospective anthology,* A Treasury of Fantasy. *His most recent books are two novels in his Bobby Dollar series;* The Dirty Streets of Heaven *and* Happy Hour in Hell. *In addition to his novels, Williams writes comic books, and film and television scripts, and is co-founder of an interactive television company.*

Here, due to a cosmic screwup, Fate sends the wrong person from our world into the world of Poul Anderson's Three Hearts and Three Lions, *with disastrous, and very funny, results.*

"DON'T FREAK OUT, Fernando," Pogo told his assistant manager. "I'm just going to the food court. You'll be fine."

Little Fernando tried to smile but it was the sickly grimace of an infantryman ordered to charge a machine gun nest. He pointed with a shaking finger at the crowd of bargain-hunters that had turned Saturday afternoon at Kirby Shoes into a battle zone. "But it's the Summer Madness Event . . . !"

Perry Como Cashman, who had been named after the singer by a soon-to-be-absent father and had been called "Pogo" by his friends since junior high school, sighed. "I know, dude. But I haven't been out of the store since I opened at seven this morning and I haven't eaten anything and I'm *starving*. Little Ed's back from his break and Big Ed's here and whatsisname—you know, Stockroom Dude—can help out if you really need another body. I'll be back in, like, twenty minutes max, so just hold your water." Pogo patted Fernando on the shoulder. "I'll bring you back something if you want."

Fernando's eyes were showing whites around the edges. "A gun or a knife, please. That lady threw a hiking boot at me!"

"Emergency!" shouted Little Ed from the other side of the store. "There's a woman climbing the display wall, trying to get the last set of kids' Adidas! Oh, man, she just clubbed somebody with a Brannock device . . . !"

Pogo was whistling as he made his way across Victory Plaza Mall. It had been a serious pleasure to leave Fernando and the others to deal with this latest crisis. For at least the next few minutes, the only thing he had to decide was whether he wanted cashew chicken, egg rolls, or both.

As he circled an ornamental fountain full of splashing toddlers, he thought he heard someone calling his name. He did his best to ignore it, but a few moments later he heard it again—*felt it* might be more accurate, since it was so faint, so distant. He turned with a grunt of irritation, expecting to see Fernando or one of his salesmen chasing after him, but saw only the usual afternoon shoppers, bored young mothers and seniors avoiding the San Fernando Valley heat in the air-conditioned mall.

Pogo . . . ! Pogo Cashman . . . !

He turned in a full circle, but nobody was even looking at him, let alone calling him. *Hunger hallucinations,* he thought. *Better get some pot stickers, too . . .*

***Pogo** . . . !*

This time the voice sounded so close he whirled, expecting to find some practical joker standing right behind him, but he was alone in the center of the shopping center concourse. An instant later, he fell through the floor, tumbling through the very fabric of reality and into a darkness that throbbed with honks and squeals like a prog rock band tuning up.

He fell for a long time. Long enough to get bored.

I really wanted some egg rolls . . . ! was his last thought before he abruptly fell back into the world. The problem was, it was not the world that Pogo Cashman had fallen out of in the first place.

"Did ye do yersel' a hurt, m'lord?" Small, rough hands pulled at him, trying to help him sit up. "Are ye wounded?"

Pogo was wondering about that himself, because everything sure smelled, sounded, and looked strange. Some shit had definitely gone wrong, either with the Victory Plaza Mall or Pogo Cashman himself. All the walls seemed to have fallen down and he was surrounded by trees instead of retail stores. Also, why was Fernando talking funny? And why was there a big, black horse standing just a few feet away?

"M'lord? What befell ye?"

"Fernando, you were supposed to . . . " But then he realized it wasn't his diminutive assistant manager standing over him but someone quite different—in fact, the stranger made little Fernando look like Kareem Abdul-Jabbar. He was a dwarf, with a nose like a brown avocado, a bushy, dirty beard, and large bare feet.

"Who are you?" Pogo asked him. "And how did I get to Disneyland?"

"I ken that land not," the small fellow said. "But ye know me sure, lord. Ludo, yer ain sworn vassal."

Pogo was really beginning to worry now. He had never had the greatest imagination (except during his youthful days of pharmaceutical exploration) and if he was imagining all this, that had to mean a pretty severe head injury.

And I never got my lunch, either, he thought sadly. *Now I'll probably spend months eating hospital food.* "Okay, Lou," he said, trying to be a good sport. "Then if this isn't Disneyland, where are we?"

The dwarf frowned, obviously concerned. "The forest of the Ardennes, Duke Astolfo. Sure ye must recollect!"

"Duke Astolfo?" The name was sort of familiar—a relief pitcher for the Angels, maybe? Professional surfer? "Hey, should somebody call an ambulance? Because I think I might have a brain injury or something. Or could you kind of steer me back to the mall, at least? I manage Kirby Shoes—you know it? Across from Orange Julius, next to J.C. Penney?"

Ludo shook his head. "This is nay guid and the dark will soon come. We maun make camp."

"Yeah. So is there a snack bar or a store or something around here? A minimart? 'Cause I never got any lunch today."

But the dwarf only shook his head again and helped Cashman to his feet. He was stronger than his size would have suggested. "Can ye ride, m'lord?"

"On a horse?" Pogo examined the huge, black beast. Horses didn't look anywhere near so big on television. "I don't know. Is it hard?"

Supervisor Fnutt had called a sudden and mandatory meeting for all management personnel. Even sub-sub-manager Quidprobe, the new kid in the office, knew that had to be a bad sign.

All the dozens of managers and sub-managers of the Crossover Division of the Department of Fictional Universes were crowded into the conference space, although most of them looked as though they would rather be pretty much anywhere else. Fnutt the supervisor was pacing back and forth at the front of the room—or what would have been the front if the Department of Fictional Universes had been in any way compelled by Euclidean geometry.

"This is bad!" Fnutt squealed. The supervisor was a small green fellow with a small green mustache and a tendency to become shrill. "Very, *very* bad!" At the moment, he was in danger of shattering every coffee cup in the room. "How could this happen?"

"Does it matter?" asked Bardler, who managed the Matter of France, his tone heavy with doom. "It's happened. It's too late now to do anything but watch the destruction!"

Quidprobe, a sub-sub-manager in the Poul Anderson subdivision, with untaxing maintenance duties in the seldom-accessed Ariosto section of Anderson's Matter of France, raised a rubbery, three-fingered hand. "I still don't understand what happened."

"One of your boss Digry's idiot clerks sent the wrong personnel request," Bardler snarled, "and so some idiot named Cashman—a shoe store manager, no less!—was dispatched to Anderson's medieval France for a tricky assignment, instead of the guy who was supposed to go, Porter Gervaise Castlemane, an English chemical engineer and former SAS officer." Bardler scratched both his noses. "Who would have been perfect by the way. Castlemane can kill a man with just his *fingertips*."

"Yes, we sent the wrong initial request," bubbled Quidprobe's boss, Digry, "but then one of *your* idiot clerks didn't see our Correction Form!" Digry was so upset his face was pressed against the window of his tank and his nicitating membranes snapped up and down like windshield wipers in a deluge. "We spotted the mistake in moments. We sent the proper MP-362A immediately. But someone in your office must have been taking a nitrogen break."

Bardler didn't seem to have an argument at the tip of his feeding tube, so he just scowled.

"*Stop!* We'll figure out what went wrong later!" Supervisor Fnutt was getting dangerously squeaky again. "Right now we have to think of something to do about this . . . catastrophe!"

"Can't we just reverse it?" asked Quidprobe. He'd been less than a century on the job—very young by departmental standards—but he was ambitious, as the young often are. As far as he could tell, the other managers uniformly loathed him for it.

"It doesn't work that way," screeched Fnutt, his mustache writhing like a caterpillar on a griddle. "Departmental regs say that once the personnel unit has been transferred into the fictional world, any change of plan has to go to the top for approval. The *very, very top*." Just the look on Fnutt's face was enough to make even the most hardened of department employees moisten with fear where his, her, or its limbs attached. "So either we call the big boys right now and tell them we have royally screwed the tetramorph or we have to leave him there."

"And if we leave him there, everything else will go wrong," said

Bardler darkly. "Roland will stay insane. Nobody will save Charlemagne from Agramant and Aelfric. Christendom will totter and fall."

"But it's only a crossover story about the Matter of France, one of Anderson's old books—in fact, what we're dealing with here isn't even an actual story by Poul Anderson!" said Quidprobe. "I was looking over the order this morning. It's only some kind of pastiche for an anthology based on his work—and not very closely based, either, I couldn't help noticing. I suspect the guy writing it is a bit of a hack. So who cares?" But when Quidprobe saw the look on the faces of his superiors his cheerful smile faltered and he blanched right down to his basal chromatophores. "Uh . . . what don't I understand?"

Supervisor Fnutt was clearly doing his best not to lose his temper, but some of the more veteran managers looked like they were already wondering if they would get time off to attend Quidprobe's funeral. "Listen . . . *youngster*. What you don't understand is that when something goes wrong enough with an important creator like Anderson's version of a world, the problem will ripple out from there."

"Ripple?" Quidprobe looked around.

"It means, you bottom-hole-breather," growled Bardler, "that when this Cashman guy fails, it'll infect the entire Matter of France. The whole thing! Not just Anderson's version, but Ariosto, the Song of Roland—which is, incidentally, the oldest surviving piece of French literature—and who knows what else." Bardler was getting angrier as he spoke, and Quidprobe was now doing his best to slide under the table, but fear had made the sub-sub-manager rubbery and he was going horizontal as much as vertical. "A few weeks from now," Bardler shouted, "Charles the Great will probably be known as Charles the Loser!"

Even Quidprobe's boss Digry looked anxious. "That bad? Really?"

"You knock the pins out from under Charlemagne and after a little while, there goes Arthur and the Round Table, too!" Bardler declared with a certain grim satisfaction. "And then—goodbye, English literature! Farewell, Western European Humanism! *So long, it was fun! Write if you find work!*"

"Enough!" squeaked Fnutt.

Bardler dropped back into his chair and subsided into scowling silence. All around the long table managers and sub-managers shifted uneasily, thanking whatever they prayed to that they were not in Quidprobe's now rather viscous seat. In fact, Quidprobe wasn't in it either: he had finally managed to slither onto the floor.

"It's your orb and your game now," Fnutt told them with dark finality. "As far as I'm concerned, this meeting never happened. And when I'm ready to send my report at the end of the day, I don't want to see any loose ends that I'll have to report to . . . *you know who.*" Fnutt rose to his full, if unprepossessing height, and marched out of the conference space, followed a moment later by his mustache.

"So . . . " said Digry at last. His bubbling voice seemed so loud in the silence after their boss's retreat that even Quidprobe, reorganizing his splayed pseudopods on the floor beneath his chair, could hear every word clearly. "What do we do next?"

"I hear there might be a few openings in the Department of Pointless Philosophical Rambling," ventured one of the sub-managers.

By the time young Quidprobe had finally managed to clamber back up onto his slippery seat, the conference space had emptied and a large, shouting mob was forming around the copying device as his fellow managers and sub-managers hurried to update and dispatch their resumés.

"Truly ye remember naught?" asked Ludo, his face scrunched in dismay like an old paper bag. "Not y'r dalliance with the fair Alcina? How the sorc'ress tired of ye and turned ye into a wee myrtle tree and the a' the hounds would make water upon ye?"

"Huh?" Cashman was doing his best to understand the dwarf, but the little fellow was clearly suffering from some kind of head injury himself: some of his words sounded like English, but the rest were gobbledygook that sounded like the excitable guy on Star Trek. "I don't know, man. Can we eat now?"

"Nae, we cannae eat yet." He hadn't called Pogo "M'lord" in a while. "I've had nae chance to find victuals, have I?"

"Vegetables? Can't we get some real food? Like burgers? Or pizza?"

"Victuals! I said 'victuals'! Are ye daft?"

"I'm not deaf. I'm not even nearsighted, dude. How come you can't talk like a normal person—like me?"

"Like ye? Like *ye*?" For a moment Ludo seemed angry enough to walk off and leave Pogo in the woods alone, but then he flopped himself down beside the sandy trail and folded his short legs under him. "Go tak up yon shield," he said.

Shield at least was a word Pogo recognized. He lifted the big hunk of wood and metal off the saddle horn of the black horse. He didn't have to reach as high as he expected to, and his hands seemed bigger and stronger than he remembered. He was beginning to wonder if the world around him wasn't the only thing that had changed. "Yeah?"

"Luik on yon painted crest. Tell us what ye see."

Pogo decided he must mean the painted front of the shield, so "crest" must mean the advertisement on the front, like the stripey Adidas flower. "Yes," he said. "The crest. I see. Very interesting." The design was weird and old-fashioned, a huge trademark of crudely painted lion-type creatures alternating with what Pogo was pretty sure was the New Orleans Saints football team logo. He stared as hard as he could, but it yielded up no secrets. "And . . . ?"

"Do ye ken it not?" Ludo asked. "The three lilies and three leopards of England? The token of your father the king?"

"My father is a king?" As far as Pogo knew, his father was a guy who painted faces on rocks he found at the beach and sold them to tourists.

"Aye, and ye have a grave duty to a' of Christendie. Can ye truly remember naught?"

The communication thing was beginning to be a problem. "I gotta be honest, Louie. I didn't understand a thing you just said."

The dwarf stared at him for a moment, then went off muttering and sat on a fallen tree, pulled out a huge pipe, lit it and began to smoke like a man who was in a hurry to achieve lung cancer.

Quidprobe was the only person left in the conference room. He might even have been the only person left in the entire building. His coworkers had hurried off to renew old friendships in other departments that might have openings, or establish alibis for where they had been when the wrong personnel requisition got approved for the Anderson world, anything but dealing with the actual problem.

Well, Quidprobe thought, *let them. I'm not like that. I'm a fellow who solves problems instead of running from them.* Also, he didn't know anyone in any of the other departments very well. In fact, after a short hundred years or so in the job, half the people in his own section still didn't know Quidprobe's name.

Fnutt's universal viewer was still sitting on the conference space table and Quidprobe was curious to see what was going on with the botched transfer. Perhaps this Cashman creature would turn out to be just as good as the one everyone had expected to enter the fiction-world instead—perhaps everything would turn out all right after all, and all the veteran department managers had panicked needlessly. And if he brought them this good news, perhaps Quidprobe himself would get some of the credit. He even let himself fantasize for a moment that this could be the start of big things for him—a raise, maybe even a promotion. By the Peerless Punctuation of Poe, wouldn't that be grand! He could get himself a new exocontainer that wouldn't break down half the time, and maybe even some top-of-the-line rigid graspers. Wouldn't the folks back home stare and jealously emit phosgene when Quidprobe came back to visit and told them he was a supervisor! And when he whipped out his fancy new graspers and . . . and grasped things, well, his old classmates would just froth themselves with jealousy.

After all, he thought, dialing through the various Poul Anderson worlds, past the speeding *Leonora Christine* and Dominic Flandry, leaving behind the modernist creations and moving farther and farther into the more primitivist inventions such as *The High Crusade* and *The Man Who Came Early*, how hard could it be to succeed in an environment as primitive as the Matter of France, where people couldn't even remove their heads without incurring permanent damage? The Pogocashman organic might not be all that advanced himself, but at least his civilization had discovered things like nuclear power and canned foods.

At last the focal window located the *Three Hearts and Three Lions* world and dilated wide so that Quidprobe could get his first look at the Pogocashman creature. The Pogocashman's Assisting Character—a construct named "Ludo"—was trying to teach him how to fight with the ancient weapon known as a sword, which apparently was the main form of social intercourse in primitive France, but the Pogocashman was sitting on the ground whimpering in pain, his hands bloody.

"You're supposed to hold the *other* end," the dwarf said wearily.

Quidprobe had a sudden powerful urge to look over his own rather slight resumé to see what needed updating. He stabbed at the button to close the focal window, but the machinery was made for more conventionally rigid digits than Quidprobe's and he wound up pressing the button beside it as well. He had only a moment to stare at the label under the accidental button, which read "INTERVENTION—Do Not Engage Without Departmental Permission!" in boldly emphatic symbols in several appropriate languages, then Quidprobe abruptly found himself drawn into an infinitely long thread and then pulled through an infinitely narrow (and infinitely painful) needle's eye before the darkness swallowed him.

Pogo could only stare. The dwarf, who a moment before had been glaring at him in that way of his which was already becoming sadly familiar, had abruptly straightened up and made a noise like a hamster clubbed with a tennis racket, then dropped to the earth in a heap. Now he was lying there looking quite dead. Pogo was just wondering if he needed to find Disneyland security or something when the dwarf groaned and sat up.

"Where am I?" the little bearded man asked, looking from side to side. Then he saw Pogo and groaned again, this time even louder. "'Intervention'! Oh, Lolitas of Leiber, I pushed the 'Intervention' button!"

Pogo wasn't sure what the little fellow was babbling about, but he was pleased by the sudden change in the dwarf's speech. "You stopped talking funny!"

The other stared for a moment, his mouth working deep in his beard, then he sighed and said, "Right. I've replaced the Assisting Character and the machines have keyed my dialect to the Main Character's own form of speech. Just as well. I never understood that detail of the original story, anyway—why would a French dwarf be speaking with a Scottish burr?"

"Huh?"

The dwarf stood up and slapped the dust and sand from his trousers. "Very well, let's figure out how we're going to get this fixed so we can both go back home. We're in some serious difficulty here, and changing dialects is the least of our problems." He turned to Pogo.

"Let me ask you one important question first, creature. Is there *any* chance at all that my managers are wrong and you're really Castlemane from the SAS? Special Air Services? Does that mean anything to you?"

Pogo thought hard. "When you're on a plane and they bring the cart with the drinks on it?"

"Excrement of Ellison." The dwarf sat down again, this time with a thump. "They were right. Ah, well, we might as well make the best of this. My name is Quidprobe . . . "

"Huh? I thought it was Lego or something."

"Never mind what it used to be, it's Quidprobe now. And you are the Pogocashman, correct?"

"Uh . . . yeah. I manage Kirby's Shoes in the Victory Mall. In the Valley . . . ?"

The dwarf shook his head. "But this still doesn't make much sense, even if someone sent the wrong form—usually the obvious mistakes get thrown back by the machines before they're executed." He turned to Pogo. "Is there a reason the multiverse should choose you instead of the right fellow, or was it just a really, really unfortunate clerical error? Have you ever been involved in dimensional slippage before?"

Pogo shrugged. "Well, I guess I experimented a bit during high school. I mean, like, didn't everybody?"

The dwarf sighed and pinched the bridge of his nose between thumb and forefinger. "I've only had a head for a few minutes, and already I have such a headache. So that means you don't know anything about the madness of Roland or Charlemagne, or any of this, do you? And I'm guessing that you don't know who Roland is, the character you're supposed to help, or Charlemagne, the character *he's* supposed to help. And so of course you also don't know how important all this is—do you?"

Pogo looked at him seriously, really trying, trying to focus on the important things. "Uh, no, not really. Hey, before you fell down and started talking normal, didn't you say something about dinner?"

"Do you understand now?" Quidprobe had put it in the simplest possible terms—words and concepts so basic that even an infant of this backward existential plane could understand it. He fixed the organic creature with a hard glare. "It's important that you do."

The Pogocashman smiled hesitantly. "Can you run that all by me again, man? I think I missed a little of it. Sorry. I'm really *hungry*, man."

Quidprobe sighed. "Very well—but pay attention this time, will you? Stop swinging that bladed weapon around before you cut your own head off."

The Pogocashman blushed and slid the sword back into its scabbard. "Sorry. Who did you say you worked for? The Department of Fixable Universes?"

"*Fictional* Universes. The Department of Fictional Universes, Crossover Division, Poul Anderson Subdivision. And you're right in the middle of three of them, at least." Quidprobe scratched at his face, distracted by the borrowed body he was wearing. It was strange to have his brain perched in a round box of bone at the top of a fleshy stalk like this, and the hairy tendrils on the dwarf creature's face itched him horribly. "This is a mess, that's what it is. The chosen Main Character was supposed to be this Castlemane fellow, who was crossing over from your organic world into a fictional universe created by the famous science fiction writer Poul Anderson, which itself was a version of the fictional universe called the Matter of France. With me so far?"

The Pogocashman looked interested. "What *is* the matter with France? I mean, some of that stuff they eat, like frog's legs . . . "

"*Of* France. The Matter of France. It's like the French version of the King Arthur stories, except instead of King Arthur and his knights, it's Charlemagne and *his* knights—Sir Roland, Sir Roger, Duke Astolfo, Holger the Dane, all those legendary characters."

The creature nodded cheerfully. "Okay. I'm totally with you, man. Sir Loin and Chateaubriand and the rest."

Quidprobe ground his teeth together for a moment—another odd sensation, like having an oral cavity full of stones. Patience, he told himself. This poor creature has to live with teeth *all the time.* "But this isn't even Anderson's version, you see—it's some other lesser writer's version of Anderson's version. And somehow when this idiot anthology writer started his story, instead of this Castlemane fellow crossing over from the real world into the Anderson universe, *you* showed up instead. So instead of a problem-solving engineer and man of action, we have . . . " He broke off. No need to rub it in. "Do you know *anything* about engineering? Physics? Anything at all?"

The Pogocashman considered. "I got a participation ribbon in science once. See, I was making this volcano for the science fair, but I was late for school, so I figured I could mix the baking soda and vinegar first and it would save time when I got there." He shrugged. "It sort of exploded—my backpack, but they gave me the ribbon anyway before they sent me home . . . "

Quidprobe winced. "Yes. Well. Science not a strong point, then. But we have bigger problems at the moment."

The creature nodded more emphatically. "Yeah, man. Like getting something to eat, right?"

"No!" Quidprobe was beginning to understand that this was going to be even more difficult than the series of impossibilities he had already conceded. "No, like figuring out how an unprepared cipher like you is going to help the great Roland get back his sanity and save this world from being conquered by the forces of Chaos. And beside your complete lack of scientific knowledge we have no other tools but Astolfo's enchanted horn and a book of useful spells—both of which are in your saddlebag, by the way, so don't lose them." But it had suddenly occurred to him that perhaps he wasn't listening to his Main Character as carefully as he should. This Pogocashman was a creature not of the symbolic plane like Quidprobe himself, but of the physical: perhaps all his talk of hunger was meaningful. Perhaps he really did need some kind of organic sustenance—perhaps he would even be more responsive once he'd taken in nutrients.

Quidprobe strode to the edge of the clearing and looked around until he detected the life-signature of a small creature, a rodent with a bushy tail. He caught it with a quick grab of his still-unfamiliar hands, carefully crushed its skull so it wouldn't suffer, and then dropped it in the Pogocashman's lap.

"Um . . . " The recipient looked with dismay at the gooey mass. The tail was still twitching fitfully. "Isn't there any way to . . . um . . . cook this?"

"I don't doubt it," said Quidprobe. "Start a fire. The oxidation process should char the meat efficaciously." He was tired—the transition into this physical body had taken a lot out of him, and carrying around the weight of a skeleton was extremely wearying. "I wish you success in your consumption."

"Huh?"

"By Howard's Holy Haunches, you do say that a lot, don't you?"

Quidprobe's patience was growing thin; he desperately wanted to rest the clumsy organic body and put his mind to work. "Go ahead and consume that. You'll need your strength—our task here won't be easy and we'll both probably die horribly." He rolled himself up in his cloak and stretched out on the soft forest earth. "Which is only slightly better than having Supervisor Fnutt angry at me. But of course, I'll likely get both."

Pogo had dropped out after the first day of Boy Scouts when he realized there were no snacks at meetings and they all seemed really fired up about taking a fifty-mile hike. Since he hadn't stuck around to earn his camping merit badge he wasn't really certain about the best way to cook a smashed squirrel.

The fire had burned down nearly to ashes, just a few smoldering coals. Pogo tossed in a couple of small twigs but they were green and wouldn't catch. He went to the saddlebag, being very careful not to startle the scary big black horse, and looked for anything useful. He found a cow horn with silver decorations on it and a seriously old-fashioned book—the dwarf had said it was something about spelling. Pogo squinted at the strange writing and couldn't make out any of it, but he didn't really care anyway—he already knew how to spell. Hell, he'd spelled "Mississippi" right once in fourth grade, in front of the whole class, which was pretty good for anybody!

He tore a page out of the book and held one corner to the coals. The piece of rough, thick paper caught with a strange green-blue flame, and for a moment he thought he could hear voices whispering in the wind, but then the page was gone and the voices were too. He wadded up several more pages and kept tossing them in until the fire was really burning, then jammed the squirrel onto a stick and poised it above the flames. It actually smelled pretty good except for the burning fur, and he began thinking it would be nice to have something to drink as well.

After a short search he found one of those Renaissance Fair squirt bags hanging on the saddle. When he squeezed it something like honey-flavored vodka jetted into the back of his throat—that which didn't go down his chin or onto his chest—and it took him a while to stop coughing. The medieval booze wasn't Southern Comfort or anything but it was still pretty good, but Pogo wished he had something less messy to drink it out of. As he sat smelling the squirrel, now bubbling nicely, he suddenly thought of the horn. Wasn't that what those old-timey guys drank from in all the movies?

He squeezed some of the honey-stuff into the horn and it promptly ran out the narrow end and into his lap. He took another messy swallow from the bag to help his imagination, and sure enough, he soon had an idea. The binding of the book was held together with some kind of glue, so he peeled some of it away, wadded it up, then poked it into the narrow end of the horn. It held pretty well, and now he could use the horn as a drinking cup.

Swigging from his horn and moving the squirrel around the fire to keep it from burning, Pogo began to feel like a true knight of the Olde Tymes. Enough honey-stuff and he didn't even mind burning his fingers on hot squirrel meat.

Food in his belly and a nice buzz starting, he sat for another hour or so drinking and feeding the rest of the book to the fire. The colors and whispers and shapes that rose up with the smoke were as entertaining as any double-feature at the Reseda Drive-In.

"Time to go," the dwarf said loudly.

Pogo skinned his eyes open a crack. For some reason, the sun was up. "Man, Quickpoop, not so loud!"

"Quidprobe. My name is *Quidprobe.*" The little guy didn't sound happy. "Get up. We have to save Roland and yesterday was all but wasted."

"Amen to that." Pogo groaned and sat up. He was lying beside the ashes of the firepit and realized he must have passed out there. The empty bag and the horn lay beside him, both covered with a surprising number of ants. He staggered to his feet, gingerly brushed off the busy little insects, then snuck the two objects back into the saddlebag. The dwarf reminded him a little of his old high-school math teacher and Pogo didn't want him any grumpier than he already was.

"You said this Roland guy went crazy?" Pogo asked when they were riding again, the dwarf perched on the saddle in front of him. Pogo didn't really care about Roland, but he was trying to distract himself from the immense, huffing monster of a horse and the way that its bumping progress made his head and stomach feel, which was not too great. "Really crazy? Was it, like, a drugs thing?"

"No, it was a 'love thing'," the dwarf told him. "For love of the fair Angelica, Roland has lost his wits. Now the greatest knight in Christendom has become a violent madman. He has killed hundreds of his own allies—destroyed whole towns! Worse than that, the pagan armies of King Agramant, aided by Duke Aelfric's evil fairies, have besieged good King Charlemagne in Paris. If Roland cannot be returned to sanity to fight for Charlemagne, more than Paris will be lost."

"Wow," said Pogo. "Like what else?"

"Everything," said the little man. "If the armies of Chaos triumph over Charlemagne here, then soon King Arthur and his Round Table will fall, too. Folktale and myth will totter. Soon all the most important tales of Western civilization will collapse. Juliet will not love Romeo. Faust will not make his bargain. Robin Hood will be executed by the Sheriff of Nottingham. Even little Oliver Twist will die a pauper."

Pogo did his best to sound intelligent. "Yeah. Wow. And that's all bad stuff, huh?"

Quidprobe made a noise of frustration. "And of course Starsky and Hutch will be killed in a fiery automobile crash."

"Oh, no! Not the Torino!" Pogo almost fell from his saddle. "All because of me?"

"Unless we can do what needs to be done, Pogocashman. Unless you can fulfill Duke Astolfo's destiny by recovering the hero Roland's wits and restoring him to sanity."

Pogo considered this awesome responsibility. "So how are we supposed to cure this Roland guy of being crazy?" he asked the dwarf. "Therapy or something? Because I don't know much about that stuff." He pictured himself taking notes on a pad while a man in armor wept on a leather couch. "Or should we just take him to a real doctor . . . ?"

"His wits are utterly lost. They must be recovered, as I told you. That means we have to bring them back to him."

"Bring them back?" Pogo frowned. "Where are they?"

"On the moon."

"So, hey, Quillpod," he asked some time later, "if we're in one of those fairytale things, why don't we just hurry up and fly to the moon?"

"My name is Quidprobe and it doesn't work that way," the dwarf explained through clenched teeth. "Quidprobe. Please remember. And the reason we can't just fly to the moon is that the rules of these things say you have to *earn* your passage. You're a knight, after all, the great Duke Astolfo of England—you have to do some courageous knightly deeds." The dwarf thought for a moment. "Or at least that's how it usually works, but I think we'd better just try to avoid getting messily killed and hope we get lucky somehow with the whole moon thing."

Messily killed. That sounded even worse than *We can still be friends*, which up to now had been Pogo's least favorite phrase. "So where are we going?"

"Well, we're making a very wide detour around the house of Caligorant the ferocious, people-eating giant, then we're heading north. Somewhere along the way you're supposed to get a flying horse and give Rabican here"—he gestured at the huge steed beneath them—"to fair Bradamant. Then you help out Prester John, King of Ethiopia, and afterward you can ride the flying horse to the Earthly Paradise. The holy folk who live there will help you get to the moon."

"Whoa. Sounds like a lot of commuting time," Pogo pointed out. "Why don't we just phone some of them and ask them to meet us somewhere?"

The dwarf shook his head and made a little gurgling noise. "That six thousand years until I retire is beginning to seem like a long time."

They rode for most of the day until the sun was low in the sky and the forest had largely given way to a flat, desolate countryside haunted by croaking ravens and the cries of other, stranger creatures. The ground on either side of them was wet and treacherous, the path so narrow that Rabican could scarcely put one hoof in front of the other. Pogo had long since digested the apples he had scavenged for lunch and was seriously wondering why no one in this place had ever thought of a restaurant, let alone a drive-thru, when the dwarf suddenly reached out and grabbed Pogo's arm.

"Rein up, Pogocashman," he said. "I think I may have made a mistake. We're supposed to be going around the swamp, but instead it looks like we're heading right into the middle of it."

Pogo was trying to pay attention to the little man but he was distracted. All day long wasps and bees had been swarming around his saddlebags and he couldn't figure out why. He kept fanning them away but they kept coming back. Right now a particularly large bumblebee was climbing his arm like an angry ball of lint. "And that's bad?"

"Balls of Blish, yes, that's bad! That also means we're heading right toward Caligorant!"

The bumblebee finally sputtered into the air and then landed on the saddlebag again and crawled inside. Pogo exhaled. "And who's he again?"

"Only the nastiest giant in all these parts, an ogre who eats knights the way the other folk eat salted nuts. He owns the unbreakable Net of Vulcan and he hides it in the dirt near his house, then chases travelers into it." Quidprobe suddenly began to squirm sideways in the saddle, trying to look back past Pogo. "And if we're in the swamp, then we're already too close to him." He stiffened. "What's that out there? Do you see that?"

Pogo turned to look over his shoulder. "What? That big boulder?"

"That's not a big boulder. This is a swamp. Have you seen any boulders this afternoon? It's a giant trying to hide in a very flat place."

Pogo felt a cold chill go up his back. "Yeah, it does sort of look like that, now that you mention it." And then the boulder stood up and began hurrying toward them, the ground shaking with each huge step. "Oh, shit, what do we do?" Pogo squealed. "What do we do? It's coming!"

"Use the book of spells!"

"The what? That book? I burned it!"

Even with the ogre bearing down on them, the dwarf turned to stare at him in astonishment. "You *burned* the book of spells?"

"I thought you said it was a spelling book! I needed to cook the squirrel."

"We're in a forest, literally *surrounded* by wood, and you burned the book of spells? You *idiot*!" Quidprobe sounded more like Pogo's old math teacher than ever. "Quick, blow the enchanted horn! Its noise terrifies everything that hears it!" A look of panic crossed his wizened face as he saw Pogo's expression. "May the Large Lizards of Le Guin defend us—don't tell me you burned that too!"

"No, no!" He pulled the horn from the saddlebag. "Here, see!"

Quidprobe stared, wrinkling his nostrils. "It stinks of mead! And why is it covered with insects?"

Pogo tried to shake off the stinging bugs, but they clung fiercely. The giant thundered toward them.

"Me so hungry!" the ogre boomed in a voice that made Pogo's bones vibrate. His mouth was huge and his teeth were yellow and jagged. "Food, don't run!"

"Blow the horn!" screamed Quidprobe. "What are you waiting for? Oh, why couldn't you have been a chemical engineer or something *useful* . . . ?"

"I'm trying!" Pogo shouted, and it was true; he had been blowing into the horn with absolutely no result. Pogo was beginning to feel that plugging the end with gooey book-glue might have been a mistake.

"Look out!" Quidprobe leaped off the saddle as the giant stretched his vast and dirty hand toward them. Pogo threw himself after the dwarf, still clinging to the magic horn.

"Little men not fall down," boomed Caligorant in a disapproving tone. "You run. Make more entertaining."

Pogo had the horn against his lips once more and was blowing as hard as he could, puffing until his cheeks ached.

The giant paused to observe him, a look of confusion and hurt on his wide, ugly face. "Why you not run? Better you run, fall in net, then me eat. Fun for everyone!"

Pogo took a moment's rest from his fruitless blowing. His head was swimming and he felt like he was going to pass out. "No . . . thank . . . you . . . " he panted. "We don't want to be eaten."

"Me think you unreasonable," said Caligorant, spreading his tree-trunk arms. "But me guess me eat you anyway."

A close-up look at the giant's hideous maw was all Pogo needed to decide to start blowing again. Just as he was certain his brains were going to fly out of his ears before he could coax even a squeak out of the horn, the hardened plug of glue popped out of Pogo's horn and, covered in confused ants and angry hornets, shot up one of Caligorant's huge and hairy nostrils.

"Owwwwooooooooo!" bellowed the giant, leaping up and down and slapping at his sinuses in dismay. "Beeeezzz izzz in nozzzzze! Beeeeeeeezzzzzz!"

Pogo and Quidprobe managed to scramble out of the way, but noble Rabican was not so lucky: the ogre came down with one foot right on top of the great black warhorse, squishing it quite flat.

"Warrrrgggggl! Warrrraaarrrrarrrgl!" thundered the giant, then ran off down the path toward his house. Pogo ran after him.

"What are you doing?" Quidprobe shouted.

"My horse is stuck to his shoe!"

A moment later Caligorant tripped over something and crashed to the ground, then began thrashing and bellowing even louder in pain and frustration, unable to get up. By the time Pogo reached him the giant was wound head to foot in a net of fine silvery mesh. The trussed Caligorant made an enormous hocking noise, then finally managed to spit out the plug of glue. It bounced away across the swamp like a hooked tee shot, ants hanging on for dear life and the yellowjackets fizzing angrily.

"Helb me!" the ogre cried, his nose swollen into a crimson volleyball. "Me caught in Vulcan's Det! Helb!"

"Why should I help you, dude?" Pogo asked. "You were going to eat me!"

The giant looked at him, considering. "You helb, me let you go, just eat your friend."

Pogo examined the mess that had been noble Rabican, knightly charger. Pretty much the only thing recognizable in the smear on the giant's heel was the saddle chased in silver, shiny once but now slightly dulled by horse juices, and a few fragments of the enchanted horn. Pogo wasn't going to be drinking out of it any more.

Quidprobe hurried up, eyeing the tangled giant warily. "Middens of Moorcock, how are we going to finish the quest?" he wailed. "Without a horse we'll never get anywhere!" He looked at the ogre and scowled. "At least we can kill this ugly big bastard now."

"Just because me try to eat you . . . ?" Caligorant grumbled. "Seem like over-reaction."

"No, we're not going to kill him," Pogo told the dwarf. He'd been thinking about how Big Ed sometimes lifted Little Ed up on his shoulders to take things off the high shelves so he didn't have to go downstairs to the stockroom for the ladder. "We're going to ride him."

"Me want to file formal protest," the ogre complained as Pogo and

Quidprobe tightened the girth strap around his neck. Quidprobe, not trusting the Pogocashman's knots, also checked to make sure the giant's hands were securely tied behind his back. "Treaty of Pax Nicephori specify no saddles on prisoners."

"You tried to eat us," the Pogocashman pointed out. "*And* you stepped on my horse. So, basically, shut up."

Quidprobe had just got used to riding atop the huge battle charger, but now they were traveling at the height of the treetops. The forest itself was pretty in a primitive sort of way, its trees, streams, and meadows as well-ordered as one of the departmental schematics Digry was always making him study, but the rest of the experience wasn't ordered at all. In fact, it was downright disturbing, especially the part about having a skeleton. How did these creatures live with these weird struts inside them? Flexibility was almost nil . . .

"Who are those guys?" the Pogocashman asked, pointing to a small group of mounted, armored men in the distance. "Oh, and there's some more over there. Wow, there's a ton of 'em. What are they doing?"

Quidprobe shrugged. "Performing quests, most of them. The Forest of Ardennes is a busy place. If we bump into any knights they'll probably want to fight, so tell them you're on a holy quest or you'll have to stop and joust every ten minutes. Do you know what that means?"

"Oh, hell yeah!" The creature nodded his head vigorously. "I took this hippie chick to the Renaissance Fair in Agoura once. I wanted to watch the jousting, but all she wanted to do was get her tarot cards read. Like three times! Two bucks a pop! I didn't even have enough left to get a turkey leg!" The Pogocashman shook his head in sad recollection. "I really wanted to try one of those turkey legs."

"Yes, very sad," said Quidprobe. "But we must keep our minds on the matter at hand. With our horse dead there's no point in meeting Bradamant because we have nothing to exchange for the hippogriff, so we might as well go straight to Prester John. The only problem is, he's in Ethiopia."

The ogre made a noise of irritation. "Me not swimming to Africa."

The Pogocashman wasn't listening—he had been distracted by a loud clanging from nearby. "What's that?" he asked.

Quidprobe listened for a moment, then felt the disturbing

sensation of his hackles lifting. "Oh dear, I completely forgot about Orrilo."

"Maybe you ride *him*," suggested Caligorant.

"What's an Oh Real Oh?" the Pogocashman asked.

"Orillo. He's an infamous bandit. Very dangerous, very cruel. And because of a magical spell, nothing can kill him." Even as Quidprobe spoke the din from the clearing ahead of them grew louder, and now they could see the shapes of armored men through the trees. Three knights, one in shiny black, the other two in more colorful outfits, were fighting with swords, the two bright against the dark one. "Poor fools," he said. "They haven't a chance against Orrilo."

"Why not?" the Pogocashman asked. "They look like they're doing pretty good."

"Watch."

Even as the dwarf spoke, one of the knights managed to cut off the black knight's arm. The Pogocashman gasped as the black knight's sword clattered to the ground, but strangely, no blood came from the wound. Even so, the other attacker took advantage of the enemy's literal disarming and lopped off Orrilo's head, but the bandit knight only bent over, picked up his arm and put it back on his shoulder, where it connected and stuck; then, as his two enemies watched in dismay, he found his head and returned that to his shoulders, where it also stuck. A moment later he was attacking the knights again.

"Why are you laughing?" Quidprobe asked the Pogocashman.

"Because I saw this movie," Pogo told him. "You know, 'I fart in your general direction!' It's those Nudge-Nudge guys!"

"I have no idea what you're talking about," Quidprobe said, "but I promise you that Orrilo is real and very dangerous." He watched the black knight hammering his enemies, who were definitely beginning to look as if they would rather be somewhere else. "Unless his spell of invulnerability is broken, nothing can kill him."

"How do you break the spell?"

"I don't know," said Quidprobe with a touch of aspersion. "I don't know because some idiot *burned* our book of spells."

"You don't have to be all vague and sarcastic," Pogo said. "I know you're talking about me."

At that moment, one of the colorful knights snuck a lucky swipe past Orrilo's guard and lopped off his head again. The force of the blow sent it rolling across the clearing. It fetched up near Caligorant's immense feet.

"Me smell something yummy," the giant said.

The Pogocashman climbed out of the saddle and jumped down to examine the bandit's head.

"Use caution—he's very dangerous . . . !" Quidprobe warned.

"Be cool, dude! I just want to check this out!"

There was no blood dripping from the severed neck, but the Pogocashman still held the head at arm's length by its feathered crest before opening the visor. The face inside was cheerful if a bit sweaty, with handsome features, a grayshot beard, and black, beetling eyebrows.

"Toss me back to my body, will you?" said Orrilo's head. "Then if you want to have a go, just stick around. I'll soon have finished carving up these two."

The Pogocashman, head dangling in one hand, climbed laboriously back onto the giant's neck.

"What if I don't?" he asked the head when he was back in the saddle. "I mean, what if I just hang onto your head up here? You won't be able to do much then, right?"

"Yes, but my body will follow you around until it gets my head back, and then you'll have to fight me anyway." Orrilo's head grinned. "I can't be killed, remember? So basically, you're in deep *merde* either way." He saw the puzzled expression on the Pogocashman's face. "That's French for 'shit'," the bandit explained.

"Oh."

The knight's armored body turned and hastened toward them at a clanking trot; the other two knights, choosing discretion over pointless valor, took advantage of the distraction to flee the clearing. Within moments the body had reached them and was jumping up and down in front of the giant trying to reach its dangling head.

"Him smell good," said Caligorant, but the Pogocashman was busy trying to work through what the black knight had told him.

"So no matter what I do, I'm going to have to fight you?"

"Pretty much," said Orrilo. "Say, you don't have a drop of claret, do you? I'm parched. Better wait until I'm back on my body, though, or it will just run out onto the ground and that would be a sad waste of wine. Ho ho!" He was amused by his own joke. "Ho, ho! Funny, eh? Too bad most people don't get to know that side of me." Orillo's head looked around as best it could while dangling in mid-air. "Now, where did my body go?" He tilted his eyes down as far as he could. "Seriously, where is it?"

"How should I know?" The Pogocashman was clearly feeling grumpy.

Quidprobe pulled on his sleeve and pointed down. "Ummm, you might . . . want to . . . "

"What? What's the problem now, little dude?"

Quidprobe pointed. "Look."

A pair of legs clad in black armor were poking out of the giant's mouth, kicking as haphazardly as a child failing a swimming test.

"Oops," said the Pogocashman. Quidprobe thought it was a bit of an understatement.

The head was beginning to get frustrated. "Oops? Oops *what*? Where's my body?"

"Spit that out," the Pogocashman told the giant. "Go on. Spit it out."

Caligorant quickly swallowed down the rest of the body. When the ogre spoke, it was in tones of perfect innocence. "Spit out what?"

"Where's my body?" shouted the head. "I'm telling you, there'll be trouble here. The Royal Assize is going to be passing through here in a fortnight or so and if someone's nipped off with my body there'll be hell to pay, sure enough!"

"Don't know what this royal ass size is," the Pogocashman whispered to Quidprobe, "but maybe we better not stick around."

"You may have something there," Quidprobe said. "In fact, I'm sure you do."

Despite the stream of invective coming from it, the Pogocashman didn't seem to remember he was still holding Orrilo's head until they were a good distance from the clearing. The giant, belly full, was whistling happily as he walked.

"I can't believe this!" The bandit's head hadn't stopped shouting for a moment. "I can't believe you just let your pet giant . . . *eat my body* like that. That's not right!"

"Is he really going to live forever like this?" the Pogocashman asked Quidprobe as the black knight's head described all of his important friends at the court of Charlemagne, as well as several more among the nobility of Faerie, and listed the various penalties that could be levied against the owners of a dangerous steed like a giant. "With no body?"

"I think so."

"Then find me something to put this damn head in."

When they found a suitable sack, still smelling of the onions that Quidprobe had hastily transferred to the saddlebag, Pogo dropped the head in.

"You're not really going to do this to me, are you?" Orrilo's head demanded.

"Damn right. Until you learn to shut up." The Pogocashman twisted the top of the sack and tied it closed.

"*Merde*," said the head's muffled voice.

"Yep." The Pogocashman looked down with no little satisfaction at the giant's distended stomach. "Sooner or later."

"Me hungry again," said the giant as he waded through the waves toward the Ethiopian shore. "Swimming hard work. Food was stringy, too."

"I'll thank you to speak a little more courteously about me," Orrilo's head complained from the sack. "Or about my body, anyway. I mean, I'm right here! How do you think I feel? And I'm not stringy—I'm sinewy."

"You say sinewy—me say stringy. Point is, not enough good stuff."

"Will you *both* shut up?" Pogo asked. The two of them, giant and disembodied head, had spent the entire swim arguing about what kind of whalefish that was, and whether the wind was nor'east or nor'south or nor'something. It was like listening to Big Ed and Little Ed endlessly stupid disputes about whether Han Solo could beat Dirty Harry in a fist-fight. "Head, if you can't keep quiet in that bag I'll put you down the back of the giant's pants instead. You think you'll like that better?"

"Charmless," said Orrilo, but fell silent.

"So what now?" Pogo asked the dwarf.

"Bradbury only knows," Quidprobe said glumly. "This is a fictional universe originally created by Poul Anderson, based on a world created by a bunch of medieval poets. But this is some *other* writer doing a cheap knock-off of Anderson's world, with characters taken from Ariosto's version. And you." He blanched. "I just had a horrid thought—what if this hack chose you as the protagonist *on purpose*? We could be in the hands of a madman!"

"Yeah," Pogo agreed, although he hadn't understood anything the dwarf had just said. Harry Ostro and Pole Anderson sounded like the names of Muppets. "So, like I said, what now?"

"If this story were being written by a real writer like Anderson I might have some idea," the dwarf said, scowling. "But with this fool in charge—well, anything could happen. And since they couldn't even send me a proper Anderson hero with a working knowledge of science and engineering and such . . . well, whatever *does* happen is bound to be pretty stupid. What did you say you did for a living, anyway?"

"Retail management," said Pogo promptly. That always sounded better than mentioning the shoe store.

"Well, that should do us a world of good." The little man didn't really sound like he meant it.

As the day wore on, the hilly slope continued to lead them upward through dry, mostly barren country until Pogo could see they were climbing the highest of a small range of rocky hills. As they neared the top of the hill, Pogo noticed what he at first thought were large birds wheeling in the air above the hilltop, although something about their shapes didn't look quite right.

"We're getting near," said Quidprobe.

"That's good, right?"

"Good in the sense that we're at the next stage of the quest," said Quidprobe. "Bad in that we're going to have to deal with the harpies somehow, and to be honest, I can't imagine what we're going to do in a million years."

"Harpies?"

"Horrible female demons. They persecute Prester John. He's blind. They steal his food."

"Whoa, I saw this movie!" Pogo said. "There were skeletons in it too. And Hercules. I think it was called Jason and the Astronauts."

The dwarf made a noise of irritation. "This is not a movie. This can kill you. But to be fair, Ariosto did steal that bit from the original Jason and the Argonauts, so in that sense you're right." A hopeful look momentarily lit the dwarf's brown, wrinkled face. "How did they deal with the harpies in this moving picture?"

"I dunno. I was kind of stoned, to be honest. I think they threw a net on them and whacked the shit out of them with swords or something. Too bad we didn't save the giant's net, huh?"

Quidprobe sighed. "Yes. And I'm guessing a proper Poul Anderson hero would have remembered that before we swam across the ocean."

"We?" inquired the giant. "Me think not."

"Yeah, it's a bummer." Pogo was getting a bit tired of the adventure now. It had gone on way too long to be just an acid flashback, at least as far as he knew, although to be fair, pretty much all he knew about flashbacks were health class warnings and what he'd seen on *Hawaii Five-O* and *Streets of San Francisco*. Also, the thing Quidprobe had said about "this can kill you" hadn't exactly made him feel warm and tingly.

Speaking of not feeling warm and tingly, the closer to the hilltop they got, the easier it was for Pogo to see that the flying shapes weren't anything like birds: they were human-sized, and their wings looked more like the kind you saw on bats. Stuff that was cool on movies and television seemed a lot less fun when it was flying back and forth not far away, letting out nasty screechy noises that echoed down the dusty hillside.

"May I just mention that it's really getting unpleasant inside this sack," announced Orrilo's head. "If I'd known I was going to spend hours smelling my own breath I would have taken up that newfangled teeth-cleaning fad."

"Why you complain?" said Caligorant. "You ride in nice bag. Me have to carry you all. Uphill, too."

"You tried to eat us," Pogo reminded him.

"He *did* eat *me*," said the head in the bag.

"Me didn't ride you," the giant said, sulky as a sixth-grader whose parents would only buy him cheap knock-off running shoes instead of Pumas. "Me play fair."

"I don't recall you being particularly fair to me when you ate my body," Orrilo said. "One moment it was just standing there, the next moment—hey-presto, it's lunchtime!"

"Me couldn't help it. Was right there, begging me eat it."

"It wasn't doing anything of the sort," said the muffled voice from the sack. "Because it didn't have a head on. So spare us the untruthful excuses."

"Me meant metaphorically."

"Well, then I wish you would have only eaten my body metaphorically too, you large oaf. Then I wouldn't be bouncing along here all day having to smell the onion I broke my fast on two days ago—and it wasn't even a particularly nice onion. If I'd known I was going to spend the rest of my life in a sack I would doubtless have been a bit more selective . . . "

Pogo smacked the bag so hard that Orrilo's teeth clicked together. "Jeez, just shut up!"

"You should be quiet too, Pogocashman," the dwarf said in hushed tones. "We're almost there and harpies have sharp ears."

As they neared the top of the hill, Pogo could see the ruins of what had once been a castle. The harpies were swooping in and out past the broken walls, busy as mosquitoes during swim trials at fat camp. Someone seemed to be shouting at them.

"Curse you, foul creatures! Why do you torment me?" But though the words were angry, the tone seemed strangely weary, even resigned, like a woman with a size nine foot trying yet again to fit into a size seven pump.

"It's coming from over there, Quitpoke," Pogo told the dwarf.

"I don't ask much," said the little bearded man, just as resigned and despairing as the mystery voice. "Just that you use my correct name. Once, anyway. Once would be nice . . . "

The climb was not an easy one, even on giant-back. "Oh, grand," called Orrilo's head from inside the sack. "Bump, bump, bump. Are you sure you can't jounce me around a little more? Maybe you could drop me and kick me like a football."

"Don't you ever stop talking?" asked Pogo.

"I might if I had something else to do. In fact, I've been told I'm actually a very good listener. But for some reason, I don't seem able to, I don't know, play a game or dance or whittle or do pretty much anything else to entertain myself. Now why is that? Oh, right—because you let your pet ogre eat my body!"

"Pet ogre?" rumbled Caligorant. "Me not pet. Me prisoner of war."

They rounded a bend in the hilltop path and now Pogo could make out a spot in the ruins where an entire section of wall had fallen away, revealing the shell of some mighty hall. It was around this crumbling structure that the harpies whirled. A pale figure cringed in a tiny alcove, partially sheltered from their attack but not from the abuse the flying creatures hurled at him—and not just abuse: the harpies also sprayed their own filth everywhere as they flew. The rocks all around were streaked with the stuff, and the buzzing of flies seemed almost as loud as the shrieks of the old man and his tormentors. They might look very much like angry old ladies, but Pogo now knew for a fact that harpies did not wear adult diapers.

"Man, that guy is screwed," he said.

"That's Prester John!" Quidprobe looked worried. "You have to save him!"

"Why? I didn't put him there."

"It's just how it works—quests, heroes. Don't you ever *read*?"

"Sometimes. Magazines and shit."

"Me want rest," said Caligorant. "Me tired and hungry."

An idea came to Pogo. "Could you eat those harpies?"

The giant made a face. "Me not eat. Taste like poopoo. Meat dry like twigs."

"Well," said Orillo's head from inside the sack, "I suppose I should be relieved that my poor body was consumed by such an epicure. I mean, I wouldn't want to be eaten by someone who'd devour just *anything* . . ."

Caligorant swiveled his head like a tank turret to look back at Pogo. "Me eat talking head now? Stop head talking?"

"We must save Prester John," said the dwarf.

Pogo frowned, trying to imagine a scenario in which he might go running through a downburst of little-old-batwing-lady crap and not being able to manage it, but even as he stared the harpies suddenly rose up into the air in a single coherent swarm, wheeled once more above the ruins, and then flew off, shrieking and cackling.

"Now!" The dwarf smacked him on the arm. "Go now!"

Pogo sighed and gave the giant a thump of his heels, setting him lumbering across the open area toward the ruined walls and the weeping, white-bearded figure that the dwarf had named Presto John.

"Dude, I totally don't get this," Pogo said as he helped the quivering, sightless man into the shelter of one of the crumbling chambers. "Why are those crazy bat-ladies out to get you?"

Presto John had been tall—you could tell he'd been a big guy once, like a football player or something—but his troubles had bent him until he looked almost like a question mark. His beard was long and fouled by stuff Pogo didn't want to think about too much. Just being next to him would have been an issue, except the whole place already stank of harpy-shit.

"I was vainglorious," the old man said. "I imagined myself as king of not only fair Ethiop, but of the earthly Paradise as well, where once Adam and his consort Eve did dwell."

"What's this old blind guy supposed to do for us?" Pogo whispered to the dwarf. "Is he a magician or something?" He figured with a name like Presto the guy must do some tricks. "I don't mean to be a dick or anything, but he can't even wash his beard."

"If you save him, he'll do a favor for Roland's allies," the dwarf whispered back. "That's all you need to know, really."

"I can hear you, bold paladin. My ears have not failed, only my orbs of vision," John said sadly. "And yes, I would gladly give you all that was in my power to give, were I free. But here I remain until someone can rescue me from these ghastly creatures, who delight only in my punishment." He shook his head. "Not only do they steal and foul my food so that I am always near starvation, they talk to me incessantly—as if a pious Christian man like me would ever bandy words with such demons of darkness!"

"Talk to you? About what?"

"Did you hear me not, Sir Knight? I said I do not bandy words with Satan's underlings. They would doubtless wish me to listen to their complaints—a rare irony!—for they claim they are bored by the very task of tormenting me. Would that I had my sight and my sword—then would I give them a challenge they would never forget . . . !" For a moment, the ancient man tried to draw himself up to his once-impressive height, but it was too painful and he curled in on himself again in despair. "But perhaps you, good Sir Knight—for I hear by your voice that you are a bold and doughty man—perhaps you could punish them and quiet their endless taunting and shrieking."

Pogo did not answer, and not just because there was no way in hell he was going to get in a fight with a bunch of magical flying crap-flingers. He was thinking, and although it was not something he did very much, he was busy at it now. The bony faces of the harpies had reminded him of a certain kind of senior citizen customer that always drove him crazy—the kind that just couldn't be satisfied, that always had one more question, one more stupid little complaint. But more important, now he was also remembering Dooley, the roving assistant manager from the Pasadena branch of Kirby Shoes who had been sent in by the main office to help when Fernando and Little Ed had both been out sick for a few days. Dooley had been a genius at dealing with old biddies, listening to them as if their confused questions and complaints actually made sense, letting them take all day to make a decision on a lousy pair of $7.99 slippers. Instead of trying to hurry them into buying or leaving, which is what Pogo and his coworkers had always done, Dooley would just gather several of the oldest customers together in one part of the store where he could chat with and flatter them all at the same time, saving time and steps. Turned out most of them were lonely and just wanted something to do, which is why they were in the mall in the first place, but if a young man in a suit and tie listened to them attentively they'd actually buy things. Dooley booked a surprising amount of sales just from such crabby, unlikely customers, and Pogo had never forgotten it.

His thoughts were interrupted by a squeak from the dwarf. "They're coming back! I can hear them!"

"They never give me rest," Prester John said sadly. "Truly, I am cursed for my damnable pride . . . "

Pogo reached into the saddlebag and pulled Orillo's head out by the hair. It blinked in the sunlight. "'Zounds! You could give a fellow some warning," the head complained.

"Here's what's going to happen," Pogo told him. "I'm going to toss you up there where the harpies are. I don't know whether they'll eat you, crap on you, or just drop you twenty or thirty times from really high up. Maybe they'll do all of that." He considered for a moment. "Although not necessarily in that exact order . . . "

"What?" The bandit's handsome face contorted in dismay. "You would murder me in cold blood?"

Pogo did feel a little bad about it, but Orrilo had been planning to carve him up too, just like he did everyone else who passed by. "Look, let's face it," Pogo told the head, "I'm not going to carry you around with me for the rest of my life. But I'll bet those harpies would love someone to talk to. So if you just make some chitchat with them, act real sweet and listen real good, they probably won't kill you. Hell, they might even be nice to you." He remembered some of the senior customers and suppressed a shudder. "Y'know, like give you hard candy with bits of Kleenex stuck to it. Show you pictures of their fat grandkids. Stuff like that."

"They're right above us!" the dwarf shouted. "We have to get to some shelter . . . !"

But Pogo had other plans. He waited until the first few harpies had swished past over their heads, shrieking and cursing and spattering the nearby stones with things too disgusting to think about, let alone describe, then he took Orrilo's head and spun it around by the hair like an Olympic hammer (which made the head yell some interesting French swear words), then threw it straight up in the air. One of the harpies turned in mid-air and snatched it in her claws like an eagle taking . . . whatever eagles took. Some other kind of bird. Except instead of a bird, this was a head that was still screaming as she carried it higher up in the air.

"Don't hurt me!" Orrilo's head shouted as it disappeared. *"Some of my best friends are harpish . . . !"*

Even as the giant left the ruins and clumped down the hillside, Quidprobe couldn't quite figure out what had just happened. "But . . . why did the harpies just . . . leave?"

"They just wanted someone to talk to," said the Pogocashman with an air of satisfaction. "Like those old guys you meet waiting for a bus. They probably won't even remember ol' Presto here," he indicated the blind man clutching the giant's shoulder nervously, "until they've told the head the same stories about their operations and stuff about ninety times."

"You have saved me, brave Astolfo," quavered the old man. "Bring me down the mountain and I will take my armies to war against wicked Agramant." John let out a dry chuckle—he was definitely perking up. "That foul Saracen dog will not enjoy besieging Paris when he learns I am burning his castles here at home!"

Quidprobe could only shake his head. The Pogocashman was proving to be more resourceful than he'd expected, but the odds were still running very high that the organic creature's dumb luck could not last, and that in the end they would be just as completely and hideously doomed as Quidprobe had always feared. Still, it was a pleasant surprise to be out in the sunshine and away from the harpies, even if he was still forced to ride a stinking giant beside an old man who was not particularly clean, either.

"So what's next, little dude?" the Pogocashman asked. "We'll drop Mr. John at the nearest town, then fly to the moon, right? With some guy named Griff the Hippo?"

Quidprobe shook his head. "I doubt the hippogriff will be available to us, since we no longer have a horse to trade for it. The fair Bradamant will not wish to ride into battle on a steed as stenchful and unpleasant as this ogre."

"Me can hear you," rumbled Caligorant from immediately beneath Quidprobe's dwarfish bottom. "Me find that hurtful."

It took them several days to find their way across the wilds of Ethiopia—or at least this imaginary version of Ethiopia—to the mountain atop which Quidprobe believed they would find the Earthly Paradise. He could only hope he was right, since this particular location had never been written into Anderson's original work, and only faintly implied by its connection to the rest of the Matter of France, but hoping and guessing was all the sub-sub-manager had been doing since he'd been thrust into this ruptured story, anyway.

The Pogocashman, buoyed by his victories, spent much of the journey explaining to Quidprobe how he had been inspired by tracts like *The Sales Pyramid* or *Think Accessories to "Add" Value.* Somehow the whole of his philosophy seemed to come down to telling people, "I have a handbag for you that would go great with those"—an eldritch phrase of indubitable power, at least according to the Pogocashman. Quidprobe could only shrug—that was one thing that having shoulders was good for, anyway—and hope their luck would continue to hold, although he thought it unlikely. For one thing, the saints that inhabited the Earthly Paradise were likely to be a fearfully rules-oriented bunch, and he suspected they weren't going to like the Pogocashman's rather freewheeling approach to the Matter of France.

His retail philosophies finally exhausted, the Pogocashman was now engaged in his newest pastime, spitting for distance and accuracy from the summit of the giant's shoulders, each expectoration accompanied by the odd, ritualistic chant, "Got you again, Vader!" It was hard to believe the Pogocashman was a genuine bull organic, his sperm coveted by all the females of his species, but there had to be evolutionary subtleties that Quidprobe could not grasp. He was beginning to think that for all his years studying them in preparation for his job, he would never really understand non-symbolic life forms.

Another trudge up another long hill, the giant moaning and grumbling all the way—"Caligorant want to lie down." "Caligorant foot hurt." "Me hungry again." It was worse than working a lonely Sunday shift with Little Ed, who had the conversational skills of a snappish dog.

"So, what's up this mountain, anyway?" Pogo asked Quidprobe.

"I told you," the dwarf said. "It's the Earthly Paradise. It used to be the Garden of Eden."

"So," Pogo said hopefully, "like a restaurant or something?"

The little man sighed. He did that a lot. Pogo was beginning to suspect the dwarf had asthma, like Little Ed. Or at least like Little Ed claimed he had: Pogo thought it was funny how Little Ed only had asthma attacks when it was time to clean the lavatory. "Not anything like a restaurant," the dwarf explained. "It's where the saints live. Is knowing that not part of your human religious rituals?"

"Don't know." The closest Pogo had ever come to church as a kid was when his electrician father had installed a forty-watt light bulb in a manger for the local church's Nativity Play. The bulb had been Baby Jesus. When the play was over, Pogo's dad had brought it home. "Here," he had told Pogo. "Go bury this in the backyard and see if it comes back to life in three days." His dad had moved out a few weeks later and Pogo had never asked him exactly what he had meant.

As they climbed, Pogo couldn't help noticing that the foliage was growing more lush, the sights more lovely, and even the smells more pleasant. Grass as green as AstroTurf grew everywhere, and bright flowers pushed their way up between the stems, colorful as an Easter sales display. The bees were big as sparrows but mellow as old hippies, and the sun shone warmly everywhere but the cool, inviting shade beneath the majestic trees growing beside the track.

"Wow," Pogo said, paying his highest compliment to natural beauty. "Somebody ought to build vacation condos here and start a time-share business. They would totally clean up."

When they reached the summit of the hill, they discovered a

grassy plain of a grandeur that matched the approach, and at the center of it a vast palace that looked to be carved from a single ruby.

"Behold," the dwarf said. "The Earthly Paradise."

"Wow," said Pogo. "That's bitchin'!"

"Me hungry again," said the giant.

As they grew closer the palace became no less amazing, sunlight glinting from every angle and facet so that the castle sat in a sparkling red glow. As they reached the palace's tall gate, it slowly rose to reveal a white-bearded man who looked to Pogo like nothing so much as a skinny Santa Claus. The man greeted them warmly, although he did seem a bit taken aback by Caligorant.

"Come," he said. "Enter and make yourselves welcome, travelers. Refresh yourselves. Your . . . steed . . . will be seen to as well. What would you eat and drink? The Lord's bounty is such we can give you whatever your heart desires."

"Little fat women," said the giant promptly. "But young. Me like them crunchy, not chewy."

The bearded man suppressed a shudder. "Perhaps we can find a suckling pig or two for your mount," he told Pogo. "So few of our guests eat pork, anyway. It's a desert-tribe thing."

"You are the holy Evangelist, aren't you?" asked Quidprobe, who was trying to brush his tangled whiskers into a more respectable shape. "John the Baptist, as some call you?"

Pogo had thought John the Baptist was some kind of southern university, but the man nodded. "It is true: I am he that trumpeted the coming of our Savior. And now that you have come to us, pious Astolfo," he said, this time talking to Pogo, "the saints and I will try to help you accomplish your quest, for your liege Charlemagne is dear to us, and his kingdom the bulwark of Christendom against both the Saracen and the treacherous fairies."

Pogo had walked past a club in Hollywood once and a very tall woman had tried to get him to come inside. He'd almost gone in, too, until he'd got close enough to see the woman's five-o'clock shadow. Pogo Cashman might not know what Saracens were, but he knew all about treacherous fairies.

The saints came out to meet them—not marching in, as Pogo had hoped, but walking like normal people. Still, they seemed nice, if a trifle on the quiet side, and the food they laid out on the long table in their splendid dining room, although a plain meal of butter, bread, honey, and some kind of vegetable soup that didn't even have alphabet noodles in it, was as tasty as anything Pogo had encountered for a long time. Thus, when they showed him and Quidprobe to a clean, warm room with two beds, Pogo was ready to drop immediately, but the dwarf seemed determined to talk. "They'll want to make certain you're a shriven and holy knight before they help you get to the moon," the dwarf said, clearly worried. "Saints are supposed to be big on things like that."

Pogo yawned. He wondered if Buzz Aldrin's golf club was still lying around up there. Maybe he'd get to hit a couple of drives. Once he'd realized that the astronauts were not going to be attacked by moon men, the golf part had been the one thing about the whole Apollo mission that had caught his imagination. But when he asked the dwarf about it, Quidprobe only seemed irritated.

"By Dunsany's Jodphurs, are you even paying attention, Pogocashman? This isn't your world and that isn't your moon—in fact, it's not even a real moon, it's a medieval moon filtered through at least two or three different storytellers. It's probably made of some kind of cheese. No, I don't mean that, and don't you dare ask me the question I can see forming even now."

Pogo grunted his disappointment. "So?"

"This religious thing truly worries me. Anderson's story-structure allows you some leeway to make mistakes, but they were expecting someone with an elementary knowledge of things like history and science that you don't seem to have."

"I'm doing all right so far . . . !"

The dwarf waved his hand. "Yes, yes. But you're going to have to talk to the saints about your love of Christ and your holy vows as a knight before they help you. How are you going to get through that with . . . what did you call it? *Guidelines for Retail Management*?"

"Well, then tell me what to say!"

"You don't understand." The dwarf was sitting on his own bed now, his feet dangling well above the stone floor. "I studied story construction. My background is in themes and influences, in the sometimes very thin line between homage and plagiarism. Religious instruction is not my field!"

"Okay, yeah. That's kind of a drag." But Pogo was too tired and too full of good food to worry about it. He only wanted to sleep. "Don't sweat it, little dude. I'll figure out something to tell them tomorrow."

"You don't 'figure out' how to talk to the saints about religion," said Quidprobe in the helpless tone of a veterinarian trying to get a particularly stupid pit bull to let go of his arm. "These are the founding fathers and mothers of the Christian religion. It's all they think about!"

But Pogo Cashman had shut his eyes.

Somehow, though, despite the great and comfortable weariness that it was his greatest wish to surrender to, Pogo couldn't fall asleep. The idea that he would have to pay for this hospitality by answering questions about something he knew next to nothing about was beginning to trouble him, too. He doubted they would consider the story of his dad's light bulb enough to get him off the hook. Also, now that he was having his first comfortable night in a while, Pogo was perversely beginning to miss his tiny apartment and especially his television and stereo, and wondering if he would ever get back. The experience hadn't been too bad for an acid flashback, which he had been assured back in high school consisted mostly of imagining you could fly and then jumping out of tall buildings, but it was definitely short on the modern conveniences. How long had he been here, anyway? How many episodes of *WKRP In Cincinnati* had he missed? John the Baptist was all well and good, but Pogo needed a weekly dose of Johnny Fever.

Quidprobe said he needed help from these religious guys to finish his quest, so he obviously wouldn't be getting to see Loni Anderson in her tight sweater unless he convinced them. He hated dealing with people who wanted him to learn a bunch of shit that only they cared about. In fact, it reminded him more than a little of one of his supervisor's Sunday Schools, a nightmarish event that happened every couple of months where he kept all the employees in the store for hours after closing time, making them take tests about stock numbers and the "Courtesy Checklist" and learn slogans like "Remember the G.S.M. FAT! (Greet, Seat, Measure—Fit, Accessorize, Ticket.)" As manager, Pogo usually had to do the lion's share of work at these meetings, and sometimes even lead them while the supervisor watched him like mall security following a shoplifter. The only way he had found to escape the worst of these Sunday School sessions was to throw another employee under the bus, usually by saying something like, "Gee, sir, I'm having trouble getting Fernando to understand the value of bringing a packet of socks with every shoe he fits. Maybe it's the language barrier." This despite the fact that Fernando had been raised in Northridge and spoke English at least as well as Pogo—better if you counted all that grammar stuff. "I'm out of my depth, sir," he would tell the supervisor while Fernando pleaded with his eyes to be spared. "Perhaps you could show us the best way to get through to him."

Which was usually enough to light an evangelical fire in the supervisor's eye, and then Pogo could kick back and watch poor little Fernando get put through two hours of hell in his place, learning how to foist off expensive tube socks on various customers who were acted out by the supervisor.

Which wasn't that bad an idea for his present problem, now that Pogo thought about it. Of course, Fernando, the perfect victim, wasn't here, and Pogo was nervous about how he would get back home without Quidprobe, but that didn't mean a suitable subject couldn't be found . . .

"Oh, yeah," he told John the Baptist when he had been ushered in to see the venerable Evangelist, "I'd totally love to talk about my holy vows and how hard I've been shrivening and everything, but first I need your help with a little religious matter. Kind of a spreading-the-faith problem, if you get what I mean."

The old man's eyes glinted like those of an avid shopper spotting a two-for-one table. "Spreading the faith? Why, yes, I suppose I'd be the one to ask!" John the Baptist tried to chuckle affably, but it had a slightly hungry sound. "Not meaning to toot my own horn, of course, but that's pretty much what I'm known for. Of course, all these centuries living here, waiting for the Last Judgement and surrounded by those who are already saints, I don't get much call to practice my trade . . . " His hand fastened on Pogo's; it was kind of alarming how hard the old man squeezed. "Tell me, how can I help, my son?"

"It's not me, sir, it's . . . it's the giant."

John's eyebrows climbed several centimeters nearer to Heaven. "Really? That monstrous creature is desirous of joining the fold?"

"Oh, sure, yeah, I think so . . . but maybe this isn't a good time, with you needing to talk to me before you send me on to the moon, and, like, Charlemagne in so much need and everything."

"Nonsense," John said firmly. "Always time to assist an errant soul looking to find its way to the bosom of our Almighty Father."

"Well, I can't help noticing that Caligorant talks about being hungry all the time, and I'm beginning to think he means in a kind of, um, spiritual way. Do giants have souls?"

"That is in dispute," said John, his eyes growing distant. "In fact, this might be a fascinating opportunity to determine . . . " He trailed off, then made an effort to focus again. "I'm sorry, but we really should discuss your quest first, then perhaps we can find time to pursue this interesting sideline afterward. Now, perhaps you can tell me about the religious training of your youth—were you a squire to a pious knight?"

"Oh, definitely." Inwardly, Pogo was cursing. He'd had the Baptist on the hook, he could tell. *C'mon, Cashman,* he told himself. *Like the Kirby Shoes manual says—"Nothing shows if you don't close."* He cleared his throat. "I mean, yeah, we totally have to deal with the important stuff first. And I'm totally going to answer your question, too. It's just that . . . well, he cries at night. When he thinks no one is around."

"The giant?" asked John the Baptist in tones of astonishment. "He laments his state?"

"Cries about all the innocent people he's eaten, yeah, absolutely. You should talk to him about it. I really think he's, like, all ready to come to Jesus." He wondered if lying like this was a sin, but since this was only a made-up version of John the Baptist, and he was lying to him about a made-up giant, too—well, how bad a sin could it be?

"Clearly I must speak with this deluded creature," said John, standing up and brushing off his crimson cloak. "Not to mention that the prophet Daniel, who has always been *very* certain of who and who would not be redeemed, would be most . . . instructed if I should convert the creature." His eyes gleamed. "And smarty-pants Isaiah would be pretty surprised, too . . . "

"Um, just to warn you, he won't . . . admit it or anything. I mean, he's really stubborn." Pogo forced a laugh. "Ha ha! You know these giants! You'll have to keep after him. It may take a while."

John seemed full of energy and high spirits. "No fear—after all, we have until the Second Coming!"

Pogo almost had to run to keep up with the ancient Evangelist, who seemed to be heading right for the stables, so keen was he to begin the ogre's conversion. "But what about me getting to the moon?"

"Don't worry," John called back over his shoulder as he broke into a run. "I'll have one of the grooms hitch up the chariot for you. Practically drives itself . . . !"

As the golden chariot was tugged into the sky by the four ruby-red horses, and the ground fell away with sickening speed, causing Quidprobe to grab the railing and gasp at the unfamiliar (and queasy) feeling of acceleration on organic skeletal structure, he could still hear the giant bellowing far below.

"No! Shut up and leave Caligorant alone! 'Suffer little children' only good part!"

Quidprobe looked down at the retreating ground once, then decided not to do that again. Instead he tried to focus on the great, pale orb of the daytime moon, which was growing larger every moment.

"Are the horses going to be able to breathe?" the Pogocashman asked. "Like, in space?"

Quidprobe shook his head, although he was mildly impressed with the question: the Pogocashman hadn't shown much interest in such practical things to this point. "This is based on the medieval imagination, not reality," he said. "Point one—these horses are magical flying horses, so they can probably breathe where we're going. And, if we're lucky, so can we."

"Huh." The Pogocashman looked down at his armor. "Hadn't thought about us. This isn't exactly an astronaut suit, is it? Pretty cool, though. I mean, if I was twelve again I'd think this was the greatest thing ever." His bemused smile didn't last long. "Right now, though, I'm just kind of wanting to go home."

Quidprobe sighed. "When I was a youngster, I dreamed of being the world's foremost jelly-tube architect. I never imagined I'd be flying around in the open air, wearing a body with bones in it."

"Poor little dude," the Pogocashman said, patting him on the head in a way that made Quidprobe's dwarf-whiskers bristle. "Don't sweat it—we'll get out of this okay. You said it's a story, right? Stories always end happy."

Quidprobe was glad none of his colleagues from the Existential Despair Division were present. Clearly the Pogocashman was familiar with only the most elemental kinds of fictional universes. A moment later, though, Quidprobe realized that he desperately wanted the Pogocashman to be right.

By the Silver Buttocks of Eddison and the Smoking Jacket of Cabell! he thought in sudden horror. *What if this is one of those stories where the companion dies?*

Quidprobe spent the rest of the ride sitting in the bottom of the chariot trying not to hyperventilate.

The surface of the moon was even crazier than Pogo had thought it would be, like the abandoned set to some ancient black and white movie, with bits of ruined walls and statues poking through shifting dunes of sand and the Earth hanging close above their heads in a most disturbing way. The saint who rigged up the chariot had told them to head toward the highest hills, and soon they were standing on the peak of the highest looking down into a bowl-shaped valley which from this distance appeared to be nothing so much as a badly tended landfill littered with a zillion odds and ends. They left the chariot on the hill and made their way carefully down the slope.

"So this is it?" Pogo asked as they neared the lake of bric-a-brac. "We're supposed to find Roland's brain in all this?"

"Everything here is something that someone on earth lost," the dwarf explained. "That was Ariosto's idea, anyway. The saints said all the lost wits are in one part."

"Ah, I got it, just got to find the right section. Like Men's Casuals, or Children's."

Quidprobe looked puzzled, but Pogo was on familiar ground now. He scrambled a little way back up the slope and began to scan the valley, looking for clues as to how the merchandise was inventoried. In his store, they kept all the similar things together, so all the men's black dress shoes were in one area, all the brown ones beside it, and a little farther away, the men's casuals and sport shoes. It shouldn't be too hard to make sense of this, if he could only recognize what the various objects were.

"Start walking around," he called down to Quidprobe. "Tell me what some of this stuff is."

The little man began an awkward tour through the mounds, calling out what he found to the best of his ability to recognize it. "Lost keys!" he shouted as he stepped through a field of clinking bronze and iron. "Letters!" he yelled, then picked one up to read a few lines. "The prose is quite romantic—think this might be lost loves." He trudged along, stopped to shade his eyes against the Earth-glare. "There's a mountain over there that looks like it's made of . . . suitcases and steamer trunks. Goodness, it's quite big!"

"Lost luggage, I bet," Pogo called. "Keep going!"

The dwarf picked his way through artifacts both real and imaginary—the collars of thousands of lost dogs and cats, a lake of corroded clocks representing lost time, and an even larger sea filled with silver and gold coins and paper money, perhaps the monetary losses of drunkards and gamblers. For a moment, Pogo considered slaloming down the sandy hill and filling his pockets with some of those coins—the gold itself should at least be worth something—but since Quidprobe kept telling him this was all imaginary stuff, he doubted it would come back with him . . . *if* he even made it back home, that was.

Immense piles of bent swords and broken arrows which might represent lost battles or lost nerve; delicate masks cracked and dirtied—Quidprobe guessed they might have something to do with lost reputations—and an immense, uneven field of toys and dolls that the little man suggested might stand for lost innocence, the dwarf listed them off and Pogo took note, trying to see something like the organizational grid he had learned in his management training workbook: *Knowing Your Inventory = Sales Power!* As the timeless day wore on and he could begin to make out some patterns, he scrambled down the slope and joined the little man. All of the saddest and most personal things seemed to be clustered at one end of the immense sea of lost wages, savings, and livelihoods, where the coins glittered like the foamy caps of frozen waves, so he led Quidprobe there and they began to search every mound, puzzling for long minutes sometimes over what the objects might represent.

"Hey, Dickrobe," he called. "I think I found something!"

"It's Quickpoop!" snarled the little man, kicking something in his irritation. "No, Quidprobe! *Quidprobe!* See what you've done! I don't even know my own name anymore!"

"Whoa. Mellow, dude. I was just messing with you." He'd actually figured out the dwarf's correct name several days ago, but it was more fun to make up new ones, especially because each time he pretended to get the name wrong, Quidprobe squeaked like a rubbed balloon. "Anyway, I think I might have found what we're looking for—it's a bunch of little jars with people's names on them." He bent and picked one up, read the carefully engraved label. "Who's Em-pee-dockles?"

"Empedocles—Greek philosopher," called Quidprobe from somewhere on the far side of a heap of lost opportunities. "Jumped into a volcano to prove he was a god."

"Was he?"

"No."

"Jackpot!" Pogo picked up another. "Pie-thuh-gore-ass?"

"Pythagoras. Another brilliant thinker, except he thought beans had little human souls in them."

"Okay, this is looking good. Joan of Arc?"

"Heard voices," said Quidprobe. "Trusted the English. Crazy as a coot." The dwarf sounded much more cheerful. "Hold on, I'll come help!"

As he and the little man clambered over the mounds of shifting glass jars, each one filled with a cloudy but slightly luminous liquid, a label caught Pogo's eye. He picked it up and examined the jar, which was larger than most of the others, although still no bigger than a soft-drink can. *CALIGULA*. He knew the name—it was a dirty movie about some emperor guy who had sex with everything that moved and a few things that didn't; there had been ads all over one of the men's magazines Pogo kept in a box in his closet. If this was that Caligula guy's wits, did that mean his memories were inside it, too? Pogo lifted the jar up and tried to stare into the shifting fluids, hoping for just the faintest visible scene of a Roman orgy, but no matter how he stared he couldn't make out anything but the cloudy liquid.

"Oh! Oh!" Quidprobe began to shout quite close by, startling him. Shamed, he hid the Caligula jar.

"What? What is it?"

"By the Hierarchies of Heinlein, I believe I've found it! Come over here!"

Pogo made his way across mounds of shifting cut-crystal jars to the dwarf's side. The little man was holding up a container nearly as large as Caligula's. Pogo squinted at the silver name-plate and shook his head in disappointment. "No, man, this belongs to some dude named 'Orlando.'"

"That's the Italian way of saying Roland," the dwarf told him. "And look at how big it is! It's his, it must be!"

By the little guy's excitement, Pogo could tell that Quidprobe was feeling ready to go home, too. "Well . . . cool, then, I guess. Let's take it and get going. Good job." But Pogo was a little sad he hadn't found it himself. After all, wasn't *he* supposed to be the hero of this story?

"Well, it was nice of those saints guys to let us hang onto the chariot," Pogo said, staring over the side as whatever ocean stretched between Ethiopia and Charlemagne-land rolled away beneath them. "So where are we headed now?"

"Paris," said Quidprobe. "The fairies and the Saracens have it under siege, and only Roland can save the day."

"Right." Pogo squinted at a sailing ship far below, so tiny he half-expected to see someone wading after it, trying to recover it and put it back into its bottle. "What's a Saracen, again?"

"The villains in this particular epic," the dwarf told him. "Non-Christians."

Pogo thought guiltily of his own meager forty-watt faith. "Right. Damn those Saracens."

After some time had passed, they swooped down over fields of ripening grain, gliding so low that Pogo could see workers looking up in astonishment. It was kind of cool, really, riding in a flying chariot. He wondered if he would be rewarded for bringing this Roland guy back his brains. Maybe Charlemagne would give him a castle of his own and a bunch of servants. If he got to keep the chariot it would be even better. All it was missing to be the near-perfect ride was a righteous sound system, so he could swoop down on bad guys blasting "Smoke on the Water" at concert volume . . .

But really, I'd rather go home, he had to admit. *Somewhere they already have stuff like James Bond movies and car stereos and onion rings. Somewhere I know how things work.*

At last, they reached Paris, where the twin armies of Islam and Faerie had surrounded the city walls like coffee grounds filling the sink around a failed garbage disposal. As they flew over, many of the enemy troops pointed up at them, shouting curses and firing arrows, but the flying horses nimbly avoided the hostile shafts and then brought the chariot swooping down over the walls to land in a commons at the center of the city where the tents of the besieged army were massed, their many colorful banners trembling in the breeze like (Pogo couldn't help thinking) the triangular pennants of the world's largest used-car lot.

When they landed, the dwarf announced who they were and they were taken by a company of armed men to the king.

Seated on his throne, armored all in gold, gray-bearded Charlemagne looked noble enough to make Pogo instantly wish to enroll in whatever management training courses he offered. Now *this* was what a supervisor should look like!

"Our thanks, noble Duke Astolfo," the king said in a voice almost exactly like the dad from Bonanza. "You have done us a great service by freeing Prester John, and soon may prove to have done an even greater one, if you can bring back the wits of our greatest paladin, Sir Roland."

Pogo mumbled that the king was welcome.

"Already the messenger pigeons tell me that Prester John has brought his armies to bear on both Duke Aelfric's Faerie and Agramant's infidel lands," Charlemagne continued. "Both have already lost much of their stomach for this siege. I think if Roland should be returned to health and bring his mighty blade Durendal back to my service, their resolve should quickly crumble."

"But where *is* Roland, your Highness?" asked Quidprobe.

"Ranging all across Paris like the madman he is, destroying property and the lives of those who try to restrain him. I have asked my bravest knights to harry him hence, with trumpets sounding, so that we may try this sovereign cure you have brought us for his broken wit." He paused. "Hark? Do you hear? Even now he comes toward us."

Pogo could hear the horns quite clearly, dozens of them all blatting and tooting excitedly, like a monster rush-hour backup on the San Diego Freeway. Charlemagne and his court got up and hurried outside in time to discover one of the strangest things Pogo had ever seen—several dozen knights in armor getting their butts severely kicked by one naked, frothing, bearded man.

It was pretty impressive, actually, like an episode of the Hulk where they'd run out of budget for green make-up. The knights were armed with shields and spears and swords and axes, and the naked guy with nothing but a massive spar that might have been the roof beam of a large house, but which he was swinging as though it were a Little League-size Louisville Slugger, bashing armored men out of their saddles and sending them flying through the air to crash in crumpled heaps that Pogo suspected would be impossible to do anything about until someone invented the can-opener.

"Ropes," shouted Charlemagne in his booming Ben Cartright voice, "throw ropes about him!" Now Pogo really did expect to see Hoss and Little Joe run out with their lariats, but instead a variety of soldiers came forward and flung loops of rope over Roland, who seemed more bemused than angry—at least until he tried to move on and found that the ropes prevented it. As he was flinging the soldiers around at the end of their cords like armored yo-yos, more soldiers ran in with more restraints until at last Roland was temporarily brought to a helpless standstill, and could do nothing but growl and snap at the air.

"Now!" said Quidprobe, shoving Pogo forward. "The crystal jar! Hurry up and make him inhale it!"

"Go to him, Duke Astolfo!" cried Charlemagne. "The fate of all the Christian world is upon thy brave shoulders!"

Pogo couldn't help noticing that even with more than two dozen men holding him, bearded crazy Roland was looking like he might break free any moment. Pogo swallowed hard, then dashed forward past the soldiers and between the straining ropes, trying to get close enough to make the mad knight breathe the fumes.

Roland fixed him with a rolling eye. "*Argle argle argh!*" he shouted, spittle flying. "*Kill!*"

"Uh, yeah. I totally would too, if I were you." Pogo reached under his chestplate and pulled out the crystal jar, then cracked it open beneath Roland's nose. Something glowing and silvery rushed out and into the knight's distended nostrils.

"*Argle! Bargle argle!*" Roland roared, then suddenly a very different look crept onto his face—an expression of surprise.

"Sweet Jove!" the great knight shouted, looking down at himself in dismay. "I am naked and hairy! What have I done . . . ?" The look of surprise quickly turned into something more severe—an expression of horrific shame. "By the Vestals—I made my *horse* a senator! *What was I thinking?* And I married one of my own sisters as well—not even the good-looking one!"

With this, Roland threw himself in the dirt and began to crawl on his hands and knees, weeping and pulling his hair. Pogo stood watching, trying to figure out what had happened. Was this what the knight was normally like when he was sane? If so, Pogo couldn't understand how he was going to be much use against the fairies and Samaritans.

While everyone else was also staring, Quidprobe sidled up next to Pogo. "Uh . . . are you certain that you gave him the right wits back? I mean, if I didn't know better, I'd swear he sounded less like Roland than like one of the crazier Roman emperors—you know, like . . . "

"Caligula!" Pogo said. "Damn! I must have pocketed his jar when you called me." He reached under the breastplate and found a second jar waiting there. He took it out and saw to his relief that this one was indeed labeled "Orlando." "So what do we do now?" Pogo asked.

King Charlemagne and his court watched in slightly uneasy wonderment as Duke Astolfo and a dwarf chased a scuttling, weeping Roland around the town square. When they caught him at last, Quidprobe managed to get a foreshortened leg-lock around one of the knight's arms so Pogo could get the vial under his nose and pull the stopper. As Roland inhaled between wails of lamentation, the silvery stuff flew up his nose. The naked man paused, as if tasting something beloved and familiar, then relaxed, smiling with relief.

"Yes!" he cried. "Praise God I am released from my madness! I am Roland again!" This time the naked man leaped to his feet with a loud cry of joy and relief, incidentally throwing Astolfo and the dwarf quite a distance, so that as the noise of celebration rose at the bold knight's return, Pogo and Quidprobe just lay on their backs and waited for the sky to stop spinning.

"Dude," Pogo said at last. "That was pretty weird. Does this mean we can go home now?"

"I think it's time to find out," said the dwarf. "Let's get out of here before these armies start killing each other all over again. Once he's done celebrating, Roland's going to be tossing Saracen heads all over the place."

Pogo nodded and helped the dwarf get to his feet. As they walked quickly away from the crowd that surrounded the noble (if still nude) Roland, Pogo examined the damage the long siege had done, at the burned and ruined houses, the countless fresh graves and the bloated corpses of animals still lying unburied in the street. "Wow. Everyone says Paris is so great, but it's kind of a dump, really. I mean, seriously, how do they ever get tourists to come here?"

Quidprobe was astonished to be both alive and in one piece, and was in a hurry to get back to the symbolic plane before the Metaverse realized how unlikely that was and decided to rejigger the odds. "Intervention over," he told the Pogocashman. "The story has been fulfilled. As soon as I get back to the Department, I'll send you home again."

"Promise, man? I mean, this is pretty interesting to visit but I wouldn't want to live here, if you know what I mean."

Quidprobe only nodded. For once he knew *exactly* what the Pogocashman meant. "I promise. I can't send you home until I get back to the Department where all the machinery is, but as soon as I get there, I'll do it." He took a breath, noting for perhaps the last time how strange it felt when the lungs inside his chest inflated. How awkward organic life was! But interesting, too. As Quidprobe began to consider the precise symbolic sequence of thoughts that would take him back, an idle curiosity floated up to him—what other sensations did organic beings have that he had never experienced on the symbolic plane?

Ah-ah, he told himself. *No use wondering because I'm never going to do something like this again. Ever.*

The Pogocashman was looking at him strangely as he finished his preparations. "What is it?" Quidprobe asked. "Have we forgotten something?"

"Naw. I'm just . . . " The organic creature was avoiding eye contact, which seemed strange. "I'm kinda gonna miss you, little dude."

Which was odd, because Quidprobe himself had been feeling something similar, although he had not realized it until just now. "Where I come from," he told the Pogocashman, extending a bony, organic hand, "we say, 'May all your stories have a proper ending'."

"And as my people say," said the Pogocashman, slapping the palm of Quidprobe's hand even as they both began to turn intangible to each other, "gimme five! And keep on truckin', baby!"

A moment later Quidprobe was tumbling down a long, whistling tunnel of different shades, temperatures, and textures of blackness. After a while, it began to resolve itself into shapes—a whole crowd of shapes, all his coworkers and managers and even Fnutt the supervisor . . . and they were all clearly waiting for him! Welcome banners! Treats and streamers! It was a party—for him! Quidprobe was thrilled. Someone had seen what he was doing and alerted his superiors! He had been noticed and now his bravery would be celebrated and he might well be rewarded for saving the Matter of France and all of Western Literature.

But although his coworkers waved and cheered as he coalesced back into the collection of symbolic solids he had worn all his life until this adventure, he saw that many of them were also laughing, although they were doing their best not to make it obvious. Then, as his familiar world came into sharper focus, he could finally read the signs.

"WELCOME BACK QUICKPOOP!"

"QUITPUNK—OUR HERO!"

"CONGRATULATIONS, QUARTPUMP!"

He stood for a moment, glowering at them. "Very funny," he said. "Did anyone notice I saved the world?"

Fnutt the supervisor stepped forward and handed him a piece of treatsweet on a disposable plate. "In all seriousness, you did very well, Quick . . . Quidprobe. Saved the Department a lot of trouble. Good to have you back."

Quidprobe thanked him. The departmental supervisor wandered off to refill his container of natured spirits, and for a moment Quidprobe just stood and soaked in the glory of his successful return, the proximity of his own office and peers and home. He stretched out one of his pseudopods and reveled in its boneless suppleness, its entirely obvious *rightness*. Yes, it was very good indeed to be home at last.

Which suddenly reminded him of his former companion, still stuck in an imaginary past for which, recent victories aside, he was probably not entirely suited. Quidprobe hurried to the office machinery center, his fingers slippery with frosting and his rubbery young soul in a hurry to get back to the party—a party in honor of him! He punched the button.

"Safe journey, my friend," he said to the image.

Somebody had put on some music—something slithery and

non-traditional. The younger workers were dancing. Quidprobe didn't stay to watch the monitor.

Pogo was just beginning to worry that the dwarf might have forgotten him when the walls of Paris began to grow faint and translucent before his eyes, as though the entire damaged city was turning into glass. A moment later he found himself hurtling down what seemed like the world's longest, driest, and coldest Slip-n-Slide.

Finally going home! was his thought as the winds between realities spun him. *Finally!* But he'd had a pretty amazing adventure and he'd done pretty damn well, if he said so himself. He really deserved some kind of reward. And to think it all happened because he got sent into the story instead of some English guy.

Yeah, that English guy. Wonder whatever happened to him . . . ?

A moment later Pogo tumbled out of the void and into the reality of his familiar world, to warmth and carpets and beautifully painted oriental screens and heavy wood furniture. And also to a slender naked woman sitting on a bed, brushing her hair with her back to Pogo.

"Hurry, darling!" she said, in one of those posh Upstairs-Downstairs PBS accents. "It's cold. I want to get under the covers with you so you can warm me up. In fact, I want you to do more than just warm me up, you amazing man . . . "

Reward . . . ! Pogo thought. *Jackpot! Hallelujah!*

But then she turned and saw him standing in the doorway. For a moment a look of confusion seized her lovely face. "You . . . you're not my husband! Who are you?" Then she began to scream, and scream, and scream.

Pogo was going to find it very difficult to explain to the village constable what he was doing in Mr. Castlemane's house.

Meanwhile, six thousand miles away, the appearance of a naked Englishman in the middle of Kirby Shoes Summer Madness Event was barely noticed. There was a *sale* going on, after all.

AFTERWORD:

I MUST HAVE discovered Poul Anderson when I first began haunting used-book stores and buying my own books. All I remember is that his fantasy hit me like a sledge hammer, particularly the grit and realism. I also was knocked out—and the best example is *Three Hearts and Three Lions*—by his idea of taking one of these magical, fairy-tale worlds and trying to figure out how it actually WORKED. This has carried over into my own work, and is one of the reasons that I often think of myself as being a "hard fantasy" writer. Because of Anderson's influence, I try to make even the craziest stuff feel as though it could really happen in a universe with rules. Later on I was hit equally hard by *Tau Zero*, which convinced me that science (or at least fictional science) could be as exciting as magic any old time. I'm sure that at some subconscious level Anderson's versatility also convinced me never to get pinned down as a writer, not to keep retreating to familiar territory but to follow an idea wherever it led without concern for genre boundaries.

(I'm sure a few of my long-suffering editors are now cursing Mr. Anderson's illustrious name for this important contribution to my waywardness.)

In later years, I read a great deal more of his work and loved it, and doubtless internalized a great deal of it to the influence of my own work, but I will forever remember my breathless first response to things like the "boiler explosion" in *Three Hearts* and the way time itself turns widdershins in *Tau Zero*. More than any other writer, I think he opened me up to how facts make fantasy more believable, and since belief is at the core of what we writers do, that was a gift beyond price. Thank you, Poul.

—Tad Williams